STANDOFF

Other Books by Patricia Bradley

STANDOFF

PATRICIA BRADLEY

Revell

a division of Baker Publishing Group
Grand Rapids, Michigan

© 2020 by Patricia Bradley

Published by Revell
a division of Baker Publishing Group
PO Box 6287, Grand Rapids, MI 49516-6287
www.revellbooks.com

Printed in the United States of America

Library of Congress Cataloging-in-Publication Data
Names: Bradley, Patricia, 1945– author.
Title: Standoff / Patricia Bradley.
Description: Grand Rapids : Revell, a division of Baker Publishing Group,
    [2020] | Series: Natchez Park Rangers; 1 |
Identifiers: LCCN 2019035671 | ISBN 9780800735739 (paperback)
Subjects: GSAFD: Romantic suspense fiction. | Christian fiction.
Classification: LCC PS3602.R34275 S73 2020 | DDC 813/.6—dc23
LC record available at https://lccn.loc.gov/2019035671

ISBN: 978-0-8007-3867-9 (casebound)

20 21 22 23 24 25 26   7 6 5 4 3 2 1

To the men and women
of the National Park Service.
You do a wonderful job
of sharing the parks with us
and keeping us safe.

PROLOGUE

What had he gotten himself into?

Brandon Marlar leaned back in his chair and chewed his thumbnail. His dad had warned him the last time he'd caught him hacking. *"Son, breaking into someone's files you have no business being in is wrong, and it's going to get you in trouble. Just don't come crying to me when it does."*

But hacking was as addictive as the heroin he'd been hooked on two years ago, and when he'd found an open port in the Boudreaux Enterprises system, Brandon couldn't help himself, not after he cracked the password in less than two minutes. Didn't make it right, though.

Brandon jiggled his legs, hesitating as the keyboard lured him. Now that he'd found one secret file, he might as well go all in. Sucking in a breath, he hunched over the computer again, his fingers flying across the keys as he unlocked another file. A spreadsheet popped up on the screen, listing banks he'd never seen in his job as bookkeeper for Justin Boudreaux. He straightened his back and massaged his tight muscles.

Just to make sure his assumptions were correct, he copied a

number in one of the columns and opened Google. Sure enough, the search engine returned hits for Fidelity Trust in the Cayman Islands. He repeated his search with numbers from another column. Another financial institution, this one in Switzerland. He totaled the accounts. At least thirty.

Brandon pulled up another file that listed dates, locations, and deposits. When he brought up both files side by side on his screen, it all clicked into place. He was looking at a classic case of money laundering. The company he worked for was blending funds and then depositing the laundered money in offshore accounts. Brandon drew in a shaky breath. "Oh, boy."

Maybe all of this was legitimate. And maybe the Golden Gate Bridge was for sale. Justin Boudreaux was a powerful man. Even with these files, who would believe a twenty-two-year-old ex-heroin junkie? And if—he mentally erased the *if*—*when* Boudreaux discovered he'd hacked into the company's computer system . . . Brandon didn't want to think what might happen.

His dad.

He'd take the information to him, and he would know what to do. Brandon removed the flash drive and shut down his computer. He could be in Natchez in three hours.

1

Brooke Danvers checked her watch. Her dad had said six and it was almost that. She quickly twisted her hair into a ponytail and then buckled her Sig Sauer to her waist. While she hadn't been sworn in as a law enforcement ranger yet, Mississippi was an open-carry state, and her dad had okayed her wearing it.

She hadn't stopped smiling since he'd asked if she wanted to ride along with him tonight. It didn't even bother her that he'd chosen Sunday night because there wouldn't be many cars out and about.

Brooke glanced toward the flat-brimmed hat that she'd worn all day at Melrose, the almost two-hundred-year-old mansion where she'd led tours. At times it felt as though the August heat and humidity would cook her head. She wouldn't need the hat tonight, though, and left it sitting on her childhood bed.

Returning home after fifteen years while contractors finished the remodel on her water-damaged apartment was proving to be an experience. She'd always heard grown children shouldn't return to the nest, and now she knew why. At her place, she came and went as she pleased without anyone asking questions. But now it was almost like she'd stepped back into her teenaged years. Not that she wasn't thankful her parents had offered to let her move into her old room, but it would be good to get back in her own apartment in a couple of weeks. The chimes from the grandfather clock sent her hurrying down the hall to her dad's home office.

It was empty. He'd said he had work to do before they left . . . She quickly walked to her mom's studio.

"Where's Dad?" she asked.

Her mom turned from her easel. "He got a call and left. Said to tell you if you still wanted to do the ride along, text Gary to pick you up."

Disappointment was swift, and Brooke ground her teeth to keep from letting it show.

"He said something about you riding with him tomorrow night."

That brightened her mood slightly. Her phone dinged with a text. Gary, the retiring ranger she was replacing.

Are you riding with me?

She quickly texted him.

Yes. What time?

Give me an hour and I'll pick you up.

She sent him a thumbs-up emoji and hooked her phone on her belt.

"Come see what I'm working on," her mom said.

Brooke edged into the room. It wasn't often she got a chance to see an unfinished work by her mother. The painting was of her very pregnant sister. "Oh, wow," she said. "That's beautiful. She'll love it."

"I hope so. Meghan's feeling kind of . . ."

"Fat? That's what she told me the other day," Brooke said. "I tried to tell her that wasn't true, and maybe this will show her."

"I'm glad you like it. I should have it finished in time to take with the others to Knoxville next month."

The baby's due date was a couple of months away, just after her mom's gallery showing of her work ended. They both turned as the doorbell rang. It couldn't be Gary already, and besides, he would just honk. "I'll get it," Brooke said and hurried to open the front door.

"Jeremy?" she said, her stomach fluttering at the sight of one of Natchez's most eligible bachelors. Had she forgotten a date?

He looked behind him then turned back to Brooke with laughter in his eyes. "I think so."

Heat flushed her face, and it had more to do with the broad shoulders and lean body of the man on her doorstep than the temperature. "I wasn't expecting you. I don't have a lot of time, but do you want to come in?"

"Since it's a little hot and humid out here, coming in would be good," he teased. "And I apologize for dropping by without calling, but I was afraid you'd tell me you were busy."

Brooke steeled herself against the subtle citrus fragrance of his cologne as he walked past her. She'd had exactly two dates with Jeremy Steele and hadn't figured out why he was even interested in her. She was so not his type. The handsome widower tended to lean more toward blondes.

"Hello, Mrs. Danvers," Jeremy said to her mother, who had followed her to the living room.

"How many times have I told you to call me Vivian?"

"I'll try to remember that," he said with a thousand-watt smile.

"Good. A thirtysomething calling me Mrs. Danvers makes me feel old," she replied. "And since I know you didn't come to see me, I'll go back to my painting."

"Good to see you . . . Vivian." Then he turned to Brooke and glanced at her uniform. "Are you working tonight?"

"Sort of," she said. "I was going to ride along with Dad on his patrol, but he cancelled and turned me over to another ranger. Why?"

"I know it's last minute, but I was hoping you'd have time to join me at King's Tavern," he said. "I have a hankering for one of their flatbreads."

Her mouth watered at the thought. Brooke hadn't eaten since lunch, and she could do last minute, at least this time. But the question of why *her* kept bobbing to the surface. Ignoring it, she said, "That sounds good. I'll text Gary to pick me up later."

"Gary?"

She grinned at him, tempted to describe the aging ranger as a hunk but instead settled for the truth. "He's the ranger I'm replacing when he *retires.*"

Red crept into Jeremy's face. "Oh, that guy. Are you even sworn in yet?"

"No, that's next week. I talked my dad into letting me get a little early practice." It helped having a father who was the district ranger, even if he wasn't overjoyed about her becoming a law enforcement ranger. Then she looked down. "I need to change first."

"You're fine like you are," he said.

Maybe to him, but she was not about to go on a date wearing a National Park Service uniform and a Sig strapped to her waist. "Give me five minutes."

After Brooke changed into a lavender sundress and slipped into sandals, she gave herself a brief once-over. While the dress showed no cleavage, it accentuated curves the NPS uniform hid. She freed her hair from the ponytail and put the elastic holder in her purse. In this heat, she might have to put it up again.

Brooke checked her makeup. She rarely wore anything other than pink gloss. Thick lashes framed her eyes and the sun had deepened her olive skin to a nice tan. Brooke wasn't sure where she got her darker complexion and hair since her mom and sister, and even her dad, were fair and blonde, but she wasn't complaining.

Tonight she wanted something more and added a shimmering gloss to her lips. Then she took a deep breath and slowly blew it out. Didn't do much good with her heart still thudding in her chest.

Why was Jeremy pursuing *her*? The women usually seen on his arm were ones who could mix and mingle with the rich and famous. Women who could further his career. Jeremy was a Mississippi state senator with his sights set on Washington like his daddy, while she was a National Park Service ranger who didn't care one thing about leaving Natchez.

Her heart kicked into high gear. Had the M-word just crossed her thoughts? Impossible. It wasn't only that she wasn't his type, he definitely wasn't hers. She was a simple girl with a simple lifestyle—nothing like the Steeles.

In the 1850s, half the millionaires in the United States lived in Natchez, and the Steeles were among them. A hundred and seventy years later, the family's holdings had increased substantially, not to mention the Steele men had a long history of public service.

Jeremy's dad was the retiring US senator and his son was poised to take his place in the next election. His photo appeared regularly in the *Natchez Democrat*, often with a beautiful woman on his arm. And never the same one.

She sighed. If they lived in England, he would be royalty, and she would be the commoner who ended up with a broken heart.

Brooke chided herself about being melodramatic and hurried to her mom's studio. "Jeremy and I are grabbing something to eat," she said.

Her mom laid her brush down. "What about your ride along?"

"I'll catch up to Gary later," she said.

When she rejoined Jeremy, his eyes widened, and he whistled. "Nice," he said.

Jeremy Steele knew how to make a woman feel special. As they stepped out of the house, she immediately noticed the ten-degree drop in temperature from when Jeremy first arrived and nodded at the thunderheads that had rolled in. "Guess that means we won't leave the top down."

"I think we can make it to the tavern before it starts."

Ten minutes later Jeremy escorted her into King's Tavern, where the original brick walls and dark wooden beams added to the mystique of the inn that had been rumored to have a ghost. The tantalizing aroma of steak drew her gaze to the open grill, but she had her heart set on one of their wood-fired flatbreads.

"Inside or out?" Jeremy asked.

"The backyard, if you don't think it'll rain," she said.

"If it does, we'll simply come in." He gave the waitress their drink order, sweet tea for both of them, and let her know where to find them. They had their choice of picnic tables and chose the one on the hill. Once they were seated, Jeremy reached across, taking her hand. His touch and the intensity in his brown eyes almost took her breath away. "I'm glad you came."

"Me too," Brooke said, trying not to sound breathy. The question worrying around in her head wouldn't wait any longer. "Why me?"

"What do you mean?"

"Why are you interested in dating me? We don't travel in the same circles."

"But we do. We've gone to church together since we were kids."

"And you sit in your family's pew clear across the sanctuary."

His eyes twinkled. "We don't have a family pew."

She laughed. "I'd hate to be the one who sat in your mom's seat some Sunday."

"You're funny," he said. "That's one of the things I like about you."

"But I'm so different from the women you usually date." There. She'd said it.

He lightly stroked the heel of her palm. "That's what I like best. You're real . . . not saying anything bad about anyone I've dated, but honestly, sometimes I think the aura of the Steele name is the attraction. That and Dad's money." Then Jeremy smiled, popping dimples in his cheeks. "But you were never like that. Even in high school you were never afraid to tell me like it was."

Heat infused her cheeks. She'd been accused of that many times, usually by someone who didn't want to hear the truth. "I'm working on not being so blunt," she said. "I hope I never hurt your feelings."

"I won't say never," he said with a wink, "but you never said anything that didn't need saying."

Okay, she'd been rude and hadn't fallen all over him because of who he was . . . Before she could ask *why* again, the waitress approached with their drinks, and Brooke pulled her hand away from Jeremy's, missing his touch immediately. Maybe she should let go of her questions and let their relationship play out.

Once the waitress left with their orders, Jeremy took her hand again. "I've looked a long time for the right person."

His brown eyes held her gaze. He surely didn't mean her. Did he? "What about Molly? I'd hate for her to get attached to me and then we stop seeing each other."

"I don't plan for that to happen. And Molly is already crazy about you."

Brooke couldn't keep from smiling. His six-year-old daughter was a sweetheart.

"How about if we take it slow?" he asked. "Get to know one another?"

"No pressure?"

"No pressure."

Her phone dinged and she glanced at the screen. A text from Gary.

Pick you up in an hour?

Brooke hesitated, torn between wanting to spend more time with Jeremy and getting practical experience on her job. If the text had been from her dad, it wouldn't even be a question—she had so much to learn from him, but Gary, not so much. She'd known him all her life and he'd always been laid-back, never wanting to climb the ladder within the park service. But if her dad thought she should ride with him . . . With a sigh, she looked up from her phone. "Can you have me back to my house in forty-five minutes?"

"Do I want to? Nope," he said. "But I can."

She texted Gary an okay, wishing it was her dad she would be riding with. Then Brooke stared at her phone a second. What had been so important for her dad to stand her up?

2

Luke Fereday's nerves thrummed like high-voltage wires as the wind from the approaching thunderstorm moaned through Windsor Ruins. He'd found the gate to the enclosure unlocked and slipped inside, concealing himself behind one of the twenty-three columns that stood like ghostly sentinels under the harsh overhead lights. The columns were all that remained of the five-story plantation that burned over a century ago.

Earlier in the day another storm had blown through South Mississippi and saturated the ground, leaving the earthy smell of wet leaves. Overhead, Spanish moss hung from live oaks and whipped back and forth in the wind that had taken a cooler turn. He hoped to be away from here before the storm arrived. With a quick tap of his watch, he checked the time. Almost midnight. Sonny was late.

All the things that could go wrong, including his cover being blown, ran through his mind. Even in the chilled air, sweat made his palms slick, and he wiped them on his jeans. It had taken four months to get a meeting with Charley Romero. Four months of baiting his hook by buying five- and ten-thousand-dollar amounts of heroin from Sonny.

Thunder rumbled again, competing with an owl's lonely hoot. Luke ignored the shiver that raced down his spine and bent to check the backup Ruger in his ankle holster. Meetings like this he always carried two guns—his Glock and the lighter-weight Ruger. Then he stood and scanned the clearing once more.

Lights flashed as a car swung into the drive, followed by more lights. They were arriving in separate vehicles. He took a deep breath and slipped into his role, this time playing himself. Luke Fereday. Made him feel exposed.

Actually it wasn't the Luke Fereday he was now, but the one who had a reputation for trouble back in his high school days. Never thought that reputation would come in handy.

A minute later a pickup and an SUV rolled into the clearing and parked beside Luke's Jeep Cherokee. He stepped out of the shadows as a lanky man climbed out of the truck holding an LED lantern. Luke would bet his next paycheck the floral Hawaiian shirt Sonny wore hid a gun tucked in the waistband.

"Hey, my man," Sonny said. The dealer glanced around. "This place gives me the willies at night."

Luke shrugged. "You picked it."

"I know, but it's still creepy."

"You're late," he said.

"My friends over here had a little business to take care of. I was about to call you when they showed up."

Sonny was twitchy. And he was talking too much. Luke tensed, shifting his stance to the balls of his feet as the driver climbed from the SUV. The overhead lights gave just enough illumination to make out the man's features.

The sixth sense honed by years of drug buys kicked in. It was hard to tell his age, but something about the cut of his shoulders and the way he held himself was familiar. Luke had seen him somewhere, maybe even had contact with him, but his photo hadn't been in any of Luke's files. What if he'd arrested him before in a drug sting?

Luke's gaze shifted as another man crawled out from the passenger side. Charley Romero purported to be second in command in an organization that had ties with a South American cartel and stretched from Natchez to New Orleans and eastward into Florida.

Romero was shorter than his bodyguard and might come to Luke's shoulders. But looks were deceiving, and he knew to treat him like the cottonmouth snakes roaming the woods around him. Very carefully.

He looked closer at the bodyguard, still trying to place him. That was the problem he always faced when he dealt with unknowns. The man could be someone Luke had busted in the past, even in a different part of the country.

"Wasn't expecting but two of you." He caught himself before he reached to smooth the full beard that was no longer there. Since he was playing himself, it wasn't needed, but he sure did miss it, along with the John Deere cap that always shaded his eyes.

"Romero here wanted his friend to tag along," Sonny said, palming his hands. "It's all good."

"Your friend in the shadows. He have a name?" The hard metal of his Glock pressed against the small of Luke's back, reminding him it was a dangerous game he played.

"Yeah," Romero said, "but you don't need to know it."

Tension crackled in the humid air. The bodyguard moved out of the shadows to join Romero, and Luke planted his feet. The bodyguard stood a good two inches taller than Luke's six feet. He inched his arm back, ready to grab the Glock in his waistband. Not much room for error. If the deal went south, he'd take out Romero first, then the bodyguard. He nodded to Sonny. "I'm only trusting them because you say they're okay."

Romero folded his arms across his chest. "How do we know you're not a narc?" His voice rose and fell in its thick Cajun accent.

"Hey, Charley, my man," Sonny said. "Luke here is okay. I know him."

Luke squared his shoulders and kept his gaze on Romero. "How do I know you won't rat me out to the law around here?"

A look passed between the bodyguard and Romero, who grinned. "You don't have to worry about the law." Romero stared at Luke a minute longer, and then he tipped his head. "I heard you're looking for some Big H."

A little of the tension eased from Luke's body. "And I heard you had some."

"Maybe. How much you want?"

"A kilo, right?" Sonny said, looking toward Luke.

"Provided the price is right."

"A kilo will cost you sixty-five Gs," Romero said.

Luke toed the ground with his ostrich-skin cowboy boots and then raised his head to pin a narrowed gaze on Romero. "Sonny said it was only sixty."

"Sonny was wrong. You want it or not?"

Luke took his time answering and shifted where he could keep his eye on the bodyguard. He didn't like the way the man had tilted his head, like he was trying to puzzle something out. Luke needed to end this and get out of here. He brought his attention back to Romero. "Can you make regular deliveries?"

"How regular?"

"Every two weeks?"

"You want a kilo every two weeks?" Romero's voice inched up a notch at the end.

Luke nodded slowly, and the drug dealer's face lit up like it was Christmas. "Can you swing it?"

The bodyguard rested his hand on a gun stuck in his waistband. "Where're you dealing that you can move that much H so fast?"

The man's Appalachian accent twanged like a note on a steel guitar, setting off warning bells. Luke couldn't place where he'd met the man before, but he was certain he had. "That, my friend, is none of your business." He turned to Romero. "Do we have a deal? Sixty Gs?"

The man's lips twitched, then his shoulders relaxed. "Deal."

"Take me a couple of days to get the cash. Got any bundles with you so I can show my people the grade?"

Romero snapped his fingers, and the bodyguard produced a bundle of small bags. Luke opened one of the pouches.

"That's some good stuff, that," Romero said.

"I'm sure it is."

The Cajun named a price, and Luke slipped a wad of cash from his front pocket and peeled off several bills.

Romero pocketed the money. "The price on the kilo is good 'til Thursday night. You don't get the cash by then, we'll renegotiate."

"Here? Same time?" Luke asked.

"Sonny will call you with the location." Romero turned to leave.

"Wait."

Romero stopped and turned around. "What?"

"I hear you're running China White up the Trace. I'd like to get in on some of the action."

"Where you hear that?"

Luke shrugged. "Here and there. What do you say?"

"I say you better stick with what you got, don't you think?"

"Maybe you want to run that up the ladder? With my connections, I can help you."

Romero eyed him. "I'll pass it by the boss, but don't be holdin' your breath."

"I'd like to meet your boss."

The drug dealer stared at him, his eyes narrow slits. "I'll run that by him too."

"Good deal." Asking about the drugs traveling the Trace had been worth a try. Maybe he should have waited, but at least he'd planted the thought, and he might get a meeting with the top man out of it. Romero turned and walked to the SUV while the bodyguard stood with his feet spread and arms folded, staring Luke down. It would be comical except that one wrong move could start a shooting war.

Sonny saluted Luke, then hopped in his pickup and waited for the SUV to drive out of the clearing before he followed. When the two sets of taillights disappeared around the curve, one going one way and the other in the opposite direction, Luke allowed himself to breathe.

Tonight he didn't have to worry about the men waiting to waylay him as he left. The roll of money he flashed wasn't enough to tempt them, but come Thursday, sixty thousand dollars could make it a different story. Depended on whether Justin Boudreaux looked at the long haul. And whether Luke figured out where he'd met the bodyguard before.

3

A waning half-moon cast a ghostly pallor over Emerald Mound. Hidden in the trees across from the ancient site, Kyle Marlar jockeyed for position on the uneven ground. He'd found a sturdy limb to steady his camera, a Canon EOS 6D with a zoom lens. Now he waited. He wasn't sure for what, other than this was the only lead he had on his son's murder. And his death definitely was murder.

If only he hadn't blown Brandon off that weekend he brought the flash drive to him. If he'd taken him seriously, his son would still be alive. But the boy had always made up wild tales—it was hard to know when he was telling the truth. To even think Justin Boudreaux was mixed up in money laundering stretched credibility.

The man was respectable. He owned a chain of grocery stores and had recently bought prime real estate for a store in Natchez. County, city, and state leaders were negotiating with Boudreaux to move his warehouse from New Orleans to Adams County. The superstore coupled with the warehouse would mean at least three hundred jobs for the area. Three hundred desperately needed jobs.

Kyle was the state representative for this district, and it was his responsibility to help bring industry to the area, not throw up a roadblock by bringing a crazy accusation based on his son's suspicions. Kyle had convinced Brandon that he was misreading the files he'd discovered. He'd even lectured him on hacking into Boudreaux's computer system.

The boy had been too bright for his own good. Kyle had kept the flash drive, intending to destroy it. Then the next week he got the call from a New Orleans detective that Brandon had overdosed on heroin.

He knew his son, and he would never have used heroin again. That was when Kyle realized the fanciful accounting story had been true and he'd followed the information on the drive to Emerald Mound.

A mosquito bit his neck, and he slapped it as a bank of clouds snuffed out the moon, plunging the area into darkness except for the far-off flashes of lightning. That no thunder followed gave him hope the rain would hold off until after the switch, but he still had to contend with the high humidity. He wiped his camera lens. If there was anything to shoot, he didn't want the photos blurred. Then he pressed the menu button and double-checked that the time stamp was set.

He jerked his head toward approaching tires. Seconds later, a car pulled into the circular drive that served as a small parking lot, and Kyle checked his watch. Eleven forty. According to the information on the flash drive, the runner was twenty minutes early. He aimed his camera at the face of the man getting out of the car.

He never would have believed it.

Emerald Mound. He stared toward the ancient mound even though he couldn't see it in the dark. The luminous minute hand on his watch crawled toward midnight. He shouldn't have come so early. He reached for antacids, and his hand brushed the two-inch piece of basswood he always carried. He popped the antacids in his mouth, then drew out his knife and the wood, and seconds later he was whittling the lines of a duck, his nerves calming.

At precisely eleven fifty-nine, he folded the bone-handled knife and slipped the wood and knife in his pocket. One minute later, a dark sedan stopped and someone handed him a package wrapped in plastic without one word being spoken.

Just as silently he walked to his car, opened the trunk, and secured the package. His hand shook as he closed the deck lid. Now all he had to do was drive the package to Jackson, where someone else would take it on to Nashville.

A twig snapped, and he jerked his head toward the sound. "Who's there?"

Silence. He stood stock-still a full minute. The only sound other than cicadas was thunder rolling toward him. He took out his phone and punched in a number. *Come on, answer.* When it went to voice mail, he hung up. What was going on? He couldn't move until he had an exact destination, and a mile from Emerald

Mound he would have no cell service. He paced by his car, his phone in his hand. Five minutes later it buzzed, and he answered.

"I have the package," he said. "Where do I drop it off?"

The caller named a place this side of Jackson along with the description of his contact's car. "Got it." He disconnected and opened his car door. Headlights caught him in their glare as a truck swung into the circle parking area. Too late to run. The driver had already identified him.

The truck pulled in front of his car at an angle, blocking a forward escape. He recognized John Danvers's truck then the district park ranger himself. Busted. He swallowed hard to keep down the bile that rose from his stomach. He'd have to talk his way out of this and waited as the ranger killed the engine and climbed out, leaving the door open.

"I was hoping I wouldn't find you here," Danvers said softly.

The ranger's words were almost snatched away by a gust of wind.

"I like coming to the Mound. There's something about being here, you know, the vibes. Have to go to Mexico to find another temple mound like this one." He was talking too fast and too much. Sweat ran down the side of his face.

"I don't need a history lesson."

"Man, what's your problem?"

"I don't have a problem, and I don't want to play games." Danvers sighed. "I know why you're here."

"I don't know what you're talking about."

The district ranger pulled his gun. "Why don't we see what's in your car before the rain hits."

This couldn't be happening. A thousand thoughts raced through his head, but only one stuck. He couldn't fail. Adrenaline surged through him, and he rushed Danvers.

He tackled the ranger, taking him down. As they struggled, a flash of lightning struck a nearby tree and thunder shook the ground. They rolled on the asphalt beside the truck, bumping against the wheel. Strength surged through him and he pushed the ranger's gun away, turning it toward Danvers's chest.

The gun fired, the sound blasting his eardrums. Danvers's body slumped under him.

For a second he didn't move. What had he done? His heart threatened to explode or stop beating altogether as he struggled to his feet and stared at the body. Maybe Danvers was still alive. He knelt and felt his neck.

Nothing.

Noooo! He held back the primal scream in his chest as blood rushed through his head, drowning out every sound. He jerked toward the road, casting a furtive glance. What if someone just happened to drive by and see him? Or someone came to investigate the gunshot. With one last look at the body he turned and ran to his car. Thirty seconds later, he raced out of the parking lot as the first drops of rain fell.

Kyle slipped through the woods, arriving at his car half a mile away from Emerald Mound before the rain hit. Maybe he should have stayed around longer, but once he'd captured the drug transfer, he'd thought it wise to leave. Hanging around would only increase the chances of getting caught, and except for that one branch, he'd been as quiet as the Native Americans who used to hunt the area.

If he'd been caught, Brandon would not get justice, and justice was all Kyle was interested in at this point. That and seeing Boudreaux and his minions spend the rest of their lives in prison.

It had taken a while, but he'd figured out what happened. Boudreaux had hired Brandon with the sole purpose of getting him hooked on heroin again so he could blackmail Kyle to vote against the upcoming medical marijuana bill in the Mississippi legislature. Brandon messed that up when he hacked into Boudreaux's computer system.

At first he hadn't understood why the cartel wanted the medical marijuana bill defeated so badly, but after a little research Kyle discovered that the cartels had poured millions into California and Colorado to block the legalization of marijuana. When the bills passed anyway, the cartels' sales plummeted. No one would risk buying from the cartel when it was easier to get it legally, and if Kyle had his way, history would repeat itself in Mississippi.

Kyle was certain the data drive contained a list of financial institutions where Boudreaux had hidden his drug money. Once Kyle learned who killed Brandon, he would hand the data drive off to someone who could nail Boudreaux for money laundering. And the photos from tonight were going to get him his information.

6

Brooke slapped at a mosquito buzzing in her ear. She and Gary had driven the Trace as far north as Rocky Springs and had pulled over at Port Gibson on the way back toward Natchez. It was a discreet place to observe traffic up and down the Trace.

"Is it usually this quiet?" Brooke asked, checking her watch. Almost midnight.

The seat creaked as Gary leaned forward and grabbed the bag on the dash. "Not really."

The bag crinkled as he pulled out a handful of chips. She clamped her mouth shut, determined not to point out how many calories he was consuming. Gary Franklin looked like he'd spent most of his years sitting in his patrol car eating chips.

"So, you think you'll like being on the law enforcement side?" he asked. "As opposed to what you do now?"

"I've always wanted to be on the law enforcement side."

"Like your daddy?"

"Yeah," she said. "I'm sure you know he didn't want me to switch. My mom, either."

"No." Surprise laced Gary's words. "He never said a word . . . seemed awful proud when you finished your training in Georgia."

Glynco, Georgia, had one of the finest law enforcement training centers in the nation, and when she graduated at the top of the class, her dad had come around. Not her mom, though. Car lights streaked past them on the Trace.

"I'd say he was doing a bit more than fifty," Gary said. He pulled onto the road with his lights flashing. "Radio in that we're in pursuit of a speeding vehicle."

The stop turned out to be nothing more than a businessman hurrying home to Jackson. Gary ticketed him and issued him a warning to slow down. "You hit a deer going that fast and your car is history. Maybe you too."

Once they were back in the Interceptor, she radioed her dad and frowned when he didn't answer. Maybe he was meeting with the person who interrupted her ride along. A few minutes later, she tried him again with no result, and then she took out her cell phone. He'd insisted she put a family finder app on her phone. A smile tugged at her lips. That worked both ways.

"He's at Emerald Mound," she said. Unease rippled through her.

"That's twenty minutes away," Gary said. "Why don't we head that way?"

7

Large drops of rain pelted Luke as he jogged to his Jeep and drove away from the ruins, taking the southern loop that passed by Alcorn State University. One of the vehicles had taken the same route while the other had gone in the opposite direction to Port Gibson. He'd been too far back to tell which was which. He took a small black phone from his glove compartment, and a quick check showed he had no reception.

Luke drove the dark and lonely road, the steady rhythm of the windshield wipers for company as he occasionally got a glimpse of headlights ahead of him. He ran out of the rain as he passed the university, and he checked the phone again. Three bars showed, along with a missed call. John Danvers. He pulled over and opened his call log. A call and a voice mail from John showed on the screen. He never called unless it was an emergency. Luke checked the time. Before he'd arrived at the ruins. He played the message.

"Got a tip there's a big drug transfer going down at Emerald Mound at midnight, and thought you'd want to be there for the takedown. Think I know who the runner is."

John's terse voice sent a chill through Luke. When they'd talked earlier in the day, John hadn't mentioned any tip, but it didn't mean one of his sources hadn't come through. Luke rubbed his hand over his forehead. He had a bad feeling about this.

Emerald Mound was twenty minutes from his current location, and it was thirty minutes past the rendezvous time. Luke tamped down the panic that squeezed his chest and shifted the Jeep into drive and gunned the motor.

Using the same burner John had called, Luke tried reaching him as he raced to the Trace. No answer. Once on the Trace, he pushed his Jeep beyond the speed limit, praying that deer stayed out of his path or that he didn't miss a curve and wrap the SUV around a tree. He slowed at the turnoff for Emerald Mound and minutes later drove past the circle drive that served as a parking lot for the ancient Indian mound. He pulled off the road and climbed out.

Luke didn't see John. His truck sat alone in the parking lot, angled in toward the split-rail fence at the base of the mound. The skin on the back of his neck prickled. Why weren't the security lights on? The area was quiet. Too quiet.

"John?" His voice cracked the silence. No answer. Luke slipped the Glock from his waistband.

With his heart hammering in his ears, he hesitated at the edge of the circle drive. The truck appeared empty, and it looked like the driver's door stood open. Luke jumped when a radio broke the silence.

"John, you at Emerald Mound?"

There were two rangers under John that Luke had yet to meet. This had to be either Clayton Bradshaw or Gary Franklin. He cocked his ear for John's answer, and again only heard silence. Either John had walked up to the top of the mounds or . . . Luke didn't want to think about the other option. His unease mounted, and he dashed to the pickup.

The truck was empty all right, because John Danvers's body lay in the shadows with a bullet hole in his chest, his handheld radio a few feet from him. He didn't have to press his finger to his friend's neck to know he was dead, but Luke did anyway. No pulse. The reality drilled down into his heart and he wanted to pound the hood of John's truck. Like that would bring him back.

"John, do you copy? We're eight minutes out from your location."

Get it together. As much as he wanted to examine the crime scene, he had to leave before law enforcement arrived or he'd blow his cover. That wouldn't help anyone. Photos would have to be his eyes on the ground, and as much as he hated doing it, Luke took out his phone and snapped pictures of the crime scene. Later he could pore over them, maybe glean something.

He ran to his SUV and pulled away from Emerald Mound, the too-bright lights of an oncoming car almost blinding him. When he reached the Trace, he raced past it to Highway 61.

Luke drove hard, but he couldn't outrun the picture of John's body on the ground. When he reached Fayette, he pulled into a service station and replayed John's phone message. A drug transfer. Had Boudreaux's men he'd met with tonight killed him? No, the timeline was all wrong. Didn't mean Boudreaux hadn't ordered it, though.

Luke had done the right thing, leaving. Keeping his cover and infiltrating Boudreaux's organization was the only way he could bring down the drug traffic on the Trace, and if the drug kingpin was responsible for John's death, Luke would nail him.

Still, the sense he'd deserted John ate at him. It didn't matter that his friend was beyond help or that it was what he would expect Luke to do. Memories of times with John bombarded him, and he dropped his head into his hands. Sorrow clouded his brain.

How was he going to face Brooke?

He parked his car in the shadows of Emerald Mound. He'd almost plowed into the car he'd met on the road. That would have taken some explaining.

Had the driver found Danvers's body? The thought dogged him as he hurried to find the knife he'd missed ten miles from the mounds when he'd checked his pocket for antacids. No. If whoever was in the vehicle had discovered John's body, he would have called 911 and then waited around for help to arrive.

Once he reached the pickup, he used the flashlight on his phone to search for the knife. His relief was palpable when he caught a glimpse of the bone handle near the front tire. He scooped the knife up and slipped it into his pocket.

His head jerked up at the distant wail of a siren, and he raced back to his car. For once, luck was with him.

8

Gary had turned on the siren a few miles back. Brooke kept telling herself there was no reason for anything to be wrong. So why didn't her dad answer?

She leaned forward in her seat as car lights crossed the Trace then disappeared.

Gary slowed as he turned off the Trace onto Highway 553, and then he veered onto Emerald Mound Road and slowed even more when a pothole jarred the SUV. They rounded the curve, and her dad's pickup came into view, almost stopping her heart.

Gary pulled the Ford Interceptor in behind it. He turned to Brooke, and she read the same dread in his face that clenched her stomach in a knot.

"You stay here," he said.

"No." She was not staying put. "You may need backup."

His shoulders sagged before he nodded once. "But stay behind me."

She pulled her gun as they climbed out of the SUV. Brooke scanned the area behind them as she followed a few steps behind Gary. He caught his breath, and she whirled around as he knelt beside her dad.

Time slowed as she took in the scene. Her dad lay stretched out on the ground. Gary stood, blocking her way as she tried to push past him.

"No," he said, grabbing her by the shoulders. "He's gone."

"You can't know that." She struggled to break loose from his hold. "We have to do something! Do CPR until an ambulance can get here."

He shook her lightly. "Listen to me, Brooke. He doesn't have a heartbeat. And the bullet wound . . . no one could survive that kind of trauma."

"I need to see him." She wrenched away from Gary and knelt beside her dad.

"Don't touch anything," Gary warned.

Blood drained from her face, leaving her light-headed. The skin around her mouth tingled. Gary was right. Her dad was beyond help.

Brooke clenched her jaw. Whoever had done this would pay.

9

Suicide.

It'd been four days since Brooke first heard that word, and now it looped through her mind in time with the wipers that scraped her dry windshield. She'd run out of a shower a few miles back, but turning off the wipers just now occurred to her.

Brooke flipped the wipers off, wishing she could turn off the images in her head from Sunday night as easily. It was bad enough that her dad had died, but for the coroner to rule it a suicide was almost more than she could bear.

Her headlights caught the mile marker on the side of the road along with several grazing deer. Twelve more miles to Natchez. She'd chosen the Trace instead of Highway 61 to drive back after she dropped off her mother and sister at the Jackson airport. This third group of deer made her question that decision, but she was almost home now.

Meghan, whose pregnancy had her hormones on a roller coaster, had huddled in the backseat, alternating between tears and total silence. To fill the void, her mom had talked nonstop about everything but their father's death, from the arrival of her granddaughter to the gallery showing of her artwork the next month. The solitude of the Trace had seemed appealing, but in reality, the drive had been too quiet with too much time to think.

She couldn't grasp the fact that she'd never hug her dad again. Or ask his advice or confide in him. He'd always been there for her. It wasn't the same with her mother. While her mother loved Brooke, Vivian Danvers had never coddled her. Still, Brooke could've used her mother's support right now.

Be fair. Her mom probably would have stayed in Natchez, but Meghan was coping even worse with their dad's death than Brooke and had asked their mom to return home with her. Mom had agreed but had deemed the eight-hour drive to Knoxville after the funeral too much for Meghan. At seven months, Meghan was still able to fly, so Mom had sent her son-in-law ahead in their car and was flying there with her younger daughter.

It had surprised Brooke how everyone's leaving had left a void in her heart. Her mother's words from years ago rang in her ears. *Buck up! You have to be strong.* If she'd heard those sentiments once growing up, she'd heard them a thousand times. But how could she be strong in the face of her father's death? Especially now that it had been ruled a suicide.

In her opinion it was a rush to judgment, a way to get his death off the books. Anyone who knew her father knew he would never commit suicide. She'd told the coroner, but he wouldn't budge, saying there was no evidence anyone else was present, he'd been shot with his own gun that had no fingerprints on it except his, and he had gunpowder residue on his hands.

There had to be another answer. Brooke pressed her lips together. She would find proof her dad hadn't taken his own life, if it was the last thing she ever did.

Fifteen minutes later, Brooke exited the Trace and drove the short distance to her parents' home, where she pulled into the drive and stared at the house she grew up in. Just hours before, it had bulged at the seams with family and friends after her father's funeral. And now it sat dark. Forbidding.

She frowned. Why hadn't she left a light burning? Not that

there was much danger in this section of Natchez. She simply hated going into a dark house.

Brooke climbed out of her Ford Escape, and with a glance next door, paused. Her neighbor, Daisy Fereday, was in rehab after knee surgery. What was a car doing in her drive? Then she noticed lights shining in the windows, and she tapped her head. What was she thinking? It could only be one person. Daisy's grandson, Luke Fereday.

Brooke didn't know why she was surprised. Luke had come to the funeral, so of course he would be staying next door. She strode to the front door, remembering too late that she could have pulled around to the new garage addition in the back and no one would know she was home. She just wasn't up to company tonight.

At the front door, she looked up at the porch light. She distinctly remembered her mother telling her she would turn it on. Maybe in getting them all out the door and into Brooke's SUV, she'd forgotten. Brooke used her smartphone flashlight and inserted her key into the lock. Once inside, she closed the door behind her and flipped on a light switch.

Everything looked okay, and she breathed easier. The faint scent of cherry pipe tobacco drew her toward her dad's office. It'd been his man cave. Maybe she'd just sit in his chair for a few minutes. She opened the door to his darkened office. Light from the hallway spilled into the room, revealing chaos.

"No!"

She couldn't believe what she saw. His office looked as though a tornado had plowed through it. Automatically she reached for her gun, but it was hanging on her bedpost.

In the split second Brooke turned to leave, she sensed a presence, and suddenly, a bright light blinded her. She threw up her hand to block it even as the faint impression of a man's silhouette formed.

He shoved her hard and she grabbed for his hand, pulling him forward, barely registering he wore gloves. He took her down with him. They crashed into a chair before hitting the floor. Brooke grabbed for his face and eyes, feeling the rough texture of a ski mask.

She caught a glint of metal before pain slammed through her head. Stars flashed and black edged into her brain, but she held on, fighting to stay conscious. He was not getting away.

He punched her in the upper part of her stomach, sending a spasm through her diaphragm. She couldn't breathe and couldn't move other than to clutch her midsection. Her assailant jumped up and ran for the hallway. She grabbed for his leg, catching air. Another spasm hit and Brooke doubled over, barely aware of the doorbell buzzing.

She tried to call for help, but all she could do was gasp for air. The doorbell rang again. Grabbing the chair that had broken their fall, she pulled up. Still holding her stomach, she staggered to the front door and jerked it open.

"Brooke!" Luke's eyes widened. "What—?"

"A man—"

"Where?" Luke rushed past her.

She pointed toward the back of the house. "Dad's office . . . he ran . . . the kitchen."

Luke stooped and pulled a small gun from an ankle holster, then edged toward the back of the house.

"No! Let him go." She didn't want to get Luke killed.

He ignored her and whipped around the corner. A minute later he returned from the kitchen, his weapon nowhere in sight. Maybe she'd just imagined it.

"Are you okay?" he asked.

"Getting better. He knocked the wind out of me." She would physically recover, but actual combat with an intruder was so different than the training at Glynco. Brooke was already rehearsing what she should have done differently.

"Can you identify your assailant?"

She shook her head. "He flashed a light in my eyes, blinding me, but I saw enough to know it was a man. He wore a ski mask . . . and gloves."

Luke scanned the living room. "Looks like nothing was bothered in here."

"He was in Dad's office." The spasms had eased, and she hurried to the study with Luke trailing her. What she found pierced her to the core. Files were scattered and pictures that had been on the wall lay in pieces on the floor. She swallowed the lump in her throat and picked up an award her dad had won for training excellence. He'd been so proud to be part of the training program for new graduates of the law enforcement academy.

A camera clicked. Luke was taking photos with his phone. "What are you doing? Why are you taking pictures?"

"I, ah, had a robbery once and regretted not doing this. I'll send them to you."

Brooke pressed her lips together. "Why are you even here?" she asked. Until the funeral it'd been years since she'd last seen Luke. Why was he showing up now all concerned when he hadn't even bothered to tell her good-bye all those years ago?

10

Red crept into Luke's face. "I just wanted to make sure you were okay." He nodded toward her phone. "Don't you think you should call the police?"

Brooke brushed aside the questions she wanted to ask him and took out her phone and dialed 911.

Soon sirens punctuated the night as vehicles piled into her drive. Crime scene techs arrived, and even Pete Nelson, the police chief, showed up. She gave her statement to him while the techs processed the house, photographing every room.

She and Luke remained outside on the wraparound porch, standing at first, then when Brooke realized it'd be a while, she sat in the wooden swing her dad had hung. Bamboo blades from an overhead fan stirred the air but did little to dispel the humidity or the mosquitos that feasted on her skin.

Even though she'd encouraged Luke to go home, he'd stuck with her and was settled in the matching rocker with his eyes closed, his head moving slightly. It was like he listened to music she couldn't hear.

He'd surprised her at the funeral earlier this afternoon. Not because he came, but because of how different he looked. Last time she saw him, he'd looked like a woolly bear. Since his eyes were closed, she took a good look at him. He'd shed the black beard and long hair, and she didn't know how much weight he'd lost, but he'd regained the chiseled jawline and defined cheek-bones she remembered from fourteen years ago. The serpentine gold chain around his neck and the black silk shirt puzzled her though. Back then he'd been more of a jeans and T-shirt guy.

Abruptly he opened his eyes, and her heart hitched from being caught. Her cell phone dinged and gave her an excuse to look away. Jeremy.

Thinking of you. Would you like company?

Warmth filled her. Jeremy had been there for her the past few days, but she was reluctant for him to come by with Luke here. She texted him back that it wasn't a good time.

"Any idea what your intruder was looking for?" Luke asked.

She looked up from her phone, heat rising in her face. "Not a clue, unless it had something to do with a case Dad was working on." Her phone lit up again and she slipped it in her pocket. It was plain rude to text in the middle of a conversation. "Or someone saw the obituary and figured they could break in while we were gone," she said.

"Sad to say that happens a lot. Shouldn't you answer your text?"

"It's a friend . . . I'll get back with him later." Did Luke's body just stiffen or did she imagine it?

"Are you familiar with any of your dad's cases?"

"Ha-ha," she said. "Like Dad ever shared anything about his work with us." The swing had stilled, and she used her foot to push it in motion again. "Why did you want to make sure I was okay? Not that I'm complaining. I'm glad you did, but I'm curious."

He lifted his shoulders in a tiny shrug. "I don't know. I saw your car and just wanted to make sure you were all right. You'd had a bad day even before the break-in."

It had definitely been a bad day. "Thanks." She fingered one of the chain links that anchored the swing to the porch ceiling.

"Did I—"

"I heard—"

"You first," she said.

"I heard you'd finished the law enforcement training in Georgia," he said. "When do you start?"

"I have one event tomorrow night as an interpretive ranger . . ." She glanced down at the award in her lap. *Excellence in Training.* "I was supposed to officially start field training Monday with Dad after he swore me in."

She'd so looked forward to that special moment with him. The air hung heavy between them in an awkward silence. Luke was like everyone else, two-stepping around the Clydesdale in the room. "My dad did not commit suicide."

For a second he didn't answer, and then he shook his head. "I never believed he did."

"Thank you." Tears burned her eyes. Finally someone besides family who agreed with her. "I was supposed to ride with him Sunday night. I keep thinking I should have tracked him down and found out why he cancelled."

"Don't blame yourself. Your dad did things his way," he said. "Is anyone investigating his death as something other than suicide?"

She shook her head. "Just me."

"I wish I could help you."

She supposed a bartender would be as good as some of the investigators she'd met. "Once I'm sworn in Monday, I'll have access to Dad's file."

"You're staying on in Natchez?"

"Absolutely. Gary Franklin is retiring, and I'm taking his place."

Again Luke was quiet. When he looked up, he said, "I'm glad your dad finally came around . . . you know, accepted you were going to be a law enforcement ranger."

"It took him long enough. Said he'd never met anyone so stubborn. And I don't know why he was opposed. Working in law enforcement is part of my DNA."

She stared at him. How did he know Dad had initially opposed her joining the law enforcement side of the park service, anyway? The question rested on the tip of her tongue, and then she pushed it away. She really didn't want to get into that subject tonight.

He tilted his head. "You were about to ask me something?"

"Did I see a gun in your hand earlier?"

His face shuttered, and she didn't think he would answer, then he shrugged.

"I have a permit to carry a concealed weapon," he said. "Never know when I might need one on the job."

When she'd bumped into him in Jackson a few months ago, he'd been coming out of the bar where he worked. "So you're still at Dave's Bar and Grill?"

"More or less."

That was an odd answer. But maybe he only worked part-time. Of all the career paths Luke could have taken, tending bar had never been on her radar. When he'd left Natchez for Annapolis, she figured he would follow in his father's footsteps. She opened her mouth to ask what happened when the front screen opened, and Pete Nelson stepped outside.

The Natchez chief of police had been off duty when she called, but he'd come anyway, dressed in jeans and a white T-shirt. With his shaved head, he reminded her of an African American version of Mr. Clean. Pete acknowledged Luke with a nod.

"The break-in is proof my dad didn't commit suicide," she said.

Pete's brown eyes softened. "There's no way to know if this has any bearing on his death. You said the intruder wore gloves. What type are you talking about? Leather, latex . . . ?"

"Not leather. Latex or maybe even vinyl."

"Was there anything familiar about him?"

She shook her head. "It was dark, but I get the sense he was taller than I am and pretty solid."

He nodded and shifted to Luke. "How about you?"

"I didn't see him at all."

"Too bad," he said and turned back to Brooke. "Do you know what cases your father was working on?"

She'd answered this question Monday when the Adams County sheriff questioned her, and she repeated her answer now. "No. He didn't share that kind of information with me."

"How about his reports?"

She pictured some of the mostly one-page reports she'd seen. "Except for the ones he had to turn in to the district office, he wrote them in a shorthand that only he understood. Have you checked to see if anyone broke into his office at Port Gibson?"

"Talked with Clayton." Pete glanced at his notebook. "He said everything looked fine."

Clayton Bradshaw. Her dad had mentioned the younger ranger was looking to move up the park service ladder, so he would probably request and get her dad's position. That meant he would be her new supervisor.

"I came out on the porch to tell you the techs would be finished in the next few minutes," Pete said. "And I'm really sorry this happened to you."

"Thanks," she said. Pete had been in her and Luke's senior class in high school. Just like never thinking Luke would be a bartender, she never would have figured Pete for law enforcement. "You didn't bother with fingerprints, did you?"

"Only the study on the hopes the intruder may have taken off the gloves briefly. There've been so many people in and out of your house the past couple of days, it would be futile to dust the whole place."

"I assume you want me to see if anything is missing."

"If you don't mind."

"I wish my mother were here to check, but she and my sister just got off a plane in Knoxville." Her mom had texted an hour ago they were on their way to Meghan's house. In turn, Brooke had phoned and informed her about the break-in.

"When will she get back?"

"I'm not sure. Her work is being featured in an art gallery all next month." Her mother's paintings had really taken off in the last few years, and one of the first galleries that had shown her work was in Knoxville. "She may not come back before the baby comes, but I can call and ask her to come home if you think it's necessary."

Pete shook his head. "Why don't you check the house out before we make a decision?"

Good. When Brooke called earlier, her mother had told her to handle the problem, and she really didn't want to call her again.

Luke checked his watch and stood. "I'm going to head out since you don't need me now, but remember, I'm right next door."

For a second his blue eyes held Brooke captive, and she smiled at him, hating the way her heart skipped. She'd learned long ago to keep Luke in the friend box, and she wasn't about to let him out. "Thanks."

Then she thought of Daisy's mail that she'd collected. "And if you talk to your grandmother, tell her I'll bring her mail tomorrow."

When Luke started down the steps, Pete said, "Hold up. I have a couple more questions to ask you."

"I'll be in Dad's office," Brooke said and walked inside the house to his study, where she surveyed the room. It would be hard to know if anything was missing since she wasn't privy to his files. She remembered the security system. Had her mom set the alarm before they left? She needed to check and see. It was a whole other ball game if the intruder had disabled it.

With a sigh Brooke took out her phone and called her mother's number again.

11

When Luke knocked on the Danverses' door, he'd never expected to find Brooke in trouble. Or that seeing her would have such an impact on him. It had taken his breath away when he realized she was in danger. And once he'd gotten his bearings, it had been her natural beauty that had left him struggling to breathe.

It was as though fourteen years had not passed. Brooke still wore her silky dark hair pulled away from her face in a ponytail. The style emphasized her huge brown eyes and high cheekbones. It was the way Luke always pictured her. Except for the one time he'd loosened the tie that held her hair and it fell around her shoulders. But they'd not been much more than kids then, and he brushed the memory away.

Luke glanced toward the house. He would love to stay and examine John's office with Brooke, but that wasn't possible—he had an appointment. Neither did he figure the role of concerned neighbor would extend that far, and he didn't want to raise a red flag, especially with the chief of police.

While he knew Pete Nelson from high school, he'd never worked with the chief. Nelson didn't know Luke was undercover, either, and he wasn't ready to reveal that yet, not until he knew for sure Pete Nelson was clean.

Sonny had indicated a few times that someone in the law

enforcement community was on the cartel's payroll, and Sunday night Romero reinforced the impression. It was Luke's job to ferret that person out. It could be a city cop, a sheriff's deputy, a ranger—even the head of one of the law enforcement agencies.

Pete jogged down the steps where Luke waited. The skinny high school senior he remembered had packed on weight—solid muscle.

"What brings you back to Natchez?" Pete asked.

"John's funeral and helping my grandmother get situated once her surgeon releases her from rehab," he said. "So, how do you like being chief of police?"

Pete laughed. "It has its moments, but I like it just fine."

His senior year, Luke had stayed in Natchez with his grandmother, and Pete and his cousins had been in his class. The cousins, a set of twins and an older boy who should have already graduated, had a reputation for trouble. Pete could have gone either way, but it appeared he'd taken the right path and somehow escaped being painted with the same brush as his cousins.

"You didn't see the intruder at all?" Pete asked.

"No. When I rang the doorbell, I heard a commotion inside. Had no idea someone was in the house other than Brooke. He was gone by the time she let me in."

"I'm glad you were around."

"So am I," he said. "But Brooke wouldn't want anyone to think she's not capable of taking care of herself."

"You know her pretty well."

"Maybe once upon a time. Not so much now." Luke had spent a lot of summers in Natchez with his grandmother, and even as a kid, he'd observed Brooke's fierce independence and the way she took care of herself and her sister, Meghan. Luke bit back a smile. Little blonde-haired Meghan had been a different story with her fair complexion and quiet ways, always striving to please everyone—not at all like her sister.

Pete looked back toward the house. "Yeah, Brooke was kind of prickly when we were in school together." He took a card from his pocket. "If you think of anything, give me a call."

"Sure thing." Luke took the card and stuck it in his wallet, then shook hands with him. "Good to see you again."

The chief started to walk away and stopped. "Maybe I shouldn't say anything . . ."

"Then maybe you shouldn't," Luke said. For a second he thought the chief would keep his thoughts to himself.

Pete rested his hand on the gun clipped to his belt. "Don't encourage Brooke to investigate her dad's death. She's only going to be hurt. The ME was adamant that John Danvers committed suicide, and as far as I've been able to tell, there's nothing to indicate otherwise."

Why was everyone so quick to write John's death off as a suicide? "There wasn't a note, so I'm surprised the ME made such a quick ruling."

Pete eyed him. "I've never known him to be wrong."

This was one time Luke was pretty sure he was, but he didn't contradict the police chief. With another nod, Pete turned and walked back to the Danverses' house.

Once Pete disappeared inside the door, Luke jogged over to his grandmother's house, his mind returning to Brooke. Just seeing her tonight took him back to their last time together. Or maybe it'd been the light fragrance of her floral-scented perfume that transported him back in time to the June evening under the magnolia tree in his grandmother's backyard where he'd kissed Brooke.

Luke's face burned as he remembered walking her to her parents' back door and then leaving, only to find her father waiting for him in the drive. He'd warned him to stay away from Brooke . . . well, he hadn't exactly warned him off, just told him he better not break his daughter's heart. Even at eighteen, Luke knew he didn't want to jeopardize his relationship with a man who treated him better than his own father. And with years ahead of him at the Naval Academy, a fling is all it could have been.

Sometimes he wondered what would have happened if he'd stayed in Natchez instead of caving to the pressure of pleasing his dad and following in his footsteps to Annapolis. Luke shook his head. That bridge had burned a long time ago. Besides, from the way she reacted to the text she'd received, it was apparent Brooke was involved with someone.

Luke's phone buzzed in his pocket as he entered the house, and he quickly glanced at it. Sonny. "Yeah?"

"Romero wants to put the deal off a week."

Luke silently groaned. He needed to get in good with Boudreaux, and the only way to do that was buy his heroin. In large quantities. "You tell Romero he's making a mistake. Sixty thousand is a drop in the bucket to what my people are ready to spend. If not with him, then someone else."

"I'm not telling him anything. The man would as soon kill me as look at me."

Luke wasn't ready to give up. "Did he say why?"

"He didn't say and I didn't ask."

"You have some idea, though."

"I figure it has to do with that ranger's death."

"It was ruled a suicide."

"For now. If the FBI investigates deeper, they may learn there was a big drop at Emerald Mound Sunday night. I figure the ranger found out about it and showed up."

Luke's heart stilled. "How did he find out?"

"I've heard Danvers had a couple of informants."

"Did Romero kill him? Is that why he's worried?"

"Romero wasn't involved in the drop. As for whether he killed the ranger or not, he's not going to share anything like that with me."

"Do you think he did it? He was late getting to the meeting the other night. Maybe that's the reason."

"Those questions are above my pay grade, and for what it's worth, they're above yours."

In other words, don't ask questions. "Thanks for the advice." He needed to be careful what he asked. Too much curiosity might make Romero skittish. "Can you get me another meeting with him?"

"Maybe."

"Give him this number and tell him to call me."

"Okay, but I wouldn't count on hearing from him."

"Just tell him my people are looking at another source to provide what we need." He was willing to bet Romero would call within the hour. "Maybe I need to talk to his boss. Can you set that up?"

"Nope. Only Romero can do that."

After he disconnected, Luke studied the photos on his smartphone. Whatever the intruder was searching for had to be small, and judging by the broken picture frames, it had to be flat. He sent the photos from his phone to the printer, and a few minutes later, he arranged them on the left side of a corkboard he'd moved into his grandmother's library. While he hated that Daisy was in rehab, being in her house by himself allowed him to set up a crime scene board without having to explain what he was doing.

On the right side of the board he pinned the photos from Emerald Mound. He took out a magnifying glass and examined the pictures one more time, looking for any kind of clue. Once he had the official crime scene photos, Luke would compare them.

12

He paced the floor. He'd found nothing in Danvers's office. No notes. No file. Maybe Danvers hadn't put anything in writing. He was famous for keeping everything in his head. His phone rang and he checked the ID. Not a number he recognized. Had to be Romero.

"I know what you're doing."

Not Romero. "Who is this?"

"A friend who wants to help you."

"Help me? I don't need any help. How did you get my phone number?"

"It's on your business card."

A lot of people had his business card. That voice. He'd heard it before. But where? "Look, you're crazy. I don't have time for this."

"You better make time. Unless you want to spend the rest of your life in jail."

"I don't have a clue what you're talking about."

"Emerald Mound. Sunday night."

His legs buckled and he sank into a chair. He'd been so careful.

"I have photos of you putting a package in the trunk of your car. They're time-stamped not long before John Danvers was murdered."

He found his voice. "He killed himself."

PATRICIA BRADLEY / 55

"No. He would never do that. Did you kill him . . . or was it someone from the cartel?"

"I-I don't know what you're talking about." He almost had the voice placed. It was older. Heavy Southern drawl. But what was more important, whoever was on the other end of the line had been at Emerald Mound Sunday night at least long enough to see the transfer.

"I think you do. And this is what's going to happen. You're going to give me information about who killed Brandon Marlar. If you don't have it, you'll get it. Then I'll give you an opportunity to make things right and turn state's evidence. If you tell the authorities what you know, unless you killed John, you probably won't have to serve a day."

Gripping the phone, he closed his eyes. He hadn't come this far to lose it now. "Are you crazy? I don't know what you're talking about."

There was a long sigh from the caller. "Let me make this plain. This can be easy or hard, but either way, you are doing it," he said. "Or the police will get those photos of you putting a package in the trunk of your car that was parked at Emerald Mound about the time Danvers died."

"How much money do you want?"

"I'm not interested in your money. I want to know who killed Brandon, and you're going to tell me."

"That happened in New Orleans. I don't know anything about it." Second time information about Brandon Marlar was mentioned. The caller could be only one person. His father, Kyle Marlar.

"But you can find out. Meet me tomorrow night at King's Tavern with the information. Seven p.m."

The man was worse than crazy, but he wasn't stupid. "King's Tavern will be packed on Friday night. If I come, how will I know you?"

"I'll know you and make contact once you get there. I would

advise you to come, or my next phone call will be to the FBI. Tomorrow. Seven p.m. King's Tavern."

The line went dead.

He swore. Then swore again.

A cold chill ran over Kyle. The flash drive was the only insurance he had that would keep Boudreaux from killing him. But he didn't like being the only one with this information.

He inserted the USB drive into his computer and downloaded the information onto another USB drive. Someone else needed to have a copy, but who? Not Pete Nelson or any other law enforcement officer—Kyle would lose what leverage he had to get information about Brandon.

Luke Fereday. If Fereday promised to sit on the information until Kyle discovered who was responsible for Brandon's death . . . but would he?

Yes. If Luke gave his word, he would keep it.

As soon as he had Luke's promise, Kyle would mail him the copy. He removed the drive from his computer and carefully wrapped it in bubble wrap, then dropped it inside a small box and sealed it with tape. Carefully, he printed an address, pausing after he added the zip code.

Should he have added the photos? Not yet. He would give the courier the opportunity to do the right thing. If he didn't show up tomorrow night, Kyle would make a copy and hand it over to Luke as well.

L uke parked his car across from the Grand Hotel behind a tour bus. He would walk to his meeting from here. He glanced across the street where tourists were still coming and going and frowned. He hadn't considered there would be so many people downtown.

When he'd first arrived in town, he thought about booking a room at the hotel instead of staying at his grandmother's because he hadn't wanted to run into Brooke. Yeah, right. That's why he'd crossed the yard and knocked on the Danverses' door. And why his heart almost stopped when she answered it. After what happened to her, he was glad he had, but he was only fooling himself if he believed that was the only reason. He was attracted to Brooke, always had been, but nothing could ever come of it. Love came at too high a price.

He pulled his thoughts away from Brooke to the man he was meeting. State representative Kyle Marlar was involved in something he had no business being in. Luke had learned from John that Marlar believed his son was murdered by Justin Boudreaux. John had asked Luke to look into it since the death happened in New Orleans and was out of his jurisdiction.

When Luke heard Boudreaux's name, his antenna went up. After he'd researched Marlar, Luke took a calculated risk and contacted the state representative, offering to help find out who killed his son. In their conversations, Marlar had blown him away when he let slip his son had given him a flash drive with information that could incriminate Boudreaux.

Marlar refused to tell him exactly what was on the drive, but Luke was pretty sure he'd figured it out. More research had revealed Brandon Marlar worked for Boudreaux as an accountant. Luke believed the boy had downloaded a second set of books, and he was here tonight to get the flash drive.

Marlar said he would meet him at the top of the steps that led down to Natchez Under-the-Hill. Luke checked his watch. Nine forty-five. It wouldn't take him two minutes to reach the spot, so he had a few minutes to kill. He couldn't think of a better place to spend it than viewing the Mississippi River from the River Walk.

When Luke opened his car door, he was met with the aroma of barbecue from up the street. After he met with Kyle, he just might have to stop by and grab a sandwich. Halfway to the top of the bluff, his calf burned, reminding him of the bullet he'd taken six months ago in a drug deal gone south that left a woman dead. His arm had taken a bullet as well and had been slower to heal.

He flexed his right fingers. Nerves had been damaged by the bullet doctors dug out of his right bicep, leaving his hand unable to even hold a gun, but within a month of getting out of the hospital, Luke had qualified at the gun range with his left hand. He was still rehabbing his grip, determined to prove wrong the doctors who said it would be another twelve months before he'd have full strength in his right hand.

"Luke Fereday? Is that you?"

His insides froze the way they always did when someone recognized him, and he slowly turned around. Jeremy Steele. Immediately Luke's memory bank provided a full résumé for Steele. Son of one of the wealthiest men in Natchez, senior class valedictorian, star quarterback, full scholarship to Ole Miss, and of late, state senator.

"Good to see you, Jeremy, or should I say Senator Steele?"

"Jeremy will do fine."

He extended his hand and Luke took it, trying not to wince when the nerves in his hand protested. "Why are so many people downtown tonight?"

"It's the third Thursday night of the month block party the mayor came up with," Jeremy said. "He thought it would generate revenue. So are you back in Natchez for good? Last I heard, you were at Annapolis."

That's what everyone remembered. Evidently Jeremy hadn't followed his career since he didn't know Luke had dropped out and joined the army. "Came back for John Danvers's funeral," he said for the second time tonight. "And I'm taking a few days to visit my grandmother."

Jeremy winced. "Terrible thing about John. Brooke is just devastated. I texted her earlier tonight, thinking she might want company, but . . ."

"Yeah. Sometimes people just want to be alone." So that's who texted her. If Jeremy was interested in Brooke, that pretty well eliminated anyone else.

"You're looking fit. Working out?"

Luke had worked hard to rebuild his body after being shot in his last undercover operation in Kentucky. "Some. You look in pretty good shape yourself."

"I'm running for the US Senate, and my PR people tell me voters like for their candidate to look healthy."

Luke hadn't heard about his US senate race. He checked his watch. Five minutes before Kyle Marlar was supposed to show.

"I'd appreciate your vote," Jeremy said.

"Afraid I'm not registered to vote in Mississippi."

"Oh, that's right." The state senator nodded. "Seems like I remember your parents lived in DC."

Why was he fishing for where Luke lived? "Mom and Dad are in London right now." He checked his watch again. "It's good seeing you . . ."

"You have to be somewhere?"

"Afraid so."

"Could I ask you something first?" Without waiting for Luke to answer, Jeremy went on. "Brooke Danvers . . . you know her pretty well, right?"

"Once upon a time," Luke said. "Why?"

"She and I have had a few dates lately, but the two of you had a thing going in high school. Is she why you came back to Natchez?"

"Like I said, I came back for her father's funeral."

Jeremy chewed the inside of his lip. "And you're not interested in her?"

"I'd like to think we're good friends."

"Nothing more?"

"What's your point?"

Jeremy shrugged. "If you two have something going, I don't want to waste my time."

"Why are you interested in Brooke? She's not your usual type." When Jeremy frowned, Luke said, "I've seen photos in the Jackson paper, and you usually have a curvy blonde in designer clothes hanging on your arm. I don't think it's ever been the same one twice."

"More PR stuff. I'm looking for someone who sees beyond the money and prestige. Someone my little girl approves of, and she definitely approves of Brooke."

Little girl? He'd totally forgotten Jeremy's first wife died right after their child was born. "I don't guess I've seen you since your wife passed. I'm sorry."

Jeremy palmed his hand. "Thanks. The cliché is true—it gets easier with time."

Something nagged at the back of Luke's mind. *Divorce proceedings.* He was pretty sure he'd read or heard the Steeles were getting a divorce before his wife died.

"Back to you and Brooke. Are you saying I don't have to worry about you when it comes to Brooke?"

"Yep." Luke swallowed the irritation that suddenly filled him. It wasn't like he had any romantic interest in Brooke, or that she would be interested in him. Not after fourteen years of silence. Jeremy Steele was a much better match for Brooke than Luke ever would be. "We're just friends," Luke said. "But as her friend, I'm warning you. Don't hurt her."

"You don't have to worry about that. She's very special to me."

"Good to know." Luke checked his watch. "Sorry, I gotta leave."

Jeremy tipped his head. "Good to see you again."

"Yeah."

Luke jogged in the opposite direction the state senator took. That had been a strange conversation. He glanced back at the state senator as he climbed into his two-seater BMW. This did not feel like an accidental meeting. He should have told Jeremy flat-out he had nothing to worry about—Brooke would never be interested in Luke Fereday.

His phone rang and he slowed to a walk to check the ID. Kyle Marlar. "Fereday."

"There's been a change of plans, son," Marlar said in his slow, south Mississippi accent. "I'm not comin'."

"Why?"

"It's complicated. I have something I need to deal with tonight. Besides, I'm not sure the two of us being seen together is a good idea."

"Are you backing out of our deal?"

"I told you I'd give you the flash drive, and I will. But first, you have to promise you won't do anything with the information until I have the name of Brandon's killer."

"What? I can't—"

"Then you won't get it."

Luke pinched his lips together. He forced himself to relax. "You don't know the people you're dealing with. Let me help you, or you could end up like John Danvers."

"I won't take the chances John did."

"What do you know about his death?" The line went silent. After a few seconds, Luke said, "Are you still there?"

"I'm here. I'm not sure what happened to John at Emerald Mound, but I do know John Danvers never killed himself."

Marlar's soft voice dropped his r's, and his slow cadence drew out each syllable.

"Were you there?"

A deep sigh came through the phone. "Yes, but I never saw him. I'd already left the area when he died."

"Why were you there?"

"I'd heard there was going to be a drug drop, and I wanted to document it with my camera."

"How did you learn that?"

"I have connections."

What kind of connections did Marlar have? Luke searched his memory, and it hit him. The community center that his nonprofit ran for kids who'd been in trouble with drugs was a perfect place to learn what was going on in the drug scene in Natchez. "You have photos of what happened Sunday night?"

"Maybe."

"How about John?" Luke's heart thumped against his ribs. "Did you take pictures—"

"No!"

"But you know something about his death."

"No, I don't. If I did, I would have gone to the sheriff."

"You knew there was going to be a drug transfer Sunday night. Did you tell John about it?"

"No. I didn't want him there. He would have arrested the courier, and that would have defeated my purpose."

"You could have gotten yourself killed. What did you hope to accomplish?"

"I thought if I discovered who the courier is, I could make him tell me who killed my son."

"Then you have to know who killed John."

"How many times do I have to tell you, I don't know what happened after I left."

"But you saw the courier." Again Marlar was silent. "Who is it?"

"If I tell you, he'll be arrested, and I'll lose what leverage I have. He's my only chance of finding out who killed Brandon."

Luke gripped the phone. He'd like to squeeze the information out of Marlar. So close, yet so far. "You're playing a dangerous game doing this alone. I can help you."

"I'm sorry, I have to do it my way."

The man was playing with dynamite. "If you think this man will spill his guts because you saw him take a package of drugs Sunday night . . . it won't happen. He'll deny it."

"I have time-stamped photos of him taking the package and putting it in his trunk. There's no way he'll wiggle out of being at Emerald Mound."

Luke massaged his temple. "Without the actual drugs, the photos are useless," he said. Still, he would like to get his hands on those pictures.

"But the photos put him at Emerald Mound about the time John was shot."

"Circumstantial." There was no point in arguing—Kyle Marlar could only see what he wanted to see. "Thing is," Luke said, "this guy probably doesn't even know what happened to your son. You want justice for Brandon? Then give me the flash drive. It's better leverage than your photos."

"You don't even know what's on the flash drive."

"Pretty sure it's a second set of books that lists Boudreaux's drug involvement."

"H-how did you know?"

"It wasn't that hard to figure out. Your son worked for Boudreaux as an accountant. So where can we meet?"

"No! Without a solid witness corroborating Boudreaux's

involvement in drugs, a fancy lawyer can get him off. Besides, if he's arrested, he'll never admit to killing my son."

It was like beating his head against a wall. The man had a one-track mind. "The runner probably doesn't even know Boudreaux."

"He knows him. The man I saw Sunday night wouldn't deal with underlings."

It was evident Marlar wasn't going to give him the runner's name, and Luke was tired of going in circles. Maybe if he came at it differently. "How did your son get a second set of books?"

Silence ticked off for a few seconds. "I'm afraid Brandon was a master hacker. Had been since high school when he got into trouble for breaking into the grading system and changing not just his grade in English, but that of several of his friends." He sighed. "I thought that had taught him a lesson, but evidently not. He hacked into Boudreaux's computer system. I don't think he ever dreamed he'd find what he did."

"Give me specifics."

"It contains a list of foreign bank accounts, delivery schedules with matching deposits, dates, places, and shell companies. And some of the shell companies he told me about are the same companies Boudreaux used to donate money to my campaign and my nonprofit."

Money laundering 101. Donate to a political figure and then threaten to expose the dirty money through rumor or even by sacrificing a shell company that could easily be replaced with another. "What's he pressuring you to do?"

There was another pause before Marlar cleared his throat. "Vote against the medical marijuana bill," he said, his voice cracking.

That made sense. If medical marijuana were legal, it would cut into the cartel's sales. "You planned to vote yes for the measure?"

"Yes. Research has proven it helps so many people with pain and nausea. And there's a kid in this district who needs it for his seizures."

"Then help me bring down the cartel. Give me the flash drive."

"Once you promise to wait until I give you the go-ahead, I'll get it to you."

"If I agree, you'll bring it to me?"

"I can't meet you tonight, but I promise, you'll get it. Is it a deal?"

It was obvious Marlar would not be deterred. "Okay, you have my word. I won't do anything with the information you give until you okay it. But we need to meet tonight."

"I told you, I can't do that."

"Meet me tonight or the deal is off." When there was no response, he checked his phone.

Marlar had disconnected and Luke was talking into dead air.

14

It had been too depressing to sit in her dad's office and go through his files so Brooke had scooped up all the papers and empty file folders and brought them to the living room sofa. She'd made little progress, and had instead replayed the break-in in her mind over and over and how she could have handled it differently. Maybe her parents were right, and she wasn't cut out to be a law enforcement ranger. She'd just wanted to make her dad proud.

Brooke brushed away thoughts of what she should have done and glanced down at the current folder. The papers for this particular file had been easy since they were stapled together and matched the name on the folder. Justin Boudreaux.

It didn't look like a case her dad had ever worked, more like a background check. *Boudreaux.* The name was familiar . . . she tried to place where she'd seen it . . . Brooke snapped her fingers. His photo had been in the newspaper recently, the grocery magnate locating a superstore in Natchez. The image of a tall, dark-haired, dark-complexioned man popped into her mind. Satisfied, she turned back to the file. There was no date, but it was possible her dad had checked him out recently—he was like that, very protective of who brought businesses into Natchez.

She set the file aside just as the doorbell rang, and Brooke glanced at her watch. Who would be stopping by her house at

10:00 p.m.? The bell pealed again, and she quickly rose from the sofa and hurried to answer it. After a quick look through the peephole, her heart kicked up a notch and she opened the door. "Jeremy?"

"I saw your lights on and figured you were still up. And I know you said you didn't want company tonight, but I was concerned about you."

She looked up, and worry was reflected in his brown eyes. "That is so sweet of you."

"Can I come in?" he asked.

Brooke hesitated. "Do you mind sitting on the porch instead? I have stuff scattered all over the living room."

When he agreed, Brooke stepped outside and sat in the swing. Like Luke earlier, Jeremy sat in the chair. "Are you okay? You look—"

"Frazzled? I am," she said and told him about the break-in, since in a town the size of Natchez, he would hear about it tomorrow anyway.

"You should've told me. I would've come sooner."

"I promise, I'm fine."

"You're sure you're not hurt?"

"I'm okay. A little embarrassed that I let him get away."

Jeremy quickly moved from the chair to the swing. "You're new at this, and experience is a fast teacher." He squeezed her hand. "Pack a bag and come stay at the house. I have a live-in housekeeper, so it wouldn't look inappropriate. There are plenty of bedrooms you can choose from."

Brooke had no doubt about that. The Steele mansion was huge, but she did not need protecting. "I can take care of myself."

"I didn't mean to imply you couldn't, but I'd feel better knowing you weren't alone."

"Thank you, but I'll be fine. I have a security system that my mom forgot to set when we left earlier. I'll make sure it's armed when you leave."

He turned her to face him. "I don't think you know how much you mean to me."

She swallowed hard. He had just kicked their relationship into high gear and Brooke wasn't sure she was ready.

"Think about staying at the house until this person is caught. Molly would love it."

He'd pulled the kid card, knowing how much she cared for his daughter. "That's not fair."

"I don't care whether it's fair or not."

He leaned forward, his gaze fastened on hers. He intended to kiss her and she froze.

Jeremy immediately pulled back. "I'm sorry. I didn't mean to make you uncomfortable."

Now she'd made him feel bad, but her feelings were all over the place. "It's not your fault. It's just that I'm so numb."

He hit his head with his palm. "That was stupid. I'm sure you're overwhelmed with your dad's death and now this break-in, and I'm only making it harder. I'm serious about you staying at the house, though, and I promise I won't put any pressure on you."

"Thank you, but I can't. I have too much to do tomorrow," she said, rising from the swing.

"And now you want me to leave."

"Since you mentioned it . . .." She grinned at him to soften her words.

Jeremy rose and took her hand. "Lock up when I leave, and don't forget to set your alarm, okay?"

"Okay," Brooke echoed.

He hesitated. "How do you feel about dinner Saturday night?"

"How about I let you know?"

He sighed and his shoulders drooped. "Would it make a difference if I said pretty please? That always works for Molly."

She laughed. "Oh, all right. Dinner Saturday night."

"Yes!" He pumped his fist.

Jeremy refused to leave until she was safely inside the house with the security system armed. As his tires crunched out of the drive, she glanced toward the papers on the sofa. She could not look at one more file and grabbed a box from the walk-in pantry to put everything in. When she was halfway down the hall, the doorbell rang again, and she retraced her steps to the door and looked through the peephole. Luke? This was getting ridiculous. Did no one in her life think she could take care of herself?

"It's me," he said.

"Hold on a sec while I turn off the alarm."

Once she keyed in the code and the green light flashed, she returned and opened the door. "Did you forget something?"

"No. I saw Pete pulling out of your drive, and then your light was on . . ."

"That wasn't Pete," she said. "It was Jeremy Steele."

"I see."

She didn't like his tone. "What's that supposed to mean?"

When he frowned, Brooke narrowed her eyes. What right did he have to disapprove of who came to visit her? She tapped her foot, waiting for an answer.

"Who you see is none of my business."

"You got that right."

Luke studied her, then a slow smile spread across his face. "I've missed locking horns with you."

"I wasn't the one who left," she said softly.

"Touché." Then he looked past her. "I thought you might like help putting your dad's office back together."

Unexpected tears burned her eyes, and she blinked them back. "Thanks, but I just can't do one more thing tonight."

He hesitated. "You look as though you could use someone to talk to. Okay if I come in?"

If she said no, he'd probably argue with her. Brooke stepped back, allowing him room to step past her, and immediately his easy confidence commanded the room like it always had. "Th-thanks."

"You want to put the papers in that box you're holding?"

Brooke looked down. She'd forgotten it was in her hands. "Sure." She handed it to him and then sighed. "I've gone through I don't know how many files, but I don't even know what I'm looking for."

"And you're sure your dad never mentioned a case—"

"I told you, I told the sheriff the night he died, and I told Pete Nelson tonight—Dad did not discuss his cases with us." Brooke took a slow breath and released it. She shouldn't take her frustration out on Luke. "I'm sorry. I've racked my brain over every detail of the past few weeks, looking for something to hang his death on, and now the break-in. And I've come up with zip."

"I'm sorry too."

Brooke felt her face flush. Wherever she turned, people felt sorry for her, and she didn't like being the object of pity.

"I'd hoped once I finished at the academy his attitude would change, and he would share information with me, but that didn't happen. Probably wouldn't have changed once he was my boss, either." Something Luke said earlier popped into her thoughts. "How did you know Dad didn't want me to become a patrol ranger?"

He picked up a file and laid it on the desk. "Your dad and I used to talk."

She couldn't believe her dad talked about her behind her back. "And he told you he didn't want me to become a law enforcement ranger?"

"Not exactly. He talked about how dangerous it could be," he said. "He didn't want you to get hurt."

"So why had he gone off like the Lone Ranger and gotten himself killed?"

"That's a good question," Luke said. "Because we both know he didn't commit suicide."

Brooke hadn't realized she'd said the words out loud. "If I could just figure out why he was at Emerald Mound."

"Maybe he was checking out a tip," he said, his voice cracking.

Her dad's death was hurting Luke as well. "I forget how close you two had been."

"Yeah. He was good to me. Pete Nelson and the other guys had Kyle Marlar, but I had your dad. No matter how bad I messed up, he always treated me like I was worth something."

That was her dad, all right.

"How come you dropped out of Annapolis?" She clapped her hand over her mouth. "I'm so sorry. That isn't any of my business."

"It's okay. It's not a secret." His red face belied his words. "I'm surprised you haven't asked Daisy."

"I have," she said and busied herself stacking papers in the box.

"What'd she say?"

Brooke paused her packing. "That it's your story to tell."

"That'd be Daisy." He tilted his head toward her. "There's really not much to tell."

"It's just that I never figured you would be—" She cleared her throat. "I'm sorry. That sounded so judgmental . . . but you were at Annapolis. That's a far cry from being a bartender."

"My heart just wasn't into a naval career," he said. "And that's what Annapolis is all about."

"I'll bet your dad wasn't happy." Daisy had told Brooke once that her son had groomed Luke from the cradle to have a career in the navy.

"I'm not sure which made the Admiral angrier—dropping out or joining the army."

"How did you get to be a bartender?" she asked and swallowed a yawn.

"There were a few career moves between Annapolis and bartending, but that's a story for another night. You look beat." He swept his arm toward the papers. "Why don't you leave this for tomorrow and go to bed? I'll help you clean all of this up in the morning."

"You don't have to," she said, feeling every hour of the long day it'd been. "How long will you be in Natchez?"

Luke made an iffy motion with his hands. "Not sure. I felt bad I wasn't here for Daisy's surgery, so I'm trying to make it up to her. How about your mom? I heard you tell Pete it'd be a while before she returned. You think she might come back because of the break-in?"

"Depends on whether Meghan needs her. Although her baby isn't due for a couple of months, Mom wanted to help with getting the nursery ready." Brooke straightened her shoulders. "She told me to take care of it."

"Well, if you need me—Wait! Meghan is having a baby? Did I miss that earlier?"

"You must have." She grinned. "It's a little girl. She's going to name her Isabelle."

"Oh, wow. Little Meghan married . . . that's hard to wrap my mind around."

"She's twenty-eight, Luke. I'm only four years older than she is."

He had the grace to blush again, which was kind of cute. "Time does get away."

That was an understatement. She was happy for her sister and planned to be a good aunt.

He touched her arm. "Like I said, if you need me for anything, just call."

"Thanks, but I don't have your cell phone number." She'd been meaning to get his number from Daisy in case anything happened to her.

"Sorry. Give me your phone and I'll put it in."

She handed over her phone, and after he keyed in the number, he said, "Now, give me your number." Once he keyed hers into his contacts, he said, "By the way, if you see Daisy, don't tell her I'm still here. I want to surprise her. She thought I was leaving right after the funeral."

Brooke assured him she'd keep his secret just as his phone rang, and Luke glanced at the screen. "I need to take this. See you tomorrow?"

"That would be great." Why did the thought of seeing him again send warmth spreading through her chest?

He hurried out the door, and she closed it behind him and walked to the kitchen to arm the security system again. It surprised her how easily they'd picked up their friendship after so many years. When Luke had talked about his dad, she'd seen past the bravado he presented to the world. He was once again the boy who had spent summers and his senior year in high school with his grandmother. And yes, the boy she'd fallen hard for that last summer before college.

15

Luke caught the phone call as he stepped off the porch. "Hello?"

"You think I'm making a mistake?"

He recognized Romero's voice as he hurried across the lawn to Daisy's house. "If you turn down my offer, yeah. Your boss going to be okay with losing not just this sixty-thousand-dollar deal but maybe a lot more? Because that's about to happen."

Romero answered him with a few seconds of silence, and then he said, "The Boss wants to see you."

Yes! "Where and when?"

"Now. Room 212. Grand Hotel."

The line went dead. Boudreaux was in Natchez? Intel should have let him know. He quickly dialed his supervisor's number. "Why didn't anyone tell me Boudreaux is in town?"

"I just found out a few minutes ago," Steve said. "How do you know?"

"I have a meeting with him right now."

"Good. Just be careful."

"Don't worry." Luke pocketed his phone as he hurried to his Jeep. Boudreaux was cautious, but the carrot of a long-term deal must have flushed him out. If he played it right, this could be a huge payoff.

Three government agencies, including ISB, had quietly been working to gather evidence against the New Orleans businessman. If the data drive Marlar had actually turned out to be a second set of books, and then they nailed him for smuggling heroin, they could seal the case. Maybe even get the people behind his organization. The cartel. But first he had to get the drive.

Ten minutes later, he parked for the second time tonight across from the Grand Hotel. This time he crossed the street and entered the hotel through the front door, then took the stairs up to the second floor. When he reached the room number Romero had given him, he knocked softly. There was a pause, then a deadbolt clicked and the door opened. The man standing in front of him was the bodyguard from Windsor Ruins.

"Come in."

Luke's mind barely had time to register a spicy Cajun aroma before the man pushed him against the wall. "Hey!" he said. "What's the deal? Romero called and said Boudreaux wanted to meet with me."

"In due time." The man released him, and then ran a wand up and down Luke's body. "Guns and phones on the table."

Luke palmed his hands. "No gun," he said.

Expecting to be frisked, he'd left both of his semi-automatics in the car. As he placed the phone on the table, Luke checked out the type of wand being used. For every listening device detector, there was a way to circumvent it, but only if he knew the brand, and he knew this one. One hurdle down, one to go. He had to somehow create an opportunity to record a conversation with the drug kingpin.

Luke never forgot a face, but he hadn't gotten a good look at the bodyguard's face at Windsor Ruins. He stared at the man with the wand. Black hair and eyes. Acne scars pockmarked his face. Sunday night a jacket had hidden the shirt-splitting biceps that formed his upper arms. But it was the snake tattoo on his neck that sent an urgent sense of déjà vu through him.

He'd seen the man and that snake tattoo before tonight. But where? The memory slammed him. Robert Wilson. Luke's stomach dipped like he was on a runaway roller coaster. Five years ago he'd arrested the man up around Nashville.

He forced himself to breathe normally. So far Wilson didn't appear to recognize him. Maybe because it'd been so long ago, or maybe because Luke had shed twenty pounds and no longer had the long curly hair and beard he'd worn back then.

Had he used his regular voice or disguised it? That undercover gig lasted over six months, and he was pretty sure he'd used his regular voice. *Just play it cool.* Luke stared the man in the eye. "If Romero isn't here, where is Mr. Boudreaux?"

"You just don't know how to keep your mouth shut, do you?"

"Look," Luke said. "Romero called me, not the other way around. I'm just looking to buy."

"They'll be here in due time."

"You have a name?" It would be interesting to know if he was using the same one.

"What are you, a game show host or something with the twenty questions? Just sit on the sofa over there," Wilson said, pointing to the red sofa against the wall.

Luke did as he was told, and five minutes later the connecting door to the adjoining suite opened, and three men entered the room. He didn't recognize two of them, bodyguards, he assumed, but the third one was unmistakable. Boudreaux. From his styled hair to tailor-made suit and Gucci loafers, the man exuded power. If Luke didn't know better, he might believe the drug dealer was the businessman he represented himself to be. Satisfaction settled in his gut. Months of buying small quantities of heroin from Sonny had finally paid off.

"Mr. Boudreaux." Luke nodded and infused just the right amount of respect into his voice as he stood and extended his hand. "Luke Fereday."

"Fereday. That's a good Louisiana name," Boudreaux said. "At last we meet."

"It's long overdue." Boudreaux's handshake was firm, but

not bone crushing, indicating the drug czar believed he was in charge and didn't feel the need to challenge Luke. Maybe even a tad overconfident. Luke shifted so he could keep an eye on Wilson, who had positioned himself by the door.

Boudreaux cocked his head. "So you think I'm making a mistake to put the deal off until next week?"

The drug czar's Cajun accent was subtle, showing up mostly in the way he put emphasis on the last word in the sentence. He was evidently proud of his roots, but didn't want to be defined by them. Luke's research indicated the New Orleans dealer was a self-made man and had started out on a shanty in the bayous.

He surrounded himself with men who were bold and fearless, even cocky. But he expected respect. If Luke impressed Boudreaux tonight, it was possible he could work his way into the organization. At least long enough to find out when the big shipment of heroin he'd heard about was arriving in the States. "I understand why you're cautious, but my people are ready to do business. You and I can work a deal that will benefit both of us."

"I like the way you think." Boudreaux slapped him on the back just as a microwave dinged. "You'll join me at the table?" he asked. "We pass a good time over a plate of boudin from Fat Mama's Tamales, eh."

That's what Luke smelled. He liked the sausage well enough and nodded as Wilson quietly moved from the door to the microwave.

"Good." The drug czar clapped his hands together.

It was as though Luke had passed some sort of test. He followed Boudreaux to the table in the far corner of the room as Wilson removed a plate of the fat sausages from the microwave and set it before them. Then Boudreaux picked up his phone, and soon zydeco music filled the room.

"Boudin should be eaten in the right atmosphere," he said. He took one of the sausages and bit into it, then pulled the casing through his teeth, squeezing the filling out. "Mmm, that's good. Almost as good as Grandmeré's, rest her soul."

Luke forked a link and bit into the boudin and followed the Cajun's example, savoring the blend of meat and rice infused with a smoky flavor. It'd been a while, and he was glad to discover he still liked the Louisiana delicacy.

"Grandmeré, she raised me, you know. In my mind's eye, I can still see that shanty houseboat on the bayou and her standing at the woodstove, boudin sizzling in the black pot." A faraway look came into his eyes, then his jaw clenched. "Living on the bayou made an old woman of her long before she took me in. When death came calling for her, I was left alone at twelve to fend for myself. More nights than not, I went to bed hungry, something I vowed once I got out of the swamp I'd never do again."

"I'm sure that was hard," Luke said. His research had included reading Boudreaux's bio several times.

"You don't have a clue, rich boy." The joviality had disappeared from Boudreaux's voice. He shoved a plate with slices of pickle on it across the table. "Here, try one of these."

The Cajun was the one who didn't have a clue. Yeah, Luke might have come from wealth, but there'd been very little love shown. "I wasn't patronizing you," he said evenly. "Having rich parents doesn't always mean you have love, at least not from them." He allowed a tiny smile to show. "But there's no love like a grandmother's, right?"

Boudreaux's black eyes narrowed. "Your folks . . . that's why you do what you do?"

Luke squared his shoulders. "I do what I do because I want to. I don't answer to anyone."

The unwavering black eyes seemed to bore right through him. Suddenly, Boudreaux clapped his hands again. "We're going to get along just fine," he said. "Now try one of the pickles."

Luke didn't like pickles, but it hadn't been a suggestion. He picked up one and bit into it. In seconds his mouth was on fire and tears watered his eyes. Swallowing a cough, he poured a glass of water and downed it.

Boudreaux laughed. "Whoever named the pickles Fire & Ice got it right, eh?"

His mouth still burning, Luke nodded and drank more water.

"Now, we get down to business. Sunday night you wanted a kilo of heroin and you wanted it on a regular basis. Is that still the case?"

"When can I get my first supply?"

"Saturday night."

He nodded. "Where and what time?"

"You'll be called. Just have your money ready—C-notes, old bills in six stacks."

Luke nodded. It was on the tip of his tongue to discuss the drugs going up the Trace. Instead he stood. He needed to get in good with Boudreaux first. And he wanted to be wearing a wire when he did.

16

He read the article on Kyle Marlar and then laid the paper down. He had a plan and searched his call log for the number Marlar had used. The state representative answered on the second ring, and he didn't sound surprised.

"I can't make it to King's Tavern at seven. How about around nine, just before closing time?" he asked, knowing Marlar would say no. The newspaper article had reported he was speaking on how to take photos of the night sky at the Perseids meteor event at Fort Rosalie at nine o'clock. The article had even provided information on where the state representative would be set up.

"Sorry, but I'll be busy then."

"I don't understand why we have to meet at all. I haven't done anything wrong."

"My photos show otherwise."

"Look, I'm not in your pictures. You have the wrong person," he said.

"I have the right person, all right," Marlar said, then he was quiet for a few seconds. "Look, I have pull. Give me what I want, and I'll see to it you don't serve any time."

"What do you want?"

"I told you—the name of the person who injected heroin in my son. And a promise to testify against Boudreaux in court."

"I have no idea about your son, and you're crazy if you think I'm testifying against anyone."

"I think you will before this is over," he said. "I have no doubt you can find out who killed my son."

"It isn't that easy."

"I don't care if it's easy or not. If you don't agree to do it—"

"You're going to show the cops a bunch of pictures that make it appear I'm doing . . . what?"

"You'll see when we meet."

"What if you dropped one of the photos and someone found it? From the way you talk, I'd be ruined."

"They're on a camera card. No one will see them except you, unless you don't show," Marlar said.

Good. The images were digital. "All right. I'll meet you at seven."

"If you don't show, tomorrow I go to the authorities."

"I'll be there."

He hung up and flexed his fingers. This had to go like clockwork. A few minutes later, he laid his tools on the table. Black leather gloves, a suppressor, and his 9mm Glock. He started the stopwatch on his phone and pulled on the gloves, removed the suppressor from the case, and fumbled as he attached it to the automatic. He had to do better than that, and repeated the process until he completed it seamlessly.

17

Brooke Danvers squared her shoulders and settled the flat-brimmed hat on her head. She checked her image in the bedroom mirror. Gray shirt, green pants, and regulation shoes. She looked the part for her last interpretive program. Not that her look would change much when she officially became an LE.

She wouldn't have to wear the flat-brimmed hat as often since at her five-feet-seven-inch height, the brim could possibly block her view when ticketing drivers, a problem the six-foot-plus rangers didn't have to deal with. The only other difference between her old uniform and the new one was the duty belt and everything that went with it—gun, extra ammo, handcuffs, flashlight, and latex gloves.

Her gaze shifted to the Sig Sauer hanging in her duty belt on the bedpost. She hadn't worn it since Sunday night. If she'd had it on last night, the intruder would not have gotten away. Brooke debated wearing it tonight, but she expected mostly families at the meteor event, and she didn't want to frighten the small children.

But it wouldn't hurt to try it on, and she carefully lifted the gun and strapped it around her waist, then turned and admired the way it looked. Just as Brooke rested her hand on the pistol grip, the doorbell rang and she jumped. She wasn't usually this edgy.

It rang again in quick succession. Only Emma laid down on the doorbell like that, and she hurried to the front door. The view through the peephole confirmed it was her best friend and fellow ranger mugging at her. "Let me in before the humidity frizzes my flat-ironed hair," she said through the door.

"I thought you were going straight to Fort Rosalie," Brooke said as she opened the door and then stepped aside to let her friend in. "And I'm afraid it's too late about your hair."

"Rats!" Emma tugged at a red curl that had sprung awry.

"So what are you doing here?" Brooke asked.

"I had a few minutes to burn, and I remembered you were making brownies for Miss Daisy. Thought you might have a few left over," she said.

"I do, and they're in the kitchen." This afternoon Brooke had turned to baking once she had her dad's office back in semi-order. "Come on," she said and led the way down the hall. "But," she said over her shoulder, "I've told you not to call her Miss Daisy! It makes her feel old."

"I always forget. But she reminds me of the Driving Miss Daisy star." In the kitchen, Emma looked her over. "How are you? Did you get your dad's office cleaned up?"

First thing this morning, Brooke had called her friend and told her about the break-in. She had not told the part about Luke. She shrugged. "Question one, I'm doing okay. Question two, the mess is cleaned up, and I even attempted to see if any of his files were missing."

"Were any missing?"

"Who knows? It doesn't look like he ever purged anything. Twenty years of cases. And he had his own filing system, mostly notes stuck in folders and filed according to dates. On the bright side, if I couldn't figure out his files, I'm pretty sure whoever broke in couldn't either." She unsnapped the top of a cake carrier and set the brownies in front of Emma. "Cup of coffee?"

Her friend waved her off. "You forget where we'll be tonight? Not many amenities." She bit into a brownie. "This is good. Any clues as to who broke in?"

"No. It was dark in Dad's office and it happened so fast, I only got a general impression of the man." It still rankled that he'd gotten away.

"That's scary," Emma said. "But I guess you'll encounter things like that every day on the new job. Are you sure you want to switch?"

"Yes, I'm sure. Besides, I'll mostly be stopping speeders and handing out tickets." And trying to prove her dad hadn't committed suicide.

"Well, even that can be dangerous. What if you stop someone doing something illegal, like running drugs?"

"You sound like Mom and Dad. I've completed twenty weeks at the law enforcement training center and once I'm sworn in, I'll have another three months of training under Clayton, at least that's who I figure will train me now."

Emma raised her eyebrows. "So last night didn't bother you?"

Brooke wouldn't go that far. "It bothered me because he got away. Can we talk about something else?"

"Sorry."

"That's okay," she said a little too quickly.

Emma glanced around the kitchen. "The cabinets look good. Your dad was doing a great job." Then her friend winced. "Sorry again. I didn't mean to bring your dad up. When do you move back into your apartment?"

"Hopefully I'll be back home in a couple of weeks."

"What if your mom decides to sell the house now?"

Brooke flinched. Other than her apartment and when she was away at college, this house had been the only place she'd ever lived, but her mom selling was a real possibility. It's what she'd wanted to do instead of remodeling, and now that Dad was gone, there was nothing to stop her.

"If she does and moves to where your sister lives, you won't leave too, will you?"

"No. My roots are here—five generations of them."

"Maybe you can buy the house."

"With what?" Her shoulders slumped. "Except for a couple thousand dollars, I spent all my savings on the law enforcement training."

"Too bad the park service didn't pay for it."

"Yeah, but since switching departments was my idea and not theirs, I had to pay."

"Speaking of the training," Emma said, pointing at the gun, "are you wearing that tonight?"

"No, I was just trying it on. Did I tell you I got Gary Franklin's job? I'll be taking the number three spot at Port Gibson."

"Don't you mean number two? I heard they were moving Clayton into your dad's job."

Social media had nothing on the park service grapevine. "I hadn't heard that."

"You haven't been in to the office." Emma broke another brownie in half. "You'll never guess who I saw when I stopped to gas up my car. Your old boyfriend, Luke Fereday."

"He wasn't my boyfriend!"

"Yeah, right. And you didn't have his name plastered on every notebook you owned along with his last name with your first one."

"I was a teenager, for Pete's sake, and probably did that to drive my mother crazy." While Luke wasn't the typical "bad boy," trouble had always seemed to find him in the form of fast cars and mostly harmless pranks. "Besides, he was here at the house last night. Even ran off the intruder."

"Get outta here," Emma said, her eyes wide.

"Yep." Heat warmed her face as her friend continued to stare at her.

"You still have feelings for him." It wasn't a question.

Brooke jutted her jaw. "I do not have feelings for Luke Fereday. It's been fourteen years since he left, and I've maybe seen him three times. We're not the same people we were then."

Emma laughed. "Methinks the lady doth protest too much."

"No, after everything that's happened this week, I'm off center." She reached for a brownie and nibbled on it. "He broke my heart when I was seventeen. He won't get a chance to do it again."

"Maybe he's changed."

"Maybe, but that doesn't change the fact Luke had commitment problems then, and from his job choice, he still does."

"What do you mean?"

"He's a bartender."

"And?"

"Most bartenders move from place to place. They have trouble committing. And how does one go from a naval career to tending bar? There's a world of difference between the two careers." She splayed her hands. "It doesn't make any difference anyway since I won't be having any further contact with Luke. He'll go his way and I'll go mine. Besides, Jeremy and I are dating now. We're going out tomorrow night."

The grandfather clock in the foyer chimed the half hour, and Brooke made a squawking noise.

"It can't be seven thirty already," she said, unbuckling the gun. "I have to stop by the rehab and drop off Daisy's mail and the brownies before I go to Fort Rosalie."

"I get the hint," Emma said, grabbing another brownie. "River bluff in the morning?"

"Not in the morning," Brooke said. "We won't get away from Fort Rosalie until well after midnight, and I won't be in any mood to get up at five thirty and run."

"Later will be too hot. Meet you at the gym around six tomorrow evening?"

"Make it five so I'll have time to get ready for my date," she said and laughed as Emma saluted. They'd been friends since first grade, and she was Brooke's greatest encourager . . . and task manager. The two saw it as their duty to keep each other in shape.

Brooke put half a dozen brownies in a Ziploc bag for Daisy

and grabbed her bundle of mail before hurrying out the door with Emma. Even though the sun hung low, the evening hadn't cooled down, and hot, humid air hit her in the face. At least with her straight hair she didn't have to worry about frizzing like Emma. Nevertheless, she was glad she'd pulled it off her neck into a ponytail.

In spite of what she'd said about Luke, she checked to see if his car was in Daisy's drive. Empty. A tinge of disappointment surprised her, and she quickly brushed it aside. Why she even looked, she didn't know. She didn't need Luke Fereday complicating her life.

She backed out of her drive. Maybe it was true that a person never got over their first love. She didn't really believe that, but it would be better if Luke weren't staying at his grandmother's.

Brooke shook her head. Why was she thinking about Luke? She had a good thing going with Jeremy. No need to mess it up.

18

Brooke pulled into the rehab, glad that practically everything in Natchez was reachable in ten minutes—fifteen at the most. She grabbed the brownies and mail and made her way inside, where she signed the guest book before walking to the east wing. She'd know soon enough if Luke had been here. If Daisy didn't mention his name, neither would she. "Knock, knock," she said and pushed open the door to room 119.

"I'd about given you up." Daisy sat on the side of her bed working on her knee exercises. "My, don't you look spiffy. What's the occasion?"

Her heart sank at Daisy's slip, but Brooke kept a smile on her lips. "Thank you, ma'am, for the compliment, and I'm on my way to the Perseids meteor showers tonight . . . remember? We talked about it."

The older woman tapped her head. "Where is my brain? Of course we did. Fort Rosalie. It will be a lovely night for it."

This wasn't the first time she'd forgotten something. Brooke hoped her fuzzy memory was from the recent surgery and anesthesia. She laid the older woman's mail on the utility tray by her bed next to a laptop. "Sorry I'm later than usual, but by the time I set up everything, I was hot and sweaty and had to go home and change. But I brought you some brownies."

"How did you know I had a hankering for some of your brownies?"

One of the nurses had remarked that Daisy had wistfully bragged on them. "I think a little bird might have told me."

As Daisy studied Brooke, a frown creased her face. "Are you sure you're okay? I hate that I had to miss your father's funeral."

"He would have understood. And I'm fine. I know it's going to take time."

"He was such a big part of your life, but God's grace will see you through."

Brooke wasn't sure she knew what that looked like. Or felt like. The question must have shown on her face.

"Right now you're numb, and your dad's death is hard to wrap your mind around," Daisy said. "But always remember God loves you."

Brooke walked to the window and stared out at the golden glow cast by the setting sun, her hands dropping to her sides. "I know that, but why did Dad have to die now? He wasn't old enough to die." She dug her nails into her palms.

For a minute the older woman didn't reply. "You may never get that answer," she said softly. "But it's okay to ask God why."

She turned. "You really think so?"

"Job did." Daisy struggled off the bed, and using her walker, she shuffled to Brooke and slipped her arm around her waist. "God's got this. You know that, right?"

"Yeah," she replied, leaning into Daisy. Brooke believed that deep down, but she missed her dad so much. She'd been his little girl, and he'd been her rock. "He's probably fishing with Saint Peter right now," she said with a shaky laugh.

For a minute neither of them spoke, then Daisy said, "When's the big day?"

Brooke helped her friend back to the bed. "Tonight is my last official act before I move to the Parkway. The chief ranger hasn't given me a start date since . . ." She bit her lip. "I expect it'll be next week."

"Who is your new chief?" Daisy asked.

"Dale Gallagher." Her dad would have been her immediate boss as district ranger, but until the park service filled his position, Dale, as the chief ranger, would be in charge.

"I remember him. He used to live in Natchez."

"Yeah. He and Dad were friends, and Mom is friends with Dale's wife."

"How is your mom? How's she handling everything?"

"Like she always does. Full steam ahead." Her mom was a force to be reckoned with and didn't let anything stop her or even make her pause. "She's in Knoxville helping Meghan and getting on with her life."

Brooke cringed as her conscience pinched like a too-tight shoe. She wasn't being fair. It's just that she and her mom were like a jigsaw puzzle that had a piece missing. Turning to Daisy's computer, she avoided her friend's all-knowing eyes.

"I meant to ask earlier," Daisy said, "have you heard back on the DNA test you and Meghan took?"

"Not yet. The brochure said six weeks, so it should come soon." Brooke didn't know if it was hormones or what, but finding their ancestral roots had become an obsession with Meghan after she discovered she was pregnant. Brooke had tried to tell her only one of them needed to take the test, but her sister insisted that she join a genealogy site and take the DNA test as well.

"Are you and Meghan still planning to fly to Europe next year?"

"England for sure, and Ireland if we can pinpoint the area where Dad's ancestors originated from." Both Mom and Dad were fourth-generation Americans, their great-great-grandparents having immigrated to America back in the late 1890s. They knew the area their mother's relatives were from in England, but the only history their dad remembered was that his ancestors were from Ireland. Even though Meghan believed the genealogy site's advertisement that they could pinpoint even the county their dad was from, Brooke wasn't so sure.

"How does your mom feel about this?"

"I'm not sure if she even knows about it. I'm assuming Meghan must've told her, but she hasn't mentioned it to me."

"Just keep in mind, regardless of what you discover, your lineage doesn't define you. Only God does that."

"I know," Brooke said as a knock sounded at the door.

"Come in," Daisy said. Her eyes widened. "Luke! I thought you went back to Jackson yesterday. You could've let me know you were still here!"

"And spoil the surprise?" he said with laughter in his voice.

Brooke was glad she hadn't said anything to Daisy about him still being here. She just wished she'd left before he arrived—being around him complicated her life, and not in a good way.

19

Brooke's gaze collided with Luke's. The surprise when he saw her morphed into . . . was that dismay? But then his lips curled upward in a smile.

"Hi again," he said. "I didn't see your car."

She nodded. "I parked on the side."

"You two have already seen each other?" When Brooke nodded, sparks flew from Daisy's blue eyes. "And you never told me he was here!"

"He made me promise," Brooke said. "I didn't know he would take all day to come see you."

"It's not Brooke's fault." Luke gave his grandmother his thousand-watt smile.

Same old Luke, always thinking he could smile and make everything rosy, and he probably could with Daisy. But he did look good in a pullover shirt and jeans. *Stop it.* She checked her watch then leaned over and kissed Daisy's cheek. "Y'all need to visit and I need to go. Do you want anything besides your mail when I come tomorrow?"

"I can't think of anything, but thanks, honey. I don't know what I'd do without you."

"Just get stronger and come home," she replied and hurried toward the door. "Good to see you again," she said and brushed past him, his crisp, clean-smelling cologne almost stopping her in her tracks. Brooke stiffened, warding off the memories.

"Wait," he said. "Don't go just yet."

Everything in her said to keep walking, that the more she was around him, the more it complicated her fledgling relationship with Jeremy, but she found herself pausing.

"Surely you can stay a minute or two longer," Daisy said.

Brooke glanced out the window. It was hard to tell Daisy no, and more than likely she would keep bumping into Luke again if he stayed any length of time. *Just keep him at arm's length.* "Maybe five minutes. I still have a few things to do at Fort Rosalie."

"Did you get the rest of the things in your dad's office put back?" he asked.

She shot him a warning look. "Yeah."

"And you set the alarm when you left?"

"Yes," she said, a little sharper than necessary.

"What are you two talking about?" Daisy asked.

"Why don't you tell her, Luke?" Since he was so dense.

When he finished, Daisy shook her head. "Do you need to stay at the house by yourself?"

"I have a gun."

"I'm sorry. I know that. You'll be just fine." She turned to her grandson. "You'll make sure of that, right?"

Brooke dropped her head. Did no one think she could take care of herself? She was tired of this discussion.

"How long are you staying?" Daisy asked.

"It's flexible," he said.

His grandmother frowned. "Since when? Greene, Blanchard, and McCoy have never been able to do without you very long."

"Greene, Blanchard, and what?" Brooke asked. "I thought you worked at Dave's Bar—"

"Whatever made you think he worked at a bar?" Daisy asked. "He's one of GB&M's top accountants."

One look at Luke was enough to know that he didn't want

Daisy to know he worked at a bar. She understood his concern, but at some point he needed to tell his grandmother the truth. For tonight, though, she went along with him. "I must be thinking of someone else."

"Must be," he murmured.

"And he works way too many hours," Daisy said, and then shot Luke a questioning gaze. "How did you get away?"

"Told them I needed a few days off to come check on you. Maybe get you moved into assisted living."

"What?" Daisy and Brooke spoke at the same time.

"She is so not ready for assisted living!" Brooke totally regretted helping him out a few seconds ago. "Not once she recovers from this knee surgery."

Luke took a step back and held up his hands. "It's just a thought." He pointedly eyed his grandmother's swollen knee with staples across the top. "One you really need to think about."

The older woman seemed to shrink before Brooke's eyes. She clenched her jaw. Luke should know that moving Daisy out of the home she'd been in for over fifty years would kill her.

"Time for me to go," she said. Brooke didn't want to say something she shouldn't. She leaned to hug Daisy once again. "Not happening," she whispered. "So don't worry."

Daisy responded to Brooke's reassuring smile with a tentative one of her own. "Have fun tonight," she said, her voice teary.

Brooke turned to Luke. "Want to walk me to my car?" she asked, keeping her voice even.

"Sure." After they closed the door behind them, he said, "You said something about helping to set up at Rosalie. What's happening there?"

"A meteor-gazing event." She bit the words off and then glanced at him, her heart reacting with a flurry of beats when she noticed how his shoulders filled out his short-sleeved shirt. Had Luke been that buff four months ago when she ran into him in Jackson?

She replayed their meeting in her mind—he'd been wearing a loose-fitting shirt and cargo pants, and her attention had been more on his hair and beard than any muscles he might have had.

Refocus. "Sorry, didn't mean to take your head off, but I will if you try to railroad your grandmother out of her house."

"She's eighty," Luke said. "I'm worried about her. The last few times I've talked with her, I've noticed her memory isn't what it used to be."

"That happens to everyone, and Daisy doesn't act a day over seventy," she said. "And why did you lie to her about what you do for a living?"

"She wouldn't think tending bar was respectable," he said and tilted his head. "Why did you back me up?"

"Because . . ." His blue eyes twinkled, and she bit back the retort on her lips. "For the same reason."

"We seem to have something in common." He held the door open for her and then followed her outside. "I see the clouds are breaking up. Should be clear skies for your event."

She turned and faced Luke, poking him in the chest. "Don't change the subject. And don't think you can ride in here on your high horse and order Daisy around. Especially since I'm sure I could count on one hand how many times you've been to see her in the last year. And even then, you were in and out so fast you made her head spin. You have no idea what she can or cannot do."

20

W hoa!" Luke backed up, wincing at Brooke's sharp jabs to his chest. Her vocal barbs hurt as well. But she had a point that he agreed with. He'd tried to tell his dad that Daisy wasn't ready for assisted living.

She planted her feet and crossed her arms. "You could also come see her more often than you do. How many times have you been here since her birthday in January?"

"I'm sorry I've been AWOL, but it couldn't be helped." He hadn't told anyone he'd spent February in the hospital, and while he had been in and out of Natchez the last four months, 99 percent of the time it had been at night well after Daisy had gone to bed. Working undercover and buying drugs from Sonny wasn't conducive to spending time with family, especially when it could put the family in jeopardy. "I phone her at least once a week."

"A phone call isn't the same thing as being here in the flesh. It's not like you live thousands of miles away." In spite of her tone and words, her rigid stance relaxed and she dropped her arms.

"I'm here now and I hope to make it up to her."

For once Brooke seemed at a loss for words. "Well . . . okay, then, as long as you understand Daisy needs to stay right where she is. In her house."

"You're right, but I'm afraid with Mom and Dad in London,

it's only me. It's hard, living in Jackson, especially with my hours. I can't always drop what I'm doing and come check on her."

"Hire someone." She looked askance at him. "And that doesn't make sense. How hard can it be to take time away from tending bar long enough to see about your grandmother only two hours away?"

If she only knew. "I'm here now," he said. "I want to thank you for checking on her every day and picking up groceries and her medicine when she needs it, but you're right. I need to hire someone to do it."

"I don't mind—"

"But it's not your responsibility."

"I do it because I want to." Then she stared at him a minute before she shook her head as if to clear it. "Oh my goodness. Listen to me. You practically saved my life last night, and here I am reading you the riot act."

"No big deal." One thing for sure, Brooke was passionate about the things she believed in. "But when did you and my grandmother get to be such good friends?"

Brooke looked back toward the rehab building. "It's hard to say. We always connected, even when I was a little girl. She listened to me. I mean, really listened. She made me feel like my thoughts were important. Then after you left that last summer, Daisy and I just gravitated to each other. She was lonely, and Mom and I weren't getting along on anything. Daisy was my sounding board." She brought her gaze back to him. "I guess she's the grandmother I never had."

He nodded. "I don't mind sharing her. She's always been my biggest booster, especially after Annapolis. Chewed my dad out after he blew his stack, not that it helped any. Looking back now, I don't blame him for being upset."

"What are your folks doing in London?"

"The first secretary to the ambassador is retiring at the end of the year, and I think Dad's going after his appointment." He would get it, too, and probably one day would be ambassador to England. Maybe he'd be happy then and get off Luke's case. He cocked his head. "Do you think you're doing the right thing, switching careers?"

"Why not?"

"Maybe because you never talked about being a law enforcement ranger when we were kids—it was always about becoming an interpretive ranger. It's dangerous, anyway."

"Driving across town can be dangerous."

"Don't give me that old cliché," he said and studied her. "You've moved up the ladder on the interpretive side. If you go the law enforcement route, you'll start off as a rookie."

"You sound like my dad," she said. "And how do you know that I'm moving up the ladder?"

"Your dad and Daisy," Luke said. "They both were proud of your accomplishments."

She stared down at her feet where she toed a rough spot on the pavement.

Suddenly, the alarm on her watch went off. "Oh! I have to get to Fort Rosalie."

Fort Rosalie. He'd decided to intercept Kyle Marlar there, but he'd have to make sure she didn't see him. "I'm glad I got to see you again tonight."

Her warm brown eyes held his, making it hard to breathe. The chemistry between them was still there—at least for him. He'd have to be careful not to let his feelings for her get out of hand. Luke nodded toward the building. "And I better get back and visit with Daisy."

Brooke stood straighter and taller, looking very official in her uniform. "Just don't go trying to run over Daisy—she's not ready to leave her home."

"I'd never hurt my grandmother."

Brooke caught his gaze and held it. "I'm sure you wouldn't intentionally, but sometimes what one person thinks is best for someone else isn't what they really need." She turned to walk away then hesitated and stepped closer to him.

"I am glad to see you, and this is for last night," she said, hugging him.

Brooke's light fragrance reminded him of the good times he'd shared with her. He almost wished he hadn't told Jeremy Steele they were only friends. Suddenly she pulled away, and the look on her face told him she'd remembered those days too.

"I better be going," she said, her cheeks flushing.

"While I'm staying at Daisy's, you don't have to pick up her mail."

"But I want to," she said. "And it's no problem. She likes getting her mail every day, and I don't trust you to remember to take it to her."

"Just because I didn't finish at Annapolis doesn't mean I'm not trustworthy," he called after her as she walked to her car.

"Never said that." Once in the driver's seat, she rolled down the window. "You're looking fit. Been working out?"

"Something like that."

"I meant to tell you last night—you look a whole lot better than the last time I saw you," she said, "especially since you shaved that horrid beard and got a haircut."

He just grinned at her. "You look terrific too."

Her eyes sparkled. "Thanks, see you around."

Luke stood in the shadows of the nursing home until her taillights disappeared around the corner, his thoughts on their accidental meeting in Jackson four months ago. He rubbed the back of his neck and let his hand trail down his shaved jaw, remembering how at first he'd missed the long hair and beard he'd worn for so long. But he hadn't expected to feel naked. When he worked undercover, his disguises had always been a barrier between him and the world he infiltrated.

A blast of cool air met him when he entered the rehab again, chilling Luke. When he tapped on his grandmother's door, her voice was strong when she bid him to come in. Maybe like Brooke said, Daisy wasn't ready for assisted living just yet. He could at least try to convince his father of that during their next call.

"You need to ask that girl on a date," Daisy said.

He chuckled. "I doubt she'd accept."

"Of course she would. Now that you've gotten rid of that frightful beard, you're right presentable."

"I think there's someone else in the picture now."

"Jeremy Steele?"

Daisy didn't miss much, and he nodded.

"Jeremy is a nice man, but being married to him would be demanding. He's running for the US Senate, and he stands a good chance of getting it. Not sure Brooke is ready to give up her career."

"You may be right, but I'm sure Brooke is looking for something permanent, and that's not me."

"You haven't always had the best examples in front of you." Daisy sighed. "I don't know where your granddaddy and I went wrong with your father. When he went away to Annapolis, his priorities changed."

"Dad is just who he is," Luke replied.

"I wish you'd known your grandfather. You're more like him." Then she shook her finger at him. "How am I going to get any great-grandkids if you don't get married?"

The life Luke lived was too dangerous to involve children. Or a wife. "How'd you like a burger from the Malt Shop?"

"Not this late," Daisy said. "I wouldn't sleep a wink. Now tomorrow for lunch . . ."

He laughed. "Okay, that's a date. I'll be here at eleven with one of their burgers. All the works?"

"Don't forget onion rings."

"I won't." Luke glanced out the window. Darkness had fallen. Time to get to Rosalie. He brushed a kiss on his grandmother's forehead. "See you tomorrow."

He'd almost made it out the door when she called his name, and he turned around.

"Brooke is going through a hard time right now," she said softly. "She needs you."

He shook his head. "I'm the last person she needs."

21

Luke Fereday. For the second time since she'd arrived at Fort Rosalie, Brooke pushed thoughts of him away. She had too much to do to think about him. She looked up and scanned the skies. Stars twinkled against a backdrop of black velvet. The low clouds that had hung around all afternoon had cleared out, just like Luke said. And there she was thinking of him again.

She shook her head and concentrated on what would be happening once Kyle Marlar finished his talk on how to take night photos. Brooke was sure he would have preferred no moon, but the crescent moon should not interfere with the viewing of the meteors when they peaked around midnight. At least the small amount of light from the moon, along with the solar lights she'd placed along the main paths, would help the public return to their spots after Kyle finished.

A breeze from the river cut through the humidity that had her shirt clinging to her back. She stopped to adjust a park service telescope for a guest. The telescopes weren't needed to see meteors but were available for anyone who wanted to use them for a closer view of Jupiter and Saturn.

"Good crowd. And the solar lights were a good idea."

She straightened up, surprised to see the chief ranger, Dale Gallagher, sweat beading his round face. It was the first time she'd seen him since her father died. "Thanks. I didn't know you were coming."

The district ranger took off his flat-brimmed hat and ran a hand through his dark hair. Even though Dale was around her dad's age, he didn't have a strand of gray hair.

"I had a meeting in Port Gibson this afternoon with Clayton," he said. "He told me about the event and that you would be here. Since I was so close, I came on to Natchez to see how you're doing . . . and to see if your intruder had been caught."

"How do you know about that?" She hadn't told him about the break-in.

"Clayton told me. Pete Nelson had called him. Besides, you know how information spreads in the park service."

Yes, she did, thinking of Emma. "I got everything cleaned up and back in place."

"All of your dad's files are there?"

"Who knows? It's not like Dad kept a list of what was in his file cabinets, but if the burglar had found what he was looking for, I wouldn't have walked in on him."

"Good point."

She studied the ranger. Deep lines creased his face, and even though he was still stocky, she could see he'd lost weight. His wife's illness had taken a toll on him. She followed Dale's gaze as he glanced toward where Kyle Marlar was speaking.

"Let me know if I can do anything," he said.

"Thanks. We were lucky to get Kyle for this."

"It won't hurt his campaign either," Dale said.

She'd almost forgotten Kyle was running for state representative again.

He dropped his gaze to the ground. "I'm sorry I didn't make it to the funeral, but Mary had a reaction to her chemo Wednesday, and we ended up in the ER, then overnight in the hospital. But at least she tolerated her infusion before we left."

Brooke had assumed something had come up with his wife. "I'm sorry. Is she better today? Did she come with you?"

He rubbed the side of his face. "No. She wasn't up to it but said to tell you hello. She insists she's coming to your swearing in, but I don't know . . ."

"I hope she can. I've been meaning to get up to Jackson and visit her," Brooke said. It was a trip she should have made weeks ago.

"Mary would like that, but call first—some days she really struggles, especially after an experience like Wednesday's."

"I'll be sure to check first." Dale looked so lost, she almost wished she hadn't asked. "How long will she have to be on this treatment?"

"The doctors haven't said. They say it's her only hope." His shoulders drooped and he shook his head. "I just wish it weren't so expensive."

"Insurance doesn't cover it?"

"I wish. They ruled it experimental. I've appealed, but you know how that goes. In the meantime, it's out of pocket."

"I'm sorry." She'd heard some of the new treatments cost tens of thousands of dollars and was pretty sure Dale didn't have that kind of money. If only there was something she could say that didn't sound like a platitude, or worse.

"When do you want to swear me in?" Brooke asked, deliberately changing the subject.

He thought a minute. "This is Friday . . . how about Monday—no, that won't work. Mary has a doctor's appointment." He tapped his hand against his leg. "I have to come back to Port Gibson tomorrow. Why don't we shoot for tomorrow morning? That way you can start bright and early Monday."

"Sounds good. Clayton still doing the field training? Or are you?"

"Clayton, unless I hear otherwise from higher up. He learned under your dad, so he knows what he's doing."

Dale turned and scanned the fort grounds, still tapping his leg. Something seemed to be bothering him, or maybe it was just his concern about Mary. Or it could be he was checking for potential problems. She followed his gaze, noting the diverse crowd from toddlers to senior citizens. Emma held a clipboard and appeared to be asking a visitor to sign in.

Beyond them, Kyle Marlar talked with several people. He must have finished his talk and soon would be headed to his spot on the bluff. Brooke shifted her attention back to Dale, puzzled that he was so tense.

"By the way, we have a new ranger coming in from the Nashville area," he said, his gaze fixed on the road.

She hadn't expected that. "I didn't think they were filling Gary's job."

"You're taking it."

"I know, but I thought they were only filling one position, that it would just be Clayton and me."

"No, the new ranger is stepping into your dad's old spot." He still avoided looking at her.

For a second Brooke couldn't speak. She hadn't dreamed the park service would fill his job that fast. She'd known they wouldn't leave it vacant long, but she figured Clayton would temporarily take her dad's place before officially getting the position.

"When?" Brooke asked.

"Ten days," Dale said. He finally turned to her, his eyes sad. "Have you thought about applying somewhere else in the park service? It has to be hard, staying here after your dad . . ."

Leave Natchez? She stared at him, stunned into silence.

"I heard your mom might move to Knoxville to be with your sister, so you could probably get a position up in the Smokies. I'd be glad to put in a good word for you."

"No," she said, finding her voice. "I want to stay in Natchez. Besides, Mom hasn't made a decision about moving to East Tennessee." If Brooke left Natchez, she could never prove her dad hadn't committed suicide. And she couldn't depend on anyone else to clear his name.

"Think about it."

"I'm sorry, but I'm not interested in transferring."

"If you don't want the Smokies, I know the chief ranger at Yosemite. He'd be a good one for you to intern under."

"You're kidding, right? Those openings get snapped up quicker than snowflakes melt around here."

"You never know," he replied.

"Thanks, but Natchez is my home. I like it here just fine." Then she cocked her head. "I don't understand why you're trying to get rid of me."

"It's just that you're young. Don't you want to travel? See new places? You've never been away from Natchez except when you went away to college."

"Maybe I don't want to travel, and maybe I like being a homebody." When his expression didn't change, she said, "You can't be serious."

"Your dad was my friend, and I don't know, I thought you might want to get away from here, start fresh somewhere else. I've lived in Natchez, and I know how it is—everyone knows every little detail of your life."

He had a point there, but that was just Natchez—a small town where people cared, and that meant they were up in your business, but not in a mean way. And she knew everyone was talking about her dad's supposed suicide, but once she proved the ME wrong, that would stop.

She lifted her chin. "Really, I don't want to leave here, but thanks for thinking about my welfare."

"Anytime you want to transfer, just let me know."

"I will," she said faintly then turned and scanned the park again.

"How is your mom?" he asked.

"Like the rest of us—still in shock. But you know her. Still doing her own thing, preparing for her showing at the art gallery. When she's not involved in that, she's focused on Meghan and getting ready for the new baby."

"She likes Knoxville?"

"I suppose." She glanced past him where people were settling into their spots, and her gaze locked on a family gathered together on a quilt, the mom laughing and the dad pointing up as a star shot across the darkened sky. How that brought back memories of her childhood. She shifted her gaze toward a bank of picnic tables illuminated by a string of low-watt bulbs. Jeremy stood talking with another man.

"I see our state senator made it tonight," she said, surprised that he hadn't sought her out.

He followed her gaze. "Oh, good. I need to talk to him. See if he can pull some strings with the insurance company." Dale patted her shoulder and then walked toward the two men.

Brooke couldn't keep from noticing how Jeremy stood out in a crowd. A head taller than most, his dark hair styled with the precision of a hundred-dollar haircut. He commanded an audience wherever he was. When he was reelected the last time, she'd read more than one newspaper article that touted his popularity with the voters.

She looked closer at the other man. He stood with his back to her, his hand resting on a gun strapped to his waist. Mr. Clean—she'd seen Pete near the gate earlier with a couple of uniformed policemen. Good to know there was plenty of security around.

22

Time inched on toward ten o'clock. He'd seen Marlar trying to break away from the crowd, and he'd taken the back way, using a small, handheld night vision scope to navigate the trees near the bluffs in the darkness. His other night vision goggles gave him a much clearer view, but their bulk made them hard to conceal. When he'd scoped the area earlier in the day, he'd found the only spot away from the crowd where Marlar could set up his camera to get decent shots of the meteors. And that spot was just ahead. He halted by one of the large oaks. Now it was just a matter of waiting for him to arrive.

From the look on Marlar's face when he exited King's Tavern, he'd been quite upset that he'd been stood up. He'd followed Marlar long enough to know he was going to Fort Rosalie instead of returning home to dispose of whatever evidence he had.

His hand shook as he brought the scope to his eye. *Don't think. Just act.* He'd never purposely killed a man. John Danvers had been an accident. Did Marlar know for sure that he'd killed John? No. He would have used it against him.

Lead lodged in his stomach. He'd read somewhere that killing a second person was easier. Evidently the author of the article had never killed anyone. His jaw ached from locking down on it, and he worked it back and forth, releasing the tension. His heart almost stopped when a narrow beam of light flickered on the path. His wait was over.

He pulled on a pair of latex gloves and used the scope to scan the area to make sure no one had wandered near them. A woman walked toward the bluff but was too far away to see or hear them. He slipped the scope in a pocket—Marlar's flashlight provided all the light he needed. He removed the suppressor from the other pocket and attached it to the 9mm Glock.

Marlar's back was to him, and his silent steps on the damp ground went unnoticed. When he was in reach, he squeezed his eyes shut and slammed the butt of the gun against his head. Marlar fell to the ground with a low grunt.

A quick search of the camera bag revealed several memory cards for the camera. Which one? It didn't matter. He pocketed all of them. He searched the bag once more, pulling out a photograph of him accepting a package from a dark sedan. Sunday night came flooding back. Marlar had definitely been at Emerald Mound. While the photo proved nothing, the Emerald Mound sign and timestamp put him at the mounds not long before John Danvers's death.

Suddenly, Marlar moved, and before he could react, the older man snatched the photo from his hand. In a knee-jerk reaction, he fired, the muffled pop loud in his ears. Marlar fell back, blood spreading across his chest. He tore the photo out of Marlar's hand.

Marlar stared straight at him. "Joke's on you . . . not the only picture . . . copies," he whispered and then closed his eyes.

He whirled around and raced silently through the trees. Minutes later he broke through the woods and leaned over. Could. Not. Breathe.

Marlar had copies of the photo? He'd killed a man for—nothing? Where could the copies be? Maybe hidden in the camera bag?

He should have brought it with him.

23

Brooke mingled with the crowd, estimating at least a hundred people had turned out. A few were using the telescopes the park service provided to view different planets and constellations, but most were here for the Perseids. She'd have to admit that after Dale swore her in as a law enforcement ranger, she would miss the hands-on aspect she enjoyed now. Brooke loved walking the grounds of the fort that had carried three different names, depending on who controlled the territory, but the first, Fort Rosalie, had stuck.

This place was so rich in history that sometimes she wished she'd chosen a career on the historical side of the park service. Digging into the lives of the men and women who'd settled this area intrigued her. First the Natchez Native Americans, followed by French fur traders, Spaniards, the English—each group had brought something different to the territory.

But it'd been the very last group, the "Kaintucks" as they were called, who made the Trace where she would soon be working what it was. After floating their goods down the Mississippi, they'd walked the trail made by bison and Native Americans to Nashville and then on to Kentucky. Sometimes Brooke drove up the Trace past Mount Locust to a section known as the Old Trace. Looking at the sunken ground, she found it easy to imagine those men walking in leather leggings, making their way home.

A pop jerked Brooke's attention and she turned around. Molly had her fingers pressed to her lips, her eyes wide.

"Ms. Brooke! My balloon popped," she wailed. "And Daddy said I could see a little bear, but I can't see anything!"

Brooke knelt beside the small girl. "Do you know where your dad went?"

Molly hunched her shoulders in a shrug. "I dunno. Aunt Cara is watching me."

Hearing her name, Jeremy's sister turned from the diaper bag she was digging in. A toddler clung to her leg. "Said he'd be back in a minute."

Brooke had somehow missed seeing Cara. She smiled at the young mother who had her hands full. "Why don't I hang around until Jeremy gets back?" she said.

"Oh, bless your heart. I should not have brought the twins."

Brooke knelt beside the telescope and adjusted the lens. "Let's see what we can find. Have you seen a shooting star?"

"Almost. Aunt Cara showed me, but when I looked, it was gone."

When another pop sounded, Brooke looked over her shoulder toward the bluffs. She didn't see who had the popped balloon this time and hoped whoever thought helium balloons were a good idea would be around tomorrow to help pick up the pieces of latex.

Molly tugged her hand again. "Where's the shooting star?"

She returned her attention to the girl. "Keep watching and maybe you'll see one." Once she had the telescope aimed at the North Star, she showed Molly how to look through the view-finder. "There. Now you should be able to find the Little Dipper."

The girl put her hands on her hips. "I thought you were going to show me a little bear!"

"They're the same thing." Brooke spent a few minutes patiently explaining about the constellation and how the bear had a really long tail and at the end of it was the brightest star ever.

"And that's where I'll see the bear?"

No, but how did she make her understand?

"Daddy!" Molly's eyes brightened as her father approached, a frown on his face. "You told me we were going to see a bear!"

"She's all yours," Brooke said, grinning.

The frown disappeared, and Jeremy winked at her as he looked over his daughter's head. "I did say you'd see the bear," he said and swung Molly up in his arms. "But I told you the Little Bear is a constellation."

She planted her fists on her little hips. "I don't want to see a conselation. I wanna see a bear."

"But the Little Dipper is really neat," Brooke said. "Let me draw it for you." It was what she should have done in the beginning. The girl was quiet as Brooke used her pen to draw the stars in Ursa Minor on her notepad.

Molly shook her head. "That's not a bear. That looks like what Mimi cooks with."

Brooke hugged Molly, then tenderly brushed a strand of hair from her face. The motherless child had burrowed deep into Brooke's heart.

"You're right, it does look like a pan," she said with a laugh and then glanced up at Jeremy. The smile he gave her lit up his eyes. She'd like to hang around, but she had work to do. "I'll leave it for you to show her the real one. And hopefully you can distract her with a shooting star."

"Do you have to hurry off?" he asked. "I mean, you're doing such a good job explaining . . ."

"I need to check and see if anyone else needs my help," she said. "Maybe I'll see you at church Sunday."

Jeremy ducked his head. "Don't forget dinner tomorrow night?"

he said softly. "There's a new place out on Highway 61. Tangle-foot."

She'd heard good things about the rather expensive restaurant. "I'm looking forward to it."

Brooke left them and wandered over to a flat area in the middle of the grounds and jumped when Clayton stepped out from behind one of the big oaks. "I didn't see you," she said.

"Sorry," he said.

"I didn't expect you to be here," she said and shined her flashlight beyond him to two scowling teenage boys.

"My sister had to work, and I offered to bring them so they can complete their science project," he said, nodding toward the two boys. "Beginning to wonder if it was a mistake."

"Maybe I can help." She turned to the boys. "What do you need for your project?"

"Uncle Clay's camera doesn't work," the older boy said.

Clayton shrugged. "I forgot the batteries. Thought I had some in the truck, but when I looked a few minutes ago, I couldn't find them."

"That's an easy fix if you need AAs," she said. "I have a brand-new package in my car. Give me a minute and I'll get them for you."

The younger boy held out his hand to Clayton. "I'm hot," he said. "Can I get a Coke?"

His uncle pulled out a couple of bills and handed them to him. "Kids are too much trouble," Clayton grumbled after they left. He scanned the skies. "But they're right, it sure is hot tonight."

"We could use a breeze for sure. I'll go get those batteries." She turned to leave, then stopped. "Dale said you're scheduled to start my field training Monday."

"That's the plan," he said. "Are you okay with me training you in your dad's place? That way you won't have to sit around trying to find something to do until the new district ranger arrives."

She definitely didn't want to do that. "I would rather have

had my dad, but since that's not possible, you're the next best thing—he trained you, and he was proud of you."

"He was the best."

"Th-thanks."

"What time—"

A woman's piercing scream drowned out the rest of his words.

24

The scream had come from somewhere behind her, and Brooke jerked around, frantically scanning the area. The woman screamed again, and she pinpointed the direction.

Clayton was on her heels as Brooke ran toward the back of the property and the bluffs. Halfway there, she recognized a woman from her church on the path, her face drained of color. Brooke searched for a name. Anna . . . Corbett.

Anna pointed in the direction of the river. "A man. On the path . . . He . . ." She gulped air. "He's just lying there."

"Call 911," Clayton yelled and took off in the direction Anna pointed.

"Did you see anyone else?" Brooke asked, punching in the numbers on her phone.

The woman shook her head and shuddered. "No! I almost stepped on him."

Brooke filled in the 911 operator as she sprinted up the path. The solar lights helped her find the man sprawled face down with Clayton kneeling over him.

"Stay with him. I'm going to check out the path," he said, pulling his gun.

Brooke knelt beside the man, feeling his wrist for a pulse. Thready. Her heart pounded in her ears. She should get him on his back in case he needed CPR. She rolled him over, and her breath caught. In the center of his bloodstained shirt was a small, neat hole. From the way he fisted his hands, he must be in pain.

She pulled her gaze from the wound to his face, and her stomach clenched. Kyle Marlar? She just saw him not twenty minutes ago. Who could have done this? She'd gone to school with his kids, graduated the same class as his middle son, attended his youngest son's funeral just a month ago. The thoughts shot through her mind like bullets.

Brooke felt his wrist again. His heart rate was even fainter. Skipping. If the ambulance didn't get here quick, he wouldn't make it. Blood spread in an ever-widening circle on his shirt. She needed to stanch the flow. But with what? She yanked the handkerchief she carried from her back pocket. Not big enough, but it'd have to do until paramedics arrived. She pressed it against his chest, and blood quickly saturated it.

Kyle groaned.

"Who did this?" She leaned in closer, straining to hear his words, but they were garbled. "Who was it?"

He winced. "Hurts bad . . ."

"Hang on," she said as a siren pierced the air. "The ambulance is almost here." The hospital wasn't that far away.

His eyes fluttered open. "B-Brooke?"

"Yes. What happened?"

"Brandon . . ."

Not good. He was thinking of the son who just died. "Just lie there."

"So sorry about your dad. I didn't know," he whispered. His eyes closed and he seemed to be gathering his strength, then he struggled to sit up.

"No! Don't move!" Brooke pressed against his chest, but blood kept flowing.

"Got to tell you. Don't trust anyone . . . Find photos . . ."

Brooke leaned closer as his voice dropped. She couldn't make out his last words. Sensing someone behind her, she looked over her shoulder. Where had Luke come from? "Do you see the ambulance?"

"It's pulling into the side street now," he said.

Brooke craned her neck toward the street as paramedics jumped out of the emergency vehicle. She turned back to Luke, and her gaze locked on the gun in his hand. "Did you shoot him?"

"Of course not," he said, slipping the automatic in an ankle holster before he knelt to the ground. "We need something bigger than your handkerchief."

"I don't have anything." She rocked back on her heels, looking for something they could use.

Without hesitation, he yanked off his shirt and pressed it against Kyle's chest. "Kyle, it's me, Luke Fereday. Who did this?"

His eyes fluttered open, and he moved his lips, forming soundless words.

"Stay with us," Luke said.

"Photos . . ." he whispered. "Drive . . ."

Luke leaned closer. "Where is it?"

The wounded man fixed his gaze on Luke as Clayton returned. "What's his condition?" Clayton asked.

Brooke shook her head at the ranger and turned back to Kyle. "Hang on!" she urged. "Help is here."

He was slipping away. He opened his eyes again. "Tell Sharon . . . I love her."

Paramedics dropped the gurney to the ground. "Move back."

As the medics took over, Brooke stood, her legs shaky. Luke must have sensed it because he put his arm around her, helping her to move from the scene. Strength returned to her legs and she pulled away from him and turned to Clayton. "Did you find anything?"

He shook his head. "It was too dark."

She looked around as Jeremy hurried toward her. "Brooke, are you all right?"

"Yeah."

"What happened?" he asked. "Who is it?"

"Kyle Marlar. Someone shot him."

"No!" He looked past her shoulder where paramedics worked on Kyle. "Why?"

Her thoughts exactly. She turned and scanned the people who had gathered off to one side. Several held lanterns, giving an eerie glow to the area. A chill raced through her. Had one of them shot Kyle? And why hadn't she heard a gun go off? "Did you hear gunfire?" she asked, looking first at Luke and Clayton, then Jeremy.

"I heard popping," Clayton said, "but I thought it was balloons."

Luke frowned. "Maybe whoever shot him used a suppressor."

"I heard those pops too," Jeremy said. "You think it was gunfire?"

It must have been. Brooke caught sight of Pete Nelson on his phone, and Dale beside him as they walked toward the scene.

"Did Kyle say who shot him?" Jeremy asked in a hushed voice.

"He didn't tell me," Luke said.

She shot a questioning gaze toward Clayton.

"I was looking for the shooter," Clayton said. "Did he say anything to you?"

Brooke shook her head. While she'd committed Kyle's words to memory, she wasn't ready to share them, not until she had a chance to ask Kyle what he meant.

"Daddy! Where are you?"

Jeremy jerked his head toward the crowd. "I better see about Molly."

Luke leaned in close. "You're sure he didn't say who shot him?"

His voice was low and urgent, and she stepped back, frowning at him. "Why do you want to know? And you never said a word about coming to Fort Rosalie when we were with Daisy."

Luke shot a quick glance at the men bearing down on them, then he shrugged. "It was a last-minute decision," he said.

Brooke stared at him. She had not just imagined the urgency

in his voice. What was going on? Before she had a chance to ask, Dale and the police chief descended on them.

"I've called in all available officers to search for suspects and question witnesses," Pete said. His eyes widened when he recognized the man on the ground. "Kyle Marlar? Who would want to shoot him?"

That was the question that everyone seemed to be asking. Brooke didn't know of anyone who harbored ill will toward him.

Don't trust anyone. Kyle had used what could be his dying breath to warn her about someone. But who? Was he trying to tell her not to trust someone close to her? That could be anyone around her, even Luke and Jeremy.

"What happened?" Pete asked.

She jerked her head to the scene behind her. "You know as much as I do."

"But you found him."

"Along with Clayton."

"He's crashing." The paramedic's voice rose.

"Bolus 1 cc—"

"Let's move to the picnic tables near the street and give them room to work," Pete said, pointing toward the road where several of his officers were piling out of cars.

With one last look at Kyle, she walked toward the tables. Pete was on his phone again as he outpaced the others to the street where his officers waited. Luke dropped back to walk beside her, and her gaze was drawn to his well-toned muscles under the ribbed tank top.

"You okay?" Luke asked.

She nodded. "I still want to know what you're doing here."

"Daisy thought I should come."

"You can do better than that."

"No. Ask her yourself."

The sincerity in his face seemed genuine. She glanced over her shoulder where the paramedics still worked on Kyle.

"How well do you know him?" Luke asked, following her gaze.

"We go to church together. His wife, Sharon, and I are friends." The weight of what Sharon was facing lay heavy on Brooke's heart. Sharon still grieved the loss of her son and now this? "Kyle made a difference in the lives of a lot of teenaged boys around here."

"Like Pete?"

She nodded. "If it hadn't been for Kyle, he'd probably be in jail like his cousins instead of being the police chief."

"It was plain Kyle was trying to say something to you before I reached you. Did he say who shot him?"

There it was again. That tightness in Luke's voice while he was trying to sound casual. "No. Just that he was sorry about my dad and something about photos."

"That's all he said?" Luke persisted.

She ignored his question. They had caught up with Clayton, and she slowed to walk with him. "You don't have to hang with us," she said to Luke.

He gave her a curt nod and walked ahead of them, pulling something from his pocket.

"You okay?" Clayton asked.

Brooke pulled her attention back to the ranger, who was attacking his thumbnail. The wiry Clayton was never still. "I keep wondering if I could have prevented Kyle's shooting."

"Don't do that to yourself. Reality is different from training."

"Still . . ."

"You have a lot to learn," Clayton said. "Consider this your first lesson."

"Do you think we'll be involved in the investigation?"

"It'll depend on a couple of things, but I doubt it."

"Why wouldn't we be involved? It happened on NPS property."

"You know Pete Nelson will claim jurisdiction," he said.

"Local law always does—another thing you'll learn. But more than likely the FBI will take over. Or someone from ISB."

"I'm sure Dale would prefer the Investigative Services Branch," she said. "Do you really think they'd send someone to investigate this?"

Clayton shrugged. "You can never tell, but I'd bet on the FBI doing the investigation."

25

When they reached the picnic tables, Luke was already seated and stood to give her his spot. Pete's officers had dispersed, and he was on his cell again. After finishing his conversation, Pete hooked his phone on his belt and nodded to Luke. "This is getting to be a habit."

She hadn't considered it, but Luke had shown up at just the right time last night and now again tonight.

Pete turned to the others. "My officers are cordoning off the crime scene and interviewing the witnesses."

"Good," Dale said. He turned to Luke. "Were you with Kyle when he was shot?"

He gave the chief ranger a sidelong glance. "No."

"How did you get to him so quickly?" Pete asked.

"I'm questioning him right now," Dale snapped.

Brooke couldn't believe they were scrapping over jurisdiction. Dale reminded her of an English bulldog guarding a bone while Pete stood with his massive arms folded.

"I've got this," the chief said. Sweat beaded his face.

Dale shook his head. "Not trying to step on your toes, Pete, but this happened on NPS property," he said. "The investigation falls under the park service jurisdiction."

"My city, my case." Pete's jaw shot out. "And this is a little more than a speeding ticket, Dale. You really don't have the manpower or the time to investigate it. Besides, in the past we've usually worked together on cases."

"Won't the FBI take it over?" Brooke asked. "Have you notified them?"

Both men frowned at her. Pete spoke first. "No. I'll call once I have the crime scene secured. Until then, I'll take the lead."

When Dale grudgingly agreed, Brooke knew it wasn't because he wanted to, but because the chief had more manpower than the park service. With Dale involved in Mary's treatment, and the Port Gibson office low on staff, it only made sense for Pete to head up the investigation with the rangers taking a secondary role.

"I want Clayton and Brooke kept in the loop," Dale said, nodding at the two of them.

"No problem with that," Pete said. He turned away from them. "A rookie. Just what I need."

She barely caught the chief's muttered words as he looked at his notes. She might be a rookie, but this time tomorrow she would be an official rookie, and she would make him eat those words.

"Now that's settled," Pete said, turning to Luke, "you never said how you got to the victim so quickly."

Luke had stood off to one side while the two men argued, and he lifted his shoulder in a noncommittal shrug then repeated what he'd said earlier.

"But why were you here in the first place? The Luke I remember from high school wouldn't be caught dead at something like this."

Brooke winced. That was a low blow from Pete. She was surprised when Luke laughed.

"You're probably right, but that was a long time ago. People do change. Besides, my grandmother said Brooke was heading it up and . . ." He glanced at her and winked. "I was looking for her when everything broke loose."

Heat crept up her neck. What was he doing? He made it sound like they had some sort of relationship.

Pete's gaze went from Luke to Brooke then back to Luke. "You just happened to be at the right place at the right time two nights in a row?"

"That's about it," Luke said.

"Did you hear any gunfire?"

"Not normal gunfire, but I did hear several pops—like maybe a silencer would make, or the noise could have been the balloons popping that Brooke said she heard earlier."

Pete eyed Brooke. "Did he tell you who shot him?"

"No," she replied. "Maybe he didn't see the person."

The chief turned and questioned Clayton with his brows. "How about you? Did you hear anything?"

"I didn't hang around long enough," Clayton said. "I wanted to make sure we didn't have an active shooter."

"Looked like to me he was shot point-blank," Luke said.

She thought of her intruder last night. "Maybe the shooter wore a mask."

Pete held up his hand. "Start at the beginning, and tell me exactly what happened."

She took a breath and went over the details of the shooting again.

Pete chewed the end of his pen. "Did he say anything that would point to his shooter?"

She shook her head and then glanced across the field to the crime scene. Someone had rigged up a couple of high-powered lights, and the medics were coming toward them with Kyle. If he'd seen who shot him, why hadn't he given them a name? Brooke sighed. Kyle was one of the good guys and she hoped he didn't die. When she turned back, Pete was frowning at Luke, but then he looked beyond him as the paramedics approached with the gurney.

"Coming through!"

Pete stopped the lead medic. "Is he going to make it?"

"It's going to be touch and go," the medic said and barely

paused while the other two hurried toward the ambulance with the stretcher. "His blood pressure is almost nonexistent. I'm afraid he's bleeding out."

None of them spoke as he turned and rushed to catch up with the stretcher. Once Kyle was loaded into the ambulance, they slammed the door and pulled away, sirens blasting. Brooke thought of Kyle's wife, remembering the pain of being told her dad was dead. She wouldn't wish that on anyone.

26

Luke's gaze followed the ambulance as it swung out of the side street and sped toward Highway 84. Another failure to notch into his heart. He shook off the memories. It did no good to revisit the case in Kentucky. Mandated sessions with a psychologist had helped him understand that he wasn't a hostage negotiator, and he wasn't responsible for the bad intel that said the drug dealer was alone at the campsite where the deal went down.

He'd learned to accept he'd done everything possible to save the drug dealer's girlfriend when the man used her as a shield then shot her when she tried to escape. While Luke had come to terms with her death, the scent of burning wood could put him right back at that campsite. He wondered what the trigger for tonight's memories would be. It seemed everything he touched turned to ashes.

The fading siren sent a shiver down his back. It didn't look good, but Luke prayed Kyle wouldn't die. He didn't know a lot about him, only that he had a wife and sons and grandchildren. Regret pressed on Luke's heart. Could he have kept this from happening?

His fingers itched to examine in more detail the paper Marlar had slipped him. Evidently Brooke hadn't seen him press it into Luke's hand since she hadn't questioned him about it. He'd gotten a brief look—it appeared to be part of a photograph—like someone had ripped all but the corner from his hand.

What if the shooter had hung around and blended with the crowd? Luke eyed each of the men sitting at the picnic table. He hadn't ruled out any of them as the shooter. Brooke nudged him and he looked up. Pete was staring expectantly at him.

"Sorry, I missed that," he said.

Pete flipped through his notebook. "Mind telling me what you're doing in Natchez?"

"You asked that question last night, and my answer is the same—visiting my grandmother."

"Just making sure." The chief wrote something in the notebook. "I heard you were an Army Ranger. Is that true?"

"I don't know what that has to do with anything. It was years ago." He frowned. "I hope you're not thinking I killed Kyle. I don't know when he was shot, but I had just arrived at Fort Rosalie when the woman screamed."

"I never said I suspected you. How well did you know Kyle Marlar?"

"I knew his sons better."

Luke held Pete's gaze. His old schoolmate seemed anxious to throw suspicion Luke's way. Why? Maybe because Pete was the guilty culprit? He'd like to know if Pete's Sig Sauer had been fired tonight. And if he had a suppressor stashed in his patrol car. He glanced down at Pete's cargo pants. Good place to hide something. Luke glanced toward Clayton and Dale. Both wore their service pistols. Clayton wore shorts with pockets big enough to conceal a silencer. Dale not so much, but his car was bound to be close by. At this point, Luke didn't trust anyone except Brooke.

Pete tapped his pen against the notebook, then with a nod he snapped it shut. "Both of you come by in the morning and sign a statement. And if you remember anything else, write it down." He took out his phone, dismissing them.

Brooke turned to Dale. "Are we taking statements from the witnesses?"

"My officers will take care of that," Pete said, moving the phone away from his ear. "You can get a copy of their reports in the morning."

"Since you know the woman who found him, why don't you interview her before you take down the telescopes," Dale said, shooting a disgruntled look at Pete.

Brooke stood, and Luke said, "I'll help you."

"Why?"

He searched for an answer she might buy. "I'm in no hurry to go home. Daisy's house is so empty without her, I'd rather stay and help you." And for once, he wasn't lying.

"I know the feeling."

Using the light on his phone, he illuminated their path as Brooke walked silently beside him. "Watch the rock," he said as the light picked up a stone jutting out of the ground. "Did Kyle have any enemies?"

"Not that I know of. I've never heard anyone say a bad word about Kyle."

"Was he still working with boys at the community center?"

"He was up until his son died. That hit him hard."

"Brandon."

"How did you know about Brandon?"

He scrambled for an answer. "Daisy. She keeps me up-to-date on what's going on in Natchez."

"Oh. Speaking of Daisy—I know you didn't come to Fort Rosalie because she encouraged it, so why were you here tonight?"

He slapped at a mosquito on his arm. Brooke was just as tenacious. "She did encourage me to come."

She eyed him suspiciously. "And before I forget, I do not appreciate you trying to make Pete think we have some sort of relationship."

"I didn't tell Pete we were a couple. If he thinks that—"

"You may not have come right out and said it, but you heavily implied it. Why?"

Because he wanted anyone within hearing distance to know someone was looking out for her. "Would that be such a bad thing?"

"Has it not occurred to you that I might be in a relationship with someone?" she asked.

So she and Jeremy Steele were a couple. Oh man, he'd stepped into it this time. "I'm sorry. I had no right to do that."

"Thank you."

"Is it anyone I know?" he asked, trying to keep his tone light. "Like maybe Jeremy Steele?"

She was quiet, keeping her gaze on the ground. "Maybe."

Brooke didn't want to talk about it and that meant Jeremy was wasting no time. "Do you think it might turn into something serious?"

Brooke stopped dead still and turned to him. "When you left here without saying good-bye and then didn't even so much as send a postcard for fourteen years, you lost the right to ask me that kind of question."

"Touché," he said, but right now it was important for her safety that he stay close to her. "Can we at least be friends again?"

She looked up at him. "I suppose, since I owe you one for being there for me last night."

"Good."

"Did you see Kyle get shot?"

"No. You heard me tell Pete I'd just gotten here when I heard the scream," Luke said.

"Most people don't run toward trouble."

"You ought to know by now I'm not most people."

She gave him a sour look. "Now how would I know that?"

"Ouch." He'd hurt Brooke by not contacting her after he left, something he regretted now. But he'd done it for her own good, at least that's what he kept telling himself. That summer, she had her plans for the future made. It wouldn't have been fair for him to mess them up, not when he didn't have a clue who he was or what he wanted from life. And what if it turned out he was like his father? Another ranger approached, saving him from saying more and making things worse.

"Hello, Luke," she said.

She looked familiar. Shorter than Brooke, curly red hair.

"I see you don't remember me. Emma Winters—from high school?"

An image popped in his mind. Cheerleader. Brainy. "Oh yeah. Of course. How are you?"

"Been better than tonight." Emma tucked a strand of her red hair behind her ear and fanned herself with her hat. She turned to Brooke. "People are asking when they can leave. Their kids are getting cranky."

"Pete Nelson is coming this way," Luke said. "Maybe you could ask him if they could leave their name with one of the officers and then go by the police department tomorrow and give their statement."

"Good idea," Brooke said. "I'll be right back."

"You think Kyle will make it?" Emma asked as Brooke walked away.

"I hope so. I always liked him."

"Me too," she said. "How long will you be in town?"

Everyone was interested in how long he would be here. "Couple of weeks."

"Don't hurt Brooke again."

The sharp edge to Emma's voice drew his attention. "What do you mean?"

"I've watched you tonight, and you're all protective, acting like you care." She narrowed her eyes at him. "She could have a good thing with Jeremy Steele. Don't mess it up."

"I don't intend to."

"It doesn't look that way to me," she said. "You hurt her when you left town that summer without so much as a 'so long, have a good life.'"

"I was young and didn't think. And I've apologized."

She placed her hand on her hip and shook her head. "And you think now that you've apologized everything will be fine? That you can pick up where you left off?"

"One kiss, that's all we ever had."

"Men," she said and held her finger up. "I'm warning you, don't get in the middle of Brooke and Jeremy."

He'd had enough of her lecture. "If me being here interferes with their relationship, then maybe he isn't the right person for her."

"And you are?"

Before Luke came up with a snappy comeback, Pete and Brooke approached.

"Can I have your attention?" Pete asked, raising his voice. "I'm going to let you give your name and contact information to one of my officers, and then you can leave. Appreciate it if you'd drop by the office tomorrow and give your statement, but if not, we'll be in contact."

A collective sigh went through the crowd, and Brooke walked back to join them. "That was a good idea," she said.

"Just made sense," Luke said. From the questioning way she looked at him, he should have kept it to himself. "Let's get the telescopes loaded."

"Emma," Brooke said, "would you help him while I interview the woman who found Kyle?"

"You want us to put everything in my truck?" Emma asked.

"If you don't mind."

They avoided further conversation about Brooke, and by the time he and Emma had the telescopes loaded in her little pickup, Brooke had finished questioning her witness and rejoined them.

Luke closed the hatch and dusted his hands. Even with low lighting, he couldn't help but notice the dark circles shadowing

Brooke's eyes. "You're tired," he said. "Why don't you let me drive you home? We can pick up my car tomorrow."

"I can take her home," Emma said with a sharp glance at him.

Brooke waved Emma off. "You live in the opposite direction. Besides, I'm going to the hospital to check on Kyle, and I can get there on my own."

He wasn't about to let her leave by herself. "Can I tag along with you?"

Brooke hesitated. "Tell me again why you're so interested in Kyle."

"It's like we made a connection," he said, which wasn't a lie.

Her face softened. "I guess I can understand that. Sure, you can join me."

"Let me grab another shirt," he said and hurried to his Jeep. Once he slipped on another pullover, he rejoined them.

"You keep shirts in your car?" Brooke asked.

"Usually at least one." He always kept a "go bag" in his car in case he had to leave a place in a hurry.

"Do you want me to come with you to the hospital?" Emma asked.

"No need in both of us losing sleep," Brooke replied. "I'll call you tomorrow about working out."

"Would you like me to drive?" Luke asked.

"Not hardly."

"You mean hardly."

"No. Not hardly—double negative for emphasis, meaning I definitely do not want you to drive."

"Aw, come on. You look exhausted," Luke said, "and I'm a good driver."

She rubbed the back of her neck and then pulled her keys out of her pocket and tossed them to him.

He caught the keys and at the same time didn't miss the warning Emma shot him.

27

He'd played it all wrong. He should've known there were more photos. Showed you couldn't trust an honest man. And how did Kyle Marlar make it to the edge of the clearing? He'd left him for dead a good hundred yards from where that woman found him.

How did it go so wrong? What if Marlar had told Brooke Danvers who shot him? No, he would already be in jail if that had happened. But he'd watched as she leaned over the man . . . Marlar told her something.

Maybe it was nothing.

He couldn't take that chance. He had to get rid of her.

He released the death grip on the steering wheel and fished the suppressor from his console, almost dropping it. With shaky fingers, he screwed the suppressor to the barrel of the automatic and placed it on the passenger seat. Just follow her and—

No! Why was Luke Fereday getting in the car with her? He forced calm through his body. He couldn't afford to panic. Just add Fereday to the casualty list. What was one more body now?

28

Brooke wasn't accustomed to riding in the passenger seat. Luke driving her car was even stranger. It was as though the years just disappeared . . . except some of his actions raised questions. She did not buy that he'd been at Fort Rosalie because Daisy encouraged it or to see her. He hadn't made the effort in fourteen years.

And by tomorrow, with Natchez being Natchez, Jeremy would hear that she'd left Fort Rosalie with Luke. She had to make sure he knew Luke was only a friend. Brooke swayed against the seat belt as Luke turned onto Highway 84. "Why do I get the feeling you're not who you claim to be?" she asked.

"What do you mean?" Luke's voice was cautious.

"Nothing adds up. You just happen to knock on my door last night and then happen to be at Fort Rosalie when Kyle Marlar gets shot. Then your suggestion that everyone give their statement later . . . it doesn't fit the image I have of a bartender."

"Coincidence and common sense, and don't forget I was an Army Ranger," he said. "I'm surprised that you're allowing me to drive. You're such a control freak when it comes to your car."

She pressed her lips together. He didn't know anything about her, not after ignoring her all these years. "Who told you I was a control freak?"

"No one had to. I remember when you got your first car—you wouldn't let anyone else drive it. I assume you haven't changed."

He remembered that? "There was a reason for that," she said. "Insurance. My dad would have skinned me alive if he caught anyone else behind the wheel."

Luke laughed. "You always were the one who followed the rules."

"And you never did. Rules were for someone else," she said.

"Did you learn anything from your friend who found Kyle?"

There he went again, sounding more like a cop than bartender. Was it because of his army background? "There wasn't anything to learn. She had wandered to the river bluff and gotten turned around when she found Kyle."

"Did she see anyone else?"

"No." The memory of Kyle lying on the ground, blood staining his shirt, was one Brooke would never forget. Was there anything she had missed? Pete had secured the area and called off the search for clues until morning, and she planned to be there tomorrow when they returned to comb the area.

"I hear your wheels turning over there," Luke said.

It was funny how some things never changed. He'd always sensed her moods, and she managed the ghost of a smile. "I was going over what happened tonight."

"I'm a good listener if you need to bounce ideas off someone."

Brooke hesitated. After the interview with Anna, she'd run an idea by Dale, but he hadn't thought much of it. She wasn't sure she wanted to get shot down again. But Luke was an outsider. He might not think her idea was so crazy. "Do you think Kyle could have been trying to tell me something when he said he was sorry about my dad? He'd told me that already at the funeral home."

Unlike Dale, Luke actually seemed to consider her question before he nodded.

"He knew his condition was critical, and that makes what he said important. What else did he say?"

She'd been puzzling over his comment about not trusting anyone. Did she really want to discuss it with Luke? She did trust him, and evidently her dad did as well to discuss things like her career moves with him. What else had they discussed? "Did you and Dad ever talk about his work?"

He flipped the turn signal on. "Sometimes. With my background in the army, your dad felt he could talk to me, and I occasionally helped him think a problem through. Why?"

Brooke bit her bottom lip. "Kyle told me not to trust anyone."

"Really. Did he name anyone specifically?"

"No."

"Maybe he believes someone in your circle is crooked. Someone you interact with."

That's what she'd thought too. But who? Since most of the people she interacted with were in law enforcement, it would have to be a crooked cop. Not something she wanted to believe.

Luke pulled into the hospital parking lot, and once he parked, he came around to her side of the car and opened the door. "Why was Kyle so far away from everyone tonight?"

"You didn't read the article in the paper?" she said.

"What article?"

"A reporter interviewed Kyle because of his photos from previous Perseids meteor showers. He's won several photography contests with his pictures," she said. "Anyway, in the article he talked about how he liked to get in his own spot, away from the crowds."

"Anyone who read the article would have known where he planned to set up?" he asked.

"Generally, yes." She followed him through the ER doors at Merit Health. It was like walking into a meat locker. "Why are hospitals so cold?"

"Keeps down germs," Luke said.

"Aren't you cold in that short-sleeved shirt?" The shirt he'd used to stanch Kyle's blood was probably in the trash now.

Luke shook his head, then just before they reached the desk in the waiting room, he turned to her. "The receptionist may not want to give us any information. Let me handle it."

They stopped at a desk manned by an older woman wearing a name badge.

"Cynthia," Luke said. "Can you tell me where I can find Kyle Marlar?"

"Are you family?"

"Do cousins count?"

Cousins? Luke was no more a cousin than she was.

The receptionist's mouth turned down. "I don't suppose it'd do any harm to tell you. He passed away right after he got here."

Brooke's breath caught in her chest, and she blinked back the unexpected tears that threatened. She'd truly thought he'd make it.

"Is some of the family still here?" Luke asked.

"They may have left, but you can check the ER waiting room."

"Thanks," he said and took Brooke by the elbow. "Come on, let's see if we can find them."

A soon as they were out of hearing range of the information desk, she said, "I can't believe you made her believe you're Kyle's cousin."

"Social engineering," he said. "It's how you get information—she wouldn't have told us if she hadn't thought we were family."

Social engineering. Baloney. "Doesn't it bother you? Lying like that?"

"I didn't lie." His face sobered. "And you don't understand. You do whatever to get what you need."

Who was this man and what did he do with Luke Fereday? Maybe Luke had been a little wild, but she'd never known him to stretch the truth.

"Do you see Kyle's wife?" he asked, scanning the waiting room.

"No."

"You're sure?"

"Yes, but I do see Kyle's oldest son," she said, pointing to a man who stood near the ICU doors.

Bill Marlar looked toward them as they approached. After the two men shook hands, Luke said, "So sorry for what happened."

"Thanks." Bill nodded as Brooke added her condolences. He ran his hand over his eyes and then blew out a deep breath. "Were you there?"

"I was one of the first to reach him," Brooke said.

"What happened?"

"I don't know other than someone shot him. Is your mom here?"

"No, one of the ladies from church took her home. She's going to stay with her until I get there. I'm waiting for whoever will take his body to Jackson for an autopsy."

Autopsy. She hadn't considered that. "Tell her I'm sorry."

"I don't know how we're going to make it through this," he said softly. "First Brandon and now Dad."

She squeezed his hand. "I'll try to get by to see her tomorrow."

Bill nodded. "Thanks for coming by."

"That's tough," Luke said a few minutes later as they stepped outside the hospital.

"Yeah." Brooke knew a little bit about things being tough, but the Marlar family had experienced more. After the air-conditioning in the hospital, the humid night air felt thick enough to spoon into a bowl. Across the street, a bank sign registered ninety-one degrees. Natchez in August.

"Mind if I drive again?" Luke asked.

"You have the keys." For once, she would rather someone else drove. Kyle's death had brought the full force of her dad's death back, and the thought of returning to her parents' empty house left a bitter taste in her mouth. "How about if we drive up the Trace first?"

"You don't want to go home either?"

She felt his gaze on her and glanced at him. The sympathy in his face almost undid her. "Not really. Do you mind?"

"Not at all."

"Just watch for deer."

Luke took a left out of the hospital parking lot, and they were soon cruising at fifty miles an hour on the Parkway. A few miles out from Natchez, she rolled her window down and opened the moon roof on the Escape, letting the lush smells of the woodlands drift in. Tree frogs serenaded them over the hum of the tires. They passed mile marker after mile marker in a comfortable silence on the deserted two-lane road.

"Why didn't you come back to Natchez after you dropped out of Annapolis?" she asked, ending the silence. What she really wanted to ask was why he'd never called after he left.

He glanced in the rearview mirror. "I don't know. I guess because I was trying to find my way. I ended up joining the army."

"Did you find your answers there?"

"I suppose. How about you? Did you never consider leaving Natchez?"

She didn't have a quick answer and glanced out her open window, briefly catching the beams of a vehicle in her side mirror. The approaching car seemed to be traveling faster than the posted fifty miles an hour. "I left once, went to college up at Starkville."

"That's still in Mississippi," he said with a laugh. "We're almost to Coles Creek. Would you like to stop and stretch your legs?"

"That sounds good." The popular tourist attraction had a paved parking area and picnic tables. But when they reached it, instead of turning in, Luke looked up at the mirror again and sped up.

"What are you doing?"

He didn't answer. Instead he reached down and pulled his pistol from the ankle holster.

"Luke!"

"There's a car right on our tail and the driver just now doused the headlights."

The Escape lurched forward. It took her a second to realize what was happening. "It's ramming us!"

"Call 911!"

Her hand shook as she yanked her phone from her pocket. "No service."

"Hold on, I'm going to outrun them."

Brooke held on to the armrest as Luke floored the gas pedal, but the Escape was built for gas mileage, not zero-to-sixty in ten seconds. She jerked against the seatbelt when the vehicle rammed them again. "Why—"

"Is there a crossroad nearby?"

She tried to think. "The Fayette turnoff should be just ahead."

The vehicle pulled beside them and Brooke clicked a mental picture. Big SUV. Dark, maybe black. Windows darkened and she couldn't see the driver or even how many were in the car.

The SUV swerved into them, and Luke slammed on the brakes, throwing her forward. The passenger window lowered and a yellow flash blazed from inside the car, followed by a *whock* and falling glass as their windows shattered.

Luke returned fire and another bullet whizzed by, embedding in the dash. The SUV rammed the Escape's front fender, and the screeching metal sent shivers through her body. Luke fought the steering wheel, but the Escape veered onto the shoulder of the road.

Brooke braced her feet against the floor as the car careened off the road into a shallow ditch. Pain ricocheted through her shoulders as they plowed over saplings and through brush, coming to a stop inches from a towering live oak.

29

Steam poured from the radiator into the already humid air, mixing with the odor of gasoline. Luke twisted in the seat looking for the gun the wreck had jarred out of his hand. He didn't see it, and he didn't have the Glock he usually carried with him.

"You okay?" he asked a dazed Brooke. Her slow nod indicated she wasn't 100 percent. Anger and frustration fueled him. He cocked his ear toward the road. The wreck had silenced the tree frogs, and in the stillness, tires screeched then transmission gears ground into reverse.

"He's coming back." Luke unbuckled his seatbelt as he spoke. When she hesitated, he unbuckled hers and then heaved his shoulder against the door. It didn't budge. Evidently one of the trees they'd sideswiped had wedged the frame into the door. A quick glance showed that a pine tree blocked her door. "We have to go out through the roof."

Brooke bolted upright, her lethargy gone. Luke didn't wait for her to agree. He gripped the edge of the opening and pulled himself up until he could stand. Once he was out of the car, he turned to help her, but she was already climbing out. He assessed their situation. The car had come to a stop a hundred feet from the road in the midst of dense woods. He'd only brought the one gun and it was somewhere on the floorboard. With no idea of how many were in the other car, they had no option but to run.

The whine of tires grew louder, and he caught a glimpse of headlights on the road. Luke hopped off the car and then caught Brooke as she jumped down. "We have to get deeper into the woods," he said. "Then we'll circle back around to the road."

"We're not far past Mount Locust. We can work our way back. Should be cell reception there," she said and sprinted ahead of him.

The crescent moon barely gave enough light for them to work their way through the dense undergrowth, but at least the darkness should make it hard to tell which direction he and Brooke took. Thorns caught his bare arms, ripping his skin. Brooke probably wasn't faring any better. Long pants protected their legs, but that would be no protection against the snakes crawling around them.

Muffled cursing came from behind. Their assailant had discovered the empty Escape. Or assailants. They were too far away to tell how many there were, and with no weapon, they couldn't hang around to find out.

They plowed through the undergrowth, and Luke knuckled the sweat off his brow. A branch slapped his cheek, and he bit back a grunt. They came to a break in the trees, and he yanked out his phone. "I have a couple of bars," he whispered.

"Call the ranger station."

He didn't know the number and instead punched in 911. His fingers hit the wrong key and he gritted his teeth and switched to his left hand. This time he was successful, and an operator answered.

"I'm on the Trace at—" What was the last mile marker he'd seen? "Mile marker 16 and my car ran off the road near Coles Creek. Please send help! I can't stay on the line," he said and disconnected. He shut his phone off so it wouldn't ring and alert whoever was after them. He heard a splash and searched for Brooke. Where was she?

"Luke!" Her frantic whisper came from below. She must have stumbled into the creek.

He cocked his ear as branches snapped behind them. Their pursuer couldn't be more than a hundred yards away. Luke grabbed hold of a small tree on the bank and used it to slide quietly in the creek into water up to his knees. Something brushed against his leg, and Luke willed it to not be a snake.

He could barely see Brooke, who had crawled under a cave-like ledge. There wasn't room for him. He clawed into the dirt until his fingers closed on a root, and he pulled himself flat against the bank.

"You all right?" he whispered and sensed her nod.

Footsteps stomped to their left. Sounded like one person, but he couldn't tell for sure. A light beam strobed overhead and swept back and forth, bouncing off the trees across the creek. His arm ached from holding the root and trying to keep his balance on the slick bank. He couldn't hold on much longer.

Was that a siren? Yes! Miles away came the definite wail of a siren. The 911 operator had sent in the troops.

Minutes later tires screeched away, and Luke released a shaky breath. "He's gone."

"You sure?"

"Yep. He must have heard the siren and took off," he said and helped her out of her hiding place. They waded in the creek until they found a place to climb out. "You want me to give you a boost up the bank?"

"I think I can make it." She grabbed hold of a tree limb that drooped near the ground and climbed out.

Luke used his left hand to pull himself up with the same limb. It didn't take long to backtrack to the wrecked Escape, where Brooke walked around it, shaking her head.

"We were lucky we weren't killed," she said. "You think there was only one person?"

"Pretty sure. The gunfire came from inside the car, like maybe the driver was the shooter." He searched the floorboard and found his Ruger and returned it to his wet ankle holster. When he looked around, she had her phone in her hand. "What are you doing?"

"I have a faint signal and I'm calling Dale Gallagher. He needs to know what happened."

Gallagher was high on his list of suspects and it was all he could do to keep from snatching the phone from her hand. But if he did, she'd want an explanation. An explanation he couldn't give. He relaxed when the call went unanswered.

"Why do you think this happened?" she asked.

He could think of only two answers. Either their assailant thought Marlar told Brooke something, or Wilson had recognized Luke and his cover was blown. Both were bad options, but if his cover had been blown, Boudreaux would have sent more than one person to take care of him. The problem with that theory was he didn't know for sure how many had been in the SUV. "How long were you with Kyle before I got there?"

"I don't know. Five minutes?"

"When I arrived, it was plain to see he was talking to you. If his shooter was watching, he could believe Kyle passed information to you."

She frowned. "That doesn't make sense. If Kyle had told me who shot him, the case would be solved."

"True, but I'm talking about perception. I figure whoever killed him is running scared. He's not thinking straight, and if he thinks Kyle told you something . . ."

She hugged her arms to her body. "Then he could have been trying to silence me."

"Yeah."

Her eyes narrowed.

"Something else is bothering me," she said. "I don't buy your 'coincidence and common sense' answer from earlier. And just now, you sounded more like a cop than I do. What's going on?"

He forced himself to not look away. "The coincidence part is true, to a point. It was a coincidence that I was at your house last night when the intruder attacked you. That I was at Fort Rosalie tonight wasn't. I wanted to make sure nothing like that happened again, so that's why I was at the event. To watch over you."

He couldn't tell if she was angry or pleased. "You deceived that woman at the hospital so easily earlier, I'm not sure I can believe you, and it doesn't explain why you sound like a cop."

"I was an Army Ranger. Comes with the territory."

The die was cast now. If Brooke ever discovered he was working undercover, she would know he played her.

30

Brooke did not need a protector, and while she hadn't forgotten he'd been a Ranger, she'd never thought about it much. But it did explain his take-charge attitude. And made it harder to understand why he worked as a bartender.

"We need to cross the ditch to the side of the road so the first responder can see us," she said as the siren drew closer.

"How are you going to handle this?"

"What do you mean?" She jumped across the water in the ditch, then scrambled up the bank while Luke followed suit.

"Are you going to investigate what happened tonight or turn it over to someone else?"

"I'm not turning this over to anyone else—it's personal."

"Then maybe we should play down the other car. Report that I swerved to miss a deer, because Dale won't allow you to investigate your own attack."

He was right. And this happened on government property. If she reported that the other car fired at their vehicle and ran them off the road, the FBI could very well take over the case. What would her dad have done? She didn't have to think long. He would've investigated it himself.

"Something keeps nagging at me," she said slowly. "The only person who could get close enough to my dad to kill him would have been someone he trusted—either a cop, or . . ." She winced. "Or a ranger."

He nodded his agreement. "You're probably on to something."

The siren grew closer. But could she lie? The right thing to do was report everything. "Maybe I'll write everything up in my report, just not turn it in right away."

A flicker of amusement crossed his eyes. "You'll learn that it's not always in your best interest to tell everything you know, especially when you're not certain who's trustworthy."

Brooke's shoulder ached even while her mind spun. Was Luke right? Flashing blue lights rounded the curve, and she stared, mesmerized. She shook her head. What was wrong with her? The SUV pulled even with them. Gary was on duty tonight.

"Having trouble?" He climbed out of his car, hitching the belt that hung below his ample belly.

"A little," she said.

Gary did a double take. "That you, Brooke?"

"It's me," she said. "Do you remember Luke Fereday?"

Gary shot him a quizzical glance, and then recognition lit in his eyes. "Played running back your senior year. What were y'all doing on the Trace this time of night? You both know how dangerous it can be, with the deer and all."

"I know." Especially the "and all" part.

"Okay, what happened?"

"Luke was driving, and . . . he swerved to miss a deer."

Gary's look said I-told-you-so. "Let me get something to write on."

He crawled back in his vehicle to retrieve a notepad. When he was ready, she gave him an abbreviated version of the accident.

"Neither of you look as though you were hurt," Gary said. "How'd you get wet?"

She hadn't thought about her wet clothes. "I fell in that ditch," she said, pointing behind her, "and Luke got wet helping me out."

A lie that is half-truth is the darkest of all lies. How many times had Daisy quoted Tennyson? Brooke took a breath. She couldn't do it. "There was another car involved, might've scraped their front fender."

"They didn't stop and offer to help?" Gary sounded incredulous.

"No," Luke said. "They kept going."

Now was the time to tell Gary the whole truth. "There—"

"No need in me writing all this up. You can make out the report and shoot me a copy."

Tell him. Before she could say anything, he turned and flashed his light over the Escape. Her heart hit triple digits again. While the wreck could have caused their windows to shatter, if he found a bullet hole, she would be in trouble and her credibility gone. But Gary seemed more interested in the front end and the radiator. Her heart slowed almost to normal when he hooked the flashlight on his belt.

"It's not drivable," he pronounced. "Want me to call AAA?"

"That'd be great," Luke said, rubbing his right shoulder. Something she'd noticed him doing off and on all night.

Two hours later as the clock inched toward 1:00 a.m., the tow truck dropped her car in the driveway after swinging by Fort Rosalie to drop Luke off at his Jeep. He pulled in Daisy's drive and walked across the yard as she handed the driver her credit card for the tow. Tonight had revealed a whole other side of Luke. The way he worked a situation—like at the hospital—he would never have done that when she knew him before. This definitely wasn't the Luke she knew from years ago.

But what about herself. She hated lies, and on the ride back to town, she'd mulled over how easily she'd lied to Gary. And her attempt to correct it had only been half-hearted. That she was able to justify it only made it worse.

The tow driver cleared his throat.

"I'm sorry, I'm a little distracted." She used her finger to sign the driver's screen. "Thanks."

The driver pocketed his phone. "You're welcome. Next time you better watch those deer better."

"We will," Luke promised.

As the tow truck's taillights disappeared around the corner, she said, "All this deception—it has to stop."

t's been a rough night. Why don't we talk about this tomorrow?"
Luke's shoulder throbbed all the way down to his wrist, and
he massaged his bicep. He should have known Brooke couldn't
fudge the line between truth and a lie. Working undercover was
a good teacher.

She had questions. He could feel them. Somehow he had to
put her off and get to Boudreaux's hotel room. Just to cover all
the bases.

"I'd rather get it out of the way now," she said. "After I get
a shower."

He scanned the area. Everything looked normal, but they
couldn't continue to stand out in the open. "Then let's talk about
it inside, but first I'd like to check out your house, make sure you
have no unwanted guests." Or bugs, but he didn't say that aloud.

She stiffened. "Excuse me, but I think I can check out my
own house."

"I'm the one with a gun, so humor me," he said. "Besides, it's
the gentlemanly thing to do."

"When I was in the tow truck, I didn't see anyone following
us," she said.

"They wouldn't have to—anyone could find out where you live."

He thought she was going to refuse, and then she shrugged.
"Okay, but let's go in the back way."

When they crossed under a bright security light, for a brief second he noticed how her damp clothes hugged her body, outlining her curves. Instantly he reminded himself that she had a boyfriend. Being thrown together in this case was not good. They rounded the back of the house, and she remotely raised the garage door from her key ring, revealing an empty space beside a Buick Regal. Luke nodded toward the Regal. "Your mom's car?"

"Yeah. Dad's truck is still at the sheriff's department."

He went in first after she unlocked the door, and once they were inside, he discreetly checked for bugs as he went from room to room. The house didn't appear to be wired. "Okay if I hang around until you get cleaned up? Then you can lock up and set the alarm after I leave."

She frowned. "I'm not some damsel in distress that you have to save. I can take care of myself."

"I know that," he said, "but it would make me feel better."

"I give up!" She started down the hall and turned around. "If you're staying, make yourself useful and brew some coffee. Everything you need is on the counter by the coffeepot." Then she paused. "Unless making coffee interferes with your macho image."

"No," Luke said. He found the coffee filters while he waited for Brooke to turn the shower on. Then he speed-dialed Steve Jackson. "I need your help. Someone ran us off the road and took potshots at us tonight," he said when his boss answered.

"Who is 'us'?"

"Brooke Danvers." Luke poured water in the drip coffeemaker and scooped coffee into the filter.

"John Danvers's daughter?"

"Yes."

"Luke . . ." Steve's voice held a warning. "You're supposed to be focused on the drug traffic."

He couldn't help it if trouble found him. "I know. Look, find out if there's word on the street that I'm undercover."

There was a brief silence, and then Steve said, "Tell me what happened."

"It's a long story. Brooke is taking a shower, and I won't have time to relate all of it right now."

"Hit the highlights."

"Kyle Marlar was murdered tonight."

"You're kidding."

"I don't kid about anything like that. Someone shot him at Fort Rosalie. Then a little later Brooke and I were on the Trace when someone shot at us and ran us off the road. We managed to get away."

"You think it was because you were compromised?"

"If I was, we'll know for sure within the hour, but there may be another explanation." Luke related what he and Brooke had discussed.

"She trusts you?"

His conscience squeezed him. "Yeah, she trusts me."

Steve was quiet a moment. "How are you going to find out if your attacker was someone from Boudreaux's organization?"

"I plan to confront him. If he thinks I'm a narc, he won't be expecting that. And if he doesn't suspect me, my righteous indignation should solidify my position."

"Just be careful. We've worked too long on nailing Boudreaux to lose him now," he said. "Do you know what Marlar told Brooke Danvers?"

"Some of it, but not all. Marlar mentioned her father, and he'd told me earlier John didn't commit suicide. I believe he knew who did it."

"The evidence—"

"I don't care what the evidence shows, John Danvers did not kill himself. Have you gotten copies of the crime scene photos yet?"

"Yes. I'll get them to you. But isn't Brooke Danvers an interpretive ranger?"

"Last month she finished her LE training and was supposed to start field training with her dad next week. With the area short staffed, she's been brought in on Marlar's case before she completes her internship."

"Does she know her father was investigating Boudreaux, and he asked you for help?"

"No." The last thing he wanted was for Brooke to discover Luke had let her dad down.

"I'll work on finding out if your cover is blown."

"Thanks." He planned to work on it as well.

"How about Sonny? Have you been in contact with him?"

Sonny was skittish. "Not yet. Any word on which law enforcement officers are in Boudreaux's back pocket?"

"No, but we're still investigating."

"One more thing. Marlar's camera may have something on it. He mentioned something about photos the last time I talked to him. The camera should be in Pete Nelson's possession."

"Got it."

The bathroom door opened. "I have to go. I'll call you in an hour. Until then, talk to your contacts in Natchez. See if anyone is talking about Kyle's murder on the streets, and I'll check with my sources," he said and disconnected.

He was looking for creamer when Brooke entered the kitchen. She'd changed into leggings and a long top. With her wet hair pulled back in a ponytail she reminded him of the girl he'd kissed so long ago. He shook the thought off. Romantic thoughts of Brooke were the last thing he needed on his mind. She glanced at him, questions in her dark brown eyes. Definitely needed to avoid looking into those eyes he could drown in. Keep it casual. "Feel better?"

"Caffeine will make me feel even better." She tugged at her ear. "I lost one of my favorite earrings tonight."

"I'm afraid it's probably gone forever."

"Yeah." She poured a cup of coffee before checking his empty mug. "Did you drink yours already?"

"Haven't had any yet." He turned and leaned his hip against the counter. "Couldn't find the creamer."

"You never used creamer before," she said. "You always drank your coffee black."

"Things change." She remembered? He'd used the creamer line to cover why his cup was empty. He didn't want her to question what he'd been doing while she was in the shower.

"That's an understatement, but I don't know why I'm surprised. Nothing else about you is the same," she said and filled his cup. "Regardless, there isn't any creamer. No one in this house uses it, although if I'd known you liked it, I would have bought some."

"Would you?"

"Get back to me on that," she said.

Luke bit back a grin and sipped the coffee, liking that it was strong. "This is pretty good black," he said. Luke glanced around the kitchen. He hadn't seen the house since John updated it and added more cabinets and modern features without downplaying its 1930s Craftsman charm.

"I like what your dad did here," he said.

His phone alerted he had a text and he checked it. Steve.

You may want to rethink a meeting with
Boudreaux tonight.

> Nothing to rethink.

It will be risky.

> Doing nothing is even riskier.

Be careful.

He definitely would, but first he had to get cleaned up and pick up his Glock.

Brooke was staring at him when he looked up. "Sorry, but I need to leave."

"You have to meet someone?" she asked.

"Kind of." He deleted Steve's message. "Call me if you need anything and be sure to set the alarm."

"Don't worry, I will." She followed him to the back door. "But who are you meeting this time of night?" Suddenly her face flushed and her eyes widened. "Oh, my goodness! Where you're going is none of my business."

The way her face colored and now she avoided his gaze . . . did she think he was going to see another woman? Briefly he thought about letting her believe that was his plan, but the flicker of disappointment in her eyes made it impossible. "I'm going to see a man about a job here in Natchez."

It wasn't a lie, but it was misleading and it bothered him. A first since he'd started working undercover.

Several emotions flitted across Brooke's face before she corralled them. She would never make a good card player.

"Really?"

Was that hope in her voice? "Daisy isn't getting any younger. In my line of work I can work as well in Natchez as Jackson." Again not a lie, but not the truth. What was she doing to him? Maybe he should have let her believe he was seeing a woman.

"She would like that."

Luke couldn't explain why, but it was important for Brooke to think well of him. Maybe to cushion the blow if she found out he was working undercover. Scratch that thought. He had to make sure she didn't discover that part of his life. He didn't want to put her in more danger than she might already be in. Brooke's cell phone rang, and he flinched.

She glanced at the screen. "It's Dale. I need to take this."

He lingered at the door. More than anything, he wanted to remind her about Kyle Marlar's warning and to be careful what she told the district ranger. Instead, he said, "See you tomorrow." On impulse, he hugged her. "Stay safe and set your alarm."

32

Brooke caught Dale's call just before it went to voice mail.

"Are you all right?" he demanded.

"Not sure how all right I am," she replied, wincing as pain radiated from her neck to her shoulder. "But I'm alive."

"I saw that I missed a call from you and when I couldn't reach you, I started calling around and finally got Gary. He told me about your accident."

"What're you doing up at two in the morning?"

"Mary gets her days and nights mixed up sometimes. This is one of those times. What happened?"

"Hold on just a sec. I need to set the security alarm." As she armed it, an internal battle warred within her. If she told Dale what actually happened, she wouldn't be able to investigate the crime, but lying wasn't in her nature. She wasn't even good at social engineering. Then there was Kyle's warning, but it couldn't apply to Dale. She'd known the man most of her life.

Brooke pushed the lock button, and after it flashed red, indicating it was armed, she took a deep breath. "Someone fired at us and ran my Escape off the road."

"What? That's not what Gary reported."

"I didn't tell him what really happened. I didn't think you would let me investigate it if I did."

"I don't understand."

"Whoever ran us off the road meant to kill us. Luke thinks it's tied to Kyle's death."

"You were with Luke Fereday? I didn't realize you two were that close."

She felt heat rising in her cheeks. "It's not like that. I've known him forever—he used to stay with his grandmother next door during the summer."

"I see," he said, his voice tense. "Did you recognize the person in the other vehicle?"

"It was dark. I couldn't see inside the vehicle. I only know it was an SUV."

"How about Luke, did he see who it was?"

"No. And I couldn't tell if it was one person or two."

"I don't like this, Brooke. First someone breaks into your house and now this. I think you should take a few days off, go visit your mom and sister in Knoxville."

"No!" She couldn't believe he'd suggested that. Or was it more than a suggestion. "You're not taking me off Kyle Marlar's case, are you?"

Silence answered her.

"Look, Dale," she said. "I don't know why these things happened, but no one is scaring me away from doing my job."

A long breath sounded through the phone. "I'll see you later this morning at the Port Gibson office, and we'll discuss it further."

He disconnected before she could respond. Not that she had anything to say that would counter his order. Brooke noticed she'd missed a text when she laid her phone on the charger and opened the app. Jeremy.

Sorry I had to leave, but I needed to put Molly to bed. You okay?

That was sweet of him. It was too late to respond now, but first thing in the morning she would give him a call. Then another text dinged on her phone and she checked it. Meghan, wanting to know how she was doing. Brooke certainly wasn't telling her about being run off the road.

> I'm fine, but what are you doing up this time of night?

Izzy won't settle down.

She smiled. Meghan gave everyone a nickname, often calling her Brookie, but this was the first time she'd referred to Isabelle as Izzy.

I tried to call you earlier—got my DNA report today.

> Mine hasn't come yet. Any surprises?

Not that I can tell—I'm 45% Irish, 47% English and 8% European. I'll scan the report and send it in the morning. Going back to bed now.

> Sleep tight.

Meghan replied with a snoring emoji. Brooke put her phone back on charge and slipped into her pajamas. Her bedroom faced Daisy's drive, and just before climbing into bed, she peeked through the blinds to see if Luke was home. The drive was empty. She frowned. It seemed an odd time to talk to someone about a job.

33

He walked around the SUV, examining the damage. Telltale white paint streaked the right fender. He fought the rising panic tightening his chest, clouding his mind. They both should be dead now, but they weren't.

Maybe he shouldn't have gone after them in the first place. Now they would be suspicious. Think. His mistake had been in focusing on Brooke Danvers. But his first impulse had been to wipe out anyone in contact with Marlar tonight. Forget about her. If she knew anything, she would have reported it. Focus on getting the photos Marlar had stashed somewhere. And getting the car repainted.

Memphis. That's where he'd take the car for repair. He stared at the fender. Who was he kidding? The likelihood of getting the car to Memphis in the next few days was zero to none. Maybe he should just park it in the shed out back for now—he rarely drove the SUV, and no one would be the wiser.

A few minutes later, the vehicle was safely tucked away, and he'd remembered a friend who did body work on the side. It was the perfect solution. His friend wouldn't get an alert to be on the lookout for a vehicle with white paint on the right front fender. And he wouldn't ask a lot of nosy questions.

Now to see what was on the memory cards he'd taken from Marlar's camera bag.

A few minutes later, he turned the computer on, his muscles tense as he waited for it to boot up. The first card had nothing but sunsets, birds, flowers. He replaced it with a second one and leaned forward. Family photos. This third card better be it, or he'd killed a man for nothing.

He stilled his jiggling legs as a time-stamped shot of the Emerald Mound sign appeared. Pay dirt. Air whooshed from his lungs. He quickly scanned the images that ended with the one he'd jerked out of Marlar's grasp.

"Joke's on you . . . not the only pictures . . . copies . . ."

His muscles tensed again. He might have the digital photos, but the printed copies were somewhere, just waiting to ambush him.

34

Once Luke cleaned up, he grabbed his other gun and drove downtown. By the time he parked, he'd psyched himself up for the meeting with Boudreaux, getting himself in the right mindset—indignant, angry. But first he had to make sure Boudreaux was in the same room.

The clerk on duty looked to be about eighteen so maybe he was in luck tonight. "I stayed in room 212 last night," he said, "and I think I left my computer bag in the room when I checked out."

The kid typed into the computer and then frowned. "You couldn't have stayed in that room. The people in it checked in two days ago. But I can check and see what room you were in, although I don't think the housekeeper turned in anything. What's your name?"

"Tony Jones." The deception rolled off his tongue. Just then the hotel phone rang and the kid held up his hand. "Let me get this."

"No problem. I'll be at the bar." Instead of the bar, he disappeared around the corner where he took the elevator to the second floor and tapped sharply on the door at the end of the hall. It opened a crack, and he recognized Robert Wilson from the night before. Luke pushed past him.

"Hey! What are you doing?"

Luke scanned the room. "Where's Boudreaux?"

"What's it to you?" Wilson sniffed the air. "Smells like a stinkin' narc in here."

In one fluid movement, Luke shoved him against the wall and at the same time yanked the Glock from the holster against his back. "Those words can get you killed," he said, putting the pistol to Wilson's head.

"You sayin' you didn't bust me a couple of years ago on cocaine charges?"

Luke shook his head. "Don't know who you think arrested you, but it wasn't me. When was this supposed to have happened?"

"Five years ago. Up around Nashville."

He thought fast. The information on the web had Luke working at a bar in San Francisco during that time. "I was in California five years ago."

"Prove it." Boudreaux's steely voice came from behind him. "And put the gun away."

Luke froze. He hadn't heard the drug boss come into the room.

Wilson's bravado returned. "And get your hands off me."

Luke released his hold on Wilson and turned to face Boudreaux. "I don't know that I can prove it. I was working at a bar and the owners could be dead by now."

"What was the name of the bar?"

"Red Horse Saloon."

Boudreaux nodded to a man who materialized from the shadows. Slight and ordinary, he was the kind of person who went unnoticed in a gathering. With his phone pressed to his ear, he stepped out onto the balcony. Tension mounted as the seconds ticked off. Luke didn't want to overplay his hand and forced himself to relax. What if Boudreaux's man called the wrong place? As far as Luke knew, there was no "real" Red Horse Saloon in San Francisco. The number listed on the website dialed straight into an undercover call service.

"How long did you work there?" Boudreaux asked.

Luke pulled his attention back to the drug kingpin. "A year, maybe longer. San Francisco is a party town and recollection of my time there is kind of blurred."

The balcony door opened and the man returned to the room. He gave Boudreaux a slight nod then whispered something in his ear. Boudreaux raised an eyebrow and turned to Luke. "What'd they call you at this bar?"

Luke startled, and then he forced a chuckle. "I hadn't thought about that in years. Grasshopper." Which was the code for warning him his cover had possibly been blown. Sweat formed between his shoulder blades. Leave or . . . he decided to push it. "What's up with this? I've been dealing with your man Sonny for four months now. I thought we'd established, if not trust, a certain respect for each other."

"I didn't get where I am by trusting people. I catch somebody lying to me . . . let's say the alligators in the bayous around here will have a good meal."

The coldness in Boudreaux's voice didn't compare to the coldness in his black eyes. Then, like a light switching on, the lines in his face relaxed, and he slapped Luke on the shoulder. "You're crazy, you know? You could have been shot, walking in here like you did. But I like to see a man with guts." He motioned him to sit in one of the lounge chairs by the sofa. "Grasshopper, huh? From that old kung fu show I watch in reruns?"

"Yeah. Back in my San Francisco days, I liked to spout Chinese proverbs. Some old guy at the bar found out I was studying judo and started calling me Grasshopper, and it stuck."

"So, you're pretty good at judo?"

"Black belt." He didn't mention he'd mastered tae kwon do as well. "Why did you send someone to shoot at me and my girlfriend and run us off the road?"

"Who said I did?"

Luke tented his fingers. He didn't deny it. That upped the likelihood that it had been Boudreaux who ordered the hit on him tonight. "The woman in the car with me—I don't want her hurt."

He didn't look away from the man's steady gaze.

"What did the man who was shot at Fort Rosalie tell her?"

Luke's insides froze. How did Boudreaux know that Brooke had found Kyle Marlar or that he'd told her anything? "Were you there?"

"I have spies everywhere. Don't ever forget that. So . . . ?"

Luke consciously kept his hands from fisting and his poker face in place. "She hasn't remembered anything important. Is Marlar's death connected to her father's murder?"

"You ask a lot of questions," Boudreaux said, "but I heard the ranger's death was a suicide."

"Don't believe everything you hear. And I like to know the people I'm doing business with, the things they're involved in. Besides, she's investigating Marlar's death. I can funnel information as I learn it . . . if that's important to you."

"All information is important. Life is like a row of dominoes—one topples and it affects all the others."

"So you are responsible for Marlar's death. Why?"

"Never said that. I don't have to be responsible to want the information. My question is, why do you want to know?"

Luke untented his fingers and brushed his hand along the rough tweed of the chair arm. "Kyle Marlar was kind to me once. I'm curious about who killed him and why."

"Curiosity has killed a lot of nosy people," Boudreaux said.

"Granted. If you killed Marlar, you had to have a reason, and I'd like to know what it is."

Boudreaux studied his fingernails and then raised his gaze to Luke. "The last time we talked, you got samples of heroin for your customers. How'd they like 'em?"

If he knew who killed Marlar, he wasn't going to discuss it. Luke's only chance of learning anything about the murders was to hang around and hope someone let information slip. "They were impressed."

"Would you like more, maybe a little something for yourself?"

It was an offer he couldn't refuse. "How much are you talking about?"

Boudreaux turned his head. "Louis, the box, please."

So that was his name. He produced a small box and handed it to the drug dealer. "How many?" Boudreaux asked.

"A couple of bags will be good." Luke paid the amount quoted, and then he stood to leave. "I'll be in touch." At the door, he paused. "Next time you have doubts about me, come to me first," he said with a glance at Wilson, who stood near the door. "And, if I get picked up by local law enforcement, is there anyone who can help me out?"

Boudreaux didn't blink. "Don't get picked up."

It'd been worth a try. Now he'd have to discover who the crooked cops were the old-fashioned way.

35

Once he was alone in the elevator, Luke released a long breath. The risk had paid off. So why did he feel like he had a bull's-eye on his back as he walked through the lobby? Because he was dealing with a bona fide psycho. He crossed the street to his car, then bypassed it and climbed to the top of the River Walk, where a breeze cooled his face and adrenaline-hyped body.

Two hundred feet below, the glassy waters of the Mississippi River belied the swift current that flowed on to New Orleans. Not unlike the current that coursed through his veins. He focused on the outward calm of the river, and bit by bit tension eased from his body. For the first time, he noticed the sweet fragrance of the white crepe myrtles all around him. He glanced south to the bridge that connected Mississippi and Louisiana where even this time of night, lights snaked across to Vidalia, Louisiana.

He shifted his gaze back to the Mississippi. The river had been here for thousands of years and would remain thousands more. It was permanent, and the One who had created it was bigger than he was. Right now he needed that reminder. He wasn't in this drug thing alone. For whatever reason, God had given him the ability to become a chameleon, to infiltrate organizations like Boudreaux's.

Laughter floated up from the casino below, and he turned from the river. He checked his watch. Daylight would be here before he knew it, and Luke would like to get at least an hour or two of sleep. He hurried to his car just as a maroon pickup slowed to turn onto the casino road and quickly disappeared down the hill. Clayton Bradshaw? Seemed a little late for him to be hitting the casino.

Luke hesitated, then decided sleep was highly overrated. He jogged down the hill to the casino to see what the ranger was up to. When he stepped through the doors, it was almost like stepping inside a kaleidoscope. Overlaying all the color was a cacophony of sounds. Bells tinkled their robotic music with electronic beeps and clangs, and occasionally a snatch of music reminded Luke of a merry-go-round. His gaze slid to the slots, where no one said a word as they lasered in on the spinning symbols. He scanned the room. Clayton had bypassed the slots for the blackjack games in the middle.

Luke stood off to one side, keeping out of the skinny ranger's line of sight. He didn't know a lot about him other than what he'd read on his employment record. At forty he looked older, with gray sprinkling his dark hair and worry lines in his face, but then, fifteen years as a law enforcement ranger could age a person, especially if he happened to be skirting the law.

Clayton placed what looked like three C-notes on the table. The dealer raked the money in and handed him a stack of chips. Luke studied the ranger's movements—his total focus on the table as the dealer kept a running patter, the way Clayton held his breath waiting for the next card. His thin body emanated tension even when he won, which wasn't often. If he had a gambling problem, and it looked like he did, the cartel could possibly own him body and soul.

It didn't take long for his chips to run out, and he leaned close to the dealer and said something. The dealer shook his head. Luke stepped back as Clayton wheeled around and made a bee-line for the ATM, but the machine spat his card out immediately. His shoulders slumped, and for a second, Luke thought he was going to kick the machine. The ranger swung around, and their gazes collided. Clayton was the first to speak.

"Fereday? What are you doing here?" he asked. "Haven't you had enough excitement for one night?"

"Couldn't sleep. Came down to the River Walk and found myself here. Can I buy you a drink, coffee, maybe?"

He hesitated. "Sure. I'm too wound to sleep too."

They walked to the almost empty bar, where Luke ordered two black coffees. "You come here often?" Luke asked, taking one of the stools.

Clayton took the barstool next to Luke. "Couple of times a week. Win more than I lose, and it helps me wind down."

It wouldn't help Luke. The bartender set their cups in front of them along with a couple of creamers and sugar. "Bad thing, what happened to John Danvers and now Kyle Marlar," Luke said.

"Yeah. They both were good men." The ranger sipped his coffee and set the cup down. "I wouldn't have a job like this in the first place if it hadn't been for Kyle. He set me on the straight and narrow. And John, he made me the ranger I am today."

"Were you at Emerald Mound after John died?"

"It was my night off." Clayton motioned to the bartender. "Could I have a shot of whiskey here?" When it arrived he poured the amber liquid into his coffee.

"You don't have to work tomorrow, or rather today?"

"Yeah, but it'll be worn off by the time I have to show up." He took a long sip and set his cup down. "What happened on the Trace?"

"Deer."

Clayton nodded his understanding.

"How'd you find out?"

"Gary. He said something about another car." Clayton cocked his head. "I'm surprised the driver didn't stop and help."

Was he fishing? "I was too. But it turned out all right." He lifted his empty cup to signal the bartender. After he refilled it,

Luke said, "I can't get Marlar off my mind. Never found someone shot before."

"I've encountered a few. Not a good thing." Clayton shot him a sidelong glance. "Why were you at the fort? I heard what you told Dale, but you don't seem the type who would be interested in meteors."

Luke forced a laugh. "Truth be told, I'm not. I thought it might impress Brooke."

"Forget that. Looks like she and Jeremy Steele have something going." Clayton studied Luke. "What've you been doing since you left Natchez?"

"A little of this, little of that. Currently working as a bartender."

"In Jackson," Clayton said and polished off his whiskey-laced coffee. "That's a long way from the Army Rangers."

"And a lot more freedom," Luke said.

"I get what you're saying." He climbed off the barstool. "See you around."

After Clayton left, Luke paid for their coffees. He hadn't learned much more about Clayton other than he seemed to know a lot about Luke's life. But it shouldn't be too hard to find out if he'd been telling the truth about his winnings. Luke put that on his mental to-do list.

36

Luke switched off the lights in his grandmother's living room and stood to the side of the window, peering through the parted curtain. When he'd parked in Daisy's drive, the Danverses' house had been dark, and no light had come on while he dug the bullet from Brooke's dashboard. Hopefully Brooke was still sleeping. Luke fingered the envelope with the bullet. He would get it to Steve later this morning.

His thoughts drifted back to Brooke. While the security system John Danvers installed was top of the line, Luke still didn't like that she was alone. He'd walked around the house, looking for easy access, and was satisfied that anyone trying to gain entry through the windows would have a hard time since they were high off the ground. He also reminded himself Brooke had been trained at Glynco.

He let the curtain fall back into place and checked the Glock tucked between his back and his belt. Luke needed sleep, but he had a report to write. Tonight had turned out much differently than he'd planned. And not just with Kyle's murder. The image of Brooke's eyes softening when she caught him watching her would not go away. The air between them had been electric. The magic was still there.

Not good, Fereday. He rubbed his palm on the side of his pants leg. He needed distance from her. No. She needed distance from him. She didn't need a man with his kind of baggage.

A board creaked, and Luke jerked his head toward the kitchen. Another creak. It hadn't been his imagination.

Someone was in the house.

Luke went on instant alert, shifting to the balls of his feet as he drew his gun. He eased to the door and then to the small hallway that held a pantry before opening up into a spacious room.

Noiselessly he swung the door open. Half the kitchen was visible. Light from the street filtered in through the windows, creating shadows where anyone could hide. To his left another board creaked.

Luke felt for the switch and flipped it, flooding the room with light as he whipped around the corner, his gun ready. "Put your hands up!"

"Just calm down." The voice came from the corner of the kitchen.

"Steve?"

What was his supervisor doing here? Then Luke saw the other two men—DEA Agent Mark Delaney, who looked more like an NFL tackle than an undercover agent, and Hugh Cortland, who looked exactly like what he was—an FBI agent.

Even as his heart rate slowed to normal, a bad feeling settled in his stomach. He'd expected Cortland to show up in Natchez, but there was only one reason an operative from the Drug Enforcement Agency would be in his house. Luke was jeopardizing his case.

"You could have gotten yourself killed," Luke muttered, holstering his gun. "How did you get in?"

"If I told you all my secrets," Delaney said, "I'd have to kill you."

That joke was old ten years ago. Luke moved the bags of heroin from his pocket to the table as the three men pulled out chairs and sat down. "Nothing like making yourself at home," Luke said, nodding at Steve and Hugh. "Why are you here?"

"We needed a meeting," Steve replied. "Sit down."

"You could've warned me." He remained standing, his feet planted.

"You should have a text on your phone," Steve said as he placed a brown envelope on the table.

Luke checked his phone. He hadn't turned his ringer on after the meeting with Boudreaux. *Bookmaking odds: Dakota Dreamer 3–1.* Bookmaking was the code name for a meeting. The three was for the time and the one indicated it was for today. He sat in the only vacant chair. "Is that the John Danvers crime scene photos?"

"Yes."

Luke pulled the small envelope containing the bullet from his pocket and tossed it on the table. "This is from the gun that fired at us on the Trace."

"I'll check for a match in NIBIN."

"Thanks." The National Integrated Ballistics Information Network had an automated imaging system that shared ballistics intelligence across the United States. If the bullet matched one of their images, it might be possible to track the gun used. "Did you get Marlar's camera?"

"No. Nelson had already checked it out. Nothing but shooting stars on it. He gave it to Marlar's widow," Steve said and glanced around the kitchen. "Got any coffee?"

"Probably." He scanned the counter looking for Daisy's electric percolator and frowned, not believing she'd bought a pod coffeemaker. He hadn't had time to look through her cabinets, but since she liked a good cup of coffee as much as he did, he was certain he'd find a bag of strong brew. Luke hit the jackpot the third door he opened and discovered a box of Colombian dark roast pods. A minute later the rich scent of coffee filled the kitchen, and he set a cup in front of the DEA agent while his boss's coffee brewed. Hugh had declined.

"Why are you here?" he repeated, joining them at the table.

"Did you get any information from Kyle Marlar?" the DEA agent asked.

"No. Didn't Steve tell you he postponed our meeting? I went to Fort Rosalie hoping to talk to him. Unfortunately he was practically unconscious when I got to him."

"And he didn't say anything before the medics arrived?"

"Nothing that could help us. But you didn't come here to ask about Kyle Marlar—that could have been done over the phone."

A look passed between his boss and Delaney, and Luke studied the giant of a man as he wrapped his meaty hands around the cup.

"You took a big chance with Boudreaux tonight," Delaney said.

Luke narrowed his eyes. There was only one way Delaney could know what happened in that hotel room. "Why wasn't I told you had someone working in his organization?"

"It was on a need-to-know basis, and until now, you didn't need to know," Delaney replied.

"You sure it's not the left hand not knowing what the right hand is doing?"

"I knew you were working the drug angle. Just never figured you'd get anywhere."

Luke had struck a nerve. "Then what's my role in all of this? I've been working this case for four months." He didn't like being kept in the dark about the investigation. It made him wonder what else was being kept from him.

"We're getting to that. The point is, I don't want a loose cannon in this operation. I need you to promise not to go off the rails again."

"It worked."

"It might not the next time."

"Look, after what happened on the Trace, I figured one of Boudreaux's men recognized me from when I arrested him five years ago. I had to do something to convince him it wasn't me. If you have a man on the inside, he should have told you that's what happened."

"I grant you it worked this time, but the Cajun is crazy. It could have just as easily gone south."

"Believe me, I won't take any risks that I don't have to. Who's your man on the inside?"

"Louis."

That surprised him. He'd figured it would be a lower-level dealer, not someone in Boudreaux's inner circle. But then, as he thought about it, Louis was very bland and nonthreatening, almost invisible, and he could see him worming his way into Boudreaux's confidence.

"Is Boudreaux the one who tried to take you out earlier tonight?" Steve asked.

"You need to be asking Delaney that question."

Delaney shook his head. "Louis says not."

"If Boudreaux ordered it, only the person who got the order knows," Luke replied.

"That's possible," Delaney said. "Just don't do anything like that again without running it by me."

"Try my best, but you know as well as I do, there isn't always time to ask permission. Is that it for tonight? I need to catch some sleep."

"No." Delaney leaned forward. "You've heard there's a big shipment coming into New Orleans next week?"

"I'd heard one was coming soon."

"We want you to make a bid for it. Right now, it's going north, maybe to New Jersey or New York."

"How big?"

"Twenty kilos of uncut heroin."

Luke whistled. The street value of twenty kilos would be at least ten million dollars. "What makes you think he'll let me have it?"

"According to Louis, he likes you. What you did impressed him." Delaney's tone indicated he didn't like admitting it. "When you pick up the kilo tomorrow, tell Boudreaux your backers are tired of nickel-and-dime sales and want to up their profits."

"And just like that, he'll let me have the shipment?"

"You should be able to talk him into it, especially since your offer will be twice what the buyers up north are offering—three million . . . three and a half if we have to."

"You don't think he'll be suspicious?"

"It'll be up to you to make sure he isn't."

The deal would be risky. Luke leaned forward, his fingers tingling from the adrenaline that shot through his body. But he'd make it work. "Did you bring the money for the shipment tomorrow night?"

Steve handed him a package. "Sixty thousand in hundreds like Boudreaux requested."

He took the money and slid it in a manila envelope. "Serial numbers recorded?"

"Yeah." Steve handed him a pen. "This should bypass the bug detector you said Boudreaux used. It activates by pressing the top, but the battery life is short, so don't switch it on until just before you meet. And the code to extract you is 'Do you have any coke?' Got it?"

"Got it." He examined the pen that looked like any ordinary ballpoint. "I doubt I'll be able to give you much lead time," he said and stuck the listening device in his shirt pocket.

"We'll be ready," Delaney said. "Even if you don't get a chance to notify us, you have a tracker on your car—we'll find your location, and it won't take long for us to set up."

37

Luke turned to Hugh Cortland, who had remained quiet while they discussed the drug deal. "Are you just getting to Natchez?"

"Yeah. I'm meeting with Pete Nelson in the morning and reviewing what he has on Marlar's case. What can you tell me about Nelson?"

"Not much. Worked hard to get where he is. Seems to be on the up and up, but he has family that isn't."

"How about Marlar?"

"I don't know what went wrong there. He was supposed to meet me Thursday night, but he called it off. He had a flash drive with a secret set of Boudreaux's books. I don't have a clue where the drive is now."

"Find it," Cortland said. "And right now, we're leaving Danvers's death as a suicide—"

"But it wasn't. I have a voice mail—"

"Let me finish. I've read your transcript of the voice mail. I figure Danvers stumbled on a transfer of drugs, and the runner killed him and made it look like a suicide. We want the killer to think he got away with it for now."

And that meant Brooke would have to continue to deal with the suicide ruling. Luke understood, though. "I'll go over the crime scene photos and call you if I find something," he said.

"Do you agree the same person who killed John probably shot Marlar?"

"That I don't know. I'm coming in late on John's investigation, and so far I haven't seen any of the evidence—will do that tomorrow. Right now as far as anyone is concerned, I'm only here to investigate Marlar's death."

Luke turned to Delaney. "What does Louis say about the murders?"

The big man shook his head. "Boudreaux was upset about Danvers's death, fearing it would bring the FBI to the area, and since it happened at the drop location, Louis thinks the drug runner acted on his own. He did say the drugs the courier passed off arrived in Nashville on time."

If the Cajun drug dealer had been upset about John's death, he was probably doubly upset about Marlar's. "Boudreaux had secured Marlar's vote against the medical marijuana bill, so I doubt he ordered him killed."

And if Boudreaux didn't order the murders, it was probably someone close to both men. Like the person transporting the drugs up the Trace. "Can't Louis find out who the drug runner is?"

"He's tried, but Boudreaux plays his cards close to the chest. The person who would know the runner's identity is Romero, and Romero doesn't like Louis. If he presses the issue, he'll jeopardize his position."

Drug dealers were paranoid, and asking too many questions could get you killed. "If you haven't sent someone from ISB to investigate these two cases, give them to me."

Steve stood and put his mug in the sink. "With Cortland here, we're not sending anyone, but you can assist him as long as you don't blow your cover."

"And on that note," Cortland said, "I'm leaving. I'd like to get a couple of hours' sleep before I meet with the police chief."

After he left, Luke figured the other two men would leave as well. Instead Delaney leaned back in his chair while Steve put away the sample bags of heroin.

"You have to understand . . ." Delaney said. "Nailing the cartel is our highest priority. Not saying the two murders here aren't important, but the heroin the cartel brings in kills thousands. We could shut down a dozen high-level dealers like Boudreaux, and heroin will continue to pour into the States." He lifted the coffee mug to his lips, drained it, then set it down with a bang. "We want the cartel."

Luke wanted that as well, but he also wanted justice for John. He rolled his shoulders, trying to loosen his tight muscles. By daylight he probably wouldn't be able to move.

The DEA agent shoved his cup toward Luke. "Got another pod?"

"Coming right up." He got the sense Delaney wanted something and it wouldn't be to his liking. Once the coffee went through the brew cycle, he turned around, and Steve was nodding to an unspoken question from the agent.

"Here you go," he said, setting the cup on the table. "Refill, Steve?"

"None for me," he said.

Since caffeine never kept him awake, Luke put in another pod for himself.

Delaney leaned forward. "Boudreaux is doing business with a drug kingpin who goes by the name Músculos. He's responsible for half the heroin coming out of Colombia into the United States."

Luke had heard the name—the Spanish word for *muscles*. He'd never seen a photo, but it didn't take much imagination to know what the man looked like. His coffee finished brewing and he took a swig. Good and hot. Then he realized Delaney was waiting for him. "And?" he said.

"We need you to convince Boudreaux that the Colombian should bring the heroin himself."

He almost spat the coffee out. "What? You have to be kidding. Or as crazy as Boudreaux." One look at both men's faces told him they were serious. "How do you propose I make this happen?"

"Tell him your people want to meet the main man."

"Boudreaux will think 'my people' are trying to take over his territory. And then he'll kill me."

"Not if he thinks he'll get something out of it—offer him a cut of everything our organization buys from Músculos. Make him think he'll be adding to his organization—whatever it takes."

Luke thought a minute. If he handled it just right, Boudreaux might buy it, especially if Louis talked it up. "Let's say that Boudreaux buys it and gets Músculos here. How will I know it's really him?"

Delaney opened his wallet and handed Luke a grainy, slightly-out-of-focus photo of a man who looked to be in his thirties when the photo was taken. His biceps strained against the T-shirt he wore.

"Is this all you have?"

"Yes."

"How long ago was it taken?"

"Maybe seven years ago."

Luke shook his head. "If Boudreaux agrees to my proposal, he could play us. He could bring in anybody with muscles and dark hair and say it was the kingpin."

"He won't know we don't have a good photo, and by the time the deal goes down, we'll have a close-up. Our agents in Colombia are working on getting one now. They're tracking Músculos as well, and they'll know if he leaves the country."

What Delaney asked was impossible. A 99 percent chance of failure.

"You don't have to do it," Steve said.

He glanced toward his boss. Nice to know he had a choice.

"But if we could arrest Boudreaux and Músculos, it would put a huge dent in the heroin traffic."

Luke pictured the last kid he'd seen strung out on heroin, his emaciated body covered in filth from the gutter he'd made his bed.

"Will you do it?" Delaney asked.

"I assume you'll have good backup to extract me if it's needed."

"A SWAT team, and we'll be close by monitoring you."

"Okay. I'll start it rolling tomorrow night."

Delaney slapped him on the back. "Great. I think you can do it."

Luke shot him a sour look as the two men prepared to leave.

"Oh, we need you to do one more thing," Delaney said at the back door.

"Which is?"

"See to it that Brooke Danvers doesn't blunder into our investigation."

"How am I supposed to do that? She doesn't even know I'm working undercover."

Delaney shrugged. "You're smart, you'll figure it out."

Luke wasn't too sure about that.

Once the two men left, he took the photos from the Emerald Mound crime scene to the study and removed them from the envelope. He was surprised Steve had even given them to him, since his supervisor didn't want him working the case. Many of the photos were similar to the ones he'd taken with his phone, and he compared them side by side.

One shot caught his attention because it had a slight variation from his, and when he examined the one taken with his phone, a light-colored object lay near the front tire of John's truck. He used a magnifying glass to zoom in closer. It was a bone-handled pocketknife, but not just any knife. The tree-brand on the handle marked it as a Boker. Luke would bet there weren't three Boker knives in Natchez.

Quickly, he flipped through every crime scene photo, looking for another angle of the same shot, and found three. None of them showed the knife. That could mean only one thing. The killer dropped the knife when he killed John and had retrieved it between the time Luke left Emerald Mound and the crime scene photos were taken. *The car with the blinding lights.* It made him sick to think maybe he'd been that close to the killer.

Or maybe the killer was one of the investigators. He'd have to find out who covered the murder.

Luke took out his cell phone to dial Steve and tell him he had additional proof John Danvers didn't kill himself. Just as quickly, he put it back in his pocket. His boss would just tell him to share the information with Cortland—let him handle it. He quickly emailed his photos to Cortland. It'd be up to him what he did with them. As for Luke, he'd be looking for someone with a Boker knife.

38

Sunlight streamed through the living room blinds as Brooke twisted the slats open, her muscles protesting every move she made. It'd been after two before she'd settled down enough for sleep to catch her, and she hadn't been happy when her alarm sounded at seven. That'd been an hour and two cups of coffee ago. Since then, she'd found bruises on her shoulder and legs and even one on her cheek, but at least she'd survived the wreck. She'd already called her insurance company and was told an adjuster would be out sometime today and to go ahead and rent a car until it was determined if hers would be totaled or repaired. Maybe she could get Luke to drop her off at the car rental after they stopped by the police department.

Luke. Brooke didn't know what to think about him. After years of not hearing from him, they were suddenly spending a lot of time together. She was a little surprised that Luke and her dad had stayed in such close touch and that he'd never talked about Luke.

She turned from the window, mentally adding a visit to Sharon Marlar to her to-do list. Maybe she knew something about her husband's death. Her cell phone rang, and she checked the ID. Her mom. Brooke's stomach tightened. What if she had decided to return to Natchez? The living room was a mess. She hadn't cleaned up after the break-in, at least not to her mother's standards. Brooke answered the call, already rehearsing reasons her mom didn't need to leave Meghan.

"Hey, Mom," she said. "It's kind of early for you to be calling. Anything wrong?"

"No, everything is fine here," she said. "Meghan has decided she doesn't like the color of the baby's room, so we're painting today. How are you?"

"I'm good." Her mom's voice was extra bright, even forced. Had she heard about last night? Brooke brushed the thought aside. Her mom couldn't possibly know what happened.

"Well, I heard Kyle Marlar was killed last night, and that you found him. And that you had a little wreck."

Or maybe she could. Nothing like a small town to spread the news all the way to Knoxville. "Yes. Who told you?"

"Dale called, afraid I'd hear it on the news." Her tone indicated disappointment, probably that Brooke hadn't been the one to let her know.

"I would have called, but it was late when I got home."

"I can be there in—"

"No! Don't do that. I'm fine, really. Meghan needs you right now . . . and I don't have time to drive to Jackson and pick you up at the airport."

"I could rent a car and drive."

"Really, Mom, there's no need."

"Are you sure you're not hurt?"

"I'm sore, but that's all. I promise."

Her mother was quiet, and then she asked, "Do they know who killed Kyle?"

"They didn't last night, and I haven't talked with anyone today." Brooke debated dropping the bomb that she would be helping Clayton with the investigation. No. If anything, her mom opposed Brooke becoming an LE more than her dad. In fact, his opposition stemmed straight from her mom. He'd never gone against anything Brooke wanted before. Anything within reason, at least.

"I hope you're not involving yourself in the case." Her mother paused to take a breath before forging on. "I just wish you'd forget this fool notion and get your old job back."

Brooke counted to twelve before answering. "It's not a fool notion. It's what I want to do. Besides, I am my father's child. Law enforcement is in my genes."

"His genes are in Meghan too, but you don't see her risking her life."

Arguing with her mother would be futile, and Brooke held her tongue, hoping she would go on to something else.

"Oh, honey, I understand that you want to be like your dad, but he's gone now. You're so good as an interpretive ranger. The people who visit Melrose are going to be shortchanged with you not there."

Her mother was good, Brooke would give her that. "There are other rangers who know as much about the historical places as I do," she said.

Silence filled the airwaves, then her mother sighed. "I hope you don't get the idea you can work on your father's case and find the person who killed him."

"There's no case, Mom. It's still ruled a suicide," she replied. Not that the ruling made a bit of difference to Brooke.

"We both know that's not true. Just be careful. I don't want to lose you."

"Mom, that's not going to—" The doorbell rang, and she said, "Hold on a sec and let me see who's at the door."

Brooke looked through the peephole in her door. The neighbor from down the street held an envelope in his hands.

"Mr. Benton, what can I do for you?" she asked after opening the door.

"The substitute carrier put this in the wrong box yesterday," he said, handing her the envelope.

She thanked him and shut the door. The return address was from the ancestry registry. Had to be her DNA results. "Sorry about that, but the carrier left my ATI Genetics results in a neighbor's box," she said, reading the label, "and he was dropping it off."

"Your what?"

"My genealogy test," she said and walked to the kitchen for another cup of coffee. "Meghan talked me into doing it. She got her results yesterday."

The phone became so quiet, she thought her mom had disconnected. "Are you still there?"

"Yes. Those tests aren't reliable. And I'm surprised you both took the test. That's like overkill. Meghan's would have been enough."

"That's what I told her, but nothing would satisfy Meghan until I agreed. Had to be a rogue hormone," she said and laughed at the thought.

"I never expected that you two would be interested in that sort of thing, especially you."

"Don't you remember the family tree I tried to make the summer after the eighth grade? I spent hours viewing census records on microfilm at the library, trying to find out when our family first showed up in Natchez."

"No, I don't remember that."

"Oh, that's right," Brooke said. "That was the summer you and Meghan spent in New York visiting art galleries."

It'd always been Meghan and her mom doing something together. Maybe that was why Brooke had been closer to her dad.

"You could have come with us." Her mom's reproach reached through the phone. "Look, I need to go. You take care of yourself, okay?"

"Sure, Mom." Brooke disconnected and stared briefly at her phone. That was an odd call even for her mother. Brooke picked up the envelope the neighbor had delivered. Inside was the key to their exact destinations next October if the company came through on their guarantee and pinpointed the regions their ancestors had originated from. Maybe the next time she talked to Meghan, she would mention asking her mom to accompany them on the trip. She poured herself another cup of coffee and tore open the envelope just as her phone rang again. This time it was Clayton.

"Morning," she said, scanning the first page of the report. "I was just going to call and let you know I'm meeting Dale at the Port Gibson station at ten."

"He called me, and we discussed your accident too," Clayton said. "Are you okay?"

She laid the DNA results on the kitchen table beside her purse. "Sore in places I didn't know I had, but I'll live."

Did Dale tell Clayton the abbreviated story or full disclosure?

"What happened? Dale didn't say much, but Gary said there was another car involved and something about a deer."

"Yeah." That answered her question. "I'm going by Chief Nelson's office this morning. Do you want me to pick up a copy of his report on Kyle Marlar's death?"

Clayton's answer was slow in coming. "Sure—if he'll give it to you. He doesn't seem too happy about sharing."

"It's his first murder case working with the park service," she said. "Wait, have you talked with Pete this morning?"

"Just got off the phone with him a few minutes ago. He indicated pretty emphatically he didn't need my help. That's why I was calling. To warn you so you don't get your head bitten off."

She swallowed the protest that sprang to her lips. "Does Dale know?"

"Not the phone call, but he anticipated resistance and said to continue our investigation alone if Natchez PD didn't want to work with us."

Brooke could do that, but she didn't understand Pete Nelson's attitude. "I'll see you at ten."

After she disconnected, she checked her watch. Too early to swing by and talk to Sharon Marlar before she met with Dale.

She'd catch her afterwards, maybe take food by. Brooke started to call Luke when a text dinged on her phone. Dale, postponing their meeting until three. Now she had the morning free, which actually might work better for Brooke since her movements were very slow. She texted him a thumbs-up emoji then dialed Luke's number.

"Good morning," he said, sounding groggy.

"Morning to you too. Sounds like I woke you."

"Mmm. What time is it?"

She checked her watch. "Eight twenty-two. Are you as sore as I am?"

"Probably. I'm surprised you're up this early."

"How late did you think I'd sleep?"

"I forgot you're Miss Sunshine in the mornings."

And he was not. She remembered Daisy complaining Luke would sleep until noon every day if she'd let him. "Think you'll have time to drop me off at a car rental after we go by and give Chief Nelson our statements?"

"I typed mine up before I went to bed. All I have to do is give my ID and sign it when we get there. And then I'll be happy to go with you to get a car."

"Great," she said. "I'll let you know when I'm ready, but first I'm going to take a hot shower and work out some of my soreness."

"Sounds good," he said. "I'll shoot you a copy of my report."

"See you in a few."

For the next few minutes, she dealt with texts from Emma and Daisy, assuring them she was fine. Daisy didn't believe her, and she phoned her, promising to pop in and see her ASAP. They discussed her mom's phone call while Brooke checked her email. After she disconnected, she opened the attachment Luke had sent. His statement was very generic, simply stating he'd heard the scream and ran to where she and Kyle Marlar were. She quickly wrote her report, detailing the steps she took from the scream until Pete arrived on the scene, hesitating when it came to what Kyle said as she tried to recall his exact words. Nothing he said had anything to do with the shooting and she recounted what she'd already told Pete. After she printed the report, she emailed it to Dale and Clayton and headed to her appointment with a hot shower.

Half an hour later, just as she started to step outside the house, her phone rang again. *Jeremy.*

"Why didn't you call and tell me about the wreck on the Trace?" he asked.

Brooke grimaced. She'd forgotten to call him. "You were next on my to-call list." She was getting a little too comfortable with "social engineering" even if she had meant to call him. "I'm fine."

"What were you doing on the Trace?"

She hesitated. How did she explain she was with Luke?

"I'm sorry, that's none of my business," he said. "The main thing is, are you okay?"

The concern in his voice touched Brooke and she relaxed, feeling like she'd dodged a bullet. "I'm fine, a little sore, maybe."

"Do you need me to take you anywhere, like to get a car?"

So much for dodging that bullet. She wasn't quite sure why she didn't want to tell him she'd asked Luke. "Thank you, but someone's dropping me off at the rental."

"Okay, but I don't want to wait until tonight to see you. Can we get together for lunch?"

Her breath caught in her chest. Jeremy had a way of making her feel cherished. "Sure, but I'm dropping off food at Sharon Marlar's around noon, so how about grabbing something quick at one? That would leave plenty of time to get to Port Gibson for my swearing in."

"You're getting sworn in today? Where and what time?"

"You want to come?" She had so not expected that.

"I sure do."

"It'll be at Port Gibson at three this afternoon."

PATRICIA BRADLEY / 189

He was quiet a minute. "The Marlars live south of town, so do you want to eat at Mammy's Cupboard?"

"That would be perfect," she said. The roadside restaurant had the best coconut cream pie she'd ever eaten, and at one the crowd should be thinned out.

After they hung up, Brooke pocketed her phone. When she stepped outside, bright sunlight nearly blinded her, and she popped on her sunshades.

Seeing the damage to her Escape made her shiver. They could've easily died last night.

39

Luke steeled himself against Brooke's nearness as they inspected her car. It didn't help that the fruity scent of her shampoo curled around him, drawing his attention to her hair bound up in a ponytail. He curbed the impulse to undo the clasp that would allow the silky dark hair to fall around her shoulders. Almost as though she read his thoughts, she stepped away from him.

"What did Dale say when you talked to him last night?" he asked.

"That he would go over the accident with me later."

Luke supposed she had no choice but to tell the ranger what happened. He pried the passenger door open. He'd been careful when he dug the bullet out last night and checked to make sure he'd left no evidence behind. "What's first on your agenda for today?" he asked.

"I was meeting Dale at ten for him to swear me in, but he moved it to this afternoon." She shifted her gaze toward the road, then back at him. "Emma will be there. Would you like to come? I mean, you don't have to, I just wondered . . ."

"I'd love to. What time?"

"Three, which means I have the morning free except for dropping off my report, getting a car, and visiting Sharon Marlar. How did your job interview turn out?"

He blanked for a second. *The cover story.* "It sounds promising," he said. "The guy said he'd let me know by the end of the week. Why are you visiting Sharon Marlar?"

"She's a friend," Brooke said. "I know Daisy would love to have you back in Natchez."

"We'll see." He nodded toward his SUV. "You ready?"

"Yeah. What will you tell her, though?" she asked as they walked across the side yard that separated the two properties. "She thinks you work for an accounting firm."

He shrugged. "I'll figure out something. I plan to stop and see her later today."

Then he had a date with Emerald Mound and his metal detector to search the parking lot. It was possible other bullets had been fired Sunday night, or maybe he could even find the pocketknife he'd seen in his photographs. There had been no mention of a knife in the sheriff's report. Sometimes what wasn't at a scene was as important as what was.

His stomach growled. He'd skipped breakfast. "Have you eaten yet?" he asked.

"Cereal."

If he remembered right, she'd never been much of an early breakfast eater. "How about some real food once we drop by the police station? I hear good things about a new coffee shop in town. I think it's called the Steampunk Coffee Roasters." She hesitated, and he wondered if it was because of Jeremy Steele. "It's not a date or anything. Just one friend to another."

"Sure. They do make great coffee," she said, "but if you're looking for bacon and eggs, we better go to the Castle. Oh wait. What time is it?"

He checked. "Nine fifteen."

"We'll still have time to get there before they shut the breakfast menu down if I put off picking up a car."

"You don't mind?"

"No, I just realized I'm starved."

"Sounds good." He'd always enjoyed eating in what was once the carriage house at Dunleith. Luke opened the passenger door of his Jeep Cherokee and waited until Brooke had her seatbelt fastened before he hurried around to the driver's side. "What kind of car are you looking for?" he asked as he backed out of Daisy's drive.

"I've been thinking about buying a Prius, and driving it as a rental will let me know if I like it."

"Good idea," he said and pulled onto the street. A few minutes later he checked his rearview mirror to see if anyone followed them. Nothing looked suspicious. "Do you really think it's the right time to question Sharon Marlar?"

"I'm taking food, not going to badger her," she said, a tinge of irritation in her voice.

"Just asking."

"If she wants to talk about her husband, I'll listen, but if she doesn't want to talk, I'll let it drop for now. Although I do want to ask if I can look at his photos, see if I can figure out what he meant last night."

Was it possible the data drive Kyle meant to give him was at the house? Luke doubted he would keep something that explosive where his wife might find it. "Did Kyle Marlar have an office?"

"I don't know. He ran the community center as a nonprofit, but I don't know if he kept his records there or at home. Something else I need to ask Sharon."

"Just be careful. Whoever ran us off the road is still out there."

They missed Chief Nelson at the jail, and Luke signed his statement while Brooke turned in her report to his secretary. Then she asked for a copy of the chief's report on Kyle Marlar's death.

"Sorry, you'll have to ask the chief for that, and he won't be back for at least an hour," the secretary replied.

"I'll be back," Brooke said.

They drove to Dunleith, arriving at the two-hundred-year-old inn before breakfast hours ended. The two-story mansion was impressive with Tuscan columns forming a colonnade around the house. A short distance away was the Castle, so named because of the turrets on each corner. Originally a carriage house, it had been turned into a restaurant sometime after Luke left for Annapolis. When the hostess greeted them, he asked that she seat them by a window.

"Thank you," Brooke said as he pulled a plaid-covered chair out for her. "It's been forever since I've been here." She placed the white linen napkin that matched the tablecloth across her lap. "Don't you just love all the wood?"

Luke took his seat across from her and followed her gaze, taking in the abundance of wood from the floors to overhead beams. "I like the brick walls," he said.

"Makes it cozy."

"I always associate eating here with Daisy," he said. It had been her favorite "special occasion" place to eat when he came home to visit.

"And not a special girlfriend?"

"Maybe I'm with her today." He loved seeing her blush and she obliged him before she turned and looked out the window.

He shouldn't have said that, but it did seem like a special day with Brooke sitting across from him. She had a way of looking at him like he was the only person in the room. If she hadn't been off limits because of her dad, Luke probably would have pursued dating Brooke when they were younger. *There's nothing keeping you from dating her now.*

The thought came unbidden, and he quickly pushed it away. His line of work didn't lend itself to having love interests, and that was the way he liked it. Besides, there was Jeremy, and Luke wasn't playing the role of spoiler, not when he had no intention of hanging around Natchez.

Unexpectedly, she shifted her gaze back to him. Busted. "Why haven't you ever married?" he asked.

She blinked and then stared at him like she couldn't believe he'd said that.

"I mean, in high school you always said you wanted a houseful of kids. What happened?"

Red crept into her face. "You said the same thing, and you haven't married, either."

"It's different with me. When I left Natchez, my priorities changed."

"Maybe mine did too." Then she straightened her shoulders. "I'm so glad you thought of this. It'll fortify me for my visit with Sharon."

She was changing the subject. "You don't have to do it."

"But I do. She's a friend, and I talked to Kyle after he'd been shot. She should know that he was thinking of her."

Anytime he'd had to notify next of kin about the death of a loved one, being able to relay the last words the victim spoke had been important. "I'll go with you, if you'd like."

"No. She doesn't know you, and I don't want that barrier."

She was right again. With him along, Brooke would lose the sense of the visit being friend to friend. He turned as the waitress approached. "You want the classic or the egg casserole? Or maybe waffles?"

She looked over the menu. "The classic with poached eggs. And coffee."

He chose the same thing, exchanging poached for scrambled eggs. "What did your mom have to say about the wreck?"

Her brown eyes widened. "How did you know?"

"Daisy said you told her about the phone call," he said. "But you knew it had to happen, with Natchez being Natchez."

"Dale called Mom, and she offered to come home, but I discouraged that option."

"Why?"

"Mom and I are on opposite ends of the spectrum. Dad was usually the buffer, and with him gone . . ."

Her eyes turned bright, and she fished in her purse for a tissue. Along with the tissue, she pulled out an envelope and laid it in her lap. "Sorry," she said, dabbing her eyes.

"Don't ever apologize for crying," he said. "And I know a little bit about family friction."

She gave him a wry grin. "Yeah, I guess you do."

"What's in the envelope?"

"It's my DNA report," she said, looking down. "That I haven't had a chance to read."

"What do you expect to learn?"

"Where our ancestors came from."

"Why didn't you just look up the genealogy records at the library?"

"I tried that already, and it's so time consuming—they're still on microfilm." She stared at the envelope.

"Well, what are you waiting for? Go ahead and open it," he said.

Brooke slipped her finger under the flap just as their food arrived. She looked from the envelope to her plate and laid the envelope aside. "I've waited this long, guess I can wait until we finish eating."

Conversation dropped off as they dug into their food. Luke bit into a warm biscuit, and it melted in his mouth. "I'd forgotten how good these are," he said.

"I know. I can't afford to come here too often, calorie-wise," she said with a chuckle.

A comfortable silence enveloped them as they enjoyed their meal. Once they finished, their server whisked their plates away then refreshed their coffee. Brooke lifted the envelope she'd laid by her purse.

"Do you want a drumroll?" he asked, picking up a spoon the waiter had left.

"No," she said, giving him a don't-you-dare look as she slipped the packet from the envelope. She scanned the papers, a frown growing on her face.

"What's wrong?"

"This doesn't match Meghan's results. It says I'm English and French and Greek." She looked up. "I don't understand. It doesn't mention being Irish at all. The company must have made a mistake."

"Let me see." He took the paper she handed him and read it. Sure enough, there was no Irish ancestry shown. "They probably got the results mixed up with someone else."

"It's the only explanation. There's a number here that I can call," Brooke said and sighed. "It'll probably take another six weeks or longer to get the correct results back."

"You could ask your mom."

She took out her phone and punched in a number. "This says they have customer service reps seven days a week. I'll try them first."

40

Brooke stuffed the ancestry papers in her purse. With the way her luck had been lately, she should have expected a thirty-minute wait for a customer service rep. She left a call-back number. Looking up, she found Luke studying her again, and her heart stuttered. Then he suddenly found his coffee very interesting.

"Thanks for breakfast," she said. "It's amazing how much better food will make you feel."

"I would say I-told-you . . . so . . ." His voice trailed off as he raised his head, and their gazes locked.

For a nanosecond she forgot everything except the electric blue eyes that drew her in. Tension as thick as the humidity outside arced between them. He hesitantly brushed her cheek, his fingertips lingering on her jaw.

"You had a bread crumb," he said, his voice husky.

Confusion clouded her mind, and she pulled back. "What just happened?"

His face flushed. "You don't know how to be anything but direct, do you," he said. Then the corner of his mouth quirked into a wry smile. "I don't know what just happened."

"You wanted to kiss me. Don't do it again," Brooke said, lifting her chin. She might as well lay it out for him. "The truth is, you broke my heart when you left for Annapolis without even saying good-bye, and then I hardly hear from you again until this week? Uh-uh. I'm not giving you a chance to do it again."

"Walking away from you was probably the biggest mistake I've ever made, and I have no excuse for not calling or at least writing you. That was just plain wrong," he said.

"At least you got that right."

He had the decency to blush. "Forgive me?"

Brooke waved him off. "A long time ago. And you didn't scar me for life. We were too young to be serious, anyway," she said. But it had taken all summer for her heart to heal. "You didn't say why you never married."

"Maybe it was because I couldn't find someone like you."

"Baloney. More like you're afraid of commitment."

Brooke nailed it. Just thinking about marriage made him sweat. He would be so bad at it.

When he was a teenager, she was the truest friend he ever had, and that one magical night he'd thought maybe they could have more. But the course of his life hadn't been his own, and by the time he took charge, it was too late.

He drew his gaze back to hers. "You were always special to me—I cared about you more than you'll ever know, but I've always known you deserved better than me."

"That's ridiculous," she said. "What's the real reason?"

He looked away, searching for an answer. Why not the truth? Luke brought his gaze back to her, wincing at the skepticism in her face. Maybe just skim the surface. "Honest? I was scared. And a little overwhelmed. Annapolis loomed, I didn't want to go, but I didn't know how to tell my dad."

Her face softened. "We could have worked that out."

Images of his parents' cold marriage bombarded him. "Not when I don't know how. My parents . . . you've seen their marriage. Mom's miserable and Dad . . ." Luke shook his head and stared straight ahead. "What if we'd gotten married and it turned out like theirs? What if we had a son, and I treated him the way my dad treats me? I couldn't risk it, so I ran."

"Look at me," she said.

Slowly he turned to face Brooke. If he weren't careful, he'd drown in those big brown eyes.

"If two people will talk, they can work out anything."

She made him want to believe it was possible, and it might have been after he got up the guts to go against his father and drop out of Annapolis. "But I didn't, and now it's too late."

"Why?"

So many reasons. They ticked off in his mind. The drug deal that went bad where a woman was killed. Kyle Marlar. He was a failure, and he didn't want to add a marriage to that list. "For one thing you're dating Jeremy Steele. He's a good guy, and he can give you what you want."

"So you're not even going to try?"

41

Brooke knew the reason he wouldn't try. Years of trying to get his parents' love had damaged him. Years of spending every holiday alone until Daisy stepped in and demanded that his parents allow him to spend Christmas with her, but by then it was too late. The hard shell around his heart was formed. "I pray someday you'll find someone you can love with abandon and that you'll go after that person with your whole heart."

Heat rose in her face as he stared at her. "Do you actually believe people love that way?"

"I most certainly do. If I ever get married, it'll be to someone who won't let anything stand in the way of making me his. I want someone who feels his life isn't complete without me."

His blue eyes twinkled. "I had no idea you were such a romantic. Do you think that will be Jeremy?"

"We haven't been dating long enough to know." Brooke took his hand. "I realized a long time ago that you would never feel that way about me, and that we could never be anything other than friends. I don't want to mess up that friendship by crossing a line we can't undo." For the briefest time, she detected regret in his eyes.

"I don't want to lose your friendship, either," he said, squeezing her hand. Then he ducked his head. "Did you know your dad saw us under the magnolia tree that night?"

"No!" She gaped at him. That explained a lot. Luke wouldn't have been the first boy her dad had read the riot act to. "What did he say?"

"He told me if I broke your heart, he'd . . . well, he never said exactly what he'd do, but I got the general idea." He smiled, his lips curling into a wry grin before it faded. "Your dad was better to me than my own dad, and I didn't want to lose that."

Good ol' Dad, always protecting her. That was one time she wished he hadn't. "Are we good now?" she asked.

He smiled. "We're good."

Brooke leaned over and kissed him lightly on the cheek. "You sure you want to come to Port Gibson later? It's just a swearing in, and Jeremy will possibly be there."

"I do. It's an important day for you, and I want to be there," he said, and then a frown creased his brow. "How well do you know Clayton Bradshaw?"

"As well as I know anyone I work with." She thought about the skinny ranger. "He's good at what he does, and Dad thought a lot of him. Why do you ask?"

"No reason, it's just that I saw him at the casino pretty late last night."

"Is that where your interview was?" Daisy would not be happy if Luke went to work at the casino. "When are you going to tell Daisy you're not an accountant?"

He stared blankly at her, then he shrugged. "Before I take a job tending bar here, but we were talking about Clayton. Do you know whether he has a gambling problem?"

"It's no secret that he frequents the casino, and he brags about his winnings all the time."

"Does he ever talk about how much he loses?"

"Does anyone who gambles?"

"Last night he lost all the cash he had on him, and when he tried to get more, the ATM turned his card down."

"Why were you watching him?"

"It's kind of hard not to watch a train wreck."

"You think Clayton has a gambling problem." If that were true . . . Brooke's thoughts automatically turned to suspicion. What if Clayton was deeply in debt? Would he turn to doing something illegal to make money? She shook the thought away. This was Clayton, one of the best law enforcement rangers she knew besides Dale and her dad. "I'll ask around," she said. "And see if anyone else thinks he has a gambling problem."

"You probably don't want it to get back to him that you're asking," Luke said. "Would you like to see about getting your rental now?"

She nodded. "I checked and Enterprise has a Prius. They're right down the street."

"Then that's our next stop."

"I think I'll wait until closer to lunchtime to get the chicken I want to bring to Sharon."

Luke motioned for the server to bring their check. "This was really nice," he said when she laid the paper on the table. "We'll have to come back."

"Thank you," she replied, "but I'm afraid Dunleith and the Castle are closing."

"Why?" Brooke asked. She'd heard rumors but had hoped they weren't true.

"It's been sold."

Sadly Brooke glanced around the cozy interior. She'd been coming here for years. The Castle would be missed.

Fifteen minutes later, Luke pulled into the car rental. True to what the salesman had told her, he had a Prius with all the bells and whistles, and it was red to boot. Once she signed the papers and had the keys, she settled herself in the driver's seat. The Prius still had a new-car smell, another enticement to buy something new if she had to replace her wrecked vehicle. She lowered the window. "I think I'll take Daisy's mail to her before I visit Sharon."

"You don't have to. I'll be going to see her later this afternoon."

"I've already had two texts from her since we talked earlier this morning. The first one asked and the second one ordered me to come by so she can see that I'm all right. Figured since the mail has probably been delivered, I might as well go now and get it over with."

"Yeah, Daisy can be persistent," Luke said with a laugh. "What time is the insurance adjuster coming?"

"Don't know. He said I didn't have to be there, that he'd get a copy of the accident report from Gary." She tilted her head. "What are you doing this afternoon, besides seeing Daisy?"

"I plan to follow up on that job I interviewed for last night."

Half an hour after picking up Daisy's mail, Brooke parked at the rehab just as her cell phone rang. Dale. "Hello?"

"Can you be at Port Gibson by three?" he asked without any preliminaries.

"That's the time we agreed on."

"What?" He groaned. "That's right. I'm sorry. I've been dealing with the insurance company all morning."

"Did they approve Mary's treatment this time?"

"No." His sigh came through the phone.

"I have a little savings," she said. Very little. "It's only a couple of thousand, but if it'd help you out—"

"Thanks, but I need at least a hundred times more than that. Don't worry about it, I've made arrangements," he said. "By the way, the FBI has arrived. Hugh Cortland. He's already digging around and will want to talk to you at some point. I heard he might look into your dad's death as well, but don't get your hopes up—it's only because both your dad's death and Marlar's were on park service property. The powers-that-be don't want any questions later."

It was also possible someone else didn't believe her dad killed himself. Maybe the agent would let her in on the investigation. They talked for a few minutes longer before Dale ended the call.

She sat in her car, processing the information she'd just heard. The FBI was actually investigating her dad's case.

A few minutes later she signed into the rehab and then hurried down the hallway, her rubber-soled shoes squeaking on the tile. When she reached Daisy's room, her friend sat in her wheelchair, an aide ready to take her to the dining room.

"About time," she grumbled.

"It's been a busy morning, and I had breakfast with your grandson," Brooke said then turned to the aide. "I can wheel her down to the cafeteria."

"And stay a minute?" The hope in Daisy's eyes morphed into surprise. "Wait a minute, did you say you had breakfast with Luke?"

"Since you only have one grandson, yes." Brooke flashed her a big grin. "But I can only stay a few minutes. I'm taking chicken by Sharon Marlar's."

Daisy shook her head. "So sad. I don't know what this world's coming to when someone like Kyle Marlar is murdered."

"Me, either," Brooke said. "Want me to put your mail beside your bed?"

She nodded, eyeing the letters and a small box. "I'll look at it later. But I'm glad to see my hearing aid batteries came. Now tell me about your breakfast. Where did you two eat?"

She placed the small package on the bedside table. "The Castle, and it was nice, but don't get any ideas about Luke and me."

"I don't have to. Luke would never take you to the Castle if he wasn't interested."

Brooke shook her head. "We're just friends. Are you ready for lunch?"

"As I'll ever be. I hope they've added salt to the food today," she said. "I reminded the nutritionist that I'm not on a salt-restricted diet."

Brooke chuckled. "Let's hope she remembered."

Once she settled Daisy and made sure her food had been

salted, she kissed her on the cheek. "Sorry to rush off, but I want to get that chicken while it's still fresh."

"Before you go," Daisy said, "I've finished the books you brought me last week, and I need something new to read. Would you bring one of the books from the bottom shelf in my library? I haven't read those yet."

"I'll bring a couple of them tomorrow. Any particular title?"

"The new romance by Rachel Hauck," she said.

"I'll see if I can find it on your shelves."

Daisy looked up at Brooke. "Oh, be sure to remind Luke he didn't bring me a hamburger from the Malt Shop when you see him."

"I will," Brooke said with a laugh.

42

He drove by Thomas Nichols Funeral Home searching for Sharon Marlar's car. It wasn't out front, but the receptionist plainly told him the Marlars had an appointment that morning. He checked out the license plate of the one car by the office. It had a Jackson tag. Of course. Sharon would have come with her oldest son, and the house would be empty.

Knowing Thomas Nichols, he could count on the family being at the funeral home a couple of hours. More than enough time to search the house for the photos. He drove to the outskirts of town and turned on the county road that went past the Marlar house. A half mile from the house he found a forestry road where he pulled his vehicle out of sight. He opened the trunk and grabbed the five-gallon can of gasoline and a small cloth bag containing a half stick of dynamite and blasting cap.

It took fifteen minutes to hike through the woods to their property line. The nearest house appeared to be a quarter mile away. Leaving the tree line, he jogged to the house. When he neared the back door, a lop-eared dachshund ran out at him, barking and nipping at his heels. "Get away!" he muttered, kicking at the dog.

It backed up, watching him, the fur on its back raised. Ignoring the dog, he tried the door. Open, like he expected. The South was like that. No need to inconvenience anyone wanting to bring food. Once inside, he oriented himself. The kitchen and living room were an open-concept design. To the right was a door, probably a hallway to the bedrooms and maybe a den. He hit pay dirt at the first door he opened off the hall. Marlar's office. Now to find the photos.

Half an hour later, he'd gone through every folder in Marlar's file cabinet and had come up with zilch. The laptop was password protected, and he didn't have time to break the code. He'd have to take it with him, but he'd leave the camera since it had nothing on it. He pulled out a desk drawer and felt under it. Where had Marlar hidden those photos? Maybe in his bedroom? He checked his watch. Not enough time to search the rest of the house.

He'd hoped it wouldn't come to this, but he'd come prepared. Working quickly, he removed the items from the cloth bag. Using his knife, he cut a three-foot strip of safety fuse, then slipped one end into a cap and crimped it. Once he had the detonator secured in the half stick of dynamite, he turned to the gas can. Needed something to keep it from rolling. He found a small book that would do and placed it and the explosive under Kyle's desk then set the can on top.

Before he could unscrew the gas cap, the front screen door scraped open, and a woman's voice floated back to him.

"See you tonight."

No! Sharon Marlar was not supposed to be back so soon. If he sneaked out through the kitchen, she'd be sure to see him. His gaze landed on the open office door. If she came down the hall, she'd definitely find him. He pulled his gun as he searched for an escape. If worse came to worst . . .

The closet. He left the gas and dynamite under the desk and slipped inside the closet just as footsteps came down the hall, the dog yapping behind.

"Hush, Toby," she said, her footsteps continuing until a door closed.

He pressed his back against shelves. There was barely enough room to shut the closet door. On the other side of the door, a low growl came from the dog's throat.

A toilet flushed just as the doorbell rang. More people arriving. He was trapped. If only he'd waited for the cover of darkness. The doorbell rang again. He held his breath as her footsteps hurried toward the kitchen, then stopped.

"What's the matter, Toby? Are you looking for Kyle?"

She was at the office door. What if she smelled the gas? He fingered the trigger of the gun in his hand. *Don't come in here.*

The distinctive click of a door shutting threw his heart into overdrive, slowing only when he heard Sharon Marlar's muffled call to the visitor that she was coming.

Cautiously he eased from the closet. With the office door closed, he had no idea what was happening, but then neither could anyone see what he was doing.

43

A car was leaving the Marlars' when Brooke rounded the curve a quarter of a mile away. She had picked up a large bucket of chicken at Annie's along with a dozen of her famous biscuits and an apple pie. Comfort food. If she weren't full from her late breakfast, the heady aroma of the chicken would have her opening the bucket and sampling it.

It was hard to think about meeting Jeremy in an hour at Mammy's Cupboard. Maybe she'd just have a salad, and leave the pie off . . . yeah, right.

Brooke turned into the drive where a modest house sat on a lot carved out of the surrounding woods. Someone had spent a lot of time tending the yard that was thick with zoysia grass. Kyle, maybe.

The circle drive was empty, but the front door was open. Brooke wanted to first check and see if Sharon was home before she took the food in. A lot of people in Natchez would be comfortable taking the chicken into the house, but she didn't like rambling around in someone's house when they weren't home.

After climbing the porch steps, she rang the doorbell while peering through the old-fashioned screen door into the darkened house. Brooke pressed the doorbell again and let a minute pass. Just as she turned to leave, she heard a faint voice.

"Coming."

Barking accompanied the footsteps that approached. A thin

wisp of a woman opened the door and stepped on the porch followed by the source of the barking. A long-haired dachshund. Brooke turned to Sharon. Dark circles under her reddened eyes spoke volumes about the kind of night she'd endured.

Sharon offered a faltering smile. "Brooke?"

"I'm so sorry," she said and enveloped the widow in a hug.

"Thank you," Sharon said, sniffing.

"I was afraid you weren't home," she said.

"My car is in the shop, and Kyle's is at police headquarters."

Brooke nodded toward her car. "I have chicken and biscuits from Miss Annie's. And pie."

Tears threatened to spill from Sharon's eyes. "Everyone's been so kind, and this will be perfect for tonight when Bill comes back with his family."

"Stay here, and I'll get it." Brooke hurried down the steps, but after she retrieved the food, she realized Sharon had followed her to the car. "Would you like me to take it to the kitchen for you?"

Sharon stared blankly at Brooke. She ran her hand through her short brown hair. "I'm sorry. What did you say?"

"Sharon, are you all right?"

"I can't do this again," she said, her face as white as flour. The tears that had threatened minutes ago spilled from the older woman's eyes, and she covered her mouth with her hand. "First Brandon and now Kyle. Why?"

Brooke had no answer. Losing her father had been awful. What if she'd lost her sister as well? She set the food on the hood of her car and gently folded Sharon in another embrace. "Go ahead and cry."

She didn't tell the widow everything was going to be all right, or that Kyle and Brandon were in a better place. Both might be true, but Brooke knew from experience those weren't the words she wanted to hear right now.

After a minute, Sharon wiped the tears from her cheeks. "I've cried until my head is stopped up, and I can barely breathe through my nose." She fished a handkerchief from her pocket and dabbed her eyes. "Everyone keeps saying it's going to be all right, but it won't. It won't ever be all right again. Brandon and Kyle . . . they were my life."

"It's hard losing someone you love."

Sharon gave a little gasp. "Oh, my goodness. I'm sorry. You just lost your father, and I'm coming apart on you."

Brooke squeezed her waist. "Don't worry about me, but I do need to get the chicken into your refrigerator. Why don't we get you back inside and then I'll put it away."

"I can't ask you to do that."

"Yes, you can." Sharon trembled as Brooke helped her climb the steps.

At the door she hesitated. "I want to sit out here."

Brooke guided her to the swing. "I'll be right back."

She was familiar with the Marlar house, and after retrieving the food she quickly walked to the kitchen and set the pie on the counter. When Brooke opened the refrigerator, it was full. She wasn't the only one who'd brought food. She found a smaller container for the chicken, and after rearranging the middle shelf, she managed to squeeze it in.

A thump came from the adjacent room. Kyle's office, if she remembered correctly. Brooke peered down the hallway. "Sharon?"

Absolute quiet answered her, and then sharp barking erupted. Her muscles relaxed. She'd wondered where the dog went. "It's just me, Toby," she called. He barked at everything. "Do you want to go out?"

The dog appeared at the kitchen door and barked again. She repeated her question, and the longhaired dachshund sat down and cocked his head, his bushy eyebrows and beard reminding her of an old man. "I guess not."

Brooke returned to the porch. "I put the chicken in a smaller container," she said and settled beside the widow on the swing. A strong gust of wind from the south held the promise of rain later. "If I can help do something else, like wash dishes or sweep, or whatever, I'll be happy to."

Sharon shook her head. "No, the food is more than enough."

"When will Todd arrive?" Bill, the son who had been at the hospital last night, lived up around Jackson. The middle son Brooke went to school with lived out in California.

"Tomorrow," she replied. "Bill dropped me off after we finished making arrangements, then he left to go home for clothes and the rest of his family."

Must have been the car she saw leave. "When's the funeral?"

"One o'clock Monday at the church. I hope it doesn't rain."

She hated for Sharon to be all alone right now. "You want me to stay a minute?"

Sharon hesitated, then her face crumpled again. Brooke didn't know what to say or do other than pat her arm.

But instead of falling to pieces again, Sharon straightened her shoulders. "Do you mind? We can stay out here on the porch. I hate being inside the house—the quiet is so loud I can't stand it. But I can't stand to hear the TV or radio either."

"No, the porch is fine." Brooke sneaked a glance at her watch. She could spare a few minutes before meeting Jeremy at Mammy's Cupboard.

They sat, neither of them speaking as Sharon stared down at her feet. Occasionally she'd give the swing a push with her foot. She lifted her head, and Brooke followed her gaze to the field across the road. "I understand you found him. Did he say anything before . . . ?"

"His last words were of Brandon and you," Brooke said. "He wanted you to know he loved you."

Sharon dabbed her eyes again. "I can't believe he won't be pulling into the drive soon." Then she fell silent again.

Brooke nodded but remained silent.

"I know I have to get a grip, be strong for my two boys that are left, but it's hard."

She sensed Sharon's eyes on her and shifted where she could see her face. "You'll make it through this."

"You understand better than most, with your dad . . ." Sharon shook her head. "Kyle didn't believe your dad killed himself. Told me so."

"Anyone who knew him won't believe it," Brooke said.

"Kyle had even been vocal about it. Told the sheriff if he didn't investigate it as a murder, he was going to get someone down here that would. Do you think that could have gotten him killed?"

Brooke's heart hitched. As a state representative, Kyle had the connections to request an investigation. "I hadn't heard that, but the investigation will uncover his killer." She hoped.

"You have to find whoever did this," Sharon said, her voice hard.

"The FBI and Pete Nelson are doing all they can to find the person responsible."

"Pete." She spat his name out. "I don't trust him. His dad was no good, and the apple doesn't fall far from the tree."

Brooke kept quiet. She didn't share Sharon's sentiments about Pete.

"Kyle told me you're a law enforcement ranger now, so why don't you investigate it? I trust you."

"Thanks for the vote of confidence, and I am on the team," Brooke said and shifted in the swing. "Are you up to answering a few questions?"

"I'll make myself be up to it."

Brooke searched for a question that wouldn't have Sharon in tears again, if there was one. "Had Kyle been acting differently lately?"

"Kyle rarely let me know if anything was bothering him," Sharon said. "But I always knew. Lately he couldn't sleep at night, and when I asked him what was wrong, he wouldn't tell me. Said it was better that I didn't know. I thought it had something to do with Brandon's overdose. His death really shook us up. But . . ."

Brooke gave her time to compose herself.

Sharon dabbed her eyes again. "I don't know if this might have to do with anything, but over a week ago, I heard him on the telephone in his office. I know I shouldn't have eavesdropped, but I was tired of his secrets." She chewed her bottom lip. "He was talking about money someone had donated. Whoever gave it to him was putting pressure for Kyle to vote against legalized marijuana."

"I understand he planned to vote for it."

Sharon nodded vigorously. "Because of that boy in town who has seizures. Kyle wanted to help him."

"Do you know who was pressuring him?"

Sharon shook her head. "Toby started barking to go out, and Kyle must have heard me. He quit talking."

"Does Kyle have a computer?" Brooke asked. If he had his financial records on it, she could possibly figure out who was pressuring him to change his vote.

"He has a laptop." Then Sharon gasped. "That had to be what he was working on."

"What are you talking about?"

She pressed her hand to her forehead. "Monday night I missed him in bed and found him in his office working, but he shut his computer down as soon as I walked into the room."

Somewhere in the back of the house, Toby barked again. "Could I look at the laptop?"

"I don't think it'd do you any good. It has a password, and I don't know what it is."

"Can I give it a try? Maybe his passwords are in a file in his office somewhere. I can take a few minutes to look."

Brooke's heart rate accelerated. This could be the break they were looking for. Except, if she found something, she'd have to leave it where it was and report it to either Pete or the FBI. But there was nothing that said she couldn't photograph anything she found. She felt her pocket for her phone and remembered

PATRICIA BRADLEY / 215

she'd left it in the cup holder. "Let me grab my phone from the car."

Photographs. She stopped at the top of the steps as the Marlars' dachshund barked at the front door. "Kyle said something about photos last night. Do you know what he might have referred to?"

"He had so many . . . most of them are on his computer."

"How about his camera?"

"There might be some in it. Pete dropped the camera off this morning, and I put it in his office." Sharon opened the door to let the dog out, and he shot past them. "Toby is going to be the death of me. He barks at everything. Probably saw a cat."

The dog tore past the house to the back of the property, his frenzied barks filling the air. Brooke turned and hurried to her car as Sharon followed her to the edge of the porch. A gust of wind pushed against her back, and for a second the scent of rotten eggs turned her stomach.

The wind must have changed, bringing the sulfur smell from the nearby paper mill. Brooke looked over her shoulder toward the porch.

She froze as time slowed.

In the yard, Toby barked, the sound hollow and far away. Sharon turned toward the house as an orange ball of flame barreled out the front door.

Her mind barely registered the *boom* a fraction of a second later. A blast of hot air knocked her backward to the ground. The buzz of a thousand hornets in her ears drowned out everything as her world turned dark.

44

Luke forced himself to breathe deeper as he turned off the Trace at Emerald Mound. He hadn't returned to the site until now. Heat shimmered off the blacktop road as images from Sunday night bombarded him.

His Jeep racing down the black winding road from Windsor Ruins to the mounds. John's pickup in the parking area. His friend on the ground . . .

Luke pulled over and uncapped a water bottle, tipping it up to wet his dry mouth. It was hard to believe it'd been just six nights ago.

He recapped the water bottle and inched his car down the road until the historic landmark came into view. Someone had laid a wreath in front of the park service sign. He bowed his head briefly, acknowledging his inadequacy. Hindsight was twenty-twenty, but even in hindsight, he didn't see how he could have changed the outcome. Luke couldn't be in two places at one time. But why was John meeting someone here without backup? Or had his backup been his killer?

He climbed out of his car and took the metal detector from the cargo area. He didn't think he would find the pocketknife shown in the photos, but stranger things had happened. Luke believed the killer dropped it and then came back for it. Or he could have been one of the investigating law enforcement officers and retrieved it during the investigation.

He was here because he believed in Locard's exchange principle—the killer brought something into the crime scene and left with something from it. With no clear-cut suspect, discovering what the killer took from the scene was almost impossible. He was looking for what the killer may have left behind.

And by being here, Luke hoped to put himself in the killer's mind. Unlike serial killers driven by a psychopathic mind and who often spent days stalking their prey and planning down to the last detail, the average killer was an ordinary Joe who got backed into a corner, usually not well organized and who often killed on the spur of the moment. At least with their first kill.

He pulled out the official report and went over it again, noting no note had been found. Odd. If John had killed himself like the ME said, wouldn't he have left a note?

After an hour under the hot Natchez sun, Luke peeled off the sweat-filled latex gloves he'd slipped on and dried his hands. So far he'd found a lot of nuts and bolts and ring tabs, but nothing else. He was about ready to give up. He made one last sweep with the detector, working toward the county road, when the detector went crazy. He pulled on another pair of gloves and used his fingers to sift through the dirt.

A bottle cap. Frustrated, he started to stand when something caught his eye. Thin, curled pieces of wood like he'd seen on Court Square when the old men sat around whittling and telling tall tales.

What if the drug runner had whittled while he waited for the drugs to arrive? And what if forensics could match the shavings to the knife in Luke's photos from John's crime scene?

Luke photographed the site then placed a marker and stepped back and snapped a photo of the site in context of the whole area. Not for court purposes, but for him personally. He picked up the marker and gathered the shavings, placing them into a paper envelope, then he grabbed the metal detector and packed everything away in his Jeep. There was no reason to risk someone driving by and reporting him for having a metal detector on government property.

He returned to where John had fallen and tried to picture possibilities. His friend believed a heroin transfer was going to happen here. Did he get here early and wait or did he pull in when it happened? Either way, Luke believed he confronted the carrier.

He looked up as a truck pulled into the parking area and Dale Gallagher climbed out. What was he doing here?

"Luke?" Dale asked when he neared. "What are you doing here?"

"I wanted to see where John died," he said.

"Didn't realize you were close to him."

"He lived next door to my grandmother and always treated me well." Better than his own father, in fact, but no need to rehash that. "It was a shock learning of his death. And no one will ever make me believe it was suicide."

Dale nodded. "I'm having trouble with the ruling too, but no evidence of foul play has surfaced."

Luke hated the way working undercover tied his hands sometimes. "How about Kyle Marlar's murder . . ."

"FBI has taken that investigation over. I requested someone from ISB but haven't heard if or when they'll arrive."

"ISB?" He shot Dale a questioning gaze. Was he testing Luke? Run-of-the mill people wouldn't know what the acronym stood for.

"The Investigative Services Branch of the park service. They specialize in this sort of thing." Dale tilted his head. "Tell me about the wreck you and Brooke had."

"Nothing much to tell. Someone tried to run us off the road—teenagers, probably, with a little too much to drink," he said.

"I didn't realize you were staying over in Natchez last night."

"I didn't. I'm just now getting here from Jackson." Then he smiled at Luke. "I'm swearing Brooke in as a law enforcement ranger at three today. You coming?"

"Yep," he said. "Why did you stop by here?"

Dale shrugged. "About the same reason you did. I miss my old friend." He glanced toward the area where John's truck had been parked the night of the murder.

"I know what you mean," Luke said. Dale seemed sincere in his sorrow. For half a second he thought about revealing why he was in Natchez. But only for half a second. If his superiors hadn't told the chief ranger what was going on, it wasn't Luke's place to break the news.

Dale's phone rang and he answered and listened for a few seconds. "What?"

Luke tensed at the alarm in the ranger's voice.

"I'll be right there," Dale said and pocketed his phone.

"What happened?"

"Kyle Marlar's house blew up."

The words hit him like a sledgehammer. "No! Brooke planned to see Kyle's widow today. Was she still there?"

"Yes. Both she and Sharon Marlar have been taken to Merit."

45

Brooke's head pounded against the bright light the doctor shined in first one eye then the other. Overhead a monitor beeped with the steady rhythm of her heartbeat.

"How many fingers am I holding up?" he asked.

"Two."

"Now?"

He'd folded one finger down. "One."

"Follow my finger?" he said, moving his hand from one side to the other. "Good." He made two syllables out of it.

"Do you know how Sharon Marlar is?" she asked.

"Another doctor is seeing after her, but I'll try to find out for you." He pressed a button, and the blood pressure cuff around her arm pumped up.

At the final beep, she asked what the reading was.

"A little high. One-seventy over ninety-eight."

Not too high for almost getting killed. The doctor had already told her the CT scan had showed no brain bleed, and that her headache would eventually ease. She had no broken bones, and a little high blood pressure shouldn't keep her in the hospital. "When can I get out of here?"

"I'd like to keep you for observation."

Brooke gingerly touched the back of her head. It was only a small bump, probably from when the blast knocked her down.

"I don't want to stay. You said the headache would leave and everything else checked out . . ."

"I'd still feel better if we could watch you. Concussions don't show up on a scan, but I believe you have one."

A knock on the door to her ER room drew both of their attention. "Come in," she said.

Pete stuck his head inside the room. "Can I ask your patient a few questions about what happened at the Marlars'?"

The doctor turned to Brooke. "If you're up for visitors, I don't have any objections."

She shrugged. "I'm good, but why are you investigating? Don't the Marlars live out in the county?"

He shook his head. "They're half a mile inside Natchez city limits."

The ER doctor cleared his throat, getting her attention. "I'll check on you in a few minutes . . . and be thinking about what I said."

She was not staying overnight.

"What happened?" Pete asked, taking his notepad out.

As long as she lived, she'd never forget the ball of fire before everything went black. "There was an explosion . . ." What else? She massaged her forehead. Details hovered around the edge of her mind, so close she could almost touch them. Finally she gave up. "That's all I remember right now."

"Did you smell anything unusual?" he asked.

Had she smelled something? If her head would just quit hurting, maybe she could think. "Rain, maybe? And something else . . ."

The chief nodded. "There was a summer thunderstorm a couple of miles away."

That didn't trigger any thoughts. "How is Sharon?"

"Very serious, but that's all I can get from the doctors. Can you remember anything else?"

Brooke stared at the floor. Something important floated close to the surface of her mind. Maybe if she talked it out. "Sharon and I were sitting on the front porch, and I went to get something from my car . . ." What was she looking for? Why couldn't she remember? "I'm afraid I can't recall much of what happened before the explosion. Was it a bomb?"

"Won't know until the state fire marshal finishes his investigation."

"How long will that be?"

"A day or two, maybe even a week. He's on his way from Jackson now. But it may be something as simple as a propane gas explosion."

She caught her breath. "Rotten eggs—that's what I smelled just before it happened, so it could have been propane gas."

He nodded. "When I talked to Sharon's son in the waiting room, Bill said his mother had complained of a funny odor earlier in the week."

Brooke closed her eyes and massaged her temples. "I keep thinking there's something else . . ." The dog barking! "I heard something in Kyle's office. Thought it was the dog, but now, I don't know."

"This is enough for now." He put away his notepad. "I won't bother you any longer, but thanks for what you've been able to tell me." Pete walked to the door. "Call me if you remember anything else."

The doctor came in as he was leaving. "Up for more visitors?" he asked.

When she nodded, he stepped out of the room, and a few seconds later, Luke stepped inside, the worry lines fading when he saw her. Right behind him was Dale, who looked paler than she felt.

"You look okay," Luke said. He glanced at the monitor. "And your heart rate looks good."

"I'm fine. At least that's what I'm trying to convince the doctor of. How did you two know?"

"Clayton called—he heard it on the scanner. It scared the daylights out of me," Dale said. "What happened?"

"Pete thinks it might have been a propane explosion." She relayed what she'd told Pete minutes ago.

"He doesn't think the fire has anything to do with Kyle's death?" Dale asked.

"You'd have to ask him . . . or the fire marshal."

"The fire marshal has been called?" Dale frowned. "Then he must be suspicious that it didn't happen naturally."

"He didn't say." Brooke craned her neck, working out some of the tightness. "Wouldn't it be normal to call in the fire marshal?"

"Sure. Don't know what I was thinking." The chief ranger shook his head. "I just hate to think someone has gotten it in for the Marlars bad enough to burn their house down. Do you know how Sharon is?"

"No one will tell me," she replied. "Could you find out for me?"

"I'll let Luke do that. I need to track down Clayton," Dale said and edged toward the door. "Looks like we'll put your commissioning off until tomorrow. That work for you?"

"Sunday?"

"Sure. Let's make it after church, say three again? That way Mary can come if she's up to it—she's really proud of you."

It was like he couldn't leave fast enough, but with his wife in and out of hospitals, Brooke shouldn't be surprised. "I hope she can make it," she said.

"I'll see if I can get an update on Sharon," Luke said and left with Dale.

When there was a hard rap at the door, she almost laughed. Her room was like Union Station with all the people coming and going. Before she could respond with "Come in," the door jerked open, and Jeremy strode inside.

"You're all right!"

"I think so, but how did you know?" she asked.

"I was on my way to Mammy's Cupboard when a friend in the 911 office called and said you were involved in an explosion at the Marlar house." He grabbed a chair and pulled it to her bedside, then took her hand. "I thought my heart would stop."

"I'm okay." Brooke squeezed his fingers. "Trying to get them to release me."

"I think you should stay here. It's much safer."

The door opened again. "They're still working on—" Luke stopped when he saw Jeremy. "Sorry, I didn't know you had company."

"I hope Brooke thinks of me as family," he said, turning a gentle smile on her. "But I am surprised to see you here."

"When I heard she was in the hospital, I wanted to see for myself that she was okay," Luke said.

Tension filled the air in the small cubicle. She wasn't sure which man sucked the air out of the room. Maybe both. They reminded her of boxers squaring off. Jeremy was a couple of inches taller and was leaner than Luke, but Luke was by no means fat—he was all muscle. Blood rushed to her face, flaming her cheeks. "You two know each other, right?" she asked, hating that she sounded breathy.

Luke extended his hand to Jeremy, and he relinquished his hold on her to shake hands with him. "Of course," Jeremy said. "We talked just the other day, and his grandmother is one of my favorite people."

"Mine too," Luke replied, and then turned to Brooke. "I better let her know you're okay. I'll just step out into the hall."

"Wait! How is Sharon?" Brooke asked.

"Haven't found out yet," Luke said.

After Luke left, Jeremy stood by her bed, shifting from one foot to the other. "So much happening lately and none of it good. I'm sorry."

"Yeah, me too." She remembered their date tonight. "I'm not up to dinner tonight."

He took her hand again. "I could play the disappointment card, but actually I was going to have to cancel on you. The governor is calling a special session in ten days, and he phoned and asked me to meet with him in Jackson this afternoon. We have lobbying to do and I'll be late getting home."

"Why is the governor calling the session?"

"It's for a special session to vote on the medical marijuana bill."

"Really?" She knew people like Dale's wife, deathly sick from chemo, would benefit from it. "Think it'll pass?"

"Of course not. Mississippi isn't ready to legalize any form of marijuana. The problem is, a few in the legislature keep calling for a vote by the constituents—they take up valuable time during the regular session. He wants it over and done when the legislature convenes in January."

"You're voting no?"

"That's right. Regardless of how I feel personally, the people who elected me expect my vote to be no. It would be political suicide for me to vote yes right now."

Jeremy was probably right about the timing, and she figured in a few years, attitudes would probably change.

"Even Kyle Marlar realized that and decided to vote no," he said. "Let's don't talk about politics. You'll be busy next week, but save some time for me. If I'd lost you . . ."

His warm brown eyes captured hers, sending the heart monitor skyrocketing. She ignored the pounding in her head as he leaned toward her.

Before he could kiss her, someone knocked at the door, and he pulled back. She caught her breath, trying to calm her heart.

"I better go," he said, running his thumb along her jawline. "But I'm worried about you. Listen to your doctor and stay here in the hospital overnight."

"I'll rest better at home."

"You are some kind of stubborn." He smiled and took her hand. "I hate to leave you like this, but I have to go."

There was another knock and she said, "Come in."

Jeremy leaned over and kissed her on her forehead. "I'll keep you in my thoughts while I'm gone."

"Thank you," she said as Luke stepped back into the room. A slight frown crossed his face as Jeremy straightened up and walked past him to the door.

"I'll see you tomorrow at church," Jeremy said.

After he left, she turned a curious glance at Luke. If she didn't know better, she'd think he was jealous. "Did you reach Daisy?"

"Yes."

"And?"

He shrugged. "She'd just gotten back from playing bingo and hadn't heard about the explosion." He raised his eyebrows. "She may not want to move back home where she'll be all alone most of the time."

A twinge stung her heart. He might be right, but the neighborhood wouldn't be the same without Daisy. "She's not alone. She has me and you, if you move back," she said.

They both turned as the doctor entered the room. Brooke looked expectantly at him. "Can I leave now?"

The physician turned to Luke. "Can you do anything with her? I'd like to keep her for twenty-four hours. It's possible she received a concussion when her head hit the ground, and that could be dangerous since she lives alone."

"I'm fine. Luke is next door, and he can keep an eye on me if that's all you're worried about." She turned to Luke. "Right?"

"I wish you would do what the doc says."

"I hate hospitals. People die here." She caught Luke's gaze and held it, practically begging him to go along with her.

"I've had some first-aid training," he said. "If she refuses to stay, I'll make sure she doesn't go to sleep for at least twelve hours."

"No need for that—keeping a concussed patient awake no longer applies," the doctor said. "In fact, sleep is good." The doctor turned a stern face toward Brooke. "I can't force you to stay, but if your headache worsens or you have a spike in your blood pressure, you need to get to the ER. Okay?"

"Yes, sir. And thank you."

"Try to keep her off her feet for the rest of the day," the doctor said as he signed her release order.

After a nurse unhooked Brooke from the monitor, she sat on the side of the ER bed, waiting for someone to bring her discharge papers. "How did you find out I was here?"

"I was with Dale when Clayton called," Luke said.

Brooke nodded and winced. Had to keep her head still. Suddenly she gasped when a memory flashed through her mind.

"What?" he asked.

"I just remembered something. Sharon was going to let me look at the files on Kyle's computer. I went to the car for my phone—that's why I wasn't on the porch."

"Why were you going to look at his computer?"

Brooke searched her memory and came up blank. "I don't know, but something inside me says to find that computer and look at those files. My impression is Sharon felt the same way." She looked toward the door. "I'd really like to find out how she is."

"As soon as you're discharged, we'll see if we can find out," Luke said just as her nurse entered the room with papers in her hand.

Brooke waited patiently while the nurse went over her instructions to not take anything stronger than Tylenol, and then repeated the warning signs the doctor had told them about.

She signed the papers, and the nurse asked if she needed a wheelchair. "No, I can walk. What room is Sharon Marlar in?"

"Twelve. It's around the corner."

A wave of dizziness hit her when she stood, and Luke grabbed her before she toppled over.

"I don't think—"

"Just let me hold on to you. I'll be fine." She held on to his arm until the dizziness passed. Maybe leaving wasn't such a good idea. She took a deep breath and blew it out. Her head cleared, and with Luke's help, she walked down the hallway to Sharon's room.

Brooke's heart plummeted when the door was open and the bed empty. She turned, looking for the nurses' station. "Where is Mrs. Marlar?" she asked.

"She's been taken to ICU."

Brooke breathed again. "Is she going to make it?" When the nurse hesitated, Brooke said, "We were in the explosion together."

"She's critical," the nurse said.

"Can I see her?"

"Probably not until they get her settled."

"Do you know what her wounds are?"

The nurse smiled apologetically, and Luke said, "She can't tell you anything more."

Brooke glared at him. Where were his social engineering skills when she needed them?

It could have just as easily been Brooke ending up in ICU with Sharon Marlar. Luke shoved down the impulse to grab Brooke's hand and whisk her away to somewhere safe. But there were two problems—she wouldn't go, and he had no idea where "safe" might be.

It was even possible she hadn't been the intended target this last time, that she'd simply been in the wrong place at the wrong time if Kyle's killer was trying to destroy evidence. But right now it was clear that she needed to find Sharon. "What room is Ms. Marlar in?" he asked the nurse.

She looked on her papers. "Two thirty-one."

"Thanks." He turned to Brooke. "Maybe you can talk with her nurse or maybe some of the family."

Brooke was quiet as they rode the elevator to the second floor. When they walked into the ICU waiting room, he asked the receptionist for information on Sharon Marlar.

"Are you family?" she asked.

"No—"

"I was with her when the bomb exploded," Brooke said. "Please, could you tell me how she is?"

"I'm sorry . . ." Then she pointed across the room. "But her son is here. Maybe he can give you an update."

Luke turned and found Bill Marlar sitting in the corner talking on his phone. He looked worse than he had last night.

"Thank you," Brooke said and struck out across the room.

He hurried to catch up with her. "Hold up a minute."

"Why?"

"Slow down. Bill's dad was just murdered, and it's only been a month since his brother's death and now his mother is critical."

Brooke winced. "Not to mention he's lost his family home. Thanks for reminding me. Sometimes I get tunnel vision."

Bill looked up as they approached and nodded. Then he turned his attention back to the person he was speaking with. "Thank you. I'll be in touch in a few days."

He pocketed his phone. "Luke," he said, holding out his hand. Then he turned to Brooke. "What are you doing out of the ER?"

Luke shook his hand. "They tried to get her to stay—"

"I'm fine," she said. "How's your mom?"

"Critical. Bruised lungs and kidneys from the blast," he said and patted the chair beside him. "But here, sit down—you look like you're going to pass out."

Brooke sank in the chair beside him and Luke sat on the sofa across from them. "How are you holding up?" she asked.

"Barely hanging on." Bill massaged his temples. "I was just talking to the funeral home, putting Dad's service on hold."

Luke didn't know what to say. "If there's anything I can do—"

"Thanks, but there's nothing anyone can do, except pray." He turned to Brooke. "What happened? The chief won't tell me anything."

She gripped the armrest. "I don't know. I'm having trouble remembering myself. Has your mom been able to talk?"

"She's on a vent and hasn't regained consciousness." He glanced toward the ICU doors. "We can't lose her."

Luke hurt for the man as he buried his face in his hands.

"It's my fault," Bill said.

"What are you talking about?" Luke asked.

He looked up. "Mom told me last week she smelled something funny, like something was dead, and it was probably propane leaking. I should have checked it out."

Luke leaned forward. Maybe the explosion had nothing to do with Kyle's death. "You think there could have been a gas leak at the house?"

"Could have been." He turned to Brooke. "Did you smell anything?"

"I thought I smelled rotten eggs."

That was one description of the smell of propane. "Did you notice anything else?" Luke asked.

She frowned. "I'm not sure . . . I may have heard someone in your dad's office. I thought it was the dog, but now I'm not so sure."

Bill's eyes widened. "If someone was there, the explosion wasn't an accident."

The thought made Luke sick. "Chief Nelson called the state fire marshal to investigate."

Bill balled his hands. "I don't know which would be worse— that there was a propane leak that I didn't check out or someone purposely blew up my parents' home," he said. "It was bad enough that someone killed my dad and brother."

Brooke fumbled in her purse, stopping to press her hand to her temple again.

"What do you need?" Luke asked.

"I was looking for my phone to make a few notes, but it's in the rental car." She turned to Bill. "Can you answer a few questions about your dad?"

"If you think it'll help catch whoever killed him," he said.

Luke stood. "I'll get something from the desk." When he returned with a notepad and pen, he said, "Brooke, why don't you ask the questions and I'll take notes?"

When she agreed, he turned to the son. "You okay with that?"

He nodded. "Not sure how much help I'll be. We were close, but we talked more about family than his work. I do know he was obsessed about my brother's death, and none of us believe Brandon started using again."

"Do you know of any enemies your dad might've had?" Brooke asked.

"He was a politician, but most people liked him. Liked what he did with the community center." Bill paused for a few seconds. "I can't think of anyone who would want him dead."

"Do you know what he was working on?"

"He said something about a special session . . ."

"To legalize medical marijuana," Brooke said.

"He was going to vote for it. Dad said there was a kid in Natchez who needed it for his seizures."

"Are you sure?" Brooke asked. "Jeremy Steele just told me your dad had changed his vote to no."

"That can't be. Dad believed it could help people."

Kyle indicated he'd been blackmailed to vote no. Had he decided to stand up to Boudreaux? And had that gotten him killed? Luke tapped his pen against the pad. "Do you know if he kept a journal?"

"I'm sure he did. It would be on his computer."

Brooke sat up straighter. "I have to get my hands on that computer," she said, and then sank back in the chair. "There's probably nothing left of it."

Luke gripped the pen. If the flash drive Kyle intended to give him was in the house, it was probably blown to smithereens as well. "Where did he keep his computer?"

"Usually in his office." Bill massaged his temple. "Look, could we do this later? I can't think anymore."

"Of course," Brooke said and stood.

Luke stood as well. "We're really sorry about what happened. Keep us updated about your mom."

Bill nodded and leaned back against the chair. "Sorry, guys."

"Don't worry about it," Luke said and took Brooke's arm. She needed rest as well.

"I want to see the house," Brooke said when they left the hospital.

"You need to go home."

"I should check on my rental car and get my phone." She looked around at Luke. "You want to take me or should I find a ride?"

"I'll take you." He wished he hadn't left her to her own devices earlier today.

He convinced Brooke to wait just outside the hospital while he walked to his car.

"What time is it, anyway?" she asked after he picked her up.

He checked his watch. "A little past three."

"Wow. Seems like it should be later. I hope the Prius is okay," she said and fastened her seatbelt. "I'd hate to call my agent for another rental the same day I got the first one."

Fifteen minutes later he parked beside the Prius in the Marlar drive. Evidently Nelson had completed his examination of the site since the area was deserted except for Brooke's car. Yellow crime scene tape cordoned off the house. The house that was in shambles. The roof on the back side had caved in and windows were blown out.

"Where were you when the blast occurred?" he asked when they were a few feet from the house.

"Right here, I think. Sharon was standing at the top of the porch steps." Brooke stared at the house a minute then nodded. "That's about it."

"Let's walk around to the back side."

Just as they rounded the corner of the house, a small dog shot out from under a shed near the back of the property, and Brooke caught her breath. "What?" he asked.

"The dog, Toby. Before the explosion, he was barking somewhere in the house, then he ran to the front door, and when Sharon let him out, he tore around to the backyard—over near the tree line." She knelt and held out her hand. "Come here, Toby, come on, boy."

The dachshund backed up a step and continued to bark. Brooke lowered her hand, and the dog cautiously edged toward her and finally sniffed her fingers.

"Come on, that's a good dog." Toby came a little closer, and she scooped him up in her arms. "Poor thing. He's shaking," she said. In response to her words, he burrowed his nose in the crook of her arm.

Too bad dogs couldn't talk. Luke stroked the quivering dog. "What are you going to do with him?"

"I haven't thought that far ahead. He's scared to death, and I hate to leave him here all alone. There's no telling when the Marlars will think to check on him."

He smiled. Luke knew exactly what Brooke would do—what she'd done with every stray dog she ran across when she was a teenager. At least this one had a real home.

"I'll keep him just until I can get in touch with Bill or Todd Marlar to see what they want me to do." She looked up. "Do you think whoever did this was in the house and Toby was barking at them before the explosion?"

"He could have been. Dachshunds are great watchdogs." Luke scanned the backyard that bordered dense woodland. Houses in this area were spaced far apart. It would have been easy enough for someone to park down the road and slip through the woods to the house without being seen.

"You've remembered the dog. Anything else?" he asked as they approached the back door. Beside him, Brooke tensed.

"That door . . . it was closed when I put the chicken in the refrigerator."

He saw what she meant and frowned. The door opened inward, and if it had been closed, the bomb blast should have splintered it and knocked it off the hinges. Someone had left it open. Someone in a hurry to get away from the house before it exploded?

He glanced toward the bombed-out shell that was the back

of the house. "If the computer survived the blast, Pete probably took it to the justice center. You want to call and ask if he has it?"

Brooke stared at Luke. "You want me to call Pete Nelson and ask about Kyle's computer?"

What was wrong with him? Brooke wasn't dumb. "Did I do it again?" he asked. He avoided her eyes. She would only buy that excuse so many times. If she were thinking clearly, she wouldn't have bought it this time.

Luke's question about the computer rang a warning bell, but Brooke couldn't lock on to why. Brain fog filled her head. Maybe the doctor was right and she did have a concussion.

Strength suddenly deserted her arms, and she almost dropped the dog. She'd been running on adrenaline, and now it was gone. "You better take him." She thrust Toby at Luke and then fished her phone from her pocket.

"You okay?"

"Just tired." Brooke stared at her phone. "Do you want me to put it on speaker?"

When he nodded, she dialed the number and was put through to Pete. "Thanks for taking my call," she said.

"Where are you? Still at the hospital?" he asked. "I'd like to get your statement."

"No. I'm at the Marlars', picking up my car."

"You're at the crime scene?"

"That's where my car is," she said. "Did you find Kyle's computer in the rubble?"

"I didn't find a computer. The bomb did a good job of destroying the back of the house and anything in it. Why do you ask?"

Why was she asking? "Luke—"

She frowned as Luke waved his hands and shook his head. "Wait! You think it was a bomb?"

"Yeah. We found a piece of metal that looked like it was from a blasting cap embedded in the ceiling tiles. You didn't answer why you're interested in Kyle's computer."

"I want to know why someone blew up his house, and Kyle's wife mentioned there might be something on his computer."

"You're not working this case, Brooke, so leave it alone."

"What could Kyle have known that is so important?" she persisted.

"If I knew that, I'd know who to arrest," Pete replied. "If you should happen to find the laptop, I expect you to bring it to me."

"Of course." After she looked at the files.

"And I do need your statement. What time do you want to come in, or should I come by the house?"

Giving statements was getting old. "How about tomorrow? I'm not up to answering questions right now."

"I'll check with you later this evening. Maybe you'll feel better by then."

"I'll call you if I do." Toby whined in Luke's arms, reminding her she needed to let someone know she was taking the dog home. "Do you have either Todd's or Bill Marlar's phone number? I found their dog."

After he gave her Bill's number, he said, "Try to stay out of danger for a while."

"Don't worry, I will." After she hung up, she turned to Luke. "Why did you cut me off?"

"Pete's not happy that you're interested in the case. How do you think he'd react if he knew I'm helping you?"

Maybe she was tired, but something about what Luke just said didn't ring true. A wave of dizziness reeled Brooke, and she grabbed his arm. "I need to sit down."

"You need to be home." He helped her to his car. "Can you hold Toby until we get there?"

"What about my car?"

"You're in no shape to drive. We'll get it tomorrow."

Brooke held Toby close to her body as Luke drove to her house.

By the time he pulled into her drive, the dog slept with his head burrowed in the crook of her arm.

"Oh no," she groaned. Her mother's car sat parked in the driveway instead of the garage.

"Isn't that your mom's car?"

"I'm afraid so." Brooke was in no shape to face her mom's inquisition.

"You didn't know she was coming?"

She blew away a strand of hair that had fallen in her face. "No. She must have rented a car in Knoxville and drove down."

He shot a sidelong glance at her. "I get the feeling you're not happy she's back."

Her face flamed. What kind of daughter was she? "It's just that she'll not react well to the bomb."

"I don't think anyone is reacting well to the bomb."

"I know, but sometimes being around Mom is like rubbing against a cactus." She chewed her fingernail. "Lately it seems like she gets upset with everything I do, even more than when I was a teenager. We both end up saying the wrong words."

"I can identify, at least with my dad."

She eyed him. If anything, his relationship with his parents was worse than hers with her mother. At least she knew her mother loved her. "It was always easier to talk to Dad."

"Your dad was special. There weren't many men like him," he said. "But I'm surprised about your mom. She was always even-keeled."

Brooke glanced toward the house. "We better go in before Mom comes to see what's keeping us."

When she climbed out of the car, pain shot from her hip to her knee. A new ache to add to the mounting list. She focused on the walkway, trying not to stumble on her wobbly legs.

"You okay?"

"Not really. I think I need an ice pack on my back, but please, don't mention it to my mother."

He nodded. "Where's your key?"

"Hanging on my purse." Before she could swing around for him to unsnap her key, her mother opened the door.

"Brooke! Thank goodness you're all right! Why didn't you answer your phone? I've been worried to death ever since I found out about the explosion, and then I get here and see the damage done to your Escape on the Trace—you could have been killed."

"I'm okay." She held Toby for support. "How did you get here?"

"I rented a car, and a nice man at the rental place brought me home when I returned it." Her mom turned on Luke. "Luke Fereday, you should have called me!"

"I'm sorry, but it's been kind of crazy," he said. "How did you know?"

"I wanted to see for myself that she was all right, so I decided to come home." She shifted her gaze to Brooke. "I was on the other side of Jackson when Daisy called and said you were in the hospital. Then when I get to the hospital, you've flown the coop and don't answer your phone." She took a breath. "And why aren't you still in the hospital?"

Thanks a lot, Daisy. Her mom had the gift of making her feel guilty when she had nothing to feel guilty about. "The doctor released me. Why didn't you tell me this morning that you were coming?"

"I think you told me to stay at Meghan's when I mentioned coming," she countered. "And what is that thing you're holding?"

"A dog." Brooke's legs gave way and she stumbled. Luke caught her, sweeping her up in his arms as Toby jumped to freedom. "Toby—"

"He's okay," Luke murmured in her ear. "He ran in the house."

"You can put me down," she said, not really wanting him to release her. Being in his arms was like being wrapped in a safety net.

"And have you fall on your face?"

"But you'll hurt your back," she protested half-heartedly.

"You hardly weigh anything," he said.

"Now I know you're crazy." But when he set her on the couch, she missed his strong arms. "Thanks," she murmured.

"Feeling better?"

"I could use a glass of water."

"I'll get it," her mother said.

As soon as they were alone, she whispered, "Do not tell her anything. I was at Sharon's offering my condolences. That's all."

"I thought you didn't believe in social engineering," he said with a wink.

Ice rattled against the glass as her mom came back into the room and handed Brooke the water, shortcutting any retort she had for him. Then her mom perched stiffly on the edge of the chair, her hands clasped so tightly, her knuckles turned white. She leaned forward, waiting. Brooke swallowed hard, hating that she had caused her mom pain. It seemed that was the one thing she was good at.

"Thanks," she said, softening her voice. Her mom had cared enough to come. "But I hate that I pulled you away from Meghan when she needs you."

"You need me more right now." Her mom fussed with the afghan on the arm of the chair. "After the wreck last night, I was worried about you."

Again shame swept through her. It shouldn't take an emergency for Brooke and her mother to relate to one another. Toby trotted into the living room and jumped up on the sofa. Brooke set him on the floor. "No, Toby. Not on the furniture."

"Where did you get the dog?" her mom asked.

"It's Sharon Marlar's dog."

"You went back to the Marlar house?"

"We were checking on my rental car and getting my phone—that's why I didn't call you. Toby was under the shed, and I didn't want to leave him to fend for himself."

The look her mom gave her was one Brooke had seen every

time she brought a stray dog home. "I'm only keeping him until Sharon gets out of the hospital."

"What if she doesn't—"

"Don't even think that!" She took out her phone and dialed the number Pete had given her for Bill. When he answered, she asked how Sharon was.

"The doctors are cautiously optimistic," he said. "She was briefly conscious a few minutes ago."

"Good. I wanted to let you know I have Toby."

"Oh, wow. I hadn't even thought about him. Do you mind—"

"That's why I was calling. I'll take care of him until your mom gets home."

"Thank you."

She glanced toward her mother, who was quietly talking to Luke. Turning away from them, she lowered her voice. "Did your dad ever mention what he kept on his computer?"

When he didn't answer immediately, she thought the call might have dropped. "Are you there?"

"Yes," Bill said. "I can't believe I forgot."

"What?"

"A couple of weeks ago Dad told me that if anything odd or strange happened to him, to get his computer to your dad and he'd know what to do."

"Have you told Chief Nelson or anyone else?"

"No . . . until you asked me just now, I'd forgotten he even said anything. And even if I had thought about it, your dad is . . ."

Dead. Even brain fog couldn't keep her from connecting the dots.

48

Opening the gas line on the propane heater in the office had been a stroke of genius. Adding it to the gasoline and the half stick of dynamite had destroyed just about everything in Kyle Marlar's house.

He set the computer on the table and turned it on. The dog had almost blown his operation. If the Marlar woman had come to see why the dog was barking, she would have caught him escaping out the back door. Too bad about her being injured, but she should have been at the funeral home. And what was Brooke Danvers doing at the Marlar house? His jaw set. She said she was offering her condolences. And that might be partially true. He didn't believe she had any hard evidence connecting him to the deaths.

But he'd worked hard to achieve what he had in life, and he wasn't going to let anyone mess that up, not even Brooke Danvers. And what about Luke Fereday? Something about him didn't gel. He was supposed to be an accountant—that's what he'd heard—but it turned out Fereday was a bartender? Definitely something fishy about that. And he seemed awfully nosy, along with sticking close to Brooke.

The computer alerted that it was booting up, and he pressed the buttons to open it in recovery mode. There he changed the password and rebooted, using the new password.

His mistake had been in underestimating Marlar. He'd had no idea the older man was even computer savvy. Now he had to find out what he was up against. He ran a scan of the files on the computer. Right away he found three locked folders and went to work cracking those passwords.

Once he had the first file opened, he swore. Empty. Marlar would not have password protected an empty file. Which meant he'd deleted the contents. Fortunately for him, deleted files were never truly lost. He installed a recovery program on the computer and quickly found the JPEG files. He stared at the first photo in the file—the photo Marlar had tried to snatch from his hand Friday night.

He leaned back in his chair. There were twenty of the time-stamped photos of him at Emerald Mound Sunday night. Marlar had alluded to other photos—were these the ones? Or were there physical ones, like the one he ripped from his hand?

There'd been nothing in Marlar's file cabinet, and the memory cards he'd found in the office were useless. Nothing but pictures of the night sky or family members. The empty file that had been password protected . . . had Marlar downloaded the pictures to a flash drive and then deleted them, thinking he was destroying the photos?

Or had he emailed them to someone? With a shaky hand, he logged into the email and scanned the sent emails. Breathing became a little easier. It didn't look as though he'd emailed the files. Mostly just correspondence about the upcoming vote on marijuana.

What if this wasn't the only account he had?

He ran another scan, looking for other email accounts, and once again relaxed when the scan didn't return a hit. Marlar was a simple man, and until Boudreaux murdered his son, he had probably never thought about withholding anything from authorities. He truly regretted his death . . . John's too, but he'd been desperate.

He shook off the melancholy. Time to look at the other two files. The first one took longer to crack, and it turned out to be a list of passwords. He shook his head. People just didn't understand that nothing on a computer was safe. The last locked file opened on the first password he tried. Emails from the state legislature. Must be something top secret. If he had more time, he'd mine them for information.

Marlar's last words indicated he had made copies of the photos, so where were they? He had to assume there was a flash drive somewhere waiting to bite him.

But what had he done with it?

Pretty sure the police didn't have it or they'd be knocking on his door. No, either he stored it in a safe place, like maybe a lockbox, or . . . what if he dropped the drive in the mail? But to whom?

Think like Marlar. Who were his friends? John Danvers. He was dead, but his daughter wasn't. What if he mailed the photos to Brooke and they hadn't arrived yet when he searched the house?

What were his options? His gut said Brooke Danvers was the key to whatever information Kyle Marlar had, and that meant he had to return to the Danverses' house.

At five thirty, Luke knocked on Daisy's door at the rehab. He held a bag from the Malt Shop that smelled strongly of beef and onions.

"Come in," she said, her voice strong.

"You sound like you feel good," he said, entering the room.

Her eyes lit up. "You brought my hamburger! Thank goodness. They're trying to starve me here," she said. "Pull up a chair and stay awhile."

"I can't," he said. "I have—" He'd almost said work to do. "I need to check on Brooke."

She pulled the burger from the bag. "You brought the onion rings too. What kind of work are you doing?"

He hoped he was as sharp as his grandmother when he reached eighty. "I'll tell you about it someday," he said, winking at her.

"How is Brooke?"

"She's going to be okay. I left her resting with her mom. Vivian is making lasagna for dinner, and I'm invited."

"Good. When do I get sprung from here?" Daisy asked. "I want to go home."

He thought of her study where he'd set up his command center and absentmindedly rubbed his right palm. "What does the doctor say?"

"Two more weeks. And what's wrong with your hand? You keep rubbing it."

Immediately he stopped. He wasn't in the mood to discuss getting shot. "Nothing," he said and looked around the room. "This isn't a bad place."

"You try it," she said, raising an eyebrow. "I've been thinking about what you said the other night, and I'm not ready for assisted living."

He nodded. "You know it wasn't my idea, right?"

"The Admiral's?"

He nodded, smiling at her use of the name they called his father behind his back. Too bad he hadn't made the army his career—General fit him much better.

"I can handle him, if you'll back me," she said.

"You got that."

"Good. Now get on to . . . seeing after Brooke," she said. "And leave me to my burger."

Luke kissed her cheek. "Love you, Gram."

"I know. Now get."

He whistled as he walked to his car. Daisy always made him feel better. A few minutes later he stood in front of his evidence board in the study.

On his way home, Steve had called and suggested that Luke get in touch with Hugh Cortland and fill him in on what had happened. He would as soon as he collected his thoughts. Luke turned back to the board and went over what he knew, starting with the drug deal almost a week ago with Romero. Although he'd been late to the meeting, Luke didn't think Romero was the person making the drug transfer John mentioned. It wasn't a job he would do in the organization.

The theory was drugs were brought into New Orleans, transferred at Natchez and maybe once again in Jackson or up north at the Alabama line, and then on to Nashville. While it took more runners, it would just about be impossible to trace. Who was the connection at Natchez?

For the hundredth time he read John's voice mail that he'd transcribed.

"Got a tip there's a big drug transfer going down at Emerald Mound at midnight, and thought you'd want to be there for the takedown. Think I know who the runner is."

John knew who the runner was. Luke wished he'd told him his name.

Luke punched in Sonny's number. "You've been hinting for a month now that someone is taking money to look the other way when drugs are moved up the Trace. Who is it?"

"Hello to you too."

"Come on, Sonny."

"I've only heard vague talk and no names."

"You sure you don't know?"

"I make it my business not to."

"How much would it take to make it your business?"

"No thanks. Just why are you interested all of a sudden, anyway?"

"This isn't a two-bit deal about to go down. My people are looking to invest a lot of money in what Boudreaux can provide us, and we need to know the law around here won't interfere. So who is it?"

"I'm not lying to you—I don't know," he said. "But I might know somebody who does."

"Good. Another thing. My organization is worried about Kyle Marlar's murder bringing the FBI's attention to Natchez. Is Boudreaux involved?" he asked.

"I doubt it. He was really upset the medical marijuana bill might pass." The sound of Sonny taking a draw from a cigarette, or maybe a joint, came through the phone followed by him exhaling. "My two cents' worth? I think he found a way to put pressure on Marlar to change his vote from yes to no."

"But Marlar was just one vote," Luke said.

"Yeah, but he'd been in the state legislature a long time and people owed him. Boudreaux expected him to call in favors to get the bill defeated, so he wouldn't want Marlar dead." Sonny took another drag. "If it passes, it'll cost the cartel a bundle. And it'll cost me. Some of my best marijuana customers are on chemo."

"Can't they get it from one of the states where it's legal?"

"Yeah, but it's a lot more trouble and way more expensive than buying it from me."

"What else have you heard? How about the bomb at Marlar's house?"

"Not much. But if you put two and two together, it's pretty easy to figure out."

"What do you mean?"

"Marlar was a photographer. Maybe he took a picture of the wrong person."

"If there are photos, do you know where they are?"

"Nah. But if I thought Marlar had pictures of me selling drugs, I'd be looking for them, and the first place I'd look is his house, and it's gone now."

"Do you know who killed him?"

"No, and if I did, I'd keep it to myself—it's how I've stayed alive all these years—keeping my nose out of things that don't concern me. It's starting to bother me why you're so interested."

A call beeped in, and he checked to see who was calling. Romero? "I gotta go," he said as his phone beeped again. Luke switched over to Romero's call. "Yeah?"

"Boudreaux said to come to his hotel room. Be there in fifteen minutes."

The deal was going down. "On my way."

Luke grabbed the money he'd stashed in his bedroom and divided it between two deep pockets in his cargo pants. He called Delaney as he drove away from the house to advise him the deal was on.

Ten minutes later Luke parked in the hotel lot and slipped

into his role of wheeler-dealer extraordinaire before he strolled inside. Anyone watching would think he didn't have a care in the world, much less a three-million-dollar deal to work out. On the ride up to the second floor, he clicked the pen on and thought about rehearsing his spiel, then discarded the idea. Luke didn't want to sound canned. Instead he took a breath and blew it out and then shook his shoulders to loosen up.

When Wilson opened the door, Luke raised his hands. "No guns," he said. Knowing he'd be frisked again, they were safe under the seat of his car.

The dour Wilson patted him down anyway as a bedroom door opened and Boudreaux came into the room followed by Louis carrying a briefcase. The small man set the case on the table where they'd eaten boudin.

"Have a seat," Boudreaux said.

Luke chose a chair that faced the door.

The drug czar sat across from him. "Do you have the money?"

Luke pulled a packet from one pocket then the other and laid them on the table. Boudreaux nodded, and Louis set the briefcase beside the money. He removed a rectangular package wrapped in plastic and handed it to his boss.

"Our finest. Uncut white heroin," Boudreaux said, placing the package beside the money. "You're welcome to open it, or weigh it, or even try a sample."

Luke waved him off. "We'll be doing business together for quite a while—I don't think you'd cheat me."

He drew the heroin closer to his side of the table while Boudreaux flipped through the cash. "Random serial numbers. You follow directions well."

Luke acknowledged the compliment with a nod. "And my people were well pleased with the samples I took them. As well as your ability to provide what I needed so quickly." Boudreaux leaned forward, and Luke paused. He'd taken the bait, now to set the hook. "I've been authorized to make you a proposition."

Boudreaux frowned, his eyes wary. "Then this . . . "—he dipped his head toward the heroin—"was a test?"

"You could call it that. The organization I represent is looking for a new source of heroin. Originally, they didn't believe you could produce what we need. It took some convincing on my part, and of course, you came through for me," Luke said, improvising as he talked. "I heard a large shipment was arriving in New Orleans next week . . ."

"Where did you hear that?"

"I have good sources." Luke smiled to soften the words. "My organization wants that shipment, and they're willing to pay top dollar."

"It's already earmarked for New York," Boudreaux said.

"So I've heard, but we'll double their offer."

"What's the name of this organization?"

"You wouldn't recognize it. It's a syndicate out of California with legitimate business enterprises. They have offices in Memphis and Jackson. It's very low-key with several layers separating the top people from the dealers. Are you interested?"

"Depends. Do they want to set up shop in Natchez or New Orleans?"

"Neither. That's your territory, and they respect you. Most of our business is from Memphis north to St. Louis. We've only branched out to Jackson in the last year, and that's as far south as we're going."

Louis leaned over and whispered something in Boudreaux's ear, and he nodded before turning back to Luke. "Your organization—they can handle twenty kilos of heroin?"

Luke nodded.

"For three million?"

Luke nodded again. "But for that kind of money, my boss will want to deal directly with the Colombian supplier. Músculos."

"How—"

"I told you, I have good sources. Is it a deal?"

"I can't speak for him, but for three mil, you can have the shipment that's coming in next week."

"It's no deal without the Colombian."

Luke didn't flinch from Boudreaux's appraising stare. "Why is that so important?"

"Like you, my people like to take the measure of whoever they do business with. We have ambitious plans and want his personal assurance he can provide for our needs."

Boudreaux's brow smoothed. "I doubt that'll be a problem. And when I explain it to him, I have a feeling he will be anxious to meet your top man." He flashed a tight smile. "Take his measure as well."

"We expect no less. It's a deal, then?" Mark Delaney should do very well in the role of top man. Luke pulled up the calendar on his phone. "Do we want to set a date?"

"I'll get in touch once the particulars of the wire transfer to an off-shore account are finalized and Músculos agrees to come."

"Are we looking at midweek? My people will want to close the deal sooner than later."

"Probably."

Luke stood and picked up the brick of heroin and stashed it in one of the pockets where he'd carried the cash. "Good deal."

50

The rattling of dishes woke Brooke from a sound sleep, and it took a few seconds to realize she was in her dad's recliner in the den. She checked her watch and was surprised to learn it was after six.

"Did I wake you?"

Brooke turned at her mom's question and brought the chair to a sitting position. "It was time. I have work to do."

"Now? You have a concussion. You need to rest. Besides, dinner will be ready soon."

"I feel better." Her headache had faded. She stretched and winced when pain rocked her shoulder. Talk about sore. Her body wasn't used to the kind of treatment it had been getting. "Where's Luke?"

"I don't know. I heard his car leave a while ago, and he hasn't returned."

Her cell phone rang with a number she didn't recognize. "Hello?" she said.

"May I speak with Brooke Danvers?"

"Speaking."

The caller rattled off her name. "I'm calling in reference to the complaint regarding your DNA profile. Something about a problem with your results."

DNA? "I'm not following you."

While the caller repeated what she'd said, the memory surfaced. "I remember now. My DNA results are wrong, and I wanted to get a repeat test."

Her mother gasped and Brooke jerked her head around, immediately regretting it. The room spun, but she focused on her mom's face. A corpse wouldn't be any paler, and her expression . . . "Excuse me," she said, bringing her attention back to the caller. "I didn't hear you."

"I said, the tests are rarely incorrect."

"These are. My sister and I took the test together and her results are different from mine. My father's family came from Ireland, and there's no mention of an Irish bloodline in my papers."

Her mom sank on the sofa, her gaze glued to Brooke. "Can I call you back?" she asked. Something was terribly wrong with her mom. After writing down the reference number of her case, she hung up. "What's wrong? You look like you're about to pass out. Can I get you some water?"

She waved her off. "Just let me sit here a minute."

A vise gripped Brooke's stomach. What if she was having a stroke? "Do I need to call 911?"

Her mom shook her head and mumbled something Brooke didn't quite catch, but it sounded like why? She tried not to hover, but she didn't know what to do, or how to help. Then her mom sat up straighter and squared her shoulders.

"I, ah . . ." She swallowed, then took a shaky breath.

"What's wrong?"

"I hate to lay this on you right now . . ."

"What are you talking about?"

Her mom clasped her hands together and took in a deep breath. "I'm afraid there's something I should—no, something your father and I should have told you a long time ago." She shifted her gaze to somewhere behind Brooke. "I wanted to, but John didn't, even after he knew you and Meghan had submitted swabs to the ancestry place . . . I should never have listened to him."

She didn't know where her mother was going with this, but Brooke was certain she wasn't going to like it.

"John isn't your biological father."

She gaped at her mother. For a second Brooke thought she'd said . . . "Not my father? What do you mean?"

"Just that. He—"

"No! That's not true. How can he not . . ." She raised her gaze until she was looking into her mother's eyes. And then she knew.

Her mom licked her lips. "I was twenty and in my second year of college at Tulane. John and I had been dating, but he got a job out West and said I needed to date other men.

"I didn't want to. John was the only man I ever loved, but I was mad at him for leaving. I was offered a blind date with a friend of my roommate's brother."

She stopped and took a breath. "I didn't know the brother that well. Didn't know his friend at all, but I said yes. It was supposed to be a double date, but he showed up alone. Said something came up with the brother." She focused on her hands, still tightly clasped. "I was so stupid."

"You don't have to tell me." Brooke wanted her mother to stop, to not say another word. It was as though she'd stepped into a nightmare, one where she tottered on the edge of an abyss that called out for her to jump. If she did, her life would never be the same.

"Believe me, I don't want to."

Brooke didn't have to hear the details. "He raped you."

She confirmed it with a nod. "I believe it's called date rape now."

"Did you report it to the police?"

"No. I just wanted to put it out of my mind. A couple of months later, I discovered I was pregnant. By then, John had returned home. When he found out what happened, he wanted to kill the man responsible, but I had no idea how to find him, and my roommate's brother claimed he'd lost contact with him."

"The man who raped you—what's his name?"

"He's not anyone you want to know." Her mother hugged her arms over her chest. "John asked me to marry him, promised he'd love you like his own. I loved him anyway, and I said yes."

Reality slammed Brooke. Her whole life had been a lie. She was a horrible mistake.

She had to get out of the house, away from her mother, away from . . . everything. She stood, palming her hands. "Stop. I don't want to hear any more," she said, backing toward the door.

"Brooke, wait—"

"No, you wait. You had to know when we sent those tests off I'd find out. When were you going to tell me?"

Her mom's shoulders sagged. "John thought he could fix any-thing. I tried to make him understand we had to tell you before the test results came back, but he kept telling me he would handle it. Then he died."

Brooke knew that side of her dad. Stubborn. Determined to do things his way. She pressed her fingers to her temples. Her whole body was numb. She dropped her hands and raised her gaze. "Were you ever going to tell me?"

"Please—"

"No!" She waved her hands. "I don't want to hear it."

Brooke bolted from the house. Ignoring the Natchez heat, she jogged to the street and turned toward town, her feet pound-ing the pavement, but she couldn't run fast enough to leave her thoughts behind.

When she'd run until she couldn't, Brooke slowed to a walk. Her phone rang. She ignored it until it stopped ringing, but then it started again. Reluctantly, she glanced at the ID. Dale. If she didn't answer, he'd probably call again. "Hello?"

"Are you still in the hospital?"

"No. I'm walking."

"Are you okay?" Dale asked. "You sound . . . odd."

"I'm fine. Did my mother ask you to call me?" she said.

"No, I'm just checking on you. Are you sure you're all right?"

No, she wasn't all right, but there was nothing Dale could do about it. Did he know? Did everyone know but her?

"Brooke, are you okay?" he asked again.

"Yeah. And thanks for coming to the hospital earlier."

"It scared me to death when Clayton called. Luke and I were at Emerald Mound and came as soon as I got the call."

She stopped short. What was Luke doing at Emerald Mound? And why did he lie to her? He'd told her he was going to check on the job he'd interviewed for.

51

Luke's cell rang as soon as he fastened his seatbelt. Steve. Rather than raise the phone to his ear, he let the car's Bluetooth pick it up. "Is the deal satisfactory?" he asked, his body still revved from adrenaline.

"Man, you did great," his boss said.

"Thanks. I think we have them." He pulled away from the parking lot. "Do you want to rendezvous and pick up the heroin? I'd like to get rid of it."

"No. We'll wait until dark. Too risky right now in case Boudreaux is having you followed. Hold on to it, and we'll make arrangements later."

"How about I hand it off to Delaney? That wouldn't make Boudreaux suspicious since he thinks Delaney is my drug boss."

"Sounds good, except he's in Jackson and won't be back to Natchez for a couple of hours."

Luke blew out a breath. He'd have to hang on to the package a little longer. "I'll touch base with him later, then, but while I'm here, I'm going to stop by Fort Rosalie and look around."

"Sure," Steve said. "Oh, the bullet you gave me—no matches anywhere."

"Did the techs compare it to the one that killed Marlar?"

"Pete Nelson still has that one. I'll see if I can get it, or at least the report," Steve said. "And I'll hang back and see if I can spot a tail on you."

Luke remembered the shavings he'd found at Emerald Mound and told Steve.

"Give them to Delaney as well," he said. "And hope we can find the knife used."

After they hung up, Luke made three turns and was at the fort. He already had a cover story if anyone saw him there—he was looking for the earring Brooke had lost. Sweat ran down his face by the time he climbed the first hill, and he stopped under the shade of a live oak to wipe his face. A light breeze swayed the Spanish moss hanging from the branches. To his right, yellow crime scene tape cordoned off where Marlar had been found, and he walked toward the area. It'd looked a lot different last night.

Marlar had fallen a good hundred feet from the tape. It had rained the day before the event and the ground was indented where the medics had loaded him onto the gurney. A small numbered marker was stuck in the ground where he had fallen, and Luke tried to remember the position of his body. Too bad police didn't draw an outline on the ground like they did on TV cop shows.

Using his phone, he took several photos of the area from different angles, then wandered down the path to the back side of the property near the bluffs and found trampled grass where Marlar had set up his camera. It was just a few feet from the path. In one direction, the path led to where Luke's car was parked. The other way led back to the crime scene.

A car door slammed, and he walked to where he could see the street. The occupants of two cars climbed out of vehicles parked beside his Jeep. Pete Nelson stood beside a Chevrolet SUV with the chief of police logo. Hugh Cortland stood beside him. While he waited for the men to reach him, he reminded himself that he'd never officially met Cortland.

"What are you doing here?" Pete asked.

"Looking for Brooke's earring," Luke said. "She lost it last night." He held out his hand to the agent. "I'm Luke Fereday, and you're . . . ?"

"Hugh Cortland, FBI," Hugh replied, showing his badge.

He doubted Pete was happy about the FBI taking over his case. Luke pointed toward the bluffs. "I assumed your men combed that area—it looks like that's where he set up to take photos of the meteors."

"They did."

"I'd like to walk the path," Cortland said.

"Mind if I tag along?" Luke asked.

Pete shot him a dark look. "Why? What's your interest?"

"I'm curious. I guess since I got to him right after Brooke found him, it's become personal."

"We can always use another pair of eyes," Cortland said.

They walked a short distance to the crime scene tape, and Pete pointed out where Marlar had fallen. The three of them stood quietly at the spot for a minute.

"It looks like he set up his camera over here," Luke said, walking toward the spot he'd found earlier. "I wonder if his killer came from the parking lot?"

"Let's see if we can find any evidence he might have come that way," Cortland said.

They walked along the back side of the property, stopping at one of several live oaks that grew on the property. "Look." Luke pointed at the grass that had been trampled around the tree.

"It looks like someone stood here for a time instead of just passing by," Cortland said. "Let's see what they left behind."

Half an hour later, Luke straightened up and pulled his wet shirt away from his body. They had examined the area around the tree, and when they fanned out, he'd followed the path along the bluff while they worked back toward the crime scene. His gaze caught a small mound of dirt where a shrub had been dug up, and he looked closer. A shoe imprint. Bingo. He quickly snapped photos, and then motioned the others over. "Is this what I think it is?"

The FBI agent knelt and examined the ground. "It's a partial shoe print. From the ridges it looks like it could be some sort of boot, or even an athletic shoe."

Pete shook his head. "I don't know how my deputies missed it," he said, taking out his phone and snapping a photo. "Not sure if it's enough to identify a particular shoe, and it could be old, maybe belongs to a worker."

"Do you think the killer could have stood here and watched Kyle set up? It's in a direct line of sight," Luke said.

"Could be." Cortland stood. He stepped to the site where Kyle's equipment had been. "Let's see if we can find any blood between here and where he was found."

They walked slowly, searching the ground. "Found a drop on this bush, I think," Luke said.

Pete examined the leaf with a rusty brown spot on it, and then examined the other branches. "Here's another leaf with blood on it," the chief said. "He must have brushed against the bushes." He stood and dialed a number. "Get the crime scene kit and come to Fort Rosalie."

They continued to search for more blood, and once his men arrived, Pete showed them what they'd missed. "How did this happen?"

Luke felt for the young detectives who appeared to be in their midtwenties. Being dressed down was bad, but to have it done in front of an audience was worse.

The older of the two scratched his head. "I don't know. There was heavy dew when we were here. Would have been hard to see the blood, but the missing print—"

"Sorry, Chief. I'm the one who missed that," the second officer said. He turned the soles of his Oxfords up. "Could it be mine?"

His shoe had the wrong pattern of ridges, and Luke glanced

at the other officer's shoes. He wore dress shoes with no ridges at all.

Pete assigned the men to cover the area along the path back to the parking lot. "And get a cast of that print." When they were out of earshot, he sighed. "We're badly understaffed. I lost two of my experienced detectives, one to Vicksburg, the other to Jackson. Been trying to raise the money to send these two to the academy, but so far it hasn't happened. Maybe this will give my efforts a little fuel."

Cortland glanced toward the setting sun and the shadows cast by the trees that lined the river. "They aren't likely to find much this time of the day."

"I know," Pete said. "But it'll be good practice for them."

The chief's phone rang, and after a brief conversation, he disconnected. "I have to get back to the station."

When they were alone, Luke turned to Cortland. "Did you get the photos I sent of the Danvers crime scene?"

The FBI agent nodded. "Shouldn't be that many Boker knives around Natchez."

Luke agreed. "I imagine most men around here carry Case knives," he said. "And unless the killer saw me at the scene, he won't realize I know about the knife."

"So he won't have any reservation about using it." Cortland scratched his jaw.

"I looked it up on the internet. It's not just any Boker—it's a special series. Cheapest one like it costs over four hundred."

"That means our killer is a serious knife collector."

"Or a serious wood carver. There's a gun and knife show starting Thursday at the Natchez Convention Center, and I thought I'd drop by there, see what I can learn."

"Good idea."

Luke checked his watch. Almost seven thirty. If he didn't leave now, he'd be late for dinner.

"See you later," he said and jogged back to his car.

He pulled away from the fort and pointed his car toward Daisy's. Two blocks from downtown he turned on a side street, and a familiar figure walked toward him, her head down, and he slowed. Brooke was supposed to be home, resting. He pulled over and lowered his window. "Want a ride?"

She jerked her head up, and he could see that she'd been crying. "Luke?"

He climbed out of his car and hurried around to her. "Are you all right?"

She hugged her arms to her waist like her stomach hurt.

"What's wrong?"

She shook her head.

"I know something's going on. What is it?"

"Nothing."

That kind of nothing always meant trouble. "I don't believe you."

Brooke drew herself up. "What were you doing at Emerald Mound today?"

Luke swallowed hard. He should have told her the truth at the hospital. "Just looking around."

"Why didn't you tell me you planned to go there? When I asked, you said you were going to follow up on that interview."

"I know." He chewed his bottom lip, searching for something to tell her. "It's just . . . it seemed important to go there."

Brooke's jaw shot out. "What were you doing there?" she repeated.

Luke didn't answer right away. "I was trying to make sense of his death and looking for something that proved he didn't kill himself."

The fight went out of her as her shoulders slumped.

"Come here," he said, taking her in his arms. "What's going on?"

"Nothing you can help with."

Whatever else she said was lost as she buried her face in his shoulder. His heart swelled with tenderness for her, and he wanted to pound whoever had hurt her. Not knowing anything else to do, he held her until she relaxed in his arms. "I'm so sorry for whatever's happened," he murmured against her soft hair.

He wished . . . what did he wish? That she loved him and he could hold her like this forever. That he could lift her face and kiss away her sadness. Instead he held her on the deserted sidewalk until she pulled away.

"Thanks for being a good friend," she whispered and looked up into his eyes.

His heart plummeted. *Friends.* Thank goodness he hadn't said anything or done something dumb like kiss her. He brushed a wayward strand of hair from her face, his gaze still locked into hers.

"Can I take you home?" he asked, almost drowning in her dark brown eyes.

She shook her head. "I don't want to go home. Take me to Daisy's."

What had happened to make her not want to go home? He walked her to the car and waited until she fastened her seat belt before he closed the door. Maybe she'd tell him. His cell phone rang as he walked around the car. Vivian. "Hello," he said, pausing with his hand on the car door.

"Would you help me find Brooke? She left over an hour ago and I thought she'd be back by now."

"She's with me," he said.

"Thank goodness. She's upset with me, but tell her . . . tell her we need to talk."

"I will," he said and disconnected and climbed in the car.

"Was that my mother?"

He nodded. Brooke turned and looked out the window. "I'm not going home."

"Okay. Would you like to get dinner?"

"The way I look? Just take me to Daisy's. I'll make a cup of hot tea."

He tried to think if he'd left anything on the kitchen table that might give away his undercover operation. Thank goodness he was obsessive about putting things away.

"One cup of Earl Grey coming up," he said.

"Thanks, and I'm sorry I went all crazy on you."

"No problem." No, his problem was losing his heart to someone he would end up hurting.

52

The blocks passed in a blur. Of all the people to find Brooke, it had to be Luke. But it'd felt so good when he held her. Like she belonged. *Stop it.* Luke was still single for a reason.

He turned into the drive, and she wouldn't allow herself to look toward their house.

John Danvers is not your father.

Like a chant, the words ran through her head, and her own voice added, *You were a mistake.* Her face burned with shame. She was the product of a—No! She would not go there.

"We're here."

She startled at Luke's voice. How would he feel if he knew?

"You sure you don't want to go to your house? Your mom sounded—"

"No! And please don't ask me again." She climbed out of the car on wooden legs before he could come around and open the door. "I just need to . . ." She had no idea what she needed. Time. A few minutes to collect herself. Then she'd decide what to do, where to go.

Brooke followed Luke inside Daisy's house. It was a mirror image of her parents' place, but decorated so differently. Daisy's furniture had been bought early in her marriage and were antiques now. "It's awfully neat," she murmured, thinking of her own apartment. If only she could go there, but it was still under construction. "I didn't know you were a neat freak."

"What can I say? There's nothing wrong with being tidy." Luke snatched a paper from the sofa. "Tea's in the kitchen. I'll just put this in my room."

"Sure." She wandered through to the kitchen and found the tin of Earl Grey, and then she looked for the teakettle and saw the Keurig. "When did Daisy get that?" she asked as Luke came into the room.

"I was going to ask you the same thing. Let's see if she has any Earl Grey in a pod."

She stepped back while he rummaged in the cabinet.

"Here you go," he said, turning the coffeemaker on.

Nothing smelled like Earl Grey. It'd been her dad's favorite tea. When she was a kid, she thought all dads had tea parties with their daughters. It wasn't until she was older that she learned most dads didn't. Brooke wrapped her hands around the hot cup of tea Luke handed her. In another minute he drank from his own cup as they leaned against the counter. They'd run out of inane conversation, and an awkward silence filled the air between them.

Brooke turned and set her cup in the sink, then pressed her hands against her temples. The heaviness in her heart was too much to carry. It'd been bad enough when Dad died, but now it was like someone had killed him all over again. Luke set his cup on the counter and wrapped his arms around her. She leaned against him.

"I don't know what happened," he said, "but it will get better. Everything gets better."

He cocooned her against his body and continued to pat her shoulders and rub her back. Safe. That's the way she felt, like when she was a little girl and her world was right side up.

But it'd all been a lie.

He lifted her chin until she was looking into eyes the color of the sea. Eyes that held desire in them. Eyes that were true and honest.

Luke cupped her face in his hands, and she closed her eyes as he brushed away her tears she hadn't realized had formed. *Walk away.*

Slowly he lowered his head and kissed her eyes and then moved down to lightly kiss her lips.

Brooke moaned and leaned into him, slipping her arms around his neck. He claimed her lips again, and this time she felt his hunger as he drew her even closer. She'd waited fourteen years for this even as she had steadily denied wanting it. She melted in his embrace.

You were a mistake.

She jerked out of his arms. "I'm sorry."

"What's wrong?"

The rawness in his voice raked her skin.

"I . . . you have to know something first."

"I don't have to know anything." He pulled her to him again and touched his forehead to hers. "I—"

"Don't say anything. You don't know . . ." She pressed her hands on his chest, pushing him away. "I have to tell you . . . John Danvers is not my father."

He snapped his head back, her words clearly shaking him. "What are you talking about? Of course he's your father."

"No." She broke away from him and paced the kitchen, spilling the whole ugly story her mom had told her. "So Dad . . ." The name was uncomfortable on her tongue. She squared her shoulders. "He married Mom so no one would know."

Brooke couldn't bear to see pity in Luke's eyes and dropped her gaze to the floor.

"I'm sorry." He gently lifted her chin. "You have nothing to be ashamed of." His eyes were tender and without a shred of pity in them.

"I'm not ashamed." She said it too quickly, like saying it would make it true. "I'm hurt no one told me."

"That would have been a hard call," Luke said. "Can't you rest in knowing he loved your mom and you?"

"If . . . if he'd loved me, he would have told me the truth."

"Maybe he was afraid of losing you. Think about it. When would have been a good time? Not when you were too young to understand, and teenage years are hard enough—I can see how each year would have made it harder to sit you down and tell you."

She hated that what he said made so much sense.

"Look at it this way. He loved your mom, he loved you and Meghan, and he didn't want you to ever feel different."

"I know what you're saying, but it doesn't change the fact that my whole life has been a lie."

53

Luke wished he could convince Brooke nothing had really changed. John Danvers had loved her as much as he loved Meghan. He was certain of that. She winced and rubbed the side of her neck.

"Neck hurting?"

"And my head."

He turned her around and gently massaged the knots in her neck and shoulders. "Why don't you go home and rest?"

"I can't. I need a little more time to think things through before I see Mom again."

"You have to be exhausted. Why don't you get in Daisy's recliner?"

Brooke glanced toward the chair. "What will you do?"

"I have plenty to do. Check my email, maybe fix a bite to eat a little later."

"Will you wake me after an hour?"

"Absolutely."

Luke found an afghan that Daisy had knitted, and once Brooke was in the recliner, he spread it over her. "Let me know if you need anything. I'll be in Daisy's study."

He closed the study door before he checked his email, then he texted Vivian to let her know Brooke was all right and that she was resting and received a reply of thanks. He glanced at the evidence board and made a note about the shoe print and blood they'd found, and then he checked on Brooke. Sound asleep. He should be able to get away long enough to transfer the heroin.

Luke dialed Delaney. "Are you back in Natchez?"

"Just got back."

"Where can we meet so I can give you the heroin?" Luke kept his voice low.

"How about your place?"

"Brooke's here."

"Can you take a walk? I'll intercept you somewhere on your block."

That should be safe enough, and hopefully Brooke would sleep through the meeting. "See you in a minute."

Luke wrote Brooke a note telling her he'd gone for a walk and left it on the coffee table. He stared down at her sleeping form, reliving the kiss they'd shared. The way she'd responded spread warmth through his chest. She'd enjoyed it as much as he had.

Jeremy Steele.

Luke winced. What had he been thinking? He could never offer the kind of relationship Steele wanted to give her. His work was too dangerous. But other undercover rangers married. Could he risk laying his heart on the line? She wanted someone who could give 100 percent. Could he do that? He never had before, didn't know that he could now. And when she discovered he was working undercover and that he'd lied to her, everything else would be irrelevant.

The afghan had slipped to the side, and Luke retucked it around her. He just hoped he hadn't messed up anything for her with Jeremy. *Maybe Jeremy isn't the right man for her.* He pushed the thought away as he slipped out the door, but it wouldn't stay gone.

54

*S*he strode toward her car and grabbed her phone. When Brooke turned around, Sharon was looking over her shoulder, staring into the house. Then she saw it. A ball of flame exploding out the front door—

Brooke jerked awake, fighting whatever trapped her arms. She gradually became aware of the soft wool afghan tucked around her. She was at Daisy's house. Safety wrapped around her like the afghan, and she snuggled in the chair, remembering Luke's lips on hers.

I'm not John Danvers's daughter. Brooke tried to block the thought, to shield herself from what her mother had told her, but the story filled her head until she thought it would burst. If only she could fast-forward six months, maybe the pain would be gone.

The room had darkened since she'd gone to sleep and she glanced around, looking for Luke, but the house felt empty.

"Luke?" she called. No answer. Where was he? Brooke returned the recliner to an upright position and stood. A paper on the coffee table caught her eye and she picked it up. Luke had gone for a walk. She smiled. Probably needed to get some fresh air. It was sweet that he had not awakened her.

Brooke stretched, feeling more rested, but at loose ends. Her phone rang. Daisy. "Good evening," she said.

"Good evening to you. How are you?" Daisy asked.

"Better."

"Good. Do you know where Luke is? He was supposed to call me back."

"Out walking. What do you need?"

"I was going to ask him to find that book I've been wanting to read."

"I'll check now. It's in your library, right?"

"On the bottom shelf."

"I'll find it and maybe we can bring it to you tomorrow."

"Are you all right?" Daisy asked. "You sound a little down."

Daisy could always read her. "Nothing I want to talk about over the phone. I'll see you sometime tomorrow."

Brooke padded down the hallway and pushed the door to the library open. The room was dark, and she flipped the switch right by the door and blinked her eyes at the bright light. The book Daisy wanted wasn't on the bottom shelf, and she scanned the other shelves, finding it on the second shelf.

She turned to go back to the living room and froze. Someone had turned Daisy's library into a . . . *command center* was the only term that came to mind. A whiteboard, a stack of files, photos pinned to a corkboard on the wall . . . She took a step toward the photos.

Blood drained from her face. It couldn't be . . . she stared from one photo to the next. Her stomach heaved. She stumbled from the library, barely making it to the bathroom before she lost what little was in her stomach.

Brooke wet a cloth and pressed it to her face. *Think.* Luke had been using the library, so what she'd seen in the room belonged to him. Her chin quivered, and she fought the rush of emotion that slammed her. *Buck up.* But how did she buck up when her whole world had turned upside down? Again.

Why did he have photos of the crime scene at Emerald Mound?

Photos of a crime scene she'd been trying to erase from her mind, but she had no delete button.

What was Luke doing with them? He wasn't a cop. Had he killed her father? Were the photos trophies? Even in her state of shock, she didn't really believe that. Did she? She needed evidence before Luke returned. If he discovered she knew about the photos, he might move them.

Brooke pulled her phone from her pocket and snapped close-ups of each photo pinned to the corkboard. She turned to take pictures of the desk. Then she quickly typed a text to Clayton and Dale, telling them she had something they needed to see.

"What are you doing in here?" Luke demanded.

She jumped, almost dropping her phone. "I didn't hear you come in."

"Obviously."

Her phone rang and she ignored it. "What is this?" She waved her hand around the room.

"You better answer that."

Brooke glanced at the ID. "It's Dale. I text—"

"You didn't tell him what's in here, did you?"

"You don't have to yell."

"If you told him anything, answer the call and tell him it was a mistake."

Brooke hesitated. She was torn between doing what she'd been taught at the academy and Luke.

"Please. I'll explain everything. Just don't tell him what you've found."

She raked her finger across the screen. "Hello."

"What is it I need to see?" Dale asked. "Can it wait until tomorrow when I swear you in? Mary is feeling better and we're going out to dinner."

"Uh, sure. It'll keep. I'm glad you found something for her nausea."

"Yeah. Sometimes her medicine works better than other times, and tonight is one of them," he said. "Oh, and you don't have to report every little thing to me or to Clayton. Trust your gut."

"Thanks. I'll keep that in mind. See you tomorrow." After she disconnected she raised her gaze to Luke, then nodded toward the photos. "Okay, tell me what this is all about. Why do you have pictures of my dad?"

55

While Brooke struggled to keep her composure, Luke wanted to kick himself for rocking her world yet again. If only he hadn't been in such a hurry to get rid of the heroin. And then Delaney wanted to rehash the meeting Luke had with Boudreaux.

She straightened her shoulders, challenging him. "I'm waiting," she said.

"Let's go into the kitchen where we can sit down and—"

"No. Right here, right now." Her eyes narrowed. "Did you take this?" She jerked one of the photos from the corkboard.

"Not that one. A crime scene tech took it." He balled his hands, and the stress caused pain to shoot from his fingers to his right bicep. That pain was nothing compared to the way his heart hurt. Deep inside, he'd known it would come to this, that one day she would hold him accountable.

"But you did take some of them. How . . . ?" Her gaze dropped to the crime scene photo. When she raised her head, disbelief filled her eyes. Then she caught her breath. "That meant you were there when he was—"

"No. I came too late, your dad was already . . ." He looked at the floor. "I'm sorry. If I'd gotten there earlier, he would still be alive."

"But there's no mention of you in the sheriff's report."

"I know. Please," he said, taking her hand. "Let me explain."

How much, he wasn't sure, but enough to make certain she didn't tell anyone what she'd seen in the study. She allowed him to lead her out of the library and down the hall to the kitchen.

"Coffee?"

"Tea."

"This won't take a minute," he said. "How about something to eat? I have sandwich meat—I could make you a sandwich."

"I've lost my appetite," she said and sat on one of the stools around the island.

So had he. Luke massaged his palm and rehearsed what he'd say while he brewed her tea, but everything sounded lame. Brooke took the cup he handed her and set it down.

"When were you going to tell me?"

He had never planned to tell her. Just find her father's killer and let the FBI take credit.

"You weren't, were you?"

Her cold accusation stabbed him. "That's beside the point now."

Throbbing started in his hand again and automatically he massaged the base of his thumb.

"What's wrong with your hand? You keep rubbing it."

He flexed his fingers. "Nothing."

"Do you ever tell the truth? I've seen you rub your palm before, so something is definitely wrong."

Luke understood her change of focus—it was her mind's way of coping, putting off the pain it knew was coming. He didn't care, he'd take the reprieve.

"I had an injury to my bicep and it affected my hand."

"What kind of injury?"

Luke took a deep breath. "It's part of what I need to tell you, but before I can, you have to promise you won't repeat anything you learn tonight. You can't tell Pete Nelson or the sheriff or even Dale and Clayton. Can you agree to those conditions?"

"I don't like making promises without knowing what I'm promising," she said, glancing toward the hallway door. "But I bet if I don't, you won't answer my questions."

"You're right," he said.

She gripped the cup, the ends of her fingers turning white. "About now I'd promise almost anything to get some answers. Unless you've done something outside the law."

He supposed he had that coming, but it hurt. "Do you think I'd do anything illegal?"

"At this point, I don't know."

"Then I'm not sure you'll believe what I have to say."

"Try me."

"Not until you agree."

"Even if I promise, what makes you think I won't tell?"

"Because I know you. You don't give your word lightly."

56

Brooke didn't know how much more she could take. The photos had stirred the memory of seeing her father's body on the ground Sunday night. Her emotions were all over the place. What should she even call him?

Not her father. Her stepfather, maybe? She shook her head. By marrying her mom before she was born, he was legally her father. Brooke rubbed her eyes. Her head felt as though it was about to burst. Nothing was as it seemed. Her dad wasn't her dad. Luke had lied to her. At this point, she didn't even know who Luke was, much less who she was.

Resolve stiffened her back. She might not be John Danvers's biological daughter, but she was a law enforcement ranger, and solving his murder would prove it. Luke had information she needed. He couldn't have changed that much from the boy he'd been. Whatever he was involved in had to be on the side of justice. "It won't go any further than this kitchen, but I want to know everything, starting with what's wrong with your hand."

Luke massaged his palm again, almost like a reflex, then took a deep breath and pushed up the sleeve on his right arm, revealing an angry red scar on his bicep.

"A while back I was shot. The bullet hit my bicep, and surgery to remove it damaged nerves in my hand, affecting my grip. I'm still rehabbing it."

Her mind took a moment to clear from the shock. "Why were you shot?"

"Because . . ." He rubbed the inside of his hand again. "I'm an undercover ranger with the Investigative Services Branch, and a drug deal went bad."

She gaped at him. Nothing he could have said would have surprised her more. "ISB? No way. Dale would know, and he would have told me."

"Dale has purposely been kept out of the loop. But you want proof? I'll be right back."

Brooke tried to wrap her mind around what he'd told her as he walked out of the kitchen. If it was true, it answered a lot of questions. Especially why he'd been sticking so close to her. Not because he cared about her, but for what he could learn.

When he returned, he tossed a badge on the counter. She stared at the National Park Service badge. "You've been lying to me, just like everyone else," she said, her voice breaking.

"Yes. But I had no choice."

"I've heard that already tonight. I didn't buy it from my mother, and I don't buy it from you."

"Okay, maybe I had a choice, but it would have meant breaking my oath as a ranger," he said.

She flinched. He'd taken the same oath she would take tomorrow to faithfully discharge her duties as a park ranger.

"If you were working undercover, you would have done the same thing."

"Okay, I get it, but you could have told me this days ago."

"You know better than that."

Of course she did, but Brooke still felt used. "How long have you worked undercover?"

"Six years. I worked out of the East Tennessee office as Evan McCord until I was shot. After I got out of the hospital, I was sent to Jackson."

"You were working undercover when I saw you outside that bar?"

"Yes. The shooting blew my cover as McCord. When an undercover agent was requested in South Mississippi, I jumped at the chance. Since I had a reputation for living on the edge back in my high school days, I used that to get in with a drug dealer here in Natchez."

"And the beard and long hair was part of your disguise?"

"In East Tennessee."

She relaxed a little. "Well, if you wanted to look disgusting, it worked."

"The day after we ran into each other, I shaved the beard and cut my hair." He rubbed his jaw. "I missed both at first, but they had to go—I didn't want an accidental meeting with someone I'd had contact with in East Tennessee to mess me up," he said, thinking of Wilson. "So here I am, a left-handed Luke Fereday who works as a bartender and is visiting his grandmother by day and by night is secretly tracking down the drug dealers moving heroin up the Trace."

His attempt to lighten the heaviness in the room fell flat, and she let it lie there while she paced the kitchen floor. He hadn't tried to defend what he'd done, she'd have to give him that. And he'd just been doing his job. So why was she upset? Was it because he hadn't trusted her enough to tell her? Heat crawled up her neck into her face. Maybe her problem was she'd made this about her.

"Try to put yourself in my shoes," Luke said. He sat at the island, fingering his badge.

"That's what I'm trying to do."

"We're on the same side, you know."

As much as she hated to admit it, he was right, and not just about being on the same side. Luke had only been doing his job. "Okay. I don't have any right to be angry with you."

He did a double take. "That seemed too easy."

"I didn't say I wasn't still angry, but I'm not afraid to admit when I'm wrong. Where do we go from here?"

Luke took his time answering. "I need your help."

That was the last thing Brooke expected him to say. She joined him at the island. "What do you want me to do?"

"I need someone to brainstorm with."

She could do that. "But why isn't Dale or Clayton or Pete Nelson in the loop on this?"

"I'll let you decide," he said. "Before I got the call four months ago, the DEA set up two raids to catch the Calla Cartel and the runners working the Trace. The heads of every law agency, including the park service, had been included in the planning, and both times the cartel got wind of what was going down. That's when I was recruited for the job."

"You think one of the three could be involved with the cartel?"

"I'm not ruling Pete out, but it could be one of his officers, or even the sheriff and his deputies."

That was hard for her to believe. "Wait, you've been working undercover in the area four months? Why haven't I seen you? Does Daisy know?"

He shook his head. "I've been working out of Jackson until this week, driving back and forth. But now we've upped the game, and I need to be in Natchez. Being at Daisy's is convenient."

She clasped her hands together and rubbed her knuckles as she sorted through the events of the past few days, the explosion, being run off the road, Kyle's murder.

Brooke looked up, and heat rose in her cheeks from the intense longing in his eyes. Instantly his eyes shuttered. "Was . . ." She pulled her bottom lip through her teeth. "When you kissed me, was that just to distract me from your undercover work?"

He hesitated.

"That's what I thought." She watched him as he looked down at the badge in his hands. "You know what else I think? You don't work undercover just to catch the bad guys. I think you'd rather live your life pretending to be someone else because you don't like being in your own skin."

He started to protest, and she palmed her hands toward him. "Don't say anything. Just think about it. And for now, let's move on. How does Kyle Marlar figure into this?"

Luke raised his gaze to meet hers, and then he rubbed the back of his neck. "Kyle's murder, your dad . . . the drugs . . . It's all related."

Her mouth dried. Briefly she'd been able to push her personal part in this aside, but now it came roaring back. "How much did he know about you?"

"Your dad? Everything. He's the one who requested that I come to Natchez."

"Dad knew you were ISB? Why didn't he ever tell me he was in contact with you?"

"What I do is dangerous, and he never wanted you involved with me."

It shouldn't surprise her. Danger was the same reason he didn't want her to become an LE. "Did the cartel kill my dad?"

"Not directly."

"Then who killed him?"

57

Luke picked up his badge and rubbed his thumb over it.

"I don't know who killed your dad."

"What happened Sunday night? You took some of those photos in the library, so you were there."

The moment of truth. Revealing his failure to help John when he needed him. He looked away from her expectant gaze. She'd nailed him with her description of why he worked undercover. Right now he'd like to be anyone other than Luke Fereday.

"Let me give you a little background first." Luke had rehearsed what he would tell Brooke about the night her dad died if he was ever forced to, and now he couldn't remember a word of it.

"I'm waiting."

Buy time. "More tea?"

"No. Just answers."

He flexed the fingers on his right hand, feeling the stiffness. *Just tell her.*

Luke fortified himself with a deep breath. "About four months ago I made contact with a dealer here in Natchez for heroin. Since then, I've been making drug buys, building my reputation with the cartel."

"And Dad knew you were doing this?"

He nodded. At least Brooke wasn't stumbling over calling John "Dad" now.

"What do you do with the drugs?"

"Turn them in and write a report. I'm building a case, and your dad was helping me," he said. "The night he died I was at Windsor Ruins setting up my biggest buy at the time—a kilo of heroin. He called me, but there's no cell reception at the Ruins, and he left a voice message. He'd learned there would be a rendezvous that night at Emerald Mound." Unable to stand the pain in her face, Luke shifted his gaze to his hands. "I didn't get his message in time. When I finally got there, he was . . . gone."

Brooke leaned forward. "But he went anyway, without backup. Was it because he didn't trust anyone else?"

"Yes, and he expected me to be there."

"Don't beat yourself up for that. You were doing your job, and when he didn't hear from you, he had to know you were tied up."

She wasn't angry with him? He swallowed. "But I failed him."

Brooke leaned across the counter and took his hands in hers. "You didn't fail him. He should have called it off when he didn't hear from you."

"I've wondered so many times why he didn't. Your dad wasn't reckless."

She released his hands, and he immediately missed the soft touch of her fingers.

Brooke stood and took their cups to the sink and rinsed them. When she turned around, she said, "How did he know there was a rendezvous Sunday night, anyway?"

"He didn't say in the voice mail."

Her brows drew together. "It's all so confusing. How does Kyle Marlar fit into all of this?"

There was much Brooke didn't know. He explained how and why he'd gotten involved with Kyle Marlar and about the information Brandon had downloaded to the flash drive. "Evidently he was something of a hacker, but why he hacked into the Boudreaux Enterprises system is a mystery. Maybe he was just honing his skills."

"Justin Boudreaux . . ." She shook her head. "I can't believe he's mixed up in drugs. He owns a chain of grocery stores that stretch cross the South. He's even building one here in Natchez."

"Grocery stores, mini marts, anything that handles cash is a good way to launder drug money."

She fell silent. "You better really have the goods on him when you arrest him."

"I know, but if I could get my hands on that data drive and hand it over to a forensic accountant, it would solidify our case," he said. "Or if I could get my hands on the photos Kyle took at Emerald Mound Sunday night."

"What photos?" She stared hard at him. "Kyle was at Emerald Mound Sunday night? Why?"

"He thought the courier might know the true story about Brandon. He admitted to being there and took pictures of the transfer. I think he might have added them to the data drive he was giving to me, but I can't find it."

"Then he knew who killed my dad."

"I'm afraid he left before your dad arrived and claimed he didn't know John was coming. His plan was to use the photos as leverage for information about Brandon. I warned him the courier probably didn't know anything about his son's murder, but Kyle thought even if he didn't know the info, he could get it."

Brooke shook her head. "It's unrealistic that a courier could get that kind of information. Do you think Kyle really had photos or was he bluffing?"

"I think he had them. The night Kyle died, he passed me a corner piece of a photo."

"When? And how?"

"Right before the paramedics arrived. It was only a small piece and I figure his killer tore the rest of the photo from his hand."

"And you never told anyone?"

"I told my boss, and the FBI agent investigating Kyle's death, . . . oh, and the FBI agent is looking into your father's death as well."

"Finally." Brooke took a deep breath. "I want to see the photos in the library now."

58

Brooke followed Luke down the hall. At the library door, he turned to her.

"Are you certain you want to see this?"

The scene from Sunday night was imprinted on her brain, and she would rather do anything in the world than look at pictures that refreshed that memory. "It doesn't matter whether I want to or not, I have to."

"It's not going to be pretty."

"Show me the ones that prove he didn't kill himself first."

Luke walked ahead of her to the board and removed two photos, and then handed them to her. "What do you see that's different?" he asked.

Her gaze was drawn to the body in spite of trying to avoid it. Briefly she closed her eyes, and when she opened them again, she focused on everything but his body and examined the picture. Then she switched to the other photo. They were the same . . . No, there was a tiny difference. "What's that?" she asked, pointing to a light-colored object.

"A pocketknife. I took this photo with my phone. The one without a knife is from the crime scene photographer."

"That means . . ." She shook off the fatigue that suddenly hit her. "The knife was there when you arrived but gone by the time Gary and I arrived and when the crime scene photographer took his pictures."

"That's right."

Someone had been with him before he died, and they dropped their knife. The only reason they returned was . . . "Whoever owns this knife killed my father."

"That's what I believe. And for the record, I always told your dad you would make a good LE."

She warmed under his praise. "You actually told him that?"

"Yep."

Brooke was learning Luke and her dad had a closer relationship than she ever imagined.

"See this mark?" He hovered a magnifying glass over the knife. "Only Boker stamps their knives with this tree-brand."

"Boker? I've never seen a knife by that name."

"It's not one you'll often see around here."

A wave of dizziness hit her and she swayed against him.

"Whoa. Are you okay?"

"The room is moving. I think I better sit down."

He helped her to a chair. "It's after eleven. You should have been in bed hours ago," he said. "But you can't stay here with me. It wouldn't look right."

It was plain that Luke thought she should go home, but that would mean facing her mother. Maybe she'd already gone to bed. No. Her mom would be waiting for her to come home. While the pain wasn't as raw as it had been, it wasn't gone. The hurt in her mother's face when Brooke walked out the door flashed in her mind. Her mom was hurting too.

She could have put you up for adoption . . . or had an abortion.

Those thoughts had lingered in the back of Brooke's mind, flashing forward briefly before she blocked them. She should be grateful her mom hadn't. And she was, or would be when she had time to process everything. It was just that she'd been close to her dad, and it really hurt that he hadn't told her.

"Would it have changed anything if you'd known the truth?"

"Now we'll never know, will we?"

"Your mom is hurting as much as you are," he said.

"I know."

"She's worried about you."

"You've talked to her?"

"Briefly, and texts. She needs to see that you're all right."

Brooke could imagine her pacing the floor, looking out the front window like she had when Brooke and Meghan were teenagers. Meghan. She had to be told. Or did she already know? Running away from the problem wasn't going to solve it, but she was in no shape to face it tonight. If only she could simply walk into the house and have everything be normal. Maybe . . .

"Will you go with me? If you're there, Mom won't say anything."

"I don't think it's a good idea for me to intrude."

"It won't be intruding," she said. "And if you don't go, then neither am I. I'll just wait and go home in the morning."

"You're not spending the night here," he said. "But I can put you up in a hotel."

"I can't let you do that. Just come with me to break the ice. You don't have to stay long—just long enough for me to tell Mom I'm going to bed."

He dipped his head, resignation on his face. "Okay."

Luke texted her mom, then locked the door and offered his arm for her to lean on. She took it gladly. "Can I ask you something?" she said as he helped her down his porch steps.

"You can ask. Not sure I'll answer."

"Why did you go into undercover work?"

He laughed. "Different reasons, but you pretty well nailed it earlier."

"I shouldn't have said that," she said. "Did you always want to do undercover work?"

"Not really. After I left Annapolis and joined the army, I ended up in the military police. When I mustered out, I applied to be a seasonal park ranger, thanks to your dad. I worked up around

Oregon and Washington and was eventually recruited by the Investigative Services Branch to work undercover. Turned out I was pretty good at it."

Why hadn't her father told her he'd kept up with Luke and that he'd become a ranger? Or that Luke had been shot—she was pretty sure her dad had known about it. "You never really told me how you got shot."

He stilled and almost seemed to quit breathing. "That's a story for another night," he said quietly.

His words hid a heap of hurt, and she hoped one day he'd trust her enough to share what happened. "How does your dad feel about your career? He has to be proud of you."

"Proud? Who knows? The Admiral envisioned me following in his footsteps at Annapolis and then a career in the navy, retiring preferably as a captain but nothing less than a lieutenant commander. He only calls when he wants to know something about Daisy."

It had always surprised her that he'd bucked William L. Fereday and dropped out of Annapolis. The austere disciplinarian she'd observed could not have made it easy for Luke to deviate from the path he'd picked out for his son. It was no wonder Luke had gravitated toward her dad. John Danvers had been a nurturer and an encourager. The world lost a good man when someone murdered him.

"Thanks for being here for me tonight," she said when they reached the steps at her parents' house. The porch light bathed them in a soft glow.

"Try to get some rest. Tomorrow is your big day."

"You're still coming to my swearing in, aren't you?" She looked up. He had the bluest eyes she'd ever seen.

"Three o'clock?"

She nodded. "We'll go to church first. Why don't you come with us?"

"As much as I'd like to, I better not. A churchgoing believer isn't exactly the reputation I've cultivated. Ready to go in?"

Not really, but she nodded and opened the door. A faint smell of tomato sauce and garlic and whatever else her mother put in lasagna lingered in the house.

"We're here," she called as they walked into the living room.

Almost immediately Toby bounded into the living room, and Brooke scooped him up as her mother appeared in the doorway.

"Good. Have you eaten?"

Brooke almost laughed. It was easy to tell her mother was raised in the South—she believed food cured everything.

"No," Luke said. "Not since a late breakfast."

"It's much too late to eat lasagna, but how about an omelet?" her mom asked with a quiver in her voice.

"Sounds really good," Luke said, breaking the awkward moment.

Her mother's gaze darted to Brooke, and the ice encasing her heart cracked. "It does," Brooke said softly. She'd never seen her mom so unsettled, almost fearful.

"Well, don't just stand there." Her mom stood in the hall doorway and motioned them to the kitchen.

Luke moved first, taking time to put his arm around her mom's shoulders. "Thanks, Vivian. I'm starved."

She surprised Brooke by leaning into his embrace. Her mom was not a touchy-feely person. And she'd never thought of her mom as fragile, but that was the only way to describe her tonight.

"I'm glad you came home," she said, softly laying her hand on Brooke's arm.

"I didn't mean to hurt you," she said, patting her mother's hand.

"I know, but let's not talk about it tonight. You need time."

The back of Brooke's throat ached. They had a long way to go, but just maybe they would get through this together.

59

Sunday morning at seven, Brooke's alarm went off. She hit snooze and rolled over, but sleep eluded her. She had much to do before church. The rich aroma of coffee brewed in a drip coffeemaker tickled her nose. No single-cup, lightning-fast coffee for Vivian Danvers.

Brooke sighed and rolled out of bed before the alarm sounded again. She wanted to get down everything she remembered about the explosion before leaving for church, as well as a few thoughts about the case.

After letting Toby out in the fenced backyard, she grabbed a cup of coffee and a warm cinnamon roll from the counter while she waited for him to come back in. Brooke hadn't seen her mom, but she'd been busy baking already. Probably getting dressed now. By the end of dinner last night, everything had nearly returned to normal—at least normal for her mom and Brooke.

She understood a little better now why they'd never had a really close relationship. Every time her mom looked at her, she probably remembered the awful night Brooke was conceived. And then to keep it secret all these years. It was a lot to think about and process, and they both needed time to heal.

After showering, she pulled her hair up in a ponytail and then stared at the dark circles under her eyes. What had she done with the concealer her mom gave her the day of the funeral?

Brooke rummaged in a drawer until she found the small box that contained what little makeup she owned and applied concealer under her eyes. Feeling awkward, she added a little mascara, and even powder and lipstick. Staring in the mirror, she nodded. "How do I look, Toby?"

He barked and wagged his tail.

She laughed. "That good, huh? But now I have to get busy."

Brooke was good at compartmentalizing and turned her total attention to the computer. She started with Kyle's murder and moved to the incident on the Trace. Next she wrote every detail she could remember about being with Sharon Marlar. As she wrote, a few puzzle pieces fell into place.

If their theory was correct about her dad knowing the identity of the drug runner, the break-in Thursday night made sense—the intruder was searching for a file her dad may have had on him. And she probably wasn't the target at the Marlar house, either. No, the killer had probably been looking for photographs Kyle may have taken. Brooke was careful not to write anything about Luke. She'd given her word that what she'd learned wouldn't leave his house.

Brooke was so focused she barely heard the light tap at her door.

"Are you about ready?"

She rubbed her eyes and checked her watch. Ten? She was almost finished.

Her mom was dropping her off at the Marlars after church to pick up her car, and Brooke checked her watch. She couldn't believe it was ten already. "Give me a minute."

"Be sure and put Toby in your bathroom," her mom called.

Brooke quickly finished the document and sent it to her printer as she grabbed her purse.

"Did you put the dog up?" her mom asked as Brooke fastened her seat belt.

"Yes, ma'am," she said. Fifteen minutes later they slipped

into their seats on the row they always sat in just as the organ music began. As they sang the first song, once again Brooke wished she'd gotten her mother's alto instead of her tuneless voice. But the pastor always said the only thing required was a joyful noise, and she could do that. When they stood for the last song before the sermon, movement caught her attention and she turned to her right. Molly Steele had her dad by the hand, pulling him to her pew. Jeremy gave a warm smile and joined in the singing.

"Hi, Miss Brooke," Molly whispered as they sat down at the end of the song.

"Hi to you too," she replied, touching her nose. "You look mighty pretty today."

The girl turned to her dad. "See, I told you Miss Brooke would like it if we sat by her."

He put his finger to his lips and nodded toward the pulpit, where the pastor waited for everyone to get settled before starting his sermon.

Heat flooded Brooke's chest as she remembered the kiss she and Luke had shared. She picked at her fingernail. There was no reason to feel guilty. But she did, especially with Jeremy sitting close by.

She shook the thoughts off and focused on the pastor's sermon. Beside her Molly fidgeted, and Jeremy handed her a sheet to draw on. When the sermon ended, Brooke leaned over to see what she'd drawn. Two large stick figures and a tiny one with a house drawn around them. A family. Her heart sank. The mama had a ponytail. Like Brooke's.

The song ended and Molly grabbed Brooke's hand. "Come eat with us," she said.

Brooke looked over her shoulder at her mother.

"Your mom is welcome too," Jeremy said.

Brooke checked the time. Noon. "I have to be at Port Gibson at three," she said. "I really don't have time today."

"Does that mean you're being sworn in today?" he asked.

She winced. "I'm sorry, I forgot to tell you that after the explosion, Dale set it up for today. You're welcome to come if you'd like, but don't feel you have to."

"Tell you what," he said. "My cook has lunch ready for us. Why don't you and your mom join us, and then I'll drive you both to Port Gibson. I'd love to be there when you're commissioned."

"Me too!" Molly cried, then frowned. "What's 'missioned?"

They all laughed, and Jeremy explained it to his daughter. Brooke didn't miss her mom's raised eyebrows encouraging her to say yes. "It sounds nice," she said, "but I have to go home and change into my uniform before the ceremony."

"You would have plenty of time to do that after lunch," her mom said.

She looked from her mom to Jeremy. This shouldn't be so hard, but the memory of Luke's kiss wouldn't go away. Then Jeremy's gaze captured hers, and briefly everything else faded away.

"Listen to your mom," he said, breaking the spell.

Even as her heart returned to normal, Brooke felt . . . like she was on an emotional roller coaster. For someone who rarely dated the same man more than three times, here she was drawn to two men. Why did that make her feel guilty?

Stop! She'd had a few dates with Jeremy and had never been out on a date with Luke. No, she'd just shared a kiss with him. And lunch with Jeremy and Molly and Brooke's mom was not exactly a date. That settled, she calculated the time. It wouldn't take any longer to drop by Jeremy's house and eat than to find a restaurant. Besides, she hadn't missed the twinkle in her mom's eyes when she smiled at Molly. Evidently one grandchild wasn't enough.

"It sounds like we'll be having lunch with you," she said, giving him a tentative smile. "But we can't stay long. And we'll meet you at Port Gibson later—that is, if you really want to be there."

"We do," Jeremy said.

"Yay!" Molly danced where she stood. "Let's go. I'm hungry."

"You're always hungry," he said, leading her out. Then he waited for them to exit. Molly grabbed her hand and walked to the car with her.

Brooke drove her mom's car, and fifteen minutes later, she followed Jeremy's BMW through the gates at Wildwood, nodding at two men stationed in the gatehouse.

"This is a beautiful place," her mom said.

Towering oaks surrounded the two-story mansion. Wildwood was one of many Civil War–era homes in Natchez and was rich with the early history of the area. It had been a hospital during the war, and while it was on the spring pilgrimage tour last year, Brooke had missed touring it.

Jeremy met them at the door. "I'd like to show you the house, but I know you're pressed for time."

"I would love to see it sometime."

"Oh, I'm sure you will," he said, winking at her.

Over a lunch of chicken salad sandwiches and fruit, she asked, "How did lobbying for your bill go yesterday?"

"Good. I think we have the votes to defeat it. Of course we'll miss Kyle Marlar's vote against it in the House. Sad thing, that was." He shook his head. "Vivian, your husband, as well. Two deaths so close together are hard to process. I'm sorry for your loss and that I missed the funeral."

"Thank you," her mother said quietly.

Brooke nodded toward the front of the house. "Those two men I saw at the gate. They looked like a security detail," she said.

"They are. With all the kooks out there, I feel better with them around."

"You can't be too careful anymore," her mom said. "Are you running for the US Senate?"

"If campaign money keeps coming in," Jeremy said. "It costs a lot of money to run."

"So I've heard," Vivian said. She turned to Molly and asked, "You want to help me with clearing the table?"

"Oh, you don't have to do that," Jeremy said.

"But I want to. Besides, that way you and Brooke can talk a while longer. Or maybe take a walk."

"How about it?" he asked, turning to Brooke. "Would you like to see the stables?"

"Briefly, then I need to get home."

As they walked toward the barn, she said, "Sorry about that. Mom was kind of obvious."

"No worse than Molly. But I'm not sorry. I enjoy being with you, and Molly is crazy about you," he said. A comfortable silence fell between them, then he said, "Where do things stand between you and Luke Fereday?"

She certainly hadn't expected that question. "We're just childhood friends."

Jeremy stopped and she turned toward him. "Are you sure you're just friends? You've seemed distant since he came back into the picture."

Brooke counted on her fingers. "My dad died a week ago, I was the first person to get to Kyle Marlar, after that someone ran me off the road, and then I almost got blown up. I'm numb to the core. I can't even get excited about this swearing in." She did not tell him she'd just discovered the man who raised her wasn't her father.

He took her hand and squeezed it. "I'm sorry. I didn't mean to add to your pain."

Now she'd made him feel bad. Brooke raised her gaze to his dark eyes so much like Molly's. "You didn't, but could we . . ." She sighed. "Could we just be in the moment? And not think about the future?"

"Come here," he said, drawing her against his chest. "Of course we can."

She relaxed against him. "Thank you."

"Miss Brooke! Wait!"

She quickly pulled away and turned. Molly was flying toward them.

"I want to show you my pony!"

Brooke's heart stumbled as the little girl ran toward them with her arms outstretched. It would be easy to love Molly like she was her own. But Molly and Jeremy were a package deal.

60

Luke crowded into the small ranger station at Port Gibson. He'd almost been late after stopping by to check on Daisy. At the front of the room Jeremy Steele stood with Brooke and her friend Emma. He'd thought Steele was in Jackson. Luke turned as Clayton approached with a soda in his hand.

"I didn't expect to see you here," Clayton said.

"Brooke and I are old friends."

"Gotcha." Then he frowned. "Uh, look . . . I'd appreciate it if you didn't say anything about seeing me at the casino, especially to Dale."

"Not a problem." He turned to Clayton, remembering the way he'd kept gambling after he started losing. "It looked like you had a bad run."

"Yeah." He flexed his fingers. "Just one more hand, and I would've won it all back." He slapped Luke on the back. "Appreciate you not mentioning it to anyone. See you around."

Luke felt bad for letting him believe his secret was safe, but it would be if Clayton wasn't their killer. Luke smiled when Brooke glanced his way, then she said something to Emma and walked over to him. The gray and green uniform looked good on her.

"You clean up well," he said, noticing the lipstick on her full lips. For Jeremy? He brushed the thought away. Even if it was, he'd encouraged the state senator to go after Brooke. Luke plainly hadn't realized at the time how much it would bother him.

She laughed. "Thanks."

"Are you ready?"

"As I'll ever be." Brooke rested her hand on the gun strapped to her waist. "Dale should be here soon. He texted a few minutes ago that he and Mary were on their way."

A small girl approached, and Brooke's smile lit up her whole face.

"Miss Brooke, can you tie my shoe?"

"Yes, ma'am." She turned to Luke. "Give me a second."

After Brooke took care of the shoelace, she took the child by the hand. "Luke, I'd like you to meet Molly Steele."

He bowed and held out his hand. "Nice to meet you, Miss Steele."

"Thank you," she said, putting her tiny hand in his. "Are you Miss Brooke's friend?"

He glanced at Brooke. "I am, and evidently, you are too."

Molly nodded vigorously. "She's going to be my mommy one day."

"Molly!" Brooke's eyes widened as her face flushed, the red spreading all the way to the tips of her ears. "That—that's . . . Why did you say that?"

"You like me, don't you?"

"Of course I do, but—"

"And I like you, so you can be my mommy."

"Oh, honey, it's not that simple." She threw Luke a look that said "help me."

"She has to like your daddy too," Luke said.

Molly frowned. It was easy to tell she was rolling his words around in her head, and then she grinned. "But you do like my daddy. You were smiling at him, and he was holding your hand at the barn today."

Brooke and Jeremy were together earlier today?

"Yes, I know, but . . . it's complicated," Brooke said.

The girl blinked her big brown eyes. "What's comp . . ." Molly dipped her head, trying to get the word out. "Compicated?"

Just then Jeremy Steele joined them, sweeping his daughter up in his arms. "You're not being a nuisance, are you?"

She shook her head. "I just told Miss Brooke she can be my mommy."

"Well, that's something we'll have to work on," Jeremy said, winking at Brooke. "Now let's get you something to drink, pumpkin."

Luke's heart sank. It didn't take a genius to see that Molly held a special place in Brooke's heart. Her ears turned pink again, but Luke couldn't tell if it was from embarrassment or anticipation. He shifted as the door opened, and Dale pushed a wheelchair into the room. The frail slip of a woman sitting in it must be his wife. She adjusted the wig on her head and said something to her husband. He shook his head, but she ignored him and attempted to rise only to sit down hard in the chair.

Luke glanced at Brooke, catching the shock in her eyes. Then she took a deep breath, and a smile appeared on her lips.

"Come with me and meet Mary," Brooke said and pulled him toward the wheelchair.

"She may not want—"

"Mary, don't get up," she said, ignoring him. "And thank you so much for coming."

"I tried to get her to stay home." Dale adjusted the pillow at his wife's back and gently patted her arm.

The man loved his wife, and Luke could not imagine the worry and fear that had to dog Dale's thoughts.

"Quit fussing, Dale. I'm getting better," she said, her shaky voice belying her words. "Besides, I've even gained a pound or two. I wasn't missing Brooke's swearing in for anything." Her gaze shifted to Luke. "And who do we have here?"

Brooke grinned. "A friend of mine. Mary Gallagher, Luke Fereday."

He leaned over to take the hand Mary offered and caught a faint whiff of a sweet odor layered into her perfume. Marijuana. Mary Gallagher wouldn't be the first chemo patient who used it to help with nausea. "It's a pleasure," he said.

Dale cleared his throat. "If everyone is ready, let's get this done."

With one last glance at Mary, Luke's heart swelled as Brooke took her place in front of Dale. This was a big day for her, and she looked every bit the professional she was. His feelings for her hit him like a thunderbolt, but it was more than being proud of her. He couldn't deny it any longer. Luke was falling in love, something he couldn't let himself do.

Mentally he ticked off the reasons why. She wanted 100 percent. On an emotional level, she couldn't depend on him. She thought of him only as a friend. Except friends didn't return kisses like she had last night.

He caught sight of the look on Jeremy Steele's face. The man was smitten, and he had a lot more to offer than Luke. As a favor to her, he should back off. If she could be happy with Jeremy, at least she'd have a good life, and a kid she evidently loved already.

Luke muscled his attention back to Dale as he said a few words before administering the oath of office. Then Brooke raised her hand, and Luke silently repeated the oath along with her, remembering his own commissioning. At the same time, memories of the dangers she faced as an LE crowded into his mind. Luke quelled the urge to stop the proceedings. He reminded himself that Brooke was well trained, and she faced more training before Dale turned her loose on her own. She would be an asset to the park service as a law enforcement ranger.

Brooke turned and faced everyone, but he felt her gaze seeking his eyes. "It's done! I'm official," she said, pumping her fist.

"Wait, let me get a picture of you and Dale," Vivian said. "And then I'd like to say something."

The two of them smiled as Vivian took a picture with her phone. "Send that to me," Brooke said.

Her mom nodded, then straightened her shoulders and smiled. "While I never wanted you to do anything so dangerous," she said, "I'm proud of you for working hard to attain this. Your dad would be proud."

Brooke's face clouded briefly, then a tenuous smile graced her lips. "Thank you."

"And, if we're done here," Vivian continued, "I have refreshments at the house to celebrate."

Half an hour later at the Danverses' house, Luke accepted a glass of punch from Brooke and sipped the tangy drink. Vivian made good punch—not overly sweet. "I can't stay long. I want to work on some of what we talked about last night."

"I would come and help you except Jeremy and Molly are still here."

Yeah. And Jeremy was sticking close to Brooke. He'd gone now to get her a glass of punch. "You can't run off and leave them."

She laughed. "That would be rude, but I doubt they'll stay long. I'll come over when they leave, if you'd like."

"No, don't do that. You need your rest." He had to push her away for her own good. "When's your first official day as an LE?"

"Tomorrow. Eight o'clock. Clayton is going to take me through orientation."

Clayton had bowed out of the party. Had he gone to the casino instead? "Too bad Mary and Dale couldn't come."

"Yeah, but Dale wanted to get her home. I had no idea she was that frail. Dale said she hadn't eaten all day. Too nauseous. I don't know what he'll do if anything happens to her."

"Do the doctors offer any hope?" Luke asked. He couldn't imagine losing someone he loved, especially to a slow death like cancer.

"Mary is taking a new, experimental drug that's not covered by insurance. And it's really expensive—probably thousands of dollars, maybe even hundreds of thousands."

"He has that kind of money?" Luke hated that his first thought was to wonder just how far Dale would go to pay for the treatment. To the cartel, perhaps in exchange for getting the heroin up the Trace?

"I don't know. He has a nice house and a few acres that he can mortgage if he has to."

The man he saw today would do anything to help his wife. He turned as laughter came from the kitchen, and then Emma and Jeremy strolled into the living room, each bearing cups. Too bad Jeremy wasn't interested in Brooke's friend.

"Here you go," Jeremy said, handing Brooke a cup.

"Molly is bringing the cookies," Emma said and offered Luke another glass of punch.

"No thanks." He dismissed the thought about Jeremy and Emma. The senator honed in on Brooke, like he was a bee and she was nectar. And Brooke didn't seem to mind that he invaded her space. "Congratulations, again," Luke said and caught her eye. "I guess I better go."

"Thanks for being here today," Brooke said.

"Wait a sec," Emma said, "and I'll walk out with you. I just have to grab my purse."

Luke was not in the mood for a lecture from Emma. Instead of waiting, he turned and walked to the door. He didn't know why he did it, but he looked over his shoulder. Brooke was laughing at something Jeremy said.

He hurried down the steps and was halfway across the yard when Emma called his name. His first impulse was to keep going, but she would probably follow him to Daisy's house. Slowly he turned around. "What do you want?"

"Just a minute of your time." She walked purposefully toward him.

He waited, tapping the side of his leg.

"It was a good day for Brooke," Emma said when she reached him. "I wish her dad could have been here."

"Me too, but you didn't follow me outside to say that."

"No, I didn't. I was watching you inside, and you got your hackles up every time Jeremy got close to Brooke."

"I never—"

"Yeah, you did. Maybe you don't realize what you're doing, but you're messing with her mind. Jeremy cares for her, but as long as Brooke thinks you two might get together, she won't give him a chance."

"I've never led Brooke on," he said.

"Maybe not with words, but can you honestly say you haven't encouraged her to think you care?"

Last night's kiss . . . but it hadn't been something he planned. If anything, he had planned not to, and he didn't intend to repeat it.

"I thought so." She pointed her finger at Luke. "It's time that you, as my granddaddy used to say, either fish or cut bait."

Her criticism stung. "Look, Brooke's a big girl. I think she can figure out what she wants without your help."

"Not when it comes to you. If you don't see a future for you two, and you care anything at all about her, get out of the picture."

"You have it all wrong. I haven't done anything to discourage her from seeing Steele. In fact, I even encouraged him to pursue her, so just butt out. If they don't get together, it won't be my fault."

"Are you saying you're not in love with her?"

He pressed his lips into a flat line.

She tilted her head. "You know what I think? I think you're not willing to risk your heart without a guaranteed payback, and guess what? There are no guarantees in love. I hope you have a good evening."

61

Brooke waved one last time to Molly then acknowledged Jeremy's jaunty wave before he climbed in his SUV. She glanced past his car to Daisy's drive. Luke's car was gone, and she glanced at her phone to see if he'd messaged her. He hadn't and she typed him a quick note.

Let me know when you want to brainstorm.

She turned at her mother's footsteps behind her. "Thank you for the party. It was nice."

"It was the least I could do after making such a fuss about you taking the training."

"You're not upset about me becoming a law enforcement ranger any longer?"

Her mom lifted her shoulder. "It's a done deal. All I can do now is what I did all the years I was married to your father. Pray you'll stay safe."

"Thank you. I'll be careful."

"I know that." Her mom twisted the wedding band on her left hand. "I asked Dale what to do about John's uniforms, and he mentioned I could donate them to the supply closet . . ."

Brooke caught her breath. He'd only been gone a week today. What was the hurry?

"I know it's quick, but it's hard seeing them every time I open the closet," she said, her voice breaking. "I'd really like to get that past me."

"I understand," Brooke said, even though she didn't. But then no two people grieved alike.

"Then you'll help me? I . . . I just don't think I can do it alone. Besides, you might see some things you want to keep."

An invisible band tightened around Brooke's chest, making it hard to breathe. It wasn't like she really had a choice. She couldn't let her mom go through the pain of packing away the clothes by herself. But as far as her keeping anything . . . there was nothing she could think of that she wanted. "Do you have something to pack everything in?"

"I picked up a couple of large tubs from the store earlier."

Two hours later, Brooke sat on the floor beside one of the tubs and laid the last pair of neatly pressed green pants in it. With a sigh, she looked up at the gray shirts hanging in the closet, still encased in the plastic bags from the laundry. She didn't know whether to remove them from the hangers and fold them to fit in the tub or leave them as they were. Even the tiniest decision overwhelmed her.

"How are you coming?"

She turned to acknowledge her mom and took the glass of tea she offered. "So-so."

"Thanks for doing this." Her mom picked up a leather belt. "It'll take a skinny ranger to use this . . . maybe Clayton?"

"It would fit him." Her mom was doing right, donating the clothes to the unofficial supply closet most districts had. She set the glass down and picked up his flat-hat, fingering the brim. Not that she could wear the Stetson, but in spite of thinking she didn't want anything, someone else wearing his hat was just wrong. "I'm keeping this."

"I hoped you would find something." Her mother joined Brooke on the floor. "He loved being a ranger, and I loved him being one until he became an LE."

"He was a good law enforcement ranger. Once I thought that was where I got it," she said, her voice breaking. She placed the hat beside his backup Sig Sauer. Pete Nelson still had his service gun. She wasn't certain she wanted it.

"I'm sorry we didn't tell you, but you have to know, he loved you like you were his own."

Her whole world was upended and she didn't know what she knew.

"Brooke, look at me."

Slowly she turned to her mother.

"We've never had an easy relationship," her mother said. "And that was mostly my fault, but partly yours too. From the time you first toddled around the house, you were so independent. Before you were even five, you wouldn't wear the clothes I bought you, preferring those raggedy jeans and T-shirts."

"Sorry I wasn't a girly-girl."

"You definitely were a tomboy." A wry smile teased her mouth.

Brooke picked up the roll of tape. "At least with Meghan you got your frilly girl."

She sealed the box, firmly pressing the tape in place. Two questions beat in her heart, two questions she wasn't sure her mom would answer. Brooke licked her lips. "Who is my father? What's his name?"

The glass slipped from her mother's hand and hit the floor with a thud, water splashing across the hardwood floor. Brooke quickly wiped up the puddle while her mom stared at it.

She shook her head. "I told you, he's not someone you want to know. You must stay away from him."

"How can I stay away from him if I don't know who he is? Why won't you tell me his name?"

Her mom palmed her hands. "Don't do this, Brooke."

"Do I know him? Does he know I'm his daughter?" Brooke persisted.

"I'm not answering those questions. It's better this way, I promise. Ask me anything else, but not that."

Brooke concentrated on taping the other box. "The . . ." She took a deep breath and released it. She tilted her head, catching her mother's gaze. "The problems we've always had . . . how did you even look at me without getting angry?"

"Oh, honey, I was never angry at you. When I first laid eyes on you, all I saw was this perfect little girl."

"Then what happened? Why did I feel you were always upset with me if it wasn't from the way I was conceived?"

Her mom raked her fingers through her hair. "I'm sorry," she whispered. "Keeping it a secret created so much stress . . . there were a handful of people who knew what had happened, and I was always terrified you'd find out the wrong way. When you were about thirteen, I wanted to tell you, but John wouldn't let me. He didn't know how it would affect you. I agreed, partly because I feared you would believe you were unwanted or that we didn't love you." Her lips curved in a tenuous smile. "Besides, your teenage years were hard enough without throwing that in the mix. I also worried about how it would affect Meghan."

Remembering all the angst of those years, Brooke sort of understood. "Meghan doesn't know?"

"No, I'll tell her when I return to Knoxville." She laid her hand on Brooke's arm. "John loved you both so much. Please believe he loved you for the unique person you are as much as he loved Meghan—he always liked to say he loved you both uniquely."

She remembered him saying that, but was it possible? Her question must have shown on her face.

"Let me ask you something." Her mom paused. "I've seen you with Molly. Do you think you could love her as much as you would love a child you birthed?"

"Of course I could." The child had wiggled her way into Brooke's heart.

"Then I rest my case."

Brooke sat very still. The feelings she had for Molly gave her a different perspective. Maybe John Danvers had truly loved her like a father.

"I have to get off this hard floor," her mom said. "Oh, I saw that Luke has returned home. Didn't I hear you tell him you'd see him later?"

Brooke scrambled to her feet then checked her messages. Why hadn't he let her know? "I did."

"What's going on with you two?"

"Nothing."

"You said that awfully fast. Are you sure? I see the way he looks at you, and you've always worn your heart on your sleeve."

"Sometimes I think he's interested, then nothing." Today had been a nothing day. Did he regret kissing her?

"Well, just be careful—he broke your heart once before."

"You knew?"

Her mom laughed. "After he left for Annapolis you moped the rest of the summer. I really don't think you ever got him out of your system."

She was probably right. Was he pulling another Annapolis on her? "We're working on a project together, and I think I'll see if he still wants my help."

Her mother pursed her lips. "Before you go, what about Jeremy? I've watched the two of you together as well, and I think at some point, you'll have to make a choice."

"I know. I really like Jeremy . . . and Molly." Brooke pulled her bottom lip between her teeth. "But I don't have to decide that tonight."

62

Luke had spent the last two hours in a strategy session with Steve and Delaney. They were ready and waiting for the heroin to arrive. After the meeting, he'd driven downtown to Bluff Park and watched the sun drop below the horizon a little before eight.

When he arrived home, he hadn't expected to feel relief that Jeremy Steele's Lexus was not parked next door. But maybe that was because Steele had whisked her away to a romantic dinner. The thought made him ball his hands as he walked to Daisy's front door.

What was wrong with him? He should be happy if that happened. Brooke deserved a man who would . . . What had she said? Love her with abandon. And that was not Luke. Did he even know how to do that? He wanted to, but years watching his parents cut each other down . . . Why had they stayed married, anyway? Actually he knew. His mother enjoyed the social position and his father needed her to run the household. At least they hadn't made two other people miserable. Just him.

Fish or cut bait. Emma's words haunted him. Luke had to let Brooke go for her own sake.

Think about something else. Like where Dale got the marijuana for his wife. He took out his cell and dialed Sonny.

"What can I do for you?" the drug dealer asked.

"You said you sold a lot of marijuana to cancer patients. Know any of the buyers' names?"

"A few."

"How about Dale Gallagher? Ever sell to him?"

Sonny didn't answer right away, and Luke didn't know if he was thinking or deciding whether to tell him the truth. "Nope, name doesn't ring a bell, but I make it a point not to ask names. The few I do know is because I know them personally. What's he look like?"

Luke pictured Dale. "Tall, heavyset, dark haired. Late fifties. Somber."

"Man, that could describe half the men I sell to. Got a picture?"

"No." He tried to think if he'd seen one on the web anywhere and came up blank. Wait. Vivian had taken one of Brooke and Dale after the ceremony. "I'll get one."

Just as he hung up, the doorbell rang. Brooke? In spite of his resolve, his heart kicked into high gear, and he hurried to the front of the house. When he threw open the door, she had her hands on her hips.

"Why didn't you text me?"

Brooke had changed out of her uniform into a T-shirt and shorts. "Because I, ah, told you to get some rest," he said. Luke couldn't keep from admiring her long legs. He brought his gaze back to her face. "But since you're here, do you want to come in?"

"I wouldn't be here if I didn't. I thought we were going to brainstorm."

"Something came up and I had to leave. We really don't have to do this tonight."

She brushed past him, and he tried to ignore the clean scent of her perfume that tantalized his senses.

"That's it? You don't need my help? Or is it you don't want my help?"

She pinned him with brown eyes that weren't so soft right now. He shifted his gaze to his shoes.

"What's going on, Luke? You've been acting strange all day."

He raised his head. "I don't know what you're talking about."

"Where do we stand? Last night when you kissed me, I thought—"

"I shouldn't have kissed you. You were vulnerable," he said. *Break it off.* "And I took advantage of the situation."

Her eyes narrowed. "Really?"

"Yes. Brooke . . ." He raked his hand through his hair. *Just do it.* "I'm the wrong person for you."

Her nostrils flared, and her lips flattened in a thin line. Then she poked him in the chest. "You know what I think? I think if you cared about me, you wouldn't let anything stand in your way. You'd find a way to be the right person. Excuse me for believing in you. Again."

With that, she whirled around and marched out the door, slamming it behind her.

He stared after her. It had worked. Now Brooke was free to find someone better suited for her, like Jeremy. He just hadn't expected it to hurt so much.

63

Brooke glanced in her full-length mirror. Other than the circles under her eyes from tossing and turning all night, she looked okay for her first official day as a law enforcement ranger.

"You look very professional."

Brooke adjusted the Sig on her belt and turned to face the doorway where her mom stood. "Thank you," she said. "You be careful driving back to Knoxville this morning, okay?"

"When have I ever not been careful?" her mom replied. "But I really feel bad about leaving on your first day at Port Gibson."

"Don't. Meghan needs you." Meghan's husband had called before daylight to tell them she was possibly having contractions, and that they were on the way to the hospital. Twenty minutes ago he'd called back, saying it was a false alarm, but that Meghan had been put on bed rest. "Are you packed?"

Her mom nodded. "I plan to leave within the hour."

"You could fly. I could take you to the airport in Jackson."

"No. I'll probably be there for the next two months and I don't want to do without my car that long."

"Give Meghan a hug for me," Brooke said and picked up her flat-hat. "And don't forget to set the alarm when you leave."

In her car, she laid the hat on the front seat, and a slight tremor shot through her. Brooke hadn't thought she'd be excited about her first day, but the way sleep eluded her last night told a different story. She was not acknowledging that her lack of sleep was because of Luke.

Brooke put the car in reverse and shot backward out of the drive, determined not to look toward Daisy's. But as she backed onto the street, she couldn't help but notice Luke's car was gone. He'd probably left hours ago. So what? She hadn't expected him to walk across before he left and say it was all a mistake.

No. The mistake had been in returning his kiss.

"I'm the wrong person for you." Heat rushed to her face. If Luke was the wrong person, was Jeremy the right one? Had she even given him a chance? Maybe if she did, their relationship could grow into something permanent. It was just that her track record with men was dismal. Within a few dates, she always found a reason to break off the relationship.

What if Jeremy had some huge fatal flaw? His image popped into her mind. No, if anything he might be too perfect. Doting father, popular with his constituents, good family . . . She squared her shoulders. Like she told her mom last night—she didn't have to decide anything right now.

Her cell phone rang. "Hello," she said and winced at her abrupt tone.

"Brooke? Chief Nelson here. Can you drop by my office sometime today?"

"For . . ."

"FBI Agent Hugh Cortland would like to interview you, and I thought it would be easier here at the department. He wants to go over the explosion at the Marlar house."

Luke had said the FBI agent was investigating her dad's murder. She'd like to ask him about it, but it would have to be out of Pete's presence—it was one of the things she'd promised Luke not to discuss. "Has he discovered anything?"

"Let's wait until you get here to discuss the matter."

"I can cut loose now."

"He'll be waiting for you," he said and hung up.

Brooke called Clayton, but he didn't answer, not even on the Port Gibson landline where she left a message letting him know she'd be late. She changed directions and drove to the police station, where Pete's secretary ushered her into his office. While she waited for him to appear, she walked around the room reading the awards and accolades for the chief. Pete had done well for himself. She looked around as the door opened and a man she didn't know stepped into the room.

Thirty minutes after Brooke pulled away from the house, he watched as Vivian Danvers pulled out of the drive. Hopefully she wouldn't be back any time soon and Brooke shouldn't return until evening. It was risky returning to the Danverses' house, but he had to be certain John Danvers had not kept a file on him.

He'd left his car two blocks away and now walked confidently up the walk to the garage door. From here only someone at the Fereday house could see him and he didn't see Luke's car. First he tried to raise the garage door, but as he expected, it was locked. Same for the outside entry door, but it didn't take ten seconds to pick the lock. Before he opened the door, he turned on a frequency jammer. Last time he was here, he got a good look at the system. The security system didn't have cameras, and everything operated on radio frequencies. He doubted he'd be as lucky as Thursday night when the system hadn't been activated.

The kitchen door was unlocked, and he slipped inside. Before he could close the door and reestablish the connection between the two sensors, a dog shot past him. He groaned. "Come here, pup," he coaxed.

The dog sat down and barked at him. He didn't have time for this. Jam the signal for too long, and someone might come to check. He'd worry about catching the dog when he finished. He left it in the garage, shutting the door so he could turn off the jammer.

The door to Danvers's office was closed, and a quick check of the frame revealed no tape across the top. Good, Brooke wasn't expecting a return visit. Inside the office were boxes and bags of clothing. He didn't bother checking the clothes but looked through the boxes, but they only contained more clothes.

A safe was the only other place Danvers might keep files, and he walked down the hall searching for one. Nothing. He found the master bedroom, and struck out there as well. Maybe Brooke's room? It took him two tries before he found her bedroom.

Her laptop sat on the small desk by the window, and he lifted the lid. Password protected. He didn't have time to bypass it. Beside it was a manila folder, and he opened it. Jackpot. Sort of. It looked like a journal Brooke had written, detailing what had happened the day of the explosion at the Marlar house.

A car door slammed. He froze as the back door opened and the alarm counted down.

"Toby, how in the world did you get into the garage?"

Vivian Danvers.

"Good thing I forgot my medicine." Her voice drew closer, and her footsteps sounded down the hallway.

He had to hide. But where? He doubted he could crawl under the bed. He stepped inside the closet and pulled the door almost shut just as she entered the room.

"I'm going to put you in Brooke's bathroom this time." A low growl came from deep in the dog's throat. "I'm sorry, but that's the way it has to be."

She crossed his narrow line of vision, the dog wiggling to get down. It growled again, then let loose a frenzy of barks. "Hush, Toby!" The dog barked again, and she said, "First you get out and now you won't hush."

The bathroom door closed, then Vivian crossed to the door, her phone in her hand. Her voice trailed down the hall as she talked with someone, probably Brooke. He wished he'd hidden in the pantry and could see the number she keyed into the security system. A few minutes later, he heard the sound of tires pulling out of the driveway, and he breathed again. He had to get out of here, though. She could return, or Brooke could come check on the dog.

He took out his phone and snapped a picture of each page, scanning them as he did. Very interesting information. It should help with his next move.

64

After introducing himself, FBI agent Hugh Cortland said, "Nelson had an errand to run."

"I'm not exactly sure why you want to talk to me," Brooke said. "You should have the written report." She'd sent Pete her statement late last night.

"Going over it again might jar a memory you've overlooked."

The FBI agent took a recorder from his briefcase. "You don't mind, do you?" he asked, nodding at the recorder.

"Feel free, but before we get started . . ." She looked over her shoulder to make sure Pete hadn't returned. "Luke told me you're looking into my dad's death."

"I am. So far I don't have anything other than the crime scene photos. I plan to talk with the ME later today, and I'm sure Luke told you not to mention the investigation to anyone. Right?"

"I haven't until just now, and if Pete had been here, I wouldn't have said anything."

"Good." Cortland laid an iPad on the conference table and sat down, motioning for her to sit across from him.

While she took her seat, the FBI agent turned the recorder on and gave the date and her name. "Now," he said. "Would you start with when you found Kyle Marlar and state exactly what happened."

Brooke bit her bottom lip as she sorted through the events

that had happened since Friday night. Cortland leaned forward and nodded, encouraging her to begin.

"Give me a minute—a lot has happened since then, and some of the events are jumbled together."

"Maybe a question or two will help," he said. "When were you first aware that something had happened?"

"When I heard the scream." That did help to put her back in the scene. She recounted everything that happened up until she and Luke went to the hospital.

"And Marlar didn't give you the name of the person who shot him?"

"No. He was worried about his wife. Do you know if the ME has been able to recover the bullet that killed him?"

"According to the report, it's been sent to Jackson for ballistics, but there's no telling when we'll hear anything."

"What caliber was it?"

He glanced at the report again and said, "Nine millimeter."

"Was a casing found?"

He shook his head. "Not yet. I understand a couple of Chief Nelson's deputies are combing Fort Rosalie now. Of course, if it was a revolver, the casing wouldn't automatically eject."

"A revolver wouldn't have a silencer on it." She thought back to Friday night. "I think some of those pops I heard were actually silenced gunfire and not balloons popping."

"Good point. Do you mind if we talk about the explosion?" When she shook her head he continued. "What were you doing at the Marlar house the day it blew up?"

Before she answered, a side door opened, and Pete joined them. "Sorry I had to leave," he said. "You're not through, are you?" He sat at the end of the table.

"No," the FBI agent said and repeated his question.

What was going on with Pete's scowl? And why was he antsy? Brooke pulled her gaze from him. "I was offering condolences along with food."

"What did the two of you discuss?"

"Funeral arrangements, when the family was coming in . . ." From the corner of her eye, she saw Pete shifting in his chair.

"How about her husband's laptop?" Pete asked, leaning forward. "You said the two of you discussed it."

She turned to give him her full attention. "Yes. She thought there might be files related to her husband's activities before he was killed. Did you find any traces of a computer in the rubble?"

"Nope."

Cortland cleared his throat. "What do you remember about the explosion?"

"Not much, only that I smelled something that may have been propane."

"You're sure?" Cortland said.

"Pretty sure. Has the fire marshal finished his investigation?"

"The report isn't in yet," Pete said.

Cortland scrolled down his iPad. "The wreck you had on the Trace after Marlar was shot. Any thoughts on it?"

She repeated the conversation she and Luke had, being careful not to give him away.

"And you didn't recognize the vehicle or the driver?"

"The Trace is really dark at night, and it happened so fast," she said.

Cortland scanned his iPad and then stopped the recorder. "That's about it for now. Thank you for coming in."

"No problem. And if there's any way I can help, let me know."

Pete shot her a deadpan look. "If you want to help, try to stay out of trouble."

Brooke palmed her hands. "Hey, I didn't ask for any of this."

65

As Brooke crossed the parking lot to her Prius, she took out her phone to turn it off silent and saw a missed call and voice message from her mom. She listened to the message and then dialed her mom. "Toby was in the garage?" Brooke asked when she answered.

"Yes. I forgot my meds, and when I returned to the house, that's where I found him. Did you come by and let him out?"

A knot formed in her belly. "No. Are you still in the house?"

"No, I'm midway to Jackson."

"Good." The knot loosened. "Could he have gotten into the garage when you were loading your car?"

"That's probably it," she replied. "I was in a hurry to get away . . . and I didn't realize he'd gotten out. I hate I bothered you now."

"No, I'm glad you did," Brooke said. "Have a safe trip."

She disconnected and opened her car door as a red Lexus SUV pulled in beside her and rolled down the passenger window.

"Hey there, good lookin'," Jeremy said. "Whatcha got cookin'?"

"Nothin'." She laughed. "You don't look too bad yourself."

And he didn't in a white shirt that showed off his tan. Jeremy was one of the few men who looked comfortable in a dress shirt and tie.

His brown eyes danced, then he said, "Seriously, what are you doing here?"

"Answering some questions for the FBI about the explosion."

"Do they have any leads?"

"As far as I can tell, they don't," she said. "I thought you were going to Jackson today."

"I don't have to be there until morning, so I'll leave late this afternoon. Right now, there's a client at the jail that I have to see."

Like a lot of the members of the state legislature, Jeremy was also an attorney.

"Are you going to be in town long?" he asked.

"I'm on my way to Port Gibson now."

Jeremy checked his watch. "Got time for an iced latte at Java Junkies?"

The way he'd revved her heart up, Brooke didn't need a shot of caffeine, but why not? She still hadn't heard back from Clayton, and there was no need for her to drive to Port Gibson if he wasn't there. She didn't have a key, so she couldn't even get into the office. "I'd love to get a latte with you."

"You want to ride with me?"

"Why don't I meet you there?"

"Sounds good. Let me notify the jailer I'm pushing my appointment back an hour."

Brooke arrived before Jeremy and put in her order for an iced latte, then chose a corner table by the window.

"I planned to buy your drink," he said when he approached the table with his own iced coffee.

She just grinned at him.

"Do you ever quit being independent?"

Brooke thought a minute. "Nope."

"That's okay. I like independent women. Molly's mom was independent, and Molly . . . Miss Independent is her middle name."

"It must be hard raising a daughter by yourself."

"It would be harder if my mom and my sister didn't help." He stared down into his iced coffee. "I'm just thankful to have Molly in my life," he said softly. "And I want her to have the best of everything."

"Then give her your time. She's a special little girl."

"Oh, I know that," he said and looked up with a grin. "And I'm not really sorry she put you on the spot yesterday wanting you to be her mom."

Heat rose in Brooke's face. "That's one reason I want us to take it slower."

He took her hand. "I'm willing to do whatever it takes to win you over."

Wasn't that what she was looking for? A man who wouldn't let anything stand in the way of getting her love?

He leaned forward. "Give me a month, and at the end of that time, if you're not convinced I'm the right person for you, I'll . . ." Then he smiled. "But that's not going to happen."

A month. That wasn't too much to ask for. *What about Luke?* What about him? He'd told her last night he was the wrong person for her. He wasn't even going to try. "Deal," she said before she changed her mind. "As long as we don't give Molly the wrong idea."

"I can do that." He grinned. "One month it is?"

She nodded. "One month."

"Good. We missed our date last Saturday night, so how about the one coming up? I'm hosting a gala at my house, actually a fund-raiser for my US Senate race. It'd be an opportunity for you to meet my friends and a few of my backers."

She stared at him. Jeremy wasn't wasting any time. "I don't have anything to wear to a party like that."

"You'll be fine. A little black dress, pearls . . ."

She had neither of those items. No way could she attend this party. "Jeremy, I don't—"

"Brooke?" Luke stopped at their table. "I thought you were working today."

She had not seen him come into the shop and looked up as he acknowledged Jeremy with a nod. Luke looked like he'd bitten into a lemon. "I had business in town at the police department. And you?"

"A meeting. Thought I'd grab a coffee first."

An awkward silence followed, and she realized Jeremy was still holding her hand. "They have good coffee here," she said, pulling her hand away. "Especially the lattes."

"I would ask you to join us, but as you can see, there are no other chairs," Jeremy said. "But Brooke is right. The iced lattes are great for this heat."

"Thanks, but I think I'll stick to their Kona blend, and leave the froufrou drinks for you connoisseurs."

She narrowed her eyes. He didn't have to be sarcastic about it. What was wrong with him, anyway?

"Nice seeing you again," he said, not sounding like he meant it at all.

Nice seeing you again? You'd think they barely knew each other. She clamped her mouth shut to keep from cracking a smart retort to his back as he walked away.

"Hey," Jeremy said, waving his hand in her face to get her attention. "How about it? Saturday night? You won't even have to bring your car—I'll pick you up at seven thirty."

She refocused. Why not? Jeremy Steele was the most eligible bachelor in Natchez. And he wanted to go out with her. Brooke could borrow her mom's pearls, and surely there was a little black dress in one of Natchez's boutiques. "Sure," she said. "But I'll get myself there."

"No, I insist. That way you won't be able to duck out on me early."

"In other words, I'll be your captive audience."

66

Luke approached the barista and gave his order. It'd looked as though he interrupted a serious discussion. And then he hadn't exactly been nice. Froufrou drink? Had he really said that? He still felt the daggers Brooke had thrown at him.

Even at that, it had taken everything in Luke to walk away. Why did he have to keep running into her? He would be glad when this case was over and he could leave Natchez.

"Here you go." The barista handed him his coffee and pointed to a sideboard. "Sugar and creamer are on the table over there."

"Don't use either, but thanks." He took a sip of the coffee, savoring its full-bodied flavor. When he looked toward the table where Brooke and Jeremy had been sitting, he saw that Jeremy was gone. Hopefully for good. But would she even talk to him now? Only one way to find out. As he approached her, Brooke stood and laid a tip on the table. Irritation flashed across her face when she turned and saw him.

"Don't go," he said. "I want to apologize for being, uh, snippy, earlier."

"Rude was more like it." But she didn't move to leave.

"Rude then. There was no call for it. Could we talk a minute?" he asked, palming his hand toward the chair she'd just vacated.

"About?"

He looked around the room. An animated conversation engaged the couple closest to them, another couple only had eyes for each other, and no one suddenly shifted eyes away from him. He leaned closer. "The case."

Instantly Brooke changed from disinterested to interested and sat back down. "Has anything changed?"

The seat opposite her had a good view of the entrance, and he took it. "No, but a few things bother me, and I'd like to run them by you." Things he should have asked last night, and would have if he hadn't let their personal relationship get in the way. He'd never let that happen before, and he couldn't let it happen again.

"What's bothering you?"

"Dale, for one. I think he's buying marijuana for his wife to combat the effects of chemo."

She frowned. "What makes you think that?"

"I smelled marijuana on Mary yesterday."

"No way," she said. "I didn't smell it."

"It wasn't a strong odor. I don't think you were close enough, and I wouldn't have noticed if I hadn't leaned in to take her hand," he said.

Her brows lowered as she concentrated. "I didn't hug Mary . . ." Brooke shook her head. "I thought she might break. Are you certain that's what you smelled?"

"I know what marijuana smells like." Luke rubbed a spot on the table. "Since it's not legal in Mississippi, Dale is most likely buying it from a drug dealer."

She winced. "A lot of high school kids have it, maybe he knows . . . What am I saying? Asking a teenager to break the law would be worse than buying it from a dealer, and he wouldn't do that."

"He could be getting it from a dealer in Jackson, but since he's well known there, I doubt he'd risk it. It'd be much easier to buy here—"

"Yeah," she said. "Pete's department is understaffed, and it's been a long time since Dale lived here, and he wouldn't be that familiar to people if they saw him buying weed."

"I need a photo of him. Didn't your mom take pictures of you and Dale yesterday at the swearing in?"

"She did, and she airdropped them to me last night." Brooke took out her phone and sent the photos to him. "I can't believe he's buying marijuana on the black market."

Luke could. The man he saw yesterday would do that and more to help his wife. "It's too bad medical marijuana isn't legal here."

"And I don't think it ever will be if Jeremy has his way."

"Do you know if any of his donors are pharmaceutical companies?"

"Why do you ask?"

"Big pharma doesn't want marijuana legalized any more than the cartel. It would cut into their sales of opioids and anti-nausea medicine."

"I hadn't thought about that," she said. "I don't know who any of his donors are, but I will after Saturday night."

"What are you talking about?"

"He's asked me to a gala, and some of his backers will be there." She held up her phone. "What are you going to do with the photo?"

"Crop you out of it and then ask the dealer I've been working with if he's sold marijuana to Dale."

"And if he has?"

Her pained stare made him pause. "I'll have to turn the information over to Cortland."

"The FBI agent, not the chief of police?"

"Just Cortland. I still don't completely trust Pete. And if Dale doesn't have anything to do with Kyle Marlar's death or your dad's, the information won't go any further."

"Surely you don't believe Dale is involved."

"I don't want to think it, but what if your dad found out Dale was buying marijuana and confronted him, maybe even threatened to turn him in."

"And if he went to jail, who would take care of Mary."

"If Dale is the courier in Kyle Marlar's photos—he could have snapped when Kyle threatened to expose him with the photos."

"You only have suspicion." Brooke clasped her hands on the table. "I've known Dale all my life, and I can't believe he's involved in any of this."

"Do we ever really know anyone? Desperate people do desperate things, and you said he was worried about money. If he's already breaking the law to buy marijuana, what's to stop him from turning to the cartel for money to pay for her treatment? Maybe in exchange for driving the heroin up the Trace? Or maybe the cartel discovered he was buying marijuana—if the cartel has their hooks in him, he'd have to do whatever they want."

"Maybe he's not buying marijuana illegally. He could be ordering it from Colorado. Or flying out there to get it." Then she fell silent. "When will you ask your dealer friend?"

"As soon as I can set it up. Had to have the photo first. And he's not my friend," he said.

"Call him now."

He punched in Sonny's number and set up a time. "Noon," Luke said after he disconnected.

"Let me know what he says."

He nodded. "I know Dale is your friend, but—"

"I'm telling you, he would have never killed my dad. Never."

Luke wasn't so sure. If Dale Gallagher was desperate enough to turn to the cartel for money, he would do whatever it took to stay out of jail.

The bells over the coffee shop jingled as the door opened. His breath caught in his chest as Romero entered the coffee shop, flicking a glance their way.

With Brooke's tense face, they did not present the picture of romance he'd painted for Boudreaux. Romero would be sure to notice and report back to the drug czar.

He leaned in closer and took her hand. "Quick! Pretend we're having a romantic moment and then leave," he said, keeping his voice low.

For half a second, she stiffened, then her eyes softened as she gazed into his eyes. A glow infused her face. Desire slammed into him, and all he wanted to do was envelope her in his arms and kiss her. He cupped her hand in his and brought it to his lips, and then said, "Are you sure you have to leave?"

"Yes."

He stood when she did and kissed her on the cheek before she turned and walked to the door.

"See you tonight?" he called after her.

"You bet," she said over her shoulder and almost ran into Romero. "I'm sorry."

"No problem. Have a nice day."

"Oh, I will," she said and turned Luke's way once more.

Her sultry gaze hit him like a thunderbolt. Even though he knew she was acting, the effect was like dancing on an electric tightrope.

Romero approached the table and appeared to pick up a scrap of paper from the floor. "Is this yours?" he asked, handing Luke the paper, then in a voice meant only for Luke's ears, he said, "There's been a delay."

Luke glanced at the writing. *The Grand. One hour.* "Yes, I believe it is," he said and stood. "Thank you."

He had an hour to kill, and once he was in his Jeep, he drove to check on Daisy. On the way, he called Sonny and changed their meeting to one. Now to figure out how to ask about Dale without raising suspicion.

67

Brooke barely took notice of the beauty along the Trace as she drove to Port Gibson. Thinking about Luke was like sticking her tongue to an ice cube when she was a kid. She knew it would hurt but somehow couldn't keep from doing it. *Luke isn't interested in you and Jeremy is. Refocus.*

That left thinking about Dale. She argued with herself about her straight-laced chief ranger buying marijuana from a drug dealer. If he was, rumors would be running rampant through the rangers in the area, right? Activities done in the dark always had a way of making it into the light. But then again, he would do anything to help Mary. Even break the law?

She passed the sign for Mount Locust and slowed. If anyone had heard rumors, it would be Emma. At the historic site, Brooke turned left and drove past the gate to a low brick building a good quarter of a mile off the Trace. She was in luck. Only one vehicle sat in the parking lot, Emma's park service truck. That meant she would have privacy to ask her loaded questions.

An air-conditioner chugged in the window, more than adequate for the small office. Emma looked up from her computer when Brooke entered. Today her curly red hair was plaited in one long braid that hung down her back.

"I'm surprised to see you today. Figured you'd be out rounding up speed demons."

Brooke laughed. "No, I had to go by Pete Nelson's office and talk to the FBI agent. Hugh Cortland."

"Really? Did you learn anything about Kyle's murder?"

"No, but I do have a question . . ."

They both turned as the door opened and a seasonal ranger entered the small room. There went any chance of asking about Dale and marijuana. She tried to place the petite blonde who was removing her hat, but nothing surfaced.

"I don't think you've met Regina," Emma said. "She started last week while you were off."

After Emma made the introductions, she turned to Brooke and said, "I usually make the rounds now—before it gets so hot. Want to walk with me?"

Perfect. "Sounds good."

Outside they walked behind the building past the old cistern and a row of dark pink crepe myrtles with Spanish moss hanging from the branches. If Natchez had a city tree, it had to be the crepe myrtle—they were everywhere.

Emma pointed to the path on the left. "Cemetery first." Without talking, they walked the narrow lane shaded by a canopy of trees. Just before they reached the cemetery, Emma turned to her. "What's going on?"

Her friend knew her well, but now that she was here, Brooke wasn't quite sure where to start. She followed Emma inside the fence surrounding the cemetery that held the remains of the original family who had started the inn at Mount Locust. "Did you notice Mary yesterday?"

Emma stood beside an alabaster angel almost as tall as the petite ranger, her eyebrows knitted together in a frown. "Yes. So sad. I hope she beats this cancer."

"Me too." Brown magnolia leaves littered the ground around the tombstones. "Did you notice anything unusual?"

"Like?"

"Like marijuana." There. She'd said it.

Emma's gaze shifted. "I didn't get that close to Mary."

There was a *but* in her voice. "You've heard something?"

When Emma didn't answer right away, Brooke said, "It's kind of a sticky subject, and you don't have to answer."

"Does this have anything to do with . . ." She swallowed hard. "All the stuff going on?"

By "stuff," Brooke assumed she meant Kyle's murder and the explosion. "It could."

She brushed a leaf from the angel statue and then took a tissue from her pocket and blotted her face. "I know Dale is buying it for her," she said, relief sounding in her voice.

It really was true. She'd hoped it wasn't, that Luke was wrong. "How do you know?"

"Let's walk up to the inn," Emma said, taking the lead on the narrow path.

Neither spoke, and Brooke wondered if she should have even asked Emma about the marijuana. On the brick pathway that led to the replica of the inn, or "stand" as it was called in the early 1800s, there were no trees to block the sun, and she backhanded sweat from her forehead. Silently they climbed the steps and stood in front of the open hallway and caught the breeze. "You really don't have to answer."

"I've wrestled with this for a couple of months," Emma said. "Almost told you a time or two, but I kept telling myself it wasn't any of my business."

It was hard to believe her friend who couldn't keep a secret had kept anything from Brooke. "What happened?"

"You know the drug houses on either side of my grandmother?"

Brooke nodded. Like all cities, Natchez had its high crime areas, and Emma's grandmother lived in one of them, although Emma had been trying to get her to move for over a year.

"I saw him leave the house two doors down, and I don't think he was visiting."

"Did he see you?"

"No. I was inside Granny's house, watching my car out the window."

"Thanks for telling me."

Emma turned and looked over the green field. "You don't really think Dale is involved in Kyle Marlar's death, do you?"

Brooke followed her gaze, wishing life was simpler. "Not really. I think he's just trying to help his wife."

"What will you do with what I told you?"

"I don't know." And she didn't. She couldn't reveal Luke's part in it without blowing his cover. Besides, it was his operation. "I'll add it to the other pieces of the puzzle."

She followed Emma as she checked the restored living quarters in the front of the inn, and then walked through the dogtrot to the room that held shovels and hoes along with pots and pans, even pottery from the 1800s. "Have there been any new developments on your dad's death?" Emma asked.

She almost blurted out about the knife Luke had seen. "Nothing concrete."

"We both know he didn't kill himself. So that means someone else did, and no one's looking for his murderer."

"I think the FBI is at least looking at the crime scene." Again she wanted to share what she knew but instead hugged her friend. "Thanks. I better get to Port Gibson—I haven't made it there today."

Emma turned toward the path to her office.

"I have to find a little black dress before Saturday," Brooke said. "Want to help me shop?"

Emma wheeled back around, her eyes lit up. "What! Where are you going that you'll need to dress up?"

Brooke quickly filled her in on the date with Jeremy.

"You go, girl!"

"But I don't have a thing to wear."

"I get off early Friday. We'll check the stores here, and if we don't find anything, we'll hit Jackson Saturday morning."

She'd known Emma would come through for her. "See you Friday, then."

When she turned out of the drive toward Port Gibson, Brooke dialed Luke's number, but he didn't answer. Soon there wouldn't be any reception and she would have to wait until she got to the ranger station to call again.

Twenty minutes later, she parked next to two white Ford Interceptors and got out. Water from the air-conditioner pooled under the SUV nearest her. Evidently Clayton just got here.

As she approached the low white building, Brooke felt like there should be a drumroll or something to mark her first day. With a contented sigh, she opened the door and stepped inside.

Clayton looked up from his computer. "So how does it feel, being a patrol ranger?" he asked and tapped his watch. "One who's late her first day."

"I called and left a voice mail when you didn't answer. The police chief and FBI agent investigating the murders wanted to talk to me," she said. "And it doesn't feel much different than being an interpretive ranger. Did you just get here?"

"That will change, and I've been here at least twenty minutes."

The oak desk where Clayton sat had seen better days. Butted against it was another desk with a stack of papers sitting on it. Together they made one big surface for them to work on. "That my desk?" she asked, indicating the empty one.

Clayton nodded. "Gary already cleaned out his stuff, and those papers are yours to fill out."

She picked up the papers, flipping through them. So much work for a simple transfer. "I didn't think Gary was leaving for a few days."

"He had enough personal time to go ahead and retire."

"When do we get started on my training?"

The corners of his mouth turned down. "I have no idea. Dale called this morning to inform me there'd been a change. The new guy will decide who will train you. I'm surprised Dale bothered to tell me at all."

She'd wondered how he felt about not getting her dad's job. Now she knew. "I suppose until he arrives, you're in charge?"

"Nope. Dale is. If you have any questions, call or shoot him an email," he said, pointing at the computer on the other desk. "Or wait half an hour and ask him in person."

"He's coming here?"

Clayton nodded. "He was in Natchez when he called earlier, said he'd drop by around noon."

"I thought he was taking Mary to the doctor today."

"I don't know anything about that."

Brooke turned her attention back to the problem at hand. If Dale didn't give the assignment to Clayton, and she had to wait for the new district ranger, she'd be little more than a glorified desk clerk until he arrived. "The SUVs outside. Is one of them mine?"

He nodded. "After your training when they turn you loose on your own. But then again, I imagine the new guy will use yours until his comes in. They ordered a brand spankin' new one for him."

The phone rang and Clayton nodded for her to do the honors.

"Port Gibson Ranger Station," she said.

"Hey," Luke said. "I tried to call your cell, about fifteen minutes ago, but it went straight to voice mail, and then I called the ranger station and no one answered. You by yourself?"

"Nope, Clayton's filling me in," Brooke said. He'd fudged about how long he'd been here. "But it's odd that you didn't reach me. There's always been cell service here."

She checked her phone. No service? "Hold on a second while I ask what's going on." Brooke put her hand over the mouthpiece. "I thought we had cell service here."

"It's been spotty lately. We only have one cell tower, and one of their servicemen stopped by Friday and said they're replacing it. Must have started on it today," Clayton said. "Take 'em a week probably."

"Sorry about that," she said into the phone.

"Did you find out anything?"

"Dinner tonight? Sounds good."

There was a hesitation on the line and then he said, "See you then."

After she hung up, she said, "Sorry about the personal call, but he couldn't get me on my cell phone."

"That had to be Luke Fereday or Jeremy Steele." Clayton put his feet on his desk and leaned back in his chair until she thought it would topple over. "Of the two, Jeremy would be the better catch."

Heat rose in her face. "What makes you think it was either of them?"

"You've had a couple of dates with our state senator, and everyone knew you had a thing for Luke back in the day, and now that he's back in town . . ." He raised his eyebrows. "Besides, he came to your swearing in yesterday—along with Steele."

She couldn't argue with his logic. "Why do you think Jeremy is a better catch? You don't like Luke?"

"It's not that I don't like him, but he doesn't seem to have a job. Neither does he seem to be hurting for money," he said. "Saw him at the casino the other night."

She laughed. "Isn't that the pot calling the kettle black? After all, you had to be there to see him."

He laughed with her. "You're right, but I'm not trying to impress you," he said. "Believe me, if I was trying to get a date with a churchgoing sweetie like you, I wouldn't go near the casino."

"You probably need to stay away from . . . that place, anyway." She'd almost said the blackjack tables.

"It's a harmless hobby. Helps me wind down."

"How can losing help you wind down?"

"That I can't answer—I never lose."

She stared at him. That wasn't what Luke told her. Was Clayton just plain lying or fooling himself?

68

A little before noon, Luke crossed the lobby of the Grand to the elevator. While it rose to the second floor, he slipped into his drug dealer role. This time he'd left his Glock locked in his glove compartment but had kept the smaller pistol and wore it strapped to his ankle. He didn't intend to be around Boudreaux and his men ever again without a weapon.

At room 212, he hesitated before knocking. Luke didn't like that there was a delay in the heroin arriving. It gave time for something to go wrong. Wilson opened the door, and Luke sauntered past him.

"Carrying?"

"Ankle holster," he replied. Better to tell the truth than to be found out.

"Let him keep it," Boudreaux said from the sofa. He was working on his laptop.

"What's going on?" Luke asked. "Is the shipment on the way?"

"Not exactly. Músculos is not coming—"

"No deal then."

"Let me finish." Boudreaux closed his computer and stood up. "He won't be here until the weekend."

"I thought it was happening sooner. What happened?"

Boudreaux shrugged. "I don't know. Does it matter?"

"I suppose not. I'll pass the word on so they won't be expecting to transfer the money just yet."

"That's what I want to talk about. Half the money will go to an account in the Caymans, the other half to a Swiss account."

"We're looking at two account numbers?"

"Which I will provide when we make the transaction."

Luke nodded. "Are we done?"

"Maybe. What's going on with the Marlar investigation?"

"Nothing as far as I can tell."

"What were you doing at the murder site Saturday?"

Luke held Boudreaux's gaze, noticing once again how flat and dead-looking his eyes were. "Looking for my girlfriend's earring."

So Boudreaux had him followed.

"The one you were in the coffee shop with earlier today?"

"Yeah."

The Cajun slapped him on the back. "Romero says you have good taste. Did you find the earring?"

What was with his questions? "No. Ran into the chief of police and an FBI agent and got sidetracked when a shoe print was found at the murder scene."

"What kind of shoe?"

Luke glanced at Boudreaux's feet. "Not the kind you're wearing." Then he focused on Wilson's chukka boots. "More like his, with a pattern."

"Did you find anything else, like, say, blood?"

Ah. That's what he was getting at. Boudreaux was checking to see if Luke was withholding information. "If you already knew, why ask me?" Who told him what they'd discovered? Only two men other than Luke were there, and he didn't believe Cortland divulged the information. That left Pete. Or possibly one of his two deputies? Maybe one of them was in Boudreaux's back pocket.

"I'll notify you by Friday when the heroin will be here," Boudreaux said.

"I'll need a two-hour lead time," Luke said. "The head of our organization is in Jackson, and it'll take him that long to get here."

Boudreaux tapped his chest. "I won't get two hours. If your man wants to meet with Músculos, you better get him set up in a hotel here."

"He's busy—"

"You think I'm not? Músculos is the one calling the shots, and he didn't get where he is playing by a rule book or a schedule."

Luke hesitated. If he pushed, Boudreaux might get suspicious. "He's not going to like it."

"Take it or leave it."

"I'll have to call him." Luke took out his phone and punched in his own number, then pretended to talk with his boss. "Okay," he said, ending the call then turning to Boudreaux. "He can't leave Jackson right now—he has another deal going down, but we have a plane and he can be here in an hour. Otherwise, he said to forget it."

The Cajun frowned. "He would call the deal off?"

Luke adopted an air of indifference. "It wouldn't be the first time when things didn't go his way."

"Is he crazy? He won't get a better deal than this one." Boudreaux's eyes widened. "Has he made a deal with someone else?"

Luke shrugged. "He didn't tell me, but he always has a backup plan. He's superstitious—once problems crop up, he's been known to drop a deal."

Boudreaux locked eyes with him. "I'll arrange it so that you have an hour. Make sure you're not late."

"We won't be." He relished playing this role.

Once Luke was in his car, he dialed Mark Delaney. "The arrival time for the shipment has been moved to the weekend. Will that be a problem for the team?" The DEA agent had a SWAT team on standby.

"No, but did Boudreaux say why?"

"I don't think he knows." Luke told him the change in the payment.

"They're both getting a million and a half."

"Sounds like it."

"Keep me updated," Delaney said.

Luke assured him he would and disconnected, then called Cortland. "Can you talk?"

"Yeah. What do you have?" Cortland asked.

"Couple of things. Boudreaux knew all about the footprint and blood that we found Saturday afternoon. That means someone told him."

"That's a problem because it wasn't me, and I'm pretty sure it wasn't you."

Luke pressed his lips in a thin line. "That leaves Pete Nelson or one of his deputies."

"Be careful what you share with the chief."

"Don't worry. Have you checked the body shops to see if an SUV has been brought in for bodywork to the right front fender?"

"Plan on doing that this afternoon. Do you really think that accident has something to do with Marlar's death?"

"It has to be someone who thought Marlar told Brooke who shot him since Boudreaux said he didn't do it."

"And you believe him?"

"I think he would have owned it if he had and just called it a little misunderstanding. Whoever ran us off the road meant to kill us," Luke said, remembering the way they'd had to hide.

"Why do you think they haven't tried again?"

He'd been puzzling that question out. "Brooke and I both have made it plain to anyone who would listen that Marlar didn't tell us who shot him. Killing someone always brings the risk of getting caught. Maybe he believes us and doesn't see the need to take another chance."

Or the right opportunity hadn't come up.

69

The next call that came into the Port Gibson office came from dispatch. Brooke turned to Clayton. "It appears there's a gator on the road near Turpin Creek, and teenagers are harassing it."

"Kids," Clayton muttered and grabbed his hat. "We better get down there before one of them gets hurt—or they do something stupid like shoot the alligator."

When Brooke signed up to become a law enforcement ranger, she hadn't considered that rounding up a gator would be part of the job description. But all reptiles were protected on the Trace.

When they arrived at Turpin Creek, two cars and an SUV were parked alongside the road, and two older teens stood near the lassoed gator that Brooke estimated to be at least four feet long.

"Okay, boys," Clayton said. "Time to turn it loose."

"Aw, come on, Clay," one of the boys said. "We wanna take it to the pond at home."

Brooke took a closer look at him. Clayton's nephew. She might have known.

"No. Your mama would kill me, and why aren't you boys in school?" he asked.

"Water main broke."

"You should have found something to do instead of harassing this gator," he said, then turned to Brooke. "Grab its tail and let's get it off the road."

Once they had the gator in the grass, Clayton secured the alligator with his own rope and a slipknot. "Wish we had a pickup bed we could get in," he said, then instructed Brooke to get on the other side of the Interceptor while he took out a pocketknife to cut the boys' ropes around the gator's body.

Brooke froze. The knife he held in his hand had a bone handle. Could it be the knife in Luke's photos? She didn't take her gaze off Clayton while he freed the gator's body. The way he held the knife kept her from seeing what kind it was. Once he was a safe distance away, he slipped the knife back in his pocket and then tugged the rope loose from the gator's long mouth.

The gator thrashed about until it realized it was free, and then it backed up a bit and stared balefully at them. "Get on!" Clayton yelled.

After eyeing them a little longer, it slowly eased down the bank to the water. Clayton turned and grinned at her. "Welcome to my world," he said.

She forced a smile. "Nice knife you had there. Boker?"

"Don't know what kind it is. It's just a knife."

Then he turned to his nephew. "You boys know better than to mess with a gator. You're lucky it didn't take your foot off."

While Clayton lectured the boys, Brooke walked toward the Interceptor, and a streak of white paint on the right fender of the nephew's dark SUV caught her eye. She crossed the road to get a better look. The vehicle had definitely scraped something. She didn't know how much damage would be on the vehicle that ran them off the road, but—

"Boy, how'd you get that scratch?" Clayton asked.

She hadn't known he was that close and jumped.

His nephew scratched his jaw. "That's a good question. Dad wanted to know the same thing, but I don't know. First time I noticed it was Saturday. Maybe somebody sideswiped a mail-box."

"Who'd you let drive it?"

He shrugged. "The key's hanging on the wall by the kitchen door. Almost anyone at the house could've used it." The boy lifted his chin. "Even you."

"You sure you're not the one who hit a mailbox?" he asked.

His nephew's face turned bright red. "Ain't nothin' but a little scratch."

Clayton shook his head and then turned to Brooke. "You ready?"

As they drove back to Port Gibson, Brooke planned how to get a sample of the paint on the black SUV. Maybe at the high school tomorrow. Dale's park service SUV sat in the parking lot when they arrived, and as much as she'd like to question him about the marijuana, she couldn't, not with Clayton hanging around. "Was Mary able to keep her doctor's appointment?"

He nodded. "Her sister took her since I had business in Nat-chez. How has your first day gone? I heard about the alligator."

She smiled. "At least I'll know how to handle the situation if I run into another one. Is there any reason why Clayton can't start my training?"

"I was going to bring that up. There's a delay in when the new district ranger will be here," Dale said. "So I'm authorizing Clayton to start your training right away."

"Good." She hadn't looked forward to spending her days only doing office work.

"You seem to be handling your first day all right, so I better get back to Jackson and check on Mary."

The rest of the afternoon went off without a hitch. They did road patrol for a couple of hours, traveling past the halfway mark to Jackson before turning and coming back. Pulled over one speeder doing sixty-five, and Clayton let her write the ticket. Of the other four they clocked over the fifty-mile-an-hour speed

limit, she gave a warning to three and ticketed the last one. This was probably her least favorite part of the job, but if LEs didn't enforce the speed limit, it wouldn't be long before the Trace would be a racetrack.

At five, Clayton told her he'd show her all the bells and whistles on the Interceptor the next morning, and then she could drive it. Brooke couldn't wait and hummed as she drove home. When she opened the back door, Toby's frenzied barks reminded her she needed to let him out in the backyard.

She keyed in the code for the alarm, and paused. What if her mom hadn't accidentally let Toby out? What if someone had broken in? While the security system had been armed just now, what if her mom had forgotten to arm the security system before she left? She'd forgotten before.

Brooke searched each room, but nothing appeared out of place, and she went to her bedroom to change. Her gaze rested on the report she'd printed yesterday. The papers were stacked awfully neat for her. She scanned them, and the thought of someone reading what she'd written made her shiver. *Stop being paranoid.* Other than Toby being in the garage, there was no evidence anyone had been inside the house. Her mom probably hadn't noticed he'd gotten out.

She would run it by Luke later, and turned to finding something to wear for her dinner with him. Brooke soon found her mood turned upside down again. Enough. This was a simple business meeting for her to fill him in on what she'd learned about Dale. Why did she care what she wore? Why hadn't she specified which restaurant? She'd at least know whether to go casual or dress up a little.

Dress up. That reminded her of her other problem. What if she and Emma didn't find a suitable outfit for Saturday night? She shot a quick text to Emma asking if they could go shopping Thursday night.

Calm down. We'll find something Friday. I saw
a cute dress in the window at JJ's that will be
perfect.

Why didn't that calm her down? Brooke practiced the Lamaze breathing Meghan had taught her. If she ever had a baby, she'd be way ahead of the game. Then she closed her eyes and grabbed two hangers. Good, a pair of skinny jeans and a white top. It'd work for business casual. Business or not, her heart jumped when the doorbell rang, and she hurried to answer it.

The peephole showed she'd chosen well. Luke was dressed in jeans and a short-sleeve T-shirt. She opened the door, and her gaze went to the basket in his hand. She raised a puzzled face to him.

"I thought a picnic would be nice. Maybe down by the river across from the convention center. And you can bring Toby, if you'd like."

Brooke didn't remember the last time she'd gone on a picnic. "You surprise me sometimes. And thanks for including Toby—I haven't had time to walk him and he needs the exercise."

She didn't expect a jolt from the lopsided grin he gave her. Maybe this wasn't a good idea.

They parked on the street and found shade near a giant crepe myrtle. Toby's leash had a long retractable line and gave the dachshund room to move around. Luke had even thought to bring a quilt and spread it on the ground. Inside the basket he had a box of Miss Annie's chicken and a small cooler of iced tea.

"I didn't get the cream potatoes and gravy," he said. "But I got her famous potato salad."

She didn't realize how hungry she was until she smelled the chicken.

"How was your first day?" he asked.

"Interesting. Clayton's nephew and his friends had lassoed an alligator, and we set it free." Brooke picked up a drumstick and bit into the crispy chicken leg. "Clayton used a bone-handled knife to set it free, but I didn't get a good look at it. When I asked about it, he brushed my question off."

"Did he act suspicious or nervous about it?"

"No, and that's not all. Clayton's nephew drives a dark SUV that has white paint on the right fender."

"Good detective work. Find out where he lives, and I'll get a scraping of the paint."

His praise warmed her. "You can probably find the SUV at the high school tomorrow."

"I'll check it out in the morning," he said.

"Let me know what time, and I'll help you locate it."

"Another good idea."

For the next few minutes, Brooke concentrated on eating the delicious food Luke had brought. The man was full of surprises. He offered her more tea and another chicken leg when her plate was empty.

"No thank you. I'm full," she said and broached the subject she'd rather leave alone. "I talked to Emma. She confirmed that Dale was buying marijuana. She saw him at a drug house near her grandmother's."

Luke winced. "I hope that's all he's doing. Where's the house? I can keep a watch on it and if I happened to be there when he came to make a buy, I could question him without involving anyone else."

She gave him directions to where Emma's grandmother lived.

"Did Jeremy send you the list of people who are attending his party?"

"Not yet. You don't think Jeremy is involved with the cartel, do you?"

"Right now, just about everyone in Natchez is a suspect." He put what was left of the chicken in the basket and then gathered the trash and stuffed it in a bag. "Want to walk along the river?"

Why not? The walk would be good for Toby, and she wasn't ready to return to her parents' empty house. She took his hand and let him pull her up. In spite of her resolve, her heart kicked up a notch when he didn't let go of her hand as they strolled the north end of the River Front Trail past several unique homes. She turned toward the river and was envious of the view the homeowners had. When they reached the end of the trail, they retraced their steps.

"How are things between you and your mom?" Luke asked.

"Better." She gave Toby a little more leash, but he trotted over and plopped in front of her, panting. "You're thirsty," she said, and poured water in her cupped hand and offered it to him.

"Should've brought a cup," Luke said. "I'm glad things are better."

Brooke stood and turned toward the west, where the sun's rays behind a bank of clouds painted the sky hues of red and yellow.

"Brooke."

Luke's quiet voice drew her, and she turned around. He had his phone out and snapped a photo of her against the fiery backdrop.

"I asked who my dad is, and she refused to tell me."

He approached her. "Did she say why?"

She shook her head. "Only that he wasn't a nice person."

"Maybe she's right. Maybe you're better off not knowing." He brushed back a strand of hair the breeze had blown across her face, his fingers lingering on her cheek. Abruptly he sighed and dropped his hand. "I'm sorry. I shouldn't have done that."

She didn't get it. It was obvious he'd wanted to kiss her, and then he didn't. "Can I ask why?"

He looked past her toward the Louisiana side of the river, then his shoulders stiffened and he brought his gaze back to her. "I'm all wrong for you. Too much baggage. You have a good thing going with Jeremy Steele, and I don't want to mess that up for you."

"I see." That made two nights in a row that he'd made his intentions plain, and it ought to be enough for her, so why did a little piece of her heart die?

"I don't think you do. When this case is over, I'll be long gone. Go have a good life with Jeremy, or if that doesn't work out, find a man who deserves you."

70

Brooke's days the rest of the week fell into a routine. Except for Tuesday morning when she met Luke at the high school to get the paint scrapings, they consisted of taking care of Toby, going to work, coming home. Next day repeat. Then Thursday at noon, she received a phone call from the rehab. Daisy had fallen and was at the ER. Brooke practically flew to Merit Hospital, and her stomach twisted like a corkscrew when she found Luke in her empty room in the ER.

"Where's Daisy?" she asked. Luke's slumped shoulders reflected exactly how she felt.

"CT scan. She hit her head when she fell."

Brooke pressed her fingers to her mouth. "What happened?"

"She'd been sitting for a while and her foot went to sleep. Didn't hold her up when she stood." He walked to the door and looked down the hall. "I thought she'd be back by now."

"Do you need to be somewhere? I'll stay here if you want to leave."

He raked his fingers through his hair. "I hate to go, but I really need to check on a dealer at the gun and knife show. He's leaving after lunch. I hope he can tell me if there are any Boker knife collectors around here."

"Daisy will understand."

Finally he nodded. "Tell her I'll be back as soon as I can."

Half an hour later, attendants rolled Daisy into the room and helped her onto the bed. "How do you feel?"

"Like I did something stupid. Where's Luke?"

"He left. Said he'd be back," Brooke said. She couldn't shake the cloud of doom hanging over her. "Did anyone tell you the results of the CT scan?"

"No. Said my doctor would tell me." She reached out her hand to Brooke. "Honey, I know you have a lot going on, but you seem sadder than usual."

A band squeezed Brooke's chest. She hadn't wanted to talk to anyone about what her mom had told her. Not even to Daisy. But maybe it was time. "Did you know John Danvers wasn't my biological father?"

Daisy was quiet, and then she patted the side of the bed. "Come sit here."

"You knew?"

She smoothed her white hair back. "Your grandmother and I were good friends, and she confided in me before Vivian married John. She was very worried about her daughter."

The band grew tighter. "How . . ." Brooke swallowed. "How many other people know?"

"John's parents, but that's all, as far as I know, and they've passed." Daisy fingered the white sheet on the bed. "I told you once that your lineage doesn't define you. That's still true."

She'd spoken those words to Brooke before she received the results from the ancestry place. "Why didn't you ever tell me?"

"Wasn't my place."

Brooke absorbed Daisy's answer. "Mom won't tell me who my father is. Do you know? And don't tell me it's not your place." When Daisy didn't answer right away, Brooke said, "You know, don't you?"

"I know," the older woman replied. "But let me think on it, and pray about it."

"Thank you." She wanted to press for more information, but it would do no good to push Daisy.

They both looked up as a man in a white coat entered the ER room. "Well, Mrs. Fereday, looks like you have a small intracranial hematoma," he said.

"English, please," Daisy said.

"When you fell, it caused a tear in the covering of your brain. We want to watch it overnight. If it doesn't get bigger and you have no symptoms, we'll simply continue to watch it."

"And if it gets bigger?"

"Then we'll talk about surgery." He patted her hand. "As soon as you're assigned a room, we'll move you, and in the morning, we'll do another CT scan, and if there's no change, we'll discharge you to the rehab."

After he left, Daisy twisted the corner of the sheet into a knot. "I hate being so much trouble."

"You are no trouble, and I'll stay with you until you get settled in your room."

"Where did Luke go?"

Brooke hesitated, not wanting to lie to Daisy.

"What's that boy up to?"

Brooke didn't know what to tell her.

Daisy sighed. "He's not an accountant, is he?"

"What makes you say that?"

"I wasn't born yesterday."

Brooke ducked her head. "You'll have to ask him what he's up to," she said and received an impatient snort.

Once she had Daisy settled in her room, she picked up her purse. "I need to leave now, but I'll be back tomorrow around lunch. Is there anything special I can bring you?"

"A burger from the Malt Shop. The one Luke brought just made me hungry for another one."

"Then that's what I'll bring." She stopped at the door. "And I hope you can give me an answer to my question when I come."

Daisy's smile faded. "I'll pray about it, child. But it really doesn't matter who your biological father is, your true father is the one who spent time with you. Taught you how to ride a bike, held you when you were hurting. That was John Danvers. He raised you, and he loved you." She hesitated. "You need to be prepared that your biological father may not want to see you."

"Trust me, I don't want to meet him, I just want to know who he is."

"I'll let you know tomorrow what I decide."

Brooke spent a restless night. She didn't understand why it was suddenly so important to know the name of her biological father, but it was like an itch she couldn't scratch. She'd always wondered why she had dark hair and olive skin tones when the rest of her family was blond and fair-skinned.

"How do you feel?" Brooke asked when she called to check on Daisy before driving to Port Gibson.

"Hungry. Don't forget my burger!"

"Have you—"

"We'll talk when you get here."

Brooke took her lunch break to go by the Malt Shop and bought them both a hamburger. She didn't get the fries, fearing they'd be cold by the time they ate.

"Here you go, missy," she said, setting the burger on the tray next to Daisy's untouched lunch.

"Real food," she said with a contented sigh.

Brooke picked at her sandwich until Daisy shook her head. "Okay, let's get this out of the way. Come sit here," she said, patting the bed.

Sitting on Daisy's bed was getting to be a habit, and Brooke did as she was told. Daisy took her hand. "First, God knew all about you before you were born. You are not a mistake. He loves you. Don't dwell on the past or something you have no control over."

When she didn't answer, Daisy squeezed her hand. "Honey,

you can either let this define you, or it can simply be a bump in the road."

Brooke turned Daisy's words over in her mind. For the past week, this mountain of a problem had consumed her.

"Does knowing the circumstance of how you were conceived change who you are?"

"No . . . but—"

"No buts. You are the same sweet, caring person you were before you learned the truth. Maybe you're not John's blood daughter, but he had a big hand in making you who you are," she said. "He helped create your moral compass. Showed you right from wrong. Loved you when you were unlovable. A lot like God.

"Except John was human. He made a mistake by not telling you the truth. My question is, are you going to let that destroy the wonderful memories you have of him?"

If she could only flip a switch in her brain. Brooke tried to swallow past the tightness in her throat. She did not want to live like this. "You're right," she said, her voice cracking.

Daisy wrapped her arms around Brooke. "It's going to be okay."

"I know." Suddenly, the chains that encircled her heart since Saturday night weren't nearly as heavy.

"And if you still want to know your father's name, I'll tell you."

Her breath stilled. Did she? The question warred within her.

"I do," Brooke said. "Maybe not for the reason I had before, but knowing me, the question won't go away."

"If you're certain."

"I am."

"His name is Justin Boudreaux."

71

Justin Boudreaux?

"The man bringing a superstore to Natchez?" The man Luke suspected of moving drugs up and down the Trace? An image of the man she'd seen in the newspaper recently popped into her mind. Yep. That's where she'd gotten her dark hair and olive coloring.

Daisy nodded. "One and the same."

"Thank you for telling me." Brooke needed space to process her feelings. She bent over and hugged the older woman, feeling her bony shoulders through the hospital gown. When had Daisy gotten so thin? "Be sure to finish your hamburger."

A few minutes later Brooke sat in her car with the motor running. Justin Boudreaux was her biological father? Grocery magnate slash drug czar? That certainly explained the file in her dad's office. She shifted the gear into drive and pointed the car toward her house. She wanted to get another look at that file.

A text dinged on her phone when she pulled into the drive. Jeremy.

Emailing you the guest list you asked for. You are brilliant!

Brooke had followed through on her idea of getting the names of people Jeremy expected at the gala, but she hadn't expected him to think her brilliant because she thought it would help her chat with them. She texted him a blushing emoji before entering the house.

Where had she put that file? Brooke searched through the first drawer without finding it. The rest of the drawers revealed no file. Brooke tapped her fingers on the cabinet. Did her mom find the file and destroy it?

She dialed Luke's number, intending to ask him if he remembered seeing the file.

"What's up, sugar?" he asked.

He must be working undercover. "Oh, nothing. Just wanted to let you know I'd seen Daisy."

"I'll catch you later, okay?"

"Sure."

"Love ya," he said before he disconnected.

If she didn't know better, she would think he meant it. She walked to her room and booted up her computer. Now that she had her father's name, she wanted to learn more about his background. Half an hour later, she leaned against the back of her chair. Justin Boudreaux seemed to be a pillar of society. Wealthy, philanthropic . . . she'd found nothing to indicate he had any dealings with drugs or a cartel. Could Luke be wrong?

Her computer alerted that she had a new email, and she opened it. Jeremy's guest list. She forwarded the list on to Luke's email and then opened the attachment. Might as well see who was coming to the party while she waited for Luke to call back. Once she had the attachment opened, she scanned it. A who's who of the wealthiest people in Natchez and a few from Jackson. Her gaze stopped halfway down the page.

Justin Boudreaux. Her father would be at the party tomorrow night.

72

Late Saturday afternoon Luke's phone rang. Delaney. He'd
spent part of the day with him and the SWAT team at a farm
out in the county before returning to Daisy's to wait for the call
from Boudreaux.

"Any word yet?" Delaney asked.

"No, but I don't expect to until after dark."

"I've checked into a motel near downtown, and the SWAT
team is ready to go," Delaney said. "But I'm kind of worried that
Louis hasn't made contact today."

There could be any number of reasons their inside man hadn't
communicated—he couldn't get away from Boudreaux, or he
didn't know anything, or he'd been compromised. Luke hoped
it wasn't the latter or that they were walking into a trap. It
wouldn't be the first time it had happened. "Last word I had
from Boudreaux was that Músculos is on his way."

"Waiting around is not my favorite thing to do."

"Tell me about it," Luke said with a dry laugh.

He'd barely disconnected when his phone rang again. Daisy.
He should have already checked on her today. But she'd been fine
last night at the rehab after Brooke got her settled.

"Sorry, I didn't mean to ignore you, but I've been kind of
busy," he said after he answered.

"I'm worried about you."

"Me? Why?" Luke paced in front of the corkboard in the study, his mind on the drug deal and where Boudreaux might set it up. He hoped it wasn't at the Grand where a bystander might get hurt.

"You're making a terrible mistake. You're pushing Brooke away and you two belong together."

That got his attention. "Gram, she deserves someone better than me."

"So you're being noble?"

"I wouldn't put it that way, but I guess, yeah, it's the right thing to do." Except walking away from Brooke had been harder than he ever imagined.

"Why is it the right thing to do?"

"I can't give her what she needs."

"You don't love her?"

Of course I do. The answer was there before he had time to even think. He caught his breath. That couldn't be true. Except it was. "Yeah, I love her," he said softly.

"Then do something about it. Put yourself out there and tell her."

Could he? All his life, he'd never risked his heart unless there was a payback. What if Brooke didn't love him? Suddenly he realized it didn't matter. Payback or not, he loved her, plain and simple. "It might be too late," he said, thinking of Jeremy Steele.

"It's never too late . . . unless she marries someone else," Daisy said.

"Thanks, Gram."

"What'd you say?"

He repeated it and she said, "Drat. The batteries in my hearing aids are gone. Hold on a sec."

"Let me just call you back," he said, but she didn't answer and he couldn't just hang up on her.

"Luke, can you hear me? I thought that package Brooke brought the other day was my hearing aid batteries, but it's some kind of computer thing."

"What?" He stood. "What does it look like?"

"There's no name and no return address."

She couldn't hear a word he was saying. Was it possible Kyle Marlar mailed the flash drive to Daisy's house, and his grandmother had it all along? He quickly texted a message that he was on his way.

He made the ten-minute drive to the assisted living in five, and barely had the car in park before he bounded out of it. After signing in, he rushed to Daisy's room.

Daisy sat in her recliner. "That was quick."

"Where's the drive?" Luke said.

"You don't have to shout," she said. "I found another pack of batteries in my nightstand so I can hear just fine." She pointed at the small box on her bedside table. "The drive is over there. The wrapping paper is on my bed."

He picked up the brown butcher paper that had Daisy Fereday and her house number in block print. No return address. Luke quickly opened the box and held up a small flash drive. "Can I use your computer?"

"It's already booted up," Daisy said, looking proud of herself. "But I want to know something. Are you working undercover?"

"We'll talk about that later." He should have known he couldn't fool her forever. Luke inserted the drive in a USB port. There were two folders on the drive, and he easily opened one. It looked like the set of books Kyle had told him about. He tried to open the other file, but it was password protected and he didn't have time to go around the password. Then he turned his back to his grandmother and called Delaney.

"Is it time?"

"No," he said, keeping his voice low. "Marlar mailed me the flash drive with the information his son downloaded and another file I can't get into. With what we get tonight, this second set of books should be enough to put Boudreaux away for good. I'll email you the files."

Luke logged into his email account and shot off an email to Delaney with the folders attached. The DEA agent would in turn send the books to the forensic accountant and the other file to a code breaker. Things were looking up. He removed the data drive and slipped it in his pocket before turning to Daisy. "Thanks for letting me know about this."

His cell rang. Boudreaux. "I need to take this," he said.

When he answered, Boudreaux said, "Músculos is here. We're meeting in an hour." Then he named the location for them to meet, a warehouse near the river.

"We'll be there."

Once he disconnected, he dialed Delaney. "Boudreaux just called and the Colombian is here." He gave him the directions to the warehouse. "There's a Shell station two blocks from it. I'll meet you there."

At least the warehouse was in an industrial area and shouldn't involve innocent bystanders. Once he ended the call, he turned to Daisy. "I have to leave."

"You mentioned Boudreaux. Were you talking about Justin Boudreaux?" Daisy asked.

"You heard?" Not good. He should have stepped out of the room, but he'd talked low and didn't think she would hear him.

"Told you I put a new battery in, and these new hearing aids are remarkable. Now tell me about Boudreaux."

"Why are you interested in him?"

She pressed her lips together. "Is he a dangerous man?"

"I don't have time to explain right now, but yes, he's dangerous."

"Oh my," she said, her face turning pale.

"What's wrong?"

"I told Brooke he was her father. What if she confronts—"

"Boudreaux is her father?"

"Yes . . . her grandmother confided his name to me years ago." Daisy pressed her hands to the sides of her face. "I never should have told her."

Luke remembered the list of donors she had emailed him. "Oh no," he said. "He's supposed to be at the gala Brooke is attending tonight."

Daisy pinned Luke with her gaze. "You said he was dangerous. You don't think he would hurt her, do you?"

"I don't know." He dialed her number, but she didn't answer. His stomach churned. What if she confronted Boudreaux?

73

Brooke lifted her hair and let Emma fasten the pearls around her neck.

"You should wear your hair down more often," her friend said.

"Too hot." She smoothed her hand over the black fabric, trying to lengthen the dress they'd found in one of the boutiques. "Are you sure it's not too short?"

"With your legs? No. Mine, yes."

Brooke wasn't sure. She liked the high neckline, though. Suddenly Toby let out a string of barks just before the doorbell rang. Jeremy was here. She checked her watch. Seven thirty. Right on time. "I guess it'll have to do."

"You look great."

"Thanks for going shopping with me." She opened the Michael Kors bag her mom had told her to get from her closet and secured her service weapon in it.

Emma gaped at her. "You're taking your gun?"

"Yep," she said. "It's the only piece of advice Dad gave me after I completed my training—once you're sworn in, don't leave home without it." She hugged Emma. "Come say hi to Jeremy."

"No, but I will stick around and lock up after you leave."

"Would you mind putting Toby in my bathroom?"

When she agreed, Brooke hurried to the front door, being careful to walk heel-to-toe in the platform sandals. That advice had been Meghan's contribution to her wardrobe tonight. With a calming breath, Brooke opened the door and relaxed slightly when Jeremy's eyes widened in approval. Maybe tonight wouldn't be a disaster.

His gaze traveled from her toes to her head. "Very nice, Ms. Danvers."

"Thanks. You're not so bad yourself." Jeremy's dark navy suit fit like it was tailor-made for him, which it probably was. Diamond cuff links showed just below his suit sleeve. He could have just stepped out of a fashion show. "You want to come in?"

"Not if you're ready. A couple of early guests were arriving when I left."

"Told you I should get myself there."

"It's not a problem," he said and placed his hand on the small of her back as they navigated the steps. "Your chariot awaits."

She looked past him, and her jaw dropped. "Is that a '97 Ferrari Spider?"

"You like it?"

"Yes. I've always wanted to ride in one."

"Your wish is my command," he said. "It belongs to my dad—he's a collector, and he lets me drive it on special occasions."

He opened the passenger door, and she slid across the seat, the rich smell of leather intoxicating. This must have been the way Cinderella felt on the way to the ball.

Jeremy hurried around to the driver's side. "I think you'll enjoy yourself tonight," he said, fastening his seat belt. "Molly will make an early but brief appearance, and she's excited you'll be there."

She lifted an eyebrow and shook her head. He was incorrigible. "I thought Molly wasn't coming."

He grinned.

"How many guests are you expecting?"

"Probably two hundred people."

"But I only researched the hundred names you emailed."

"Those are the most important guests, and you probably know

everyone else. It's come and go, although a few will linger longer than others. I'm hoping to get enough donations to my campaign to formally announce my candidacy next month."

"I, ah, noticed Justin Boudreaux was on your list. How well do you know him?"

"He's a friend and he's been very supportive of my run for the senate with money and advice. I'll introduce you."

She clasped her hands together so Jeremy wouldn't notice the slight tremble in her fingers. Her case of nerves surprised her, but it wasn't every day that she met the man who contributed to her DNA. And if Luke was right, one of the biggest drug dealers in the South. The thought sent a shiver through her body.

"Cold?" Jeremy asked. "I can turn the air off."

"No. I'm fine," she said as they turned in to the long drive that circled in front of his home. The sun had set and it was that dusky time of evening. Floodlights shone against the Greek revival house, and it stood like a beacon in the countryside. Cars stopped in front then were driven away as guests walked to the front door.

"Valet parking?" she said. "Where are you putting the cars?"

He laughed. "There's a flat field around back, but this baby goes into the garage." Jeremy passed the line of cars in the drive and pulled around to a barn-like structure. "Back when the house was first built, this was the carriage house."

What would it be like to live in a house so rich with history? So rich, period. Brooke couldn't imagine it. After he opened her car door, he took her hand and tugged her toward the house.

"We'll go in the back way, and I'll give you an abbreviated tour of the downstairs."

"You don't have time for that," she said, glancing up at him.

"I'll make time." He winked at her. "Sometime during this 'month' you've given me, you'll have to come back and get the whole tour."

Brooke had a feeling the month would be unlike any she'd ever known. They entered through the huge kitchen that she'd seen on

Sunday. Tonight a caterer was busy with preparation for the guests, and Jeremy stopped for a word with him, then he turned to her. "We'll start with the front of the house and end with my study."

"Don't you need to greet your guests?"

He checked his watch. "Not just yet. Mom and my campaign manager can take care of the early birds." He led her down a long hall.

He showed her the downstairs bedrooms, the elegant dining room, and a huge living room large enough to be a ballroom. Each fully deserved to be featured in *House Beautiful*, even Molly's room with her two-story dollhouse and stuffed animals.

He led the way to the other side of the house and opened a door.

"And this is my study," he said.

"Oh, wow." A massive cherry desk in the center of the room drew her eye first, but it was the floor-to-ceiling shelves filled with leather-bound books that held her attention. "Beautiful," she murmured, rubbing the top of a soft brown leather chair that was one of a set.

"I like it in here," he said. "It's calming."

He turned at a knock on the open door. "Ah, Justin. Just the man I want to see. I'd like you to meet Brooke Danvers."

For five surreal seconds, she didn't breathe.

"You have a nice crowd gathering," Boudreaux said before turning to Brooke and extending his hand. "Ms. Danvers, a pleasure to meet you."

His words jolted her from her daze. She took his hand, noting the firm handshake. "Thank you. I've looked forward to meeting you ever since I discovered you'd be here tonight."

Did she detect a hint of surprise in his eyes? Or was it something else? When he turned to Jeremy, she studied Boudreaux's profile. She had his straight nose, and there was something about his eyes . . .

Boudreaux glanced toward Jeremy. "I have to leave right away, and I need a word with you in private."

Jeremy turned to her, his mouth curled in a tiny wince. "Could we finish our—"

Heat flushed Brooke's face. "Don't worry about me. I need to visit the powder room anyway."

"Go through here," he said, opening a side door that led into another bathroom.

Once she closed the door, she fanned her face. If Justin Boudreaux knew who she was, he did a good job of covering it. And what was so important that he had to tell Jeremy before he left? She eased to the door and put her ear against it, barely making out their words.

Luke Fereday. She heard that plainly. Why would they be discussing Luke? Maybe if she cracked the door just a tiny bit. The doorknob turned silently, and she eased the door open a fraction of an inch.

"You just make sure the medical marijuana bill does not pass."

"Don't worry, it won't." That was Jeremy's voice. "What's the deal with Fereday?"

"It's none of your concern, but Luke Fereday and his organization will be taken care of tonight."

Brooke sucked in a breath. Luke was in danger! She yanked her cell phone from her purse just as the hallway entrance opened. Brooke jumped, bumping the study door as she turned around. A woman she didn't know hesitated in the doorway.

"Oh, I'm sorry," she said. "I didn't know anyone was in here."

"I'm finished." Brooke speed-dialed Luke as she stepped out into the hall. *Pick up.* It went to voice mail. He must be where he couldn't talk. Quickly she ended the call and tapped out a text message. *You're walking into an ambush.* Before she could send it, her phone vibrated in her hand. *Luke.* She pressed the answer button. "It's—"

"I'll take that," Boudreaux said, snatching her phone from her hand. Then he shoved Brooke inside Jeremy's office.

74

Brooke complied as Boudreaux motioned for her to move over by the desk. She scanned the room, searching for Jeremy, but he was nowhere in sight. Was he part of Boudreaux's organization? She hoped not, for Molly's sake.

"Your eavesdropping skills need improvement," he said.

"What are you talking about? And why did you take my phone?" She gripped the purse hanging from her shoulder. Her gun was tucked inside, but could she get to it?

"Don't play games with me. Who were you calling?"

"A friend."

"Now you're being cute." He looked at her phone.

This was her only chance. While he found the message on her phone, she pulled her gun and leveled it at him. "Give me my phone," she said.

His eyes widened when he saw the automatic. "You are full of surprises, ma chère." A sardonic smile curled his lips. "You wouldn't shoot your father, would you?"

She stiffened. So he did know who she was. "Don't try me," Brooke said grimly. "Just because you contributed to my DNA does not make you my father."

The words had barely left her mouth when she realized how true they were. Her mom and Daisy were right. Her father was the man who taught her to ride a bike, who had tea parties with her, who held her hand and fed her ice cream after she had her tonsils out.

Justin Boudreaux was not her father, but one way or the other, he was responsible for her true father's death. Her hand tightened on the gun. "Hand over my phone."

He gave her the phone, and she kept the gun on him while she opened the call app.

"Give me the gun."

She flinched at the voice from behind. Something hard jabbed into her back.

"I think we have a standoff," she said, not lowering her automatic.

"I don't think we do," Boudreaux said. "You won't shoot an unarmed man, but Romero, on the other hand, would have no qualms about shooting you. And don't think anyone would hear—the room is practically soundproof, and my friend has a silencer." He nodded to Romero. "Take her gun."

When she didn't immediately hand it over, Romero jabbed her again. "Give it to me."

Slowly she lowered the gun. *Buy time.* Brooke shifted where she could keep an eye on Boudreaux's henchman, but he was too quick for her. Pain exploded in her head and she staggered, fighting the blackness spreading through her brain. The last thing she heard was Boudreaux saying he had a meeting to get to.

His phone rang and he groaned. Boudreaux. He was tempted to not answer it. Like it would do any good. The drug czar knew he had him where he wanted him. "Hello?"

"I have a package I need for you to pick up and take to Emerald Mound."

"What are you talking about?"

"I didn't think I'd have to spell it out for you."

"I think you better."

"Brooke Danvers is locked in the closet at Jeremy Steele's home office. I want you to get her and take her to Emerald Mound—make it look like a suicide, just like you did her father. Is that plain enough?"

He gripped the phone. "Yes," he said, his voice flat.

"Steele will let you in the back door and show you where she is. He also has her service revolver. Don't let me down."

If only he'd never gone to Boudreaux in the first place. His shoulders sagged. "Have I ever?"

75

Luke had recognized Boudreaux's voice before Brooke's phone went dead. He didn't sound happy, and Luke knew what the drug czar was capable of. He quickly called her back, but it went straight to voice mail. At the crossroads, every fiber in his body said to turn right and drive straight to Jeremy Steele's house and make sure she was all right.

If he did, what he'd worked for the past four months would be for nothing. And the cartel would go right on smuggling heroin into the States. More people would die.

Brooke was at Steele's house and there were at least a hundred guests there—Steele wouldn't let anything happen to her in front of his donors. Reluctantly, Luke turned and drove toward the warehouse. Get this done first. But what if Steele was part of the cartel?

Luke called Cortland. If anyone could get into Steele's house and check on Brooke, the FBI agent could. "I need you to make sure Brooke Danvers is safe. She tried to call me, but something happened. She's at Steele's house—he's having some sort of party."

"How long ago did she call?"

"Five minutes."

"On it," Cortland said.

A few minutes later, the gas station came into sight. Two blocks beyond it was the warehouse. Delaney had parked his car in the side lot, and Luke pulled in beside him and climbed from his Jeep. They would go on foot to the warehouse from here.

"Are you wearing a vest?" he asked the DEA agent. The lightweight body armor was practically undetectable unless they were patted down.

Delaney nodded. "You?"

"Yeah. If they search us, we'll tell them it's a precaution. They'll probably all be wearing as well."

Luke placed the listening device shaped like a pen in his shirt pocket. "Is the SWAT team in place?"

"The commander indicated they would be ready when we walked through the doors of the warehouse." Delaney checked his watch. "Which is in five minutes. You ready?"

Luke blew out a breath. "As ready as I'll ever be."

He scanned their surroundings as they jogged to the warehouse. The land next to the warehouse looked like a graveyard for old earthmoving equipment. Anyone could hide in the shadows, waiting to pick them off.

"It's awfully dark," Delaney said.

"Yeah. Hey guys, I hope you can hear me," he said into the pen in his pocket. "When Delaney asks to buy coke, that's your cue to come in."

They'd gone over the instructions at least a hundred times, but once more didn't hurt. The side door to the warehouse was almost hidden in the shadows of the roof overhang. Luke pushed against the cold metal, and the door scraped open. Inside it was even darker except for a light at the back of the building.

Delaney followed as Luke took the lead. Even as his heart pounded against his rib cage, adrenaline supercharged Luke's body, sharpening his vision and hearing. His muscles tensed, ready for whatever might happen.

When they drew closer, Boudreaux stepped inside the light followed by a beefy, dark-haired man. "That's Músculos," Delaney said softly.

Luke scanned the sidelines for Louis and relaxed a tiny bit when he found him in the shadows. But Louis wasn't alone. Luke stiffened when the DEA undercover agent was surrounded by at least four other men. His gut screamed setup.

He eased his hand to the gun tucked in his waistband. Even though he was certain Boudreaux would do nothing until the transfer was complete, he wanted to be ready.

"What's with the entourage?" Luke asked, nodding toward the men with Louis.

"They're friends of Músculos," Boudreaux said. "Do you have a problem with it?"

"Not if they keep their hands where I can see them. Tell them to come into the light, or the deal is off."

The Colombian's eyes narrowed, then he gave a slight nod and the men eased out of the darkness. "This your man?" he asked.

"Yes."

Delaney stepped forward and planted his feet. "Do you have the heroin?"

Again the Colombian barely nodded, and one of the men rolled a suitcase in the middle of the circle and opened it. It was filled with plastic-wrapped bricks. Delaney knelt and used his knife to open one of them. Pure white heroin. They had the goods.

"Looks good," Delaney said and stood.

"Then we're ready to do business?" Boudreaux asked.

"Absolutely," the DEA agent replied. He turned to the Colombian drug dealer. "How about coke? Can you provide that as well?"

"No problem," Músculos said, grinning.

Suddenly, the window above Luke shattered, and the explosion from a flash bang rocked him. He pulled his gun and dove for cover.

Músculos's men reacted with gunfire as the SWAT team kicked in the doors.

"POLICE! SEARCH WARRANT!"

Luke returned fire, barely feeling a sting in his thigh. Músculos went down. Delaney and Louis took out three of the drug dealer's men as more SWAT members poured into the warehouse.

"GET ON THE GROUND!" They brandished AR15s. "DO IT NOW!"

Luke searched for Boudreaux through the smoky haze, and saw him running for a side door and sprinted after him. In the parking lot, the drug dealer raced toward a Hummer. Luke reached him just as Boudreaux grabbed the door handle. The Cajun spun around and executed a perfect roundhouse kick, knocking Luke's gun from his hand.

He kicked at Boudreaux's midsection but only landed a glancing blow. A wicked grin crossed the drug dealer's face. "You're not so good at this."

For an answer, Luke turned and leaped in the air, kicking the other man in the chest. Boudreaux flew back against the Hummer, and Luke closed in, grabbing for his gun.

He wasn't quick enough, and the drug dealer leveled his gun at Luke's chest. "Back off."

"And if I don't?"

"You can join your girlfriend," Boudreaux said.

"You had your daughter killed?"

A flicker of emotion crossed the Cajun's face and he hesitated. The hesitation was all Luke needed, and he rushed Boudreaux.

The drug dealer fired, hitting Luke in the chest. The impact of the bullet on the Kevlar vest almost knocked him down, but he charged ahead and karate chopped Boudreaux's wrist.

The gun hit the ground and skittered under the Hummer. Boudreaux slammed his fist toward Luke's temple. He ducked and headbutted the drug dealer in the stomach.

Boudreaux doubled over and Luke brought his knee up, smashing into his chin. Boudreaux slumped to the ground. Luke pounced on him. "Where's Brooke?" he demanded.

"Dead. Just like the man she thought was her father."

76

Pain throbbed through Brooke's head. She had no idea how long she'd been out. Long enough for her arms to ache from her hands being bound behind her. Tape covered her mouth.

The room she was in was small, stuffy. Had to be the closet in Jeremy's study. Jeremy. He hadn't been present when Boudreaux knocked her out, but she'd bet almost anything he was in on it. She pushed that thought aside for now. Getting away before Boudreaux or his henchmen returned was more important.

If her hands were in front, she stood a better chance of getting the restraints off. Brooke tried to pull her hands over her hips, but the binding around her wrists was too tight and her arms were too short. If she could stand, maybe she could get the door open. Using the wall to brace herself, she struggled to her feet.

A soft click outside the door reached her ears. Was someone in the other room? Should she pound the door or keep quiet? What if it was Jeremy? But it could be someone who could help her. Brooke kicked the door and tried to make as much noise as the tape would allow.

The door swung open, and she blinked as light flooded into the small space. Dale? What was he doing here?

"Brooke! I've been looking everywhere for you." He pulled the tape from her mouth.

"Ow!" Then she sucked in a deep breath. "How did you know?"

"I'll explain later. Right now we have to get out of here." He pulled her toward the door.

"Wait, untie my hands."

He turned her around. "They used zip ties. I have a knife in my truck." He cracked open the door. "It looks clear. Come on."

She hesitated. What if Dale was part of Boudreaux's ring? Her heart hammered against her ribs. No. She'd known Dale since childhood. There was no way he could be crooked. Besides, she didn't have much choice. The sounds of people partying filtered down the hall as they eased toward the kitchen. Maybe she should just start screaming. But what if one of Boudreaux's henchmen reached them first? And killed not just her, but Dale as well. Even if Pete Nelson or one of his deputies were here, could she trust him? No. Her best bet was to stick with Dale until she was out of the house and got her hands loose. Then she could make a run for it.

"Go out the side door here," Dale said just before they reached the kitchen.

Once they were outside, he guided her toward his truck. "How did you know I was here?" she asked.

"Jeremy called. He was scared for your life and asked if I'd come get you. I'm afraid he's gotten involved with the wrong people."

"Why didn't he help me?"

Dale shrugged. "I guess he's afraid of Boudreaux."

Hearing Boudreaux's name made her skin prickle. "Let's get my hands free," she said. "And get out of here."

He hesitated briefly, and then nodded. "Of course. Turn around."

Wait. How did Dale know about Boudreaux? As she turned, he slipped a bone-handled knife from his pocket. The same kind of knife she'd seen in Luke's photos with a tree stamped in the handle. Her breath stilled in her chest.

Stay calm. When her hands were free, she rubbed her wrists.

Out of the corner of her eye, she saw Cortland, the FBI agent, but he couldn't see her. She had to get his attention somehow, but first distract Dale. "How's Mary?"

"She's actually better," Dale said. "The doctors say she has a good chance of beating this if she stays on the new medicine. Get in the pickup, and we can get out of here."

Brooke tensed her muscles, getting ready to run.

"I wouldn't do that," Dale said.

Something in his voice made her turn toward him. Her stomach lurched. He held a gun, pointed at her. Her gun.

"Get in. And forget about the FBI agent. I told him you'd left."

Her shoulders drooped and she climbed into the pickup. Dale waited until she fastened the seatbelt and then he took out his handcuffs and cuffed her to the seatbelt strap. "I don't want to kill you, but I will if you so much as move a finger while I get in the driver's seat. Got it?"

Brooke nodded. What a mistake she'd made. "Where are you taking me?" she asked as he pulled out of the drive.

"You'll see."

"Why are you doing this?"

"I don't have any choice."

"It's because Boudreaux is paying for Mary's medicine, isn't it?"

He didn't answer, but in the low light she could see the muscle in his jaw working at a furious pace.

"You won't get away with it," she said.

"But I will. Mary's life depends on it. And there's nothing that will tie me to your death."

He said it so matter-of-factly that it sent chills over her. Then he looked over at her. "I don't want to do this, but it's the only way Mary can live. I'm sorry. So just shut up."

When they reached the Natchez Trace, she was surprised that he turned onto it, and then it dawned on her. There were sloughs and bayous where he could dump her body, and it would never be found. She wanted some answers before he killed her. "Why did you kill my dad?" When he ignored her, she said, "You owe me that."

"It was an accident," Dale said. "If John had just looked the other way . . ."

"My dad could never do that."

"Yeah," he said softly. "And it got him killed."

He turned off at the Emerald Mound exit, and what he planned became crystal clear. He didn't plan to hide her body. "No one will ever believe I killed myself."

"Yeah, they will after I tell them how despondent you were over your dad's death."

Would they? No. Luke would never buy it. If only he were here now. What if Boudreaux had killed him? She blocked those thoughts. Luke could take care of himself. He'd make it. And so would she. She just didn't know how.

Dale parked in the circle at Emerald Mound. "Time to get out."

Luke fumbled as he cuffed Boudreaux. Now that he had the drug dealer, sharp pain where the Kevlar vest caught the bullet stabbed with every breath. Probably a broken rib. "Where's Brooke? Is she at Steele's?"

"I doubt it."

He winced as he took a breath. "Who has her?"

"You'd like to know that, wouldn't you? But it's too late for you to save her. And that's too bad. She was feisty—a chip off the old block." He cocked an eye at Luke. "But then again, since she is my daughter, she may have the smarts to live."

Luke clenched his jaw. It took everything in him to not pulverize the man. "Where is she? You're going to jail, but tell me where she is, and I'll try to help you."

Boudreaux laughed. "Yeah, right."

One of the SWAT team members approached to take Boudreaux away.

"Come on, man," Luke said. "This is your daughter we're talking about. Your own flesh and blood." The man had to have some feeling.

Boudreaux stared hard at Luke. "Try Emerald Mound. If she does have my genes, you might get there in time to help her. If you don't bleed out first." He nodded toward Luke's leg.

The DEA agent approached as Luke glanced down. Blood saturated his pants.

"Man, you better get that taken care of," Delaney said.

He'd been hit and hadn't even realized it. The bullet hadn't hit the femoral artery or he'd be dead. Luke didn't know which was worse, the pain in his chest or his thigh that throbbed like an abscessed tooth. At least with blood saturating the back of his leg as well as the front, he figured it was a through-and-through and something he could deal with once he had Brooke safe.

He pushed past the DEA agent. "Later. I've got to get to Emerald Mound. Brooke is in trouble—send some of the SWAT team to meet me there. And send an ambulance. But no sirens." If she was still alive, he didn't want her captor alerted.

Luke didn't wait for the SWAT team and sped off, heading to the Natchez Trace. The two-lane road would be faster than the highway with its traffic lights. On the Trace, he pressed the pedal to the floorboard, slowing only to take the curves. He flew off the exit at Emerald Mound and parked at the first crossroad. Luke ignored the pain in his leg and chest as he pulled his gun and ran toward the Mound.

He had to get there in time.

A pickup sat in the circle drive, and Dale held Brooke at gunpoint. Everything clicked into place. The marijuana. The money for his wife's treatment. And who would suspect the chief ranger of moving drugs up the Trace?

Luke swallowed down the fear that gripped him. Dale and Brooke stood in the same exact spot where he'd found John Danvers. He couldn't get a clear shot at Dale without hitting Brooke.

He needed to get behind Dale, but the ranger faced the road and would see any movement Luke made. Unless he walked around the base of Emerald Mound.

Chills swept over Luke, and his leg throbbed. He glanced down. Blood pooled on the ground. His leg was still bleeding, and the way around the mound was grueling. Could he do it? He had to.

Luke eased to the fence rail around the mound and found a break in it. Working as quickly as his body would allow him, he climbed over rocks and through briars. Soon he was close enough to hear them talking.

"Come on, Dale. You don't have to do this," Brooke said.

"You don't understand," he replied. "Boudreaux won't give me the money if I don't kill you, and without the money, Mary will die. I'm sorry."

"You're sorry?" She stared at him. "You know what? If you're going to kill me, you'll have to shoot me in the back, because I'm not going to stand here and let it happen."

When Brooke turned and walked away from Dale, Luke's heart leaped in his throat. He raised his gun, but what if his shot caused Dale to squeeze the trigger? Distract him! He picked up a rock and hurled it against the pickup door.

When Dale swung his gun hand toward the truck, Luke fired.

78

Brooke planted one foot in front of the other, expecting a bullet in her back. She never thought this would be the way she would die. And not this young. Her biggest regret was not telling Luke how she felt about him.

A gun fired, and she dove for the ground. When there wasn't another shot, she looked over her shoulder. Dale lay on the ground. Luke kicked his gun away from his crumpled body.

Brooke scrambled to where Luke already knelt beside Dale. He turned to her and shook his head. "It looks bad. Are you all right?"

She nodded. "You came. How did you know?"

"Boudreaux."

"He—he told you where I was?" She didn't understand. Boudreaux had ordered her death. "Why—"

"I don't know. Conscience, maybe."

He swayed, and for a moment she thought he'd topple over. Then she saw the blood. "Luke! You're hurt!"

"I'll be all—"

He collapsed beside her just as bedlam broke out and men in SWAT gear poured into the area.

An hour later, Brooke paced the waiting room of Merit Health. She'd had a CAT scan and while there was no permanent damage, her head still throbbed. Luke had been taken to surgery to make sure no bullet fragments had been left in his leg when the bullet passed through. She stopped her pacing as Pete Nelson approached.

"How is he?" Pete asked.

"Doctors say he'll recover with no permanent damage."

"Good. Thought you'd like to know, Jeremy Steele has been arrested for his part in this, thanks to what you reported. And he's singing like a mockingbird."

Brooke was sad for Molly, but she had her grandparents and her aunt. It made her furious that people thought they could get away with breaking the law. They only ended up hurting their families and ruining their lives.

"Any word on Dale Gallagher?" The receptionist would not tell her anything about his condition.

Pete dropped his gaze. "I'm afraid he didn't make it. I'm leaving in a few minutes to drive to Jackson to inform his wife."

How Brooke wished it had been a different outcome. She nodded. "Thanks for going the extra mile."

Not long after Pete left, a nurse led her to a small room, and soon the surgeon stepped in.

"Luke is doing great," he said. "No bullet fragments. But he does have a broken rib from the impact of the bullet on the Kevlar vest."

"Can I see him?"

"As soon as they take him to his room, probably in half an hour. He may be a little groggy." He stopped at the door and smiled. "But he's already asking for you."

Luke glanced toward the clock again. Where was Brooke? Had she left after they told her he'd be okay? He wouldn't blame her. When he thought Dale might shoot her, one of his regrets had been that he hadn't told her he loved her. Even now, the thought of loving someone who might not return his love gave him cold sweats. But he would never know if he didn't try.

He turned his head toward the door as it opened.

"You awake?" Brooke's soft voice asked.

"Barely," he croaked and raised the head of his bed. "Come on in."

She eased into the room and stood at the side of the bed. He'd never seen a more beautiful sight.

They both spoke at the same time, and she said, "You go first."

His throat and mouth were so dry. "Are there any ice chips?"

She startled. "That's what you wanted to say?"

The monitor over his head went into overdrive. His heart had to be hitting a hundred. "No. But my mouth is dry."

"I'll see what I can do." She left the room and returned a few minutes later with a cup of ice and a spoon. "Want me to . . . ?"

He nodded, and she spooned a small amount of ice into his mouth. "Much better." He closed his eyes briefly, then opened them and reached for her hand. "I'm sorry for being such a jerk." When she didn't reply, he pulled her closer. "I . . . I was so scared when I saw Dale holding that gun on you. I thought I was going to lose you."

Her eyes widened, and she opened her mouth to say something.

"Wait until I finish. I hated that I never told you how much I love you." There, he'd said it.

She blinked. "Did I just hear you say you love me?"

Luke didn't blame her for the skepticism in her voice. "You did, and it's not the morphine talking."

"You're sure?"

He nodded. "I'm sure. Someday, if you'll have me, I'd like to marry you."

Brooke blinked back tears. "Are you talking years?" she asked softly.

"Nope. Just however long it takes you to say yes."

"Are you sure that's what you want?"

"I am."

"Then yes, when the time is right, I'll marry you, Luke Fereday."

Peace settled in his heart. "I can't promise I'll always be able to tell you what I'm doing, jobwise, but—"

"Hush, and kiss me."

READ ON FOR A SNEAK PEEK
from Book 2 in the

NATCHEZ TRACE PARK RANGERS
Series

The January warm spell had definitely ended in South Mississippi. Emma Winters zipped her National Park Service jacket against the biting north wind as she hiked the quarter mile from the gate to the Mount Locust Visitors Center on the Natchez Trace. A hike that wouldn't have been necessary if she hadn't forgotten the gate key. Or the folder she needed to finish a report due by midnight.

Forgetting things wasn't like her, but her mother's resistance to tracking down her brother had Emma off-center. Her cell phone broke the silence, and she checked her caller ID. She wasn't sure she was ready for her mother's reaction to the email Emma had sent and let two more rings go by. In fact, she was tempted to not answer her mother's call at all because she just didn't want to hear her objections. But just before it went to voicemail, Emma punched the answer button. "Hello," she said, forcing a cheery note in her voice.

"Oh, good, I caught you," her mother said. "I received the flyer you emailed."

"And? What did you think?"

"Honey, I think you'll get a lot of nutcases if you send it out. Like you did before when you offered money for information on Ryan."

"But someone might know some—"

"Your brother's choices in life are his. I hate to see you throw good money after bad."

"It's my money," she muttered. As each year passed, finding her brother pressed deeper into her heart, but she should have known her mother would kick up about the flyer. If she knew the whole story . . .

"What are you doing? You're breaking up."

"Walking to my office," Emma said.

"You're . . . Mount Locust . . . night?"

"Mom, we have a bad connection," she said. "I'll call you when I get home."

Emma ended the call and shrugged off the sense of failure that seeped into every fiber of her being whenever she and her mother discussed Ryan. But it wasn't so easily shrugged off. She glanced toward the sky just as a pale sliver of moon broke through the clouds, giving off enough light to cast eerie shadows on the ground.

A shiver ran over her body. Maybe next time she would ask someone to come with her. Or bring a gun. *Not likely.* She'd never desired to be a law enforcement ranger and was quite satisfied being on the interpretive side of the National Park Service.

The hair on the back of her neck rose as she approached the stone and wood building. *Come on. Don't get all spooked.* She worked here, and Mount Locust was as familiar as the backyard where she'd grown up. And it wasn't like being here after dark was something new. From November until the days got longer, she locked up every day in the dark. Besides, she'd never been afraid of the dark. In spite of that, she scanned the area, trying to shake the sense she wasn't alone.

Nothing moved as she scanned the grounds, her gaze stopping at the lighted maintenance building visible through the bare trees. Probably should check on the ground-penetrating radar machine that arrived earlier today. Tomorrow she was supposed to begin the preliminary mapping of the historic quarters and the adjoining cemetery.

Emma had left word for the new district law enforcement ranger on the Natchez Trace to have someone swing by every few hours to check for trespassers. Now would be a good time for a ranger to arrive . . . as long as it wasn't Samuel Ryker. Emma hadn't seen her once-upon-a-time boyfriend since he returned to Natchez and had avoided talking directly to him on the call.

But eventually she would have to face him, and she might as well make peace with it.

Something rustled to her right. Emma froze with her hand on the doorknob. She turned just as a bottle rolled from the open passageway separating the office from the restrooms.

"Who's there?" She tried for commanding, but the tremor in her voice destroyed the effect.

A bedraggled gray and white tabby limped around the corner and sat down, its baleful stare almost as pitiful as its meow. Emma released the breath caught in her chest and leaned against the door. "Where did you come from?"

The cat stretched and then rubbed against her leg, and Emma stooped to pick it up. She could count the poor thing's ribs. With it still in her arms, she turned and unlocked the door. There was half of a roast beef sandwich in the little refrigerator under her desk. Maybe the cat could eat the meat.

As she bent to retrieve the beef, Emma's gaze landed on the file she'd come for. Beside it, the landline blinked with a message. She would feed the cat first, then listen to the voice mail. Emma shredded the meat and set it on the floor. The kitty sniffed the food, then tore into it, making little growling noises as it ate. When it finished, the cat sat down and looked up at Emma as if to say, "Where's the rest?"

"That's all I have," she said. Funny how having another living thing with her made the place seem less scary. "I'll bring you something in the morning—how about that?" she asked and punched the play button on the phone. "Or maybe I'll take you home with me tonight."

The cat wound around her ankles again as Corey Jackson's voice echoed in the empty room.

"Emma, where are you? You're not answering your cell phone. Give me a call before you begin your excavation."

She groaned. Corey would be the death of her. Not the attorney exactly, but his client, whoever that might be. Corey wouldn't reveal who was objecting to the study of the slave quarters. Emma straightened her shoulders. It would take more than a phone call to stop the work that promised to get her out of Natchez. It wasn't like she was going to excavate the cemetery. That was the purpose of the GPR machine—to locate and determine once and for all the number of graves there.

Conflicting reports had abounded for years that some bodies had been missed in the research project conducted in 2000, and that bothered Emma. Every grave should be found. Even though by all accounts the slaves who lived and worked at Mount Locust had been well treated, being owned by another person just wasn't right. She wanted to make sure each person received the dignity and recognition that had eluded them in life.

It was hard to understand why anyone objected to the research project anyway, but she didn't have time to worry about Corey's client tonight. "Come on, Suzy," she said, deciding the tabby was female, and then grabbed the folder.

Suzy shot out the door, and Emma followed suit, locking it behind her. A screeching sound jerked her attention to her right, and she fisted her hands. Another gust of wind whistled through the trees followed by the screeching sound again, and she identified the source. A branch scraping against the window on the side of the building. Adrenaline left as fast as it had come.

What was wrong with her tonight? If Brooke Danvers were here, she would have a ball teasing Emma. But Emma was the first to admit she wasn't as brave as her best friend. A tree frog seemed to agree as he serenaded her with his song and then was joined with a chorus of other males, each one vying to outdo the other. Poor things were singing for nothing. The last two weeks of warm weather had them confused and singing to the female frogs who were not in the mood to answer them in the middle of January.

Another sound overrode the frogs, and Emma cocked her head toward it. Someone was operating machinery. The maintenance supervisor must have come back after supper to work on some of the equipment. She frowned. The noise sounded more like it came from the inn than the maintenance shed.

Maybe it was those kids she'd run off earlier. Just before closing time, she'd caught three teenaged boys pulling up the flags she'd staked out around the area of the slave cabins. Had they come back and hotwired one of the backhoes? That's what it sounded like rather than one of the mowers.

"Stay here," she said, as if the cat would. This time she would get names and call the parents. Flipping on her flashlight, she marched up the brick path that led to the restored inn, which was really just a three-bedroom log cabin with a dogtrot in the middle for ventilation in the summer.

Instead of remaining behind, Suzy followed her up to the deserted log structure. Emma cocked her ear again. The motor had quit. She swept the area with her light toward the maintenance building. The equipment looked untouched. Then she flashed the light across the wooded area to her left, revealing only stark tree trunks and bare limbs.

Wait. On the other side of the trees in the slave cemetery, the light revealed a yellow backhoe. Yep. Evidently those kids had returned. Emma flexed her fingers on her free hand. While she wasn't afraid of the teenagers, there was such a thing as common sense, so she checked her cell phone for service. One bar and it was faded. Doubtful she could get out.

She would try 911 anyway and let whoever answered the call deal with the boys. Preferably anyone but Sam. When the operator answered, Emma could only make out a couple of words. She identified herself and asked for a patrol ranger to come to Mount Locust, hoping the operator understood the call.

When the operator didn't respond, she checked her phone again. The call had dropped. She'd try again as soon as she had better reception near the maintenance building. Since she didn't hear anything, maybe whoever was trespassing had left.

Emma hopped off the porch just as a rifle report split the night air, and a bullet splintered the wooden post where she'd just stood. She dove for the ground and scrambled under the house. Her heart stuttered in her chest as another rifle report sent a bullet kicking up dirt a few yards from her hiding place.

Why was someone trying to kill her?

Like that mattered at this moment. She had to move or be trapped in the crawl space. Frantically she looked for the cat. If it had any sense at all, it had hightailed it back to the visitor center.

Emma scanned the area, looking for a way to escape. She couldn't go back the way she'd come—it was too open—but there was ground cover from the side of the house to the edge of the woods only thirty feet away. If she could make it to the trees and then to the maintenance shed, she would find better reception as well as a landline. Emma belly crawled to the nearest tree, scraping her hand on a rock.

A dry twig snapped to her left. Her attacker was coming after her.

Emma hoisted the rock and flung it away from her before she darted in the opposite direction toward the maintenance building. Another shot rang out, and the bullet embedded in a nearby tree.

With her heart exploding in her chest, she ducked under a live oak limb that dipped down to the ground and pressed against the huge trunk. Her lungs screamed for air. Couldn't make any noise. Heavy footsteps stomped through the dead leaves, and she pressed closer to the trunk, biting back a cry as the bark poked her back.

A faint siren reached her ears. The 911 operator had understood her!

The footsteps halted. Her stalker had heard it as well. But where was he? She dared not peer around the tree and remained absolutely still, surprised that he couldn't hear the pounding of her heart. Seconds later, footsteps retreated toward the service road. Then a motor roared to life, and the car sped away.

Emma's knees buckled, and she braced against the tree, her fingers shaking as she dialed 911 again.

ACKNOWLEDGMENTS

As always, to God, who gives me the words.

To my family and friends who believe in me and encourage me every day.

To my editors, Lonnie Hull DuPont and Kristin Kornoelje, thank you for making my stories so much better.

To the art, editorial, marketing, and sales team at Revell—especially Michele Misiak, Karen Steele, and Erin Bartels, thank you for your hard work. You are the best!

To Julie Gwinn, thank you for your direction and for working so tirelessly with me and for being my friend.

To the National Park Service rangers for answering my questions. Hopefully I didn't stray too far afield.

To the people of Natchez who opened their arms to me and made me want to move there, thank you!

Patricia Bradley is the author of three series—the Logan Point series (*Shadows of the Past*, *A Promise to Protect*, *Gone Without a Trace*, and *Silence in the Dark*), the Memphis Cold Case novels (*Justice Delayed*, *Justice Buried*, *Justice Betrayed*, and *Justice Delivered*), and the Natchez Trace Park Rangers (*Standoff*). Bradley is the winner of an Inspirational Readers Choice Award and a Carol Award finalist. She is cofounder of Aiming for Healthy Families, Inc., and she is a member of American Christian Fiction Writers and Sisters in Crime. Bradley makes her home in Mississippi with her two fur babies, Suzy and Tux. Learn more at www.ptbradley.com.

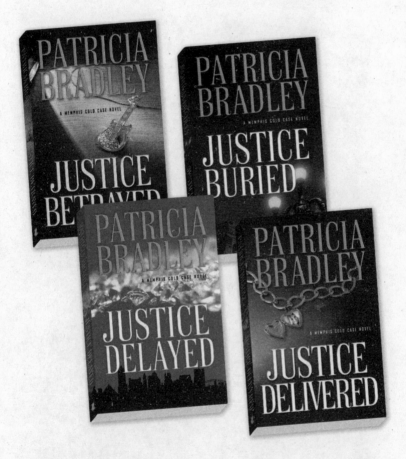

Also by
PATRICIA BRADLEY . . .

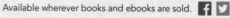

Meet
Patricia BRADLEY

www.ptbradley.com

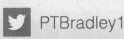 PTBradley1

Patricia Bradley Author